⊙ꜰDAWN &
DARKNESS

Will Wight

Books by Will Wight

THE TRAVELER'S GATE TRILOGY

House of Blades

The Crimson Vault

City of Light

The Traveler's Gate Chronicles

THE ELDER EMPIRE

Of Sea & Shadow   *Of Shadow & Sea*

Of Dawn & Darkness   *Of Darkness & Dawn*

CRADLE

The Fox & The Phoenix

OF DAWN & DARKNESS

THE ELDER EMPIRE: SECOND SEA

WILL WIGHT

HIDDEN GNOME PUBLISHING

To Ian, who first asked me when the book was coming out.

Welcome, Reader.

Right now, you're reading the second book in the Elder Empire series.

*But it's not the **only** second book.*

***Of Dawn and Darkness** was written in parallel to **Of Darkness and Dawn**, which takes place at the same time from a different perspective.*

*If you've read **Of Sea and Shadow**, then I'm sure you already know how these books work. In case you don't, I'd advise you to back up and read the first story in this series.*

And now that you have…

Welcome back to the Elder Empire.

CHAPTER ONE

Elder cults find their recruits in the ways you would expect: through bribery, misinformation, brainwashing, preying on the emotionally weak, and exploiting the uneducated.

But we've discovered a few, a very few, who join such cults because they truly believe that the Elders will somehow save us.

— FROM THE NAVIGATOR'S GUILD REPORT
ON SLEEPLESS ACTIVITY IN THE AION SEA

TWENTY YEARS AGO

Jyrine Tessella held her father's hand as they walked down the street. She'd never been to this city before, but she didn't think she liked it—everything smelled like fish, and the people didn't know how to walk. An old man passed them, covered in a full-body cloak of burlap, limping like his left leg was broken. Every time he took a step, something wet slapped against the pavement. She pictured him wearing fish on his feet like shoes, and she giggled.

The town was in even worse shape than its citizens. Each building had been cobbled together from driftwood and parts scavenged from shipwrecks, so Jyrine and her father walked between walls of warped wood and crusty ropes. Many of the houses had collapsed or sunk down into the earth, but someone else just built another one on top of the pile. The result was an entire town that looked more like a model built by a little boy out of scraps he gathered in his back yard.

Strangest of all was the way they treated gold. They weighted their fishing nets with mismatched golden idols the size of her fist, and gold statues of the Emperor sat on boats as anchors. Half-clothed children ran through the mud in a ditch, tossing golden pebbles at each other. Thousands of goldmarks worth of precious metal, treated like trash.

"It's not *real* gold, is it?" Jyrine asked, looking at a woman sweeping gold flakes out of her doorway.

Her father's tattooed cheek crinkled as he smiled. "Just because it's valuable to us doesn't mean it's worth the same to everyone. Gold, on its own, is worthless. Only a few things have real value." He rubbed her head, and she smiled back, because she knew he was talking about her.

His tattoo was far more complex than hers, a squirming web that covered the entire left half of his face and rolled down the left side of his body, wrapping his whole leg. Hers stretched from the bottom of her left ear to her ankle, telling the world the history of their Vandenyan family.

She'd asked him once why his was so much bigger, and he'd laughed. *"Secrets take a lot of ink,"* he'd said, which in her opinion didn't answer the question.

A cloaked figure stepped out of an alleyway and blocked their way forward, so quickly that Jyrine instinctively moved to stand behind her father. The fish smell was stronger now that this man—at least, she guessed it was a man—stood so close to them. He breathed too loudly, as though he sucked each breath through clenched teeth.

"You are Larrin Tessella." That was her father's name, but the man pronounced the words all wrong, like he was choking out a demand instead of asking a polite question. She wasn't sure he meant it as a question at all, and he hissed in and out after each word.

Her father's hand tightened slightly on hers, but he forced a smile. "I am. What may I call you?"

The man jerked his head to one side, limping away, his burlap covering dragging in the muck behind him. There was a lump like a camel's between his spine and left shoulder, though it squirmed as he moved. She imagined him hiding a cat under there, and she almost laughed.

Her father didn't seem to find the man funny. He pulled her closer to him as they followed the man deeper into the town.

The farther they went, the worse it seemed to get, though that could have been the dying light. The sun was going down, so the light was worse and worse with every passing second. Light and shadows played tricks on her eyes, which was no doubt why some of these people looked like they had webs between their fingers. And why some of the children watching her from open doorways had eyes that reflected light like a cat's. A few times, she heard what she thought was the call of a distant bird, followed by what could have been screams or loud laughter.

She drew so close to her father that she was almost hugging his leg.

Finally, the hunchbacked man stopped at a towering gold temple that rose above the surrounding. He bowed them forward like an usher bowing them into an opera, though Jyrine couldn't see if he was smiling or not.

She knew it was an old temple because it looked exactly like the pictures in her schoolbooks. Made of almost pure gold, the temple was blocky and fluid at the same time, like some architect had tried to build a rearing snake out of bricks. It was adorned by dangling flags of every color, on which were written words she didn't understand.

Her father pulled her inside, though she was more interested in staring at the entrance. They passed between two statues that looked like they could have represented the Emperor, except they each had a snake's head resting on a man's shoulders. As far as she knew, the Emperor had a normal head.

Fires burned in braziers standing against the walls, lighting their way in and filling the air with a more pleasant smell, almost like pine and cinnamon. They only walked a short way before her father unlocked a perfectly ordinary door, which opened onto a much larger chamber. A strange golden statue stood against the far wall: most of it looked like a snake, though it had the tail of a scorpion, the head of a lion, and the talons of a huge bird. She supposed it must be a Kameira of some sort, but she couldn't tell which one. She hadn't studied natural history yet.

In front of the statue, gathered around a fire-pit full of stacked, unlit wood, were five figures in hooded robes. Other than the hoods, none of the robes had anything in common; one was black and plain, another blue and richly decorated, and she was suspicious that a third was really just a bathrobe with a cowl sewn on. At the sight of her father, the bathrobe man lowered his hood and grinned. He was a very ordinary-looking old man, obviously older than her father, with a red, round face and a ring of wispy white hair.

"And the cavalry's here!" he shouted, spreading his arms wide. "Light and life, Larrin, it's been an age! Worms take me! We're getting ready to begin, just waiting on you, but we've got a little time. Why don't—"

He seemed to notice Jyrine for the first time, and he leaned down to put his hands on his knees, looking at her on her level. "I'm sorry, little lady, they say manners are the first thing to go. What is your name?"

"Jyrine," she said, happy to meet a normal person in this town.

"You must be hungry, Jyrine. Why don't you get something to eat?" He gestured over to the wall, where a perfectly ordinary service table had been set up, carrying all the bite-sized delicacies she would have expected to see in the Capital. It was bizarrely out of place here, something from polite Heartlander society over here in the middle of a wilderness temple off the Izyrian coast.

But she was happy for a meal, so she looked up at her father for permission.

"I tell you what," he said, amused. "Why don't you have a seat over there? I want you to watch what we do tonight, but just to watch, okay? Eat what you want, but don't make a sound."

She nodded impatiently; he'd explained as much to her many times over the weeks aboard the Navigator's ship. *"Don't make a sound. Pay attention, but if your head starts to feel strange, it's okay to close your eyes. You need to be brave, and look closely, but not* too *closely."* Most of her instructions she didn't entirely understand, but she'd committed them to memory anyway. She was afraid that he'd start reciting them all if she didn't escape, so she scurried over to the snacks.

Her father and the others began to talk, and she started to relax. The food was delicious, if a little less than fresh, and her father laughed and joked with these people. Three were women and two men, all much older than her parents, which made her father the youngest person in the circle. That was a strange thought: her father, *young*.

Jyrine was just starting to get bored when her father gestured to her to stay where she was. She almost jumped out of her chair with excitement.

She didn't know what was about to happen, nor why they'd traveled for weeks across the ocean, but she was finally about to find out.

Maybe she would learn why her mother had tried to stop her from coming.

Her father had changed into a brown robe, though his hood didn't quite cover his face. All the robed figures knelt around the stack of wood, speaking in another language. That was strange in itself; everyone in the world spoke Imperial, according to her tutors. There was a time when the Emperor had imprisoned people for speaking the wrong words, or even for having too much of an accent, though that was a long time ago. Now tutors like hers, under the supervision of the Witness' Guild, made sure everyone could understand each other.

Wherever her father had picked up this strange language, she wasn't sure she liked it. He and his friends sounded like they were imitating the hunch-backed man outside, hissing in through their teeth, though the sound was mixed in with clicking tongues and a few words that she thought she could *almost* understand. All in all, it was like listening to a snake trying to have a conversation with a swarm of bugs.

Something caught her eye, and she glanced down at the pile of sticks. A green light kindled inside, like the world's smallest quicklamp. She'd seen shows before where they used strange-colored quicklamps to set the mood, but those were expensive. So expensive that she was surprised to see one here.

The light spread, and she realized it wasn't a quicklamp after all. It was a fire. But rather than the comforting, homey orange light she was used to, this was a poisonous green flame that cast everything in harsh shades of emerald.

But she wasn't paying attention to anything else, because the fire was *fasci-*

nating. How had they done that? Did they burn some alchemy to change the color of the flames, or was one of the robed figures a Soulbound?

She hoped so. She'd always dreamed about meeting a Soulbound.

Jyrine was staring into the fire when the world seemed to blink out. It startled her enough that she looked around the room, to see if the older men and women had reacted, only to find that the room had left her behind.

She wasn't looking out into the chamber of a golden temple anymore. Instead, she sat on top of a high mountain, surrounded by towering clouds and piles of flawless snow. She knew it was cold from the snow flurries and the howl of the wind, though the temperature didn't touch her.

Jyrine tried to get up and look over the edge of the peak, but she couldn't move. She stifled her moment of panic. *It's like watching a play,* she thought. *I'll sit back and enjoy the show, just like they always say.*

Put that way, she could think of this like a holiday. No play had ever created such a vivid picture as this one, and maybe she'd get to see something that even her father had never seen.

She looked around, enjoying the scenery, when she noticed that there were other peaks around her. There must be miles in between the mountains, because they were hazy with distance, but one in particular caught her eye. It loomed over all the others, and there was something strange about its shape. Jyrine focused on it, and suddenly she could see it clearly, as if she'd moved closer.

This mountain was riddled with holes, like someone had drilled dozens of mines everywhere they could, and *something* wove in and out of each one. At first she thought it was a giant snake, burrowing through the mountain, but she quickly realized that the skin was too smooth for scales. And its body was segmented in lines, like an earthworm.

It was a giant worm, woven in and out through the rocky peaks as though the mountain were nothing more than a rotten apple.

And as she watched, the worm began to move. It slid forward, displacing rocks in an avalanche, slithering and squirming deeper. It was repulsive to watch, certainly, and her mother would probably have told her to look away. But it was the kind of disgust that meant she *couldn't* look away; she was too horrified and too fascinated all at once.

A sense of hunger, of growing dread, suffused the vision like someone else's emotions were pressing down on her.

"YOU ARE ONLY A PILE OF MEAT," a voice declared, deafeningly loud and yet somehow still a whisper. Jyrine leaned forward as the mountain rumbled, eager to see the worm's giant, repulsive head emerge.

Just as she was sure it was about to pop out, the scene shifted.

This time she floated above a field of flowers. Once she adjusted to her disappointment at missing the end of the last dream, she enjoyed the new one; even the scent of flowers seemed to drift up, as delicate and pure as the most expensive perfume. She looked between the petals and realized that the flowers weren't planted in grass, but rather floating on lilypads. And under the lilies, a red pool.

A coppery smell reached her, underneath the more pleasant notes of the flowers, and she wondered if it was a sea of blood.

Hands reached up from between flowers, dripping scarlet, like human hands but six-fingered and wrong. They groped for the sky, and the scene shifted again.

This time, Jyrine couldn't contain her impatience. "Go back!" she complained, but no one responded. Were all of these visions going to end just before something good happened?

The third one did the same. She was inside a dim cave, which had been filled by a mound of bleached bones. Tens of thousands of bones surrounded her in waves and piles, and the only sound was a distant crunching sound. It grew louder, until she could see something rushing toward her beneath the bones, like a mole burrowing through the soil. It rushed closer with the speed of a galloping horse, and just when she was sure it would reveal its hideous body in a spray of skulls, the sight changed again.

She'd expected it, but was still disappointed.

More images flashed in front of her, some for only an instant and others for a quarter of an hour. They were all somewhat disturbing, either grotesque or so strange that they left her squinting. One and all, they ended before her greatest curiosity was satisfied.

The rush of images ended in black.

Painted darkness enfolded her, an infinite void filled with swirls of distant colors that shivered and danced. It was like drowning in an ocean of stars, if the stars were dyed like quicklamps for a festival.

Phantom noises drifted behind her, out of sight, and she shivered in a mixture of fear and delight. Something clashed beside her hair, like massive jaws gnashing inches away from her skin, and she spun around. She hoped to catch sight of some nasty monster this time, but was frustrated to see only more dancing lights.

A thin voice whispered to her, and she would have sworn she felt lips against her ear. *"What would you ask for, given the chance?"*

The colored stars froze, awaiting her answer.

Distantly, she thought she heard older voices responding, including her father. She couldn't quite make out the words, but their cooperation gave her courage.

"Can you make it go back?" she asked.

The utter silence rang in her ears like a bell. Maybe it hadn't understood her.

"I want to see the first one. With the giant worm. Would you allow me to see the rest of it, please?" If she was speaking to Elders, as she now suspected, she may as well be polite.

"Why?" the voice whispered, breath stirring the back of her neck.

She clapped a hand to the spot and spun around, though she caught no one. "I wanted to see its face."

The voice murmured something else, something she didn't catch, and then even that vision ended. It didn't cut off instantly, as the other scenes had, but slid down her eyes like rain washing away paint.

On the other side of the abyss was the temple room, where the old men all waited in a circle. Her father was sprawled on his back, chest heaving as though he'd run a great distance. One of the older members of the group had a hand clapped to his eye, and blood oozed between his fingers.

Only four robed figures were gathered around the green fire now. They had started with five.

Jerri found herself wondering whether the others had seen the same things she had. She was willing to bet that *they* were allowed to see the giant worm's face.

The four remaining leaders of the cabal gathered themselves, each composed and kneeling before the fire. One of the men spoke up. "Great Ones, show us our guide."

From the center of the flames, a jewel rose up, flashing with light. It was an emerald, shining like a star as it hovered in the air above their heads. They whispered to each other in excitement, clapping one another on the shoulder as they watched it. Jerri's father was ecstatic, his grin as wide as she'd ever seen it, eyes fixed on the gem.

It hung there for five minutes. Ten. Fifteen. After twenty minutes of silence and green light, the circle of adults began to shift uneasily on their knees.

"Should we…should we take it?" an old woman asked.

Five more minutes passed before anyone tried it. Jerri's father rose slowly to his feet, reaching a hand out for the jewel. It didn't fly away and it didn't slap his hand down, so Jerri was sure he'd grab it.

Then the emerald became a stream of light, flashing away. In an instant, it appeared in front of Jyrine's face.

She jerked back in shock, almost knocking over her chair. If this was some kind of an attack, she had no idea what to do about it.

That whispering voice from the void returned, and though it sounded quiet, it swallowed the room. *"You look back. She looks forward. She will guide you into the future."*

The trinket fell as though a string had been cut, falling into Jerri's lap. It was so hot that it felt like it would burn her even through her skirt.

"Bind this to her soul," the voice said, and then a soft wind filled the chamber. As the wind left, the fire died.

The adults murmured to one another, glancing at her in confusion. Only her father seemed like he was on the verge of laughter. After another hour of discussion, during which Jerri fiddled with her gem and snacked on the food from the service table, the old men and women began to file out.

One by one, the three strangers put a hand on her shoulder and said words of farewell. She didn't entirely understand what had happened today, but she knew enough to mind her manners, and she responded to each one.

Her father was last. He knelt in front of her, gathering her hand up in both of his. "Are you all right?"

She nodded impatiently. "Of course I am. But what *happened?*" She had waited over an hour to find out, and with curiosity burning a hole in her, it had felt like three days.

He patted her hand gently. "It will take a long time to explain, but I'll do the best I can. The most I can say is that you're going to be very important someday, Jerri. Very, very important."

CHAPTER TWO

When Calder climbed up the ladder and onto *The Testament's* deck, no one stood at the wheel. Andel was nowhere to be seen, and a pile of ropes sat at the base of the mast.

Foster hurried up to him, blood running down into his beard from a split lip. The gunner spoke only two words:

"She's loose."

Then the darkness of Urg'naut himself descended over Calder's vision, and something slammed into his back with the force of a stallion's kick. He buckled and fell, his belly pressed against smooth, seamless wood. His spine felt as though someone had run a carriage into it, and trying to catch a breath felt like inhaling a lung full of needles. The recent injury to his shoulder screamed, and he had unhealed bruises over practically every inch of his body.

His sense of time had shattered, so he didn't know how long it took him to return to coherent thought. Only a handful of seconds, most likely, but it felt longer. With his brain returned to its proper position, he understood his situation in full clarity.

Someone was sitting on him. Someone with an arm wrapped around his eyes and a cold point of metal against the back of his neck.

He left his mouth to steer itself, hoping to say something witty, but all that came out was a sort of muffled grunt. The assassin on his neck sensed this and shifted her weight slightly, enough to allow him to breathe without unfortunate pain in his chest.

"I'm sorry, Captain," the Consultant said, from her position on his back. "I can't allow you to call on your Vessel, or I might have to kill you before we've had a chance to talk. Please understand."

If I have to be assassinated on my own deck, at least she's polite about it, he thought. Out loud, he said, "Quite understandable." His voice came out as an animal noise, closer to the squeal of a pig than to human speech.

She flipped him over without allowing him to respond, knocking his wounded shoulder and the back of his head on the deck again. He scrambled for his bearings, staring up at the stretched, green-veined skin of his sails—translucent in the sunlight—that loomed above him. Before he gathered himself again, she had her knee pressed to the base of his throat and the tip of a bronze-bladed dagger under his chin.

"My name is Meia, Captain Marten," she said. "We're going to renegotiate the course of this ship." Her voice was businesslike and professional, but her eyes were the vertical-slitted orange of a draconic Kameira. They had been blue only days before, when he'd fought her in the crumbling corridor of a Gray Island prison. Her blond hair hung loose, though short enough that it stayed out of her eyes, and she wore tight clothes of unrelieved black. One bronze knife was entirely too close for comfort, pushing as it was against his skin, and she held the other reversed in her left hand. Free for use, he supposed.

"I remembered your name, Meia," he said, and his voice came out reasonably human this time.

"You should, since you abducted me. That's a new crime for you, isn't it?"

"As the offender, yes. I've been the victim of abductions, however temporary, more times than I would like to admit."

"That should give you some sympathy for my position." The cold edge of bronze pressed harder under his chin, and he couldn't ignore the Intent that leaked out from the weapon.

The man begs for mercy, but mercy is not called for, so the blade draws his blood.

Agitated and drunk, the soldiers attack, but they do not know their opponent. The blade draws their blood.

The child of death and unnatural life lets out a howl, shrieking as it wraps its fleshy tentacles around the woman's leg. Bronze flashes, and the blade draws its blood.

Over and over, Calder Read the history of violence. The visions came with the weight of endlessness, as though he could dig forever and always unearth some older death at the end of this assassin's blade. Intent and significance hung heavy in the bronze, such that it took everything he had to shut them out.

So heavy that the weapon almost seemed to have a mind of its own. It wasn't Awakened, he would have sensed that, but it was only one technicality away. He was afraid he might Awaken it with a stray thought.

Awakening would change the physical shape of the blade, likely resulting in his throat slit. As that was the exact situation he was currently endeavoring to avoid, he corralled his mind as tightly as possible.

"...for the Island," Meia finished, waiting on his response.

The Reading hadn't taken long, relatively speaking, but long enough that he'd missed whatever the Consultant had tried to say. He gave her a smile before realizing that even that much movement brought a flare of pain from the dagger's tip. He gave up smiling.

"I apologize, Consultant Meia, I was distracted by your weapon. Would you mind repeating that? Please?" He had no choice but to pray to the Unknown God that she found it easier to persuade him than to throw his body overboard. She could sail the ship, with enough motivation. As long as the Lyathatan beneath the ship remained quiet, *The Testament* would function as well as anything else on the water. It would be a bit undermanned, but he was certain Meia would find her way around that minor obstacle.

Her hand on the knife flexed, muscles unnaturally bulging and shifting. Veins stood out blue against her pale skin, and her nails extended half an inch. Orange eyes flared.

But she gathered herself with a visible effort, and no strain or anger dyed her voice when she spoke. "This ship will return to the Gray Island immediately, where you will deposit me and surrender yourselves to the Consultant's Guild. You will not be killed, nor even harmed, only detained and questioned. Gently. You will remain a prisoner, but a safe one, if you cooperate now and set course for the Island."

"Attractive," Calder said. "I can see what happens if I don't oblige." He could feel blood leaking out around her weapon's tip.

"I'd prefer it if you did."

"Very well. I give you my word of honor that I will sail back to the Gray Island without resistance. Furthermore, I will not harm you, and I will remand myself into the custody of the Consultant Architects upon our arrival."

Meia withdrew her dagger, and her eyes faded to blue. It was a disturbing sight. She let up pressure on his chest, leaving only a throbbing ache, and stood. "You've made things much easier for all of us, Captain Marten. It would have been a waste to kill you when you can make the journey so much faster."

We're being very polite to each other for a couple of liars, Calder thought. For one thing, he harbored no illusions about what would happen to him if he returned to the headquarters of the Consultant's Guild. He'd just launched an attack on their Island, during which—due to no fault of his—most of the landscape was destroyed. On top of that, a Consultant assassin had pursued him for the last several months. He couldn't imagine they would let an outstanding contract go, if only for the pride of their Guild.

Meia was certainly lying about his treatment...which was just as well, because he had no intentions of returning.

Foster and his bloody beard stumbled over, watching the retreating Consultant's back carefully. "She's a polite one, but you shouldn't take her lightly. Play it quiet for now."

"Where's Andel?" Calder asked.

"Play it quiet for now," Foster insisted. "You're ignoring me, and that makes me edgy."

Calder sat up glanced over the deck. No one but Foster and the Consultant. "Is he okay?"

"You're still ignoring me, and I'm starting to sweat. I'm thinking you're going to try something, Captain, which would be a *bad idea*. Captain. *Captain*."

With a wince, Calder hauled himself to his feet. He knew it was going to hurt, and it did—a lance of pain shot up from his bandaged leg. As he climbed to a standing position, he shot his Intent down into the ship.

The ship has only a dim sense of who travels within it, besides the Soulbound, who flares like a beacon in The Testament's *awareness. Two ordinary humans walk on the deck, near the Soulbound captain. Two more ride below. The smaller one is tucked away in the corner of a passenger cabin, while the larger waits in the hold.*

"Why is he in the hold?" Calder asked.

"He, uh..." Foster squinted in the distance and scratched his gray-bearded chin, avoiding Calder's gaze. "He thought the Consultant might be hungry."

Calder braced himself against the mast as though trying to push it over. He'd lost Urzaia and Jerri both—the second memory burned hot—and now what crew remained had given in to the demands of an enemy. Petal he could understand; she was crouched in her room, distracting herself with alchemy. He'd expect nothing less. But Foster would oppose anyone given the slightest excuse. And Andel? Calder would have thought the Quartermaster would go to his grave before he surrendered.

Meia had retreated to a polite distance, keeping her eyes on the sea, and it occurred to Calder that she was being *respectful*. Giving the Captain a moment with his crew member. An assassin should know better than to lower her guard.

"...you've got that look, Calder, and it's not going to lead us anywhere wise. You hearing me?"

Calder focused once again on the Intent bound into his ship, the power that fused each dark green board together into a smooth whole. His mind slid down below the hull, to the bolts that anchored the first links of two ancient chains.

The chains were invested to restrain an Elder, to restrict its powers and bend them to the will of the ship's captain. They connected to a pair of manacles, which wrapped around a monster's wrists.

With a thought, Calder ordered the Lyathatan to rise.

Next to the ship, the water darkened and swelled. A head the size of a longboat crested the waves, its deep blue scales glistening in the sun. Six black eyes emerged in two rows of three, gills on its neck flapping in the air. It opened a shark's mouth and hissed, revealing endless legions of jagged teeth. Webbed spines flared up on its back. Its torso was like a man's, covered in the pale skin of a fish's belly, and its muscular arms ended in taloned hands.

The sea was more than deep enough to submerge the Lyathatan completely, but it stood as though the waves were only waist-high. Calder had never clearly seen its legs, but from what he'd glimpsed, they looked like a combination of human legs and a pair of fish tails. Like some sort of bizarre, Elder-spawned echo of a mermaid.

Meia had begun to turn as soon as the ocean surface bulged, but Calder's mind was already in the ship. It was easier than flipping a finger to wrap her in the ship's lines, binding her while the Lyathatan made its entrance.

The ropes lasted exactly no time at all, as two bronze blades flashed. For a heartbeat he couldn't believe it, even as he watched shredded pieces of rope float down. Her knives had been sheathed, and she'd been facing the other direction. She couldn't have sensed the ropes coming. It wasn't possible, even for a Reader.

He started to tip *The Testament* even as the Lyathatan reached out, but it was too late; Meia had already reached him. One bronze knife sliced his belt, which slid to the deck, carrying with it the sword he'd tried to draw. It was an Awakened blade, granted to him as part of a deal with a Great Elder, but it did him precisely as much good as a bent wooden stick. Her other knife was back in its sheath, but just as he noticed, he realized that her empty hand was coming up to his throat anyway.

Not empty. The sunlight glinted off a needle pinched between her fingers.

Calder winced at the pain in his neck as she struck like a scorpion. He'd been poisoned by one of these needles before, so he knew exactly what to expect.

Only two seconds later, he collapsed. Every one of his injuries burst to life again. The agony swallowed him, but at least he had one thing to look forward to: soon, he would pass out.

From his angle lying on his side, he could just see the Lyathatan's chest and elbow, but he still felt its Intent. It had stopped as soon as he was incapacitated, and Calder wasn't sure whether that came from concern for his well-being or a cruel sense of humor.

A strange Intent crawled up the chains. In addition to the Elder's usual distant calculations and slow rage, it was now feeling something new. Something almost like...amusement.

The Lyathatan opened its mouth, though Calder could only see its lower jaw, and let out a hissing laugh.

Even the Elders were laughing at him.

Foster knelt by Calder's side and rapped him on the forehead. "Well, that was the most stupid thing I've ever seen you do. And that's a prestigious record, I don't say it lightly. She fought Urzaia, you're not going to catch her off guard."

You could have reminded me sixty seconds ago, Calder thought, but nothing made it out of his paralyzed mouth.

Andel emerged from below deck, climbing out with a bottle of wine in one hand and a basket in the other. "The bread is relatively fresh, and we have some seasoned fish and olives to go with it. I'm not quite sure about the wine, with Petal...ah, I see the Captain is here."

Meia sighed. "He tried to set his Elderspawn on me. Evidently he mistook my mercy for idiocy."

"The Captain's inadequacies aside, we're about to have a problem." Andel turned to the Lyathatan, which spat out laughter even as it slowly descended into the ocean, its six black eyes trained on Calder. If the Elderspawn weren't completely capable of destroying this ship and everyone on it, Calder would have sought revenge for this humiliation.

Come to think of it, why did he have to witness this scene at all? Why was he still conscious?

"*The Eternal* will have seen that," Andel continued. "They're only minutes out. We intended to follow them to the Capital, but now that they've seen something's wrong, I'm sure they will send someone over."

Meia's soft footsteps padded past Calder's ears as she stepped over his head. "So the Elderspawn was a signal. Nice try, but if Shera were in my position, she would have killed the captain immediately. He's lucky to be alive."

Calder hadn't thought of using the Lyathatan as a signal, but he appreciated the results. When he discussed this with Andel in the future, he would pretend this was his plan all along.

The Consultant leaned over, pulling Calder's spyglass from inside his jacket. She turned to the railing, and metal scraped as the spyglass slid open. She must be inspecting Cheska Bennett's ship. "Who's onboard?" Meia asked.

"Three Guild Heads," Andel answered grimly, and the assassin let out an involuntary growl. An actual *growl*, as though Calder was lying at the feet of a massive hunting dog.

She didn't give any sign that she'd done anything out of the ordinary, but

Calder wished he could exchange glances with Andel and Foster. "How long before they get over here?"

"Not long," Bliss said.

Calder's hopes soared.

The Head of the Blackwatch Guild slid into his view—actually *slid*, skating over the portion of the deck that had been splashed in the wake of the Lyathatan's rise. He hadn't seen her arrive on the ship, but that was no surprise. He doubted he would have seen anything even if he could still turn his head.

Bliss looked exactly the same as always: her long hair a shade closer to white than her skin, wearing a black coat that hung down to her ankles. The row of silver buttons down the middle each bore the crest of the Blackwatch: six inhuman eyes on a bed of tentacles.

She fixed her gaze on a point over and behind Calder. "Oh? Calder Marten said you were tied up."

"I was, at the time," Meia responded. Calder's spyglass fell as she dropped it, hitting him on the chest. It struck him *right* in the bandaged shoulder, and a weak groan escaped from his chest.

Why wasn't he unconscious yet? His vision wasn't even fading; nothing new seemed to be happening to him, but he was still locked in paralysis with his burning injuries.

Bliss slid sideways on the slick deck without taking her eyes from the Consultant. "You look strange. Do you know Nathanael Bareius?"

"I've never met him, but I'm familiar with his handiwork." Meia's hand flexed, stretching further. Muscles rippled up her arm, and her nails extended into claws.

"Hmm. We need Calder Marten, we've all agreed, but I don't know what I should do with you. You're not supposed to be here, you know. I—"

Bliss was cut off when Meia launched herself explosively across the deck. Calder could actually feel his Vessel tense beneath him at the force of her leap, and she descended on the Guild Head an instant later with bronze in one hand and claws bared in the other.

Calder had to strain his eyes to catch what happened next, and it still took several long seconds for his brain to piece it together. Meia's dagger plunged down before her feet had even met the deck, and Bliss' hand moved. The knuckles of her fist struck the flat of the blade, then the hand unfolded and pushed against Meia's wrist. The Guild Head's other arm came down straight onto Meia's, pushing the clawed hand down and away.

As a result, the assassin landed with both arms pushed wide apart, as though she meant to wrap the shorter woman in an embrace. While Calder was still puzzling over their first exchange, Meia pushed her arms together, trying to overpower Bliss with sheer strength.

But Bliss released her immediately, skating backwards on the wet deck. Meia stopped before she drove a knife into her own palm.

"I see now," Bliss said, calm as ever. "They've given you some supplementary systems. That's very sad for you. How do you deal with the voices?"

Meia had stopped where Calder could see her face, and her Kameira eyes blazed with orange light. "You're an artificial. I'd heard the rumors, but I never checked your file." The Consultant's face reddened and her shoulders trembled with palpable rage, but her expression remained focused and her knife steady. The combination made her seem much less human, giving the impression that her body was shaking *without* her. Like her flesh bore an anger that her mind could not touch.

By contrast, Bliss grew cold, her entire demeanor freezing over. "That's a very rude thing to say. It suggests that I am an object, which I do not appreciate."

Meia spent a long moment struggling, clearly trying to find the right words. "This is a waste of time for both of us," she said at last. "I need transportation back to the Gray Island. Give me control of this ship for two days, and we can go our separate ways."

Bliss squinted at Meia. "You're suggesting that you will kill Calder Marten if I don't comply. You could, I suppose. It would take me an instant to reach you, and he's very close. You could step on his neck from there, or drive your dagger into his brain, or tear his head off, or kick him and break his spine, or crush his skull, or poison him, or constrict his windpipe..."

Calder wasn't sure what Bliss intended, but he wished he could move enough to ask her to stop.

"Those are all options," Meia agreed.

"That would be inconvenient for me," Bliss allowed. "And I suspect Calder Marten wouldn't like it very much either. Where would we find another Emperor at this hour?"

Meia went very still, and Calder would have groaned if he had any control over his voice. The last thing he needed was for Bliss to give the Consultants another reason to kill him.

"You want *him* to sit on the throne?"

Bliss nodded once, very precisely. "Well put. Yes, that's exactly what we want him to do."

The Consultant's eyes flickered from Bliss to Calder, and Calder strained to move. He could practically hear Meia trying to decide if it would be worthwhile to assassinate him, even with the Guild Head there. Bliss' litany rolled through his head, taunting him with all the ways he could die: *crushed skull, collapsed throat, severed head, pierced brain...*

With all his willpower focused on his body, Calder managed to lurch a few degrees to the side. He heaved himself over until most of his weight rested on his injured shoulder, sending lightning lancing through his arm and his entire chest. *Perfect. Now I'll be in even more pain before she kills me.*

From his new perspective, he couldn't see Bliss at all. Meia's black shoe rested close to his head, and Andel stood at the other end of the ship, cradling the food and wine in his arms. He had stayed completely silent during the entire exchange, Calder noted, but at least he had the decency to look concerned. Foster was nowhere to be seen, but *he* hadn't challenged Meia either. Surely he should have been able to line up a shot by now.

The rest of Calder's view was taken up by the green-black of the deck and a stretch of bright, rolling ocean. The red outline of *The Eternal* bobbed like a toy in a bathtub as it headed toward him, which was *almost* a relief; Cheska Bennett would arrive just in time to leave him a stirring eulogy.

He left those thoughts behind, searching for some way out before the Consultant's blade descended on his neck. He wasn't dead yet, so there had to be some options.

Focusing his awareness, he prepared to Read the ship. Any unnatural movement would surely alert Meia, so he had to be careful...

At that moment, his new point of view proved to be an advantage. Just as he started to send his Intent down into *The Testament*, he caught a glimpse of motion around *The Eternal*. He moved his eyes up, concentrating on the crimson ship.

The Guild Head's flagship was a deep blood-red, and made of seamless wood just as Calder's own Vessel. Its sails were a bright red as well, and alchemical flames trailed along the bottom of the hull as the ship set the ocean alight wherever it sailed.

But as Calder stared, that spot of scarlet began to *twist*, warped as though by heat. The air shifted in a visible spiral, forming into a bubble of distorted space that engulfed half the ship.

This was the Aion Sea, where the bizarre was more commonplace than the natural, but still...Calder had never seen anything like this. Was this an attack, or some strange attempt on Cheska's part to rescue him?

He got his answer an instant later, when the bubble popped, tearing *The Eternal* in half.

The bow stayed entirely intact, but the stern vanished in a spray of debris. Not an explosion but a dismantling, like the twisting bubble had taken the vessel apart piece by piece.

The sound reached Calder's ears a second later, like a cannon-shot. Deceptively slowly, *The Eternal* filled with water, its mast tilting backwards like a felled tree. Its nose twisted up, angling toward the sky.

Then he heard the screams.

CHAPTER THREE

ELEVEN YEARS AGO

Jyrine Tessella whispered her secrets into the fire, and madness answered.

"Where are his bonds?" a voice croaked from the flickering shadows. The steady chirp of the insects outside went utterly silent in the presence of that voice, and the cave dropped a few degrees.

"We have taken *The Testament*," Jerri responded. "Calder has been released unharmed, and soon we will return to the ship."

She wanted to say that the Emperor had spared him from execution, but mentioning the Emperor was tricky business when you used Elderspawn as your messengers. They knew the Emperor well enough to fear even his name.

Emerald flames blazed, illuminating the smooth dome of stone wrinkled with crystal. It looked as though some ancient traveler had polished the inside of a natural rock formation, painting lines of quartz on the ceiling like a road map.

In the influence of the voice and the flames, those crystals seemed to slither.

"Can you capture the Lyathatan?" the voice asked, creaking like the mast of a ship in high wind.

"No need. Calder works for us. He works *with* us, though he doesn't know it."

The fire bunched in on itself, like a man folding his arms to think. "Explain."

She was delighted to. "He carries with him a Bellowing Horror, a spawn of Othaghor that often declares death. But he doesn't fear it. He treats it as a beloved pet."

A short, stubby little creature, like a foot-tall fat man with a pair of undersized bat's wings. Its eyes were orbs of pure black hate, its mouth masked behind writhing tentacles, and it spoke with the voice of doom itself. They called it Shuffles.

"He is hunted by the Blackwatch, just as we are. He was exiled from their number for consorting with Elders." He was removed from the Guild as part of an Imperial decree, owing to his attempt to rescue his father. The attempt that had resulted in almost two dozen deaths, and his expulsion had nothing to do with 'consorting with Elders.' Phrasing it this way would be more persuasive.

The men and women on the other end of the flame murmured thoughtfully among themselves, and the Elderspawn translated it as the babble of madmen, trickling from the fire like drool from the lips of an imbecile.

Impatience took root inside her, and her Soulbound Vessel started up again.

They don't believe you, it said, hot with rage. *They will never believe you. But you're stronger than they are. You don't need them. You can burn them. Burn it, melt it, turn it all to slag!*

Her mind filled with visions of acid-green flame, consuming the stone walls of the cave, leaving nothing more than a pool of molten rock behind her. It would help nothing, wouldn't even touch the cabal, but her body ached for the destruction. Her Awakened earring, bearing the mated power of a Kameira and a notorious Elder, crooned in her ear. Its match, hanging from her other ear, was silent. It was invested only as protection, a false duplicate meant to counter and contain the power in her *real* Vessel.

The copy did very little to quiet the whispers, the constant urge to push a tiny fraction of the world toward ruin. But Jerri was sixteen; more than old enough to handle a little insanity.

She fed a little more of her power into the fire, to keep her Vessel content, as she waited for the Sleepless cabal to stop deliberating.

"He could be an asset," the flame finally said. "But it is not our decision. We must consult the Great Ones."

At even an indirect mention of a Great Elder, the voice of the transmission quivered.

"Oh, did I not mention?" Jerri had been saving her best card for last. "He has the approval of Kelarac."

The fire dimmed to a green spark, the crystal in the walls flared with light reflected from some other place, and a thousand unseen messengers whispered at once.

"Kell'arrack."

"The Collector of Souls."

"Great One."

"Blinded and bound."

"Great One..."

Jerri waited, projecting a nonchalance she didn't feel, keeping a tight grip on her Soulbound power. She fiddled with her braid as the cabal struggled to regain control of the void transmission.

"He made a bargain to escape Candle Bay," she went on, when the voices went silent. "Kelarac provided the Lyathatan as our guide. If he trusts Calder, why should we not?"

"The situation is changed," croaked the bullfrog-voice from the fire. "The will of Kelarac is paramount. If the former Blackwatch has a connection to the Great Ones, he could be our greatest step forward in an instant—" The voice layered over itself, as though correcting itself while speaking. "—a moment—" It stuttered again.

"—a year—"

"—an age—"

"—a day—"

"—a century."

Elderspawn messengers often had trouble translating time.

"May I introduce him to the Sleepless?" Jerri asked, fluttering with fear. More than anything, she wanted to tell Calder everything and have him approve. Approve, and join her in unlocking the secret wisdom of the Elders. But when she imagined his reaction, she could only picture his horror and disgust.

So she would make sure he understood, and *then* she would tell him the truth.

"We must proceed carefully," the voice said. "Our old enemy is still in control of himself, and we cannot afford his interference" Jerri was sure they meant the Emperor. "We must seek guidance."

"From whom?" Jerri asked, though she assumed they would seek communion with Kelarac. Hopefully, the Great Elder would support her endorsement of Calder.

"Our other patron," said the fire, and again a thousand whispers joined in. They were joyful, this time, instead of hostile and competing.

"The Overseer."

"He who knows all."

"Sees all."

"The Father of Knowledge."

"Ach'magut."

The Sleepless respected the supernatural wisdom of all the Elders, but two Great Elders were revered above the rest. Kelarac, for his willingness to help and support humanity, was considered by many in the Sleepless to be their best hope for human and non-human interaction.

But a close second was Ach'magut, the Overseer.

The Lord of a Thousand Eyes sought knowledge above everything, at any cost. It was said that the Emperor learned Reading in the halls of Ach'magut, and that the birth of human civilization could be traced back to this one Elder. More importantly, his goals did not involve the malicious destruction of humankind, as Nakothi or Urg'naut would desire. He simply wanted to learn everything, and then to move on. Whether humans survived or not was irrelevant.

Which made him a great resource, but not an ally.

There was only one problem. "Kelarac is still free to act," Jerri said. "Ach'magut is dead."

"As you should know," croaked the green flame, "that is only a minor inconvenience."

CHAPTER FOUR

The Emperor destroyed my home today, and he never left his palace. Am I the only one who wonders how?

—FROM THE SCRAPS OF A REBEL PRISONER'S PERSONAL JOURNAL.

From the wreckage of *The Eternal,* screams echoed over the water. Piercing, agonized screams, like those of a dying horse. The sea was littered with debris, and dark shapes fell over the side as at least a few of the crew escaped certain death.

But the screams continued. Too loud for a single human.

Calder saw the jeweled gleam of a thousand feathers scattered on the waves before he figured it out: General Teach's personal Kameira, the near-mythical Windwatcher, had been aboard that ship. And now it was dying.

Behind him, boots slammed against the board and Andel shouted orders, but Calder didn't listen. He didn't need to. Whether he controlled his body or not, as long as he was conscious, he could move his ship.

He left the pain of his wounds behind, shut out the death-screams of the Windwatcher, and ignored the debates of his crew. Once again, he sent his Intent down to the Lyathatan.

Save them, he ordered, focusing his will into a specific picture: the Elder cradling the remains of Cheska Bennett's ship in its clawed hands.

The Lyathatan's amusement hasn't faded, and laughter rekindles as the human gives it an order. The human is still immobile, and likely to die. If the human is killed so early, Kelarac will consider the Lyathatan's service finished, and all plans will advance. The stars wheel, the earth turns, and humans die. It is the way of the universe, and the Lyathatan looks forward to it, as much as it looks forward to anything.

As the Reading broke, Calder had to throttle his frustration and impatience. The Elder would sense those, and they would weaken his bargaining position. What could he offer the Lyathatan that would tempt it to help? How could he save those people?

A figure in black-and-red armor staggered onto the slanted deck, marching up the incline as though pushing against the force of a hurricane. General Teach. She had someone thrown over her shoulder, someone in mismatched clothes whose long, red hair spilled over the General's back. Cheska Bennett.

Teach slipped, falling onto her armored chest, one arm thrown out to grip the deck. Somehow she found a handhold, and she was barely able to keep Cheska from falling further, from plunging into the Aion Sea.

Calder owed Jarelys Teach nothing, but Cheska...Cheska had been his Guild Head for many years, and his friend for more than a few. He couldn't lose another friend, not so soon, not when he was so close. He *wouldn't*.

The six-fingered handprint on his arm grew warm.

This time, when Calder returned his Intent to the Lyathatan, he carried with him something older. His voice carried the echo of a Great Elder, and the lesser spawn had to stand aside.

Save them, he ordered, and the Lyathatan shook with an emotion even stranger than amusement: shock. It was still not a perfect approximation of the emotion, like something mimicking human feelings that didn't quite understand them, but it was shock nonetheless.

I obey, the Lyathatan sent back, and the simple Intent was layered with meaning. It submitted with reluctance, resentment, curiosity, calculation, and smoldering rage. Its reasons were tangled in such a knot that Calder knew his mind would tear like delicate lace before he comprehended the smallest part.

But the Lyathatan obeyed.

The Testament creaked as the Elder forcibly towed it closer to the other Navigator's vessel, Foster shouting as he stumbled over the shifting deck. As they drifted closer to the sinking ship, Meia knelt by Calder's head. She hadn't been thrown off-balance, of course. She was the same as Urzaia, somehow, and whatever Champion gift allowed the man to stay balanced even during the roughest storm, she had it too. Calder wondered if he'd be able to buy that power, when he was Emperor.

"Did you damage their ship?" Meia asked softly.

Calder managed to awkwardly lurch his head to one side until he could see her reaction. That meant the poison was wearing off, which came as a relief. "Not...me." He had no idea what could have caused a twisted explosion like the one that had torn *The Eternal* apart, but the two ships were clearly alone out here. He would attribute this to the mysteries of the Aion.

Good thing he had turned to see her face, because she paled a shade when she heard that. She nodded absently, as though she'd expected his answer, and then turned from him. "Guild Head," she called, and Calder did what he could to roll over and watch her. His wounded shoulder complained.

Bliss stood with her back to Meia and Calder, watching the sky. "It's coming again. Secure all hands." She glanced back at Calder. "Isn't that what you're supposed to say?"

It wasn't, but Calder was in no mood to correct her.

"Guild Head," Meia repeated, even as the air over *The Testament* warped and began to twist. "Who controls the Optasia?"

Bliss looked back to the sky, watching space bend like folded glass. "I thought no one did, but that's clearly not true, is it? Calder Marten, I suggest you turn the ship."

He didn't need *her* to tell him that. His Intent was already traveling to the Lyathatan, frantic and demanding, layered with the voice of Kelarac.

The Elder jerked the ship to starboard, sloshing waves of freezing water over the side and dousing Calder in a shocking storm of ice. The ship's lines bound him in place, securing the rest of his crew at the same time. Bliss could no doubt take care of herself, and if Meia was pitched overboard, that would solve several problems at once.

But no ship was designed to leap sideways. The stress tore at the boards, springing leaks in a dozen places, lancing through *The Testament* like a hammer-blow. The bolts fastening the Lyathatan's chains strained at the surrounding wood, beginning to pop and splinter.

Calder could fix everything, given raw materials and a little time, and he had greater concerns at the moment. As another scream from the dying Windwatcher split the air between the two ships, a bubble of force popped into existence over *The Testament*.

This close, it looked like a soap bubble, a transparent sphere of energy that warped and twisted everything seen through it. If he hadn't dragged the ship to the side, an explosion like the one that had destroyed *The Eternal* would have uprooted his mast. It wouldn't have been a lethal blow, but a crippling one. Calder would have to rely on the Lyathatan to take them *anywhere*, which was not a winning proposition over the long term.

More importantly, if they had lost their mast, they would have been delayed. Perhaps long enough to prevent them from rescuing the crew of *The Eternal*. Fortunately, Bliss' warning had come in time.

The Head of the Blackwatch had one hand stretched out to point at the bubble, which popped a second later with a deceptively quiet, empty sound.

"How is this possible?" Meia asked, her voice harsh and demanding.

Bliss turned to her. "My Watchmen must be dead, and something else has taken control of the palace. I must immediately return to the Capital, because that is my job, and I will be taking Calder Marten with me. He is now a very valuable replacement part."

Calder didn't particularly like the sound of that.

"I see," Meia said, nudging Calder with her foot. "Can he handle it?"

"It's better than leaving the weapon in the hands of an enemy."

"True." The Consultant watched the wreckage of *The Eternal*, which lurched closer and closer as the Lyathatan pulled them over. "I propose a truce, Guild Head. It seems I need to visit the Capital after all."

"Your Architects have not ordered you to the Capital."

Meia sheathed both of her knives behind her back. "If they knew what I know, they would."

When the Lyathatan reached Cheska Bennett's ship, it first reached under the hull with its clawed hands and slowly lifted. Water poured out of the shattered vessel, the deck stabilized, and survivors in the water swam away from the monster in renewed panic. Most of them paddled desperately for *The Testament*, trying to escape the rise of the giant Elderspawn.

Calder made sure that rope ladders had been unfurled down the sides to meet them. Andel and Petal were on hand for first aid, and Calder himself was huddled under a blanket against the railing. He sipped on an alchemical concoction of Petal's that was supposed to reduce the poison's control over his body, but was primarily making him feel as though the whole world was upside down.

In the end, the Lyathatan was able to rescue both Guild Heads and three of Teach's crew, none of whom had the strength to stand once they reached *The Testament*. Evidently surviving a shipwreck really took the wind from your sails. So to speak.

Cheska had a nasty cut over one eye, her breathing was shallow, and she didn't look likely to wake any time soon. Petal was currently fussing over her, carefully lowering a glowing syringe to the woman's throat.

The crew members were in varying states of panic or insensibility. Only Jarelys Teach seemed to have her wits about her, and she was still visibly exhausted and soaking wet.

By now, the screams of the Windwatcher had gone silent.

Calder's crew took care of the survivors, but Calder himself kept his mind focused on the ship. The Lyathatan strode through the water ahead of them, carrying the remnants of *The Eternal* in its clawed hands. The Elder tugged their ship behind it, but considering the beating *The Testament* had taken, it was all Calder could do to hold his Vessel together.

He would have had an easier time if he could have left the remaining half of *The Eternal* behind, but he knew what that would do to Cheska. *"A captain's ship is his life. A Navigator's ship is his soul."* That had once been a common saying, though the origin was long lost.

Every passenger cabin and half the hold was filled with cargo from *The Eternal,* from food stores to clothes to weapons. They'd salvaged everything they could, but now *The Testament* felt stuffed to the brim. Teach leaned against a trunk full of books with her eyes closed, arms resting on sacks of powdered soap. Foster sat cross-legged on a massive roll of blankets, tinkering with a cannon and muttering into his beard. And Bliss popped up from behind a cask like a prairie dog, glanced around, and slowly hid herself again.

The Guild Head slid from cask to crate to giant basket, weaving her way across the crowded deck like a child taking a game very seriously.

When her head rose out of a box next to him—he had no idea how she'd managed to get inside the box without him seeing, but he'd learned to stop asking pointless questions—he nodded to her.

"Good evening, Guild Head," he said.

She turned to him, solemnly inclining her head from over the rim of the box. "Good evening, Calder Marten. Are you sick?"

He took a sip from the mug in his hands, which tasted like lemons and cinnamon and lightning. The world lurched around him, as though reality were trying to stand on its head, but by now he'd grown used to the effects of the alchemy. "Just tired. I was poisoned earlier, and now I'm holding the ship together."

"I see." She pointed to the blanket wrapped around his shoulders. "I've noticed that people often wrap blankets around the injured and the sick. Does it help somehow?"

"At least I won't be tired, shaky, *and* cold."

She rubbed her chin as she considered. "I see. I'll remember that."

The Guild Head started to lower her head back into the box, a clockwork toy rewinding itself, but Calder stopped her with an outstretched hand. He was actually going to touch her shoulder, but reminded himself at the last second that he might want to keep the hand.

"Bliss. Who attacked us?"

He'd been planning on waiting for Meia to disappear so that he could talk to Bliss without interruption, but that plan had worked entirely too well. Meia had vanished almost immediately after the survivors of *The Eternal* had been rescued, and he hadn't seen her since. He would have sworn that she'd left, if there had been anywhere else for her to go. A cursory Reading of the ship didn't reveal her, though he couldn't spare much attention or Intent for a thorough search.

As far as he knew, the Consultant could be lurking over his shoulder, listening to every word. But that couldn't be helped. If she overheard him, so be it; he had to know what they were sailing into.

Bliss' brow furrowed. "That's a good question. I don't know, though I'm certain the Elders are involved if they've taken over the Imperial Palace. You know how difficult it would be for a human to use the Optasia."

Calder reminded himself that his mother treated Bliss with endless patience, and tried to summon some of that for himself. "No, in fact I don't. What is the Optasia?"

"It's the Emperor's throne," she said, levering herself over the edge of the box to crouch face-to-face with Calder. "He used it to control a network of amplification devices all over the world, so that he could use his Intent anywhere, instantly. An ingenious system. Too bad it was so terribly flawed."

Calder waited for her to continue, but she seemed to think that she'd explained enough. After a few awkward seconds, he prompted her. "Flawed?"

"Yes."

Nothing else.

"*How* was it flawed, Bliss?"

She moved her head from side to side like a snake, searching his face from every angle. "You must have wondered why we were willing to let someone so young, inexperienced, naive, emotional, under-educated, and generally unsuitable call himself Emperor."

Endless patience. "I hadn't thought of it in quite those terms."

"As we explained before, we need someone to sit on the throne. Not the blocky chair in the audience hall, although I'm sure that you will have to host an audience at some point, and you should be prepared for that. We need someone on the *real* throne. The Optasia. So while there are any number of other qualities that we would like in an Emperor, all we want is a Reader strong enough to use the Optasia to magnify their talents. And to not go insane, of course."

Calder was having enough trouble wrapping his mind around the reality of a device that allowed the Emperor to cast his will across the world. Was that how he had become so much more powerful than any other Reader? Did he have an artificial, world-spanning system propping up his powers?

No, that wasn't likely. Calder had Read enough of the Emperor's trail to know that the man invested objects just by walking down the same street. An Intent like that couldn't be faked.

But then, Calder would never have thought such an Intent could be magnified either.

"I'm sorry, Bliss, but I feel like I've been invited to a play in the third act. How does this device work? What did he use it for? Why does it have to be the Emperor who uses it, and not someone else? Most importantly, how is it going to drive me insane?"

The Guild Head smiled at him with obvious pity, patting him softly on the top of the head with one hand. "There, there. No need to apologize. The throne is linked to amplification devices created by the Emperor and scattered all over the world. They're in the shape of statues, I believe. They took his Intent and focused it wherever necessary, so that he could deal with threats without leaving the Capital. I should think it would be obvious why we're restricting its use: we're handing control of the Empire over to the first powerful Reader who sits in the chair. That requires quite a bit of caution."

Using both hands, she reached out and snatched his mug of softly glowing alchemical medicine, taking a brief sip. She made a face like a little girl who had bitten into a lemon, looked all around her, and then took another sip.

"What about the insanity, Bliss?"

"You're very stuck on that. It's not good to be too focused on one thing. Well, the Optasia was constructed so that the Emperor could respond to any of the Great Elders who acted up. Indeed, some of my predecessors in the Blackwatch wondered why they were necessary at all, if the Emperor could blast Elders to pieces from his seat in the Capital."

"That's another thing. How does anyone blast anything with their Intent? That doesn't seem possible."

She shrugged. "He's the Emperor."

In hindsight, it had been a stupid question.

"But the Emperor used the Optasia only rarely, for the greatest hazards, and in the last twenty years of his life I can only prove that he used it one time. Why is that, do you think?"

Bliss stared at him quizzically, as though genuinely wondering if he had the answer.

"If he had to focus his Intent on a Great Elder every time it popped up, he would be staring madness in the face. I don't know how he *ever* did it without going insane; that sounds like it would be worse than Reading an Elderspawn directly." And everyone knew you couldn't Read an Elderspawn directly unless you were tired of keeping your personality intact. Or unless you had Kelarac's handprint on your arm. Before that, when Calder sent his Intent down to the Lyathatan, he was very careful to Read only the Intent in the manacles and chains. Like looking at a reflection in a mirror.

Bliss beamed at him, patting him on the head again. "Very good! If I were grading you, I would give you full points. And I am grading you. Secretly."

"Then what do you want *me* to do with it? If this Optasia was too difficult for the Emperor, then I'm more likely to kill us all." Calder questioned many things about the late Emperor, may his soul sink down to Kelarac: his character, his decisions, his concern for the people of the Empire. But Calder had never questioned the man's power as a Reader. If the Emperor hadn't figured out a way to use the Optasia safely, then Calder would do nothing but die.

Bliss lowered herself into the box, shutting the lid over her head. Her voice came from inside, muffled and indistinct. "Don't worry. We know you can't force Urg'naut back into his seal, or keep Ach'magut from rebuilding his library, or do anything *useful.*"

Every conversation with Bliss was an exercise in not taking offense. Calder happened to think he was doing quite well so far.

"We need eyes," the Guild Head continued from within her box. "Through the Optasia, even when the Emperor couldn't confront a threat directly, he could tell us what was happening with any of the Great Elders at any time. On our own, we can't keep track of it all. And you'll be able to send messages to our agents anywhere in the world. We'll deal with all the real threats, as long as you keep us informed."

That made a certain amount of sense. And he supposed he should be grateful; if the Guild Heads hadn't needed someone to bear the risk of sitting on the throne, they would never have allowed him the chance to act as Emperor. The chance he'd always wanted. The chance he'd been promised.

Bliss spoke again, and this time her voice was coming from a different cask, this time on his left. He didn't question it, just shifted his position so he was facing the Guild Head's new container. "And, of course, the others want a figurehead to keep the people happy. A puppet. A pretty doll to put on parade so that the children feel protected."

Now he was sure Bliss was trying something. "Are you insulting me on purpose?"

She popped up from the inside of the cask, a coil of rope on her head. "That's ridiculous."

He still had the Emperor's crown, and the candles of the Witness in charge of Imperial finance. Access to power and funds both. But then, the Guild Heads could have any team of Readers unlock the secrets in Naberius' wax-sealed memories, and Teach could take the crown from him without much trouble.

His only asset, it seemed, was being disposable.

He could use that.

"So when we reach the Capital, what's the plan? You clear the way to the Optasia, and I sit on it, and everything's better again?"

"That depends on one very troubling factor," Bliss said, staring off into the horizon.

"What's that?"

"Who's using it now?"

Jerri's hand hovered inches away from the throbbing gray-green flesh that walled her inside the room. The bulbous meat that enveloped the walls would have been disgusting, if she hadn't been trained to look past its appearance and into what it *represented*: an advance in knowledge and technology so complete that humans might never understand it.

Besides the Elders, who had the power to instantly grow a life—real, living flesh—and bend it to their will? Even the Emperor couldn't do that. The Elders controlled life and death, memory and knowledge, space and time. The merest fraction of their expertise would improve the lives of people all over the Empire.

Put that way, it was hard to understand why anyone *didn't* want to learn from the Elders. Distasteful as they might seem, they embodied the clearest road into the future.

But thoughts of the distant future would only distract her for so long when she was more concerned with today.

"How long must I wait?" Jerri asked.

The room's only other occupant, a dark-skinned Heartlander man who might have been a native of the Capital, sat on the corner of the Emperor's bed. A softly glowing bulb, dangling from the new-grown flesh overhead, cast shadows on his face. Jewels gleamed at his neck, on his fingers, in his ears, in his hair—it seemed that he had crammed gold and gems anywhere he could fit them. Only his eyes were plain and unadorned, covered as they were by a steel blindfold that seemed to have been bolted to his face.

She'd seen other Elder cults who believed in mutilating their bodies, demonstrating their dedication to the Great Ones, but no one else had gone so far as to blind themselves. Especially not to these gruesome extremes. It looked as though he'd driven steel screws straight into his own eyes.

But he smiled broadly at her question. "If you wish to learn from the Elders, patience is the first and most valuable skill. There are beings who will not begin a conversation without observing the other party for at least a year, and whose names take a man's lifetime to properly pronounce."

This was another characteristic of the absurdly devout: they always pretended to know more than they did. "You haven't answered my question."

"To understand the answer, you must first understand the question."

Fury flowed into her from the Vessel on her ear, and both earrings lit up. One shone with the power of unreleased flame, and the other restricted that power, protecting her from its corrosion. To some degree.

Green fire played around her fingers, and she examined her fingertips as though searching for the proper words. "I owe a debt to the Great One who freed me from captivity, not to you. I owe you nothing. I do not know you, nor do I know what I'm doing here, and until I *do* I'm afraid I can't cooperate. If it is your job to guide me, as you claim, then I suggest you start doing so. Otherwise...well, I am a Soulbound. And you're not."

That was an assumption on her part, but a good one. She wasn't a Reader, so she couldn't sense if one of the man's rings or necklaces might secretly be his Soulbound Vessel, but she doubted it. The Sleepless had only one true combat-capable Soulbound in their membership, and the cabal valued her highly because of it. He may have been a mercenary Soulbound hired by the cult for this one task, but then he wouldn't have been so secretive about the nature of that task. Besides, only a true fanatical believer would blind himself.

The man stroked his thin beard like a sage in thought. "By definition, I cannot be a Soulbound. One requires something to bind, after all."

Before Jerri could think too hard about that statement, the room shook. The flesh of the walls quivered, and the living light flickered. "That one was closer," she said.

"Closer," her companion agreed, "but they are not yet striking at the heart. It's merely a flesh wound, as they say." He smiled to himself, revealing two teeth capped in gold.

It had been perhaps three days since Jerri had been stuck in this room, though it was hard to tell the exact time without access to natural light. She remained surrounded by skin and muscle as though she'd been swallowed by a great Elder whale, food oozing through disgusting openings at regular intervals. Her transmission through the void had taken her directly here, and she'd waited in the dimness for instructions. In vain, so far.

Yesterday, the blind man had appeared next to her, presumably through a void transmission similar to her own.

It was he who explained exactly where they were: the center of the Imperial Palace, inside the Emperor's personal rooms.

That knowledge had distracted Jerri for hours, as she explored the suite of flesh-covered rooms in a new light. This was the bed where the Emperor had slept. Those paintings were favored by the Emperor. The decorative swords on the wall, if they had ever been used by the Emperor in self-defense, would count as some of the greatest weapons in history. She wished Calder was here, so that he could appreciate the rich stores of Intent that no doubt lingered in this room.

As always when she thought of Calder, pain and sickness and anger rolled through her. She had handled him badly, she knew. Almost as badly as she ever could have. The assassin Shera had shown up at the worst possible time, before any of her plans had borne fruit. When Jerri finally saw Calder again, she had been forced to act out her duty as a member of the Sleepless. She could hardly have made a worse impression.

But still, he had abandoned her in a cell. Her own *husband*. It hurt.

Make him listen, her Vessel demanded, indistinguishable from her own thoughts. *He cannot stop you.*

To distract herself, to keep her from another fight with her own Soulbound Vessel, she turned her attention to the one object in the room she didn't understand. Behind a shattered section of wall, inside what must once have been a hidden closet, there was a knot of gray-green flesh the size of her entire body. More than anything, it reminded her of the Heart of Nakothi, as though the Heart itself had grown a hundredfold and swallowed something inside.

Between the folds of its flesh, she caught a glimpse of silvery bars and wires. Like an intricate cage of polished steel, packed into Elder flesh.

She'd examined it for two whole days with no result, and had only barely resisted the temptation to burn it away with her Soulbound power. But she'd forgotten to ask her new, unhelpful guide about it. Until now.

Jerri pointed to the mass of metal and meat. "Is this what they're after?"

Her companion turned to her, studying her through sightless eyes. "So even blind humans can find the truth if they root around long enough."

She gripped fistfuls of her red pants to keep her irritation in check. No one had ever nettled her quite so thoroughly as her blindfolded guide; even with a Vessel that provoked her to rage, she had maintained an agreeable disposition for years. She thought of herself as quite a gentle person, though she longed to blast this man to smoking pieces. "You would be the expert on blindness, I suppose."

"Indeed, thank you for noticing," he said gravely. "I can tell Readers apart from the blind, though most cannot. It's a skill I spent much of my life perfecting."

As with most everything he'd said, that statement tied her brain in knots. He could tell the difference between Readers and ordinary people? How? Calder was one of the more skilled Readers she'd ever known, and even he couldn't do that. Perhaps only the Emperor could.

She examined him more closely. His skin was dark enough, he was the right build, and he spoke in oblique riddles. Perhaps he was a royal; one of the direct descendants of the Emperor. That would certainly explain his attitude.

The room shook again, and this time the air between Jerri and the hidden silver cage rippled. It was almost invisible, as though someone had thrown a rock and managed to disturb space, and for a moment an image of another place flickered in front of her eyes. It was so vivid that it swallowed all of her senses—she smelled burnt wood, tasted the salt of the ocean, saw sunlight on waves—and so quick that she couldn't make out details.

It was the vision of a Reader, shared with her for a split second. She'd seen such things before.

"Did you see that?" she demanded.

"I'm not permitted to, I'm afraid. Safeguards."

She pointed to the flesh-covered steel again. The gesture didn't help anything, since he couldn't see it, but she felt like pointing. "What *is* that? Why do they want it?"

"It's the key that controls the world," he said softly. "Almost obsolete now, but it has its uses."

Jerri was going to wring answers out of this man if she had to sift them from his ashes. "*What* uses?"

"At this moment? In this place?" He smiled again, his gold teeth gleaming. "It's bait."

The room continued to shake as the enemies outside—the Imperial Guard, she supposed—kept launching their attacks. No matter how she pleaded, or demanded, or threatened, her guide gave her no more answers.

Which was fine, she eventually decided. If no one would tell her what she was supposed to do in this overgrown room, she would decide for herself. And she'd already decided where she would start: by burning her way out.

CHAPTER FIVE

Two Imperial Guards dragged Calder Marten out of the Emperor's palace. He had been kept in a room, not a prison cell, but he was still a prisoner. His eyes burned from a night spent weeping over his father instead of sleeping.

His father, who had been killed on the Emperor's orders. Right in front of his eyes.

One of the Guards was a slender woman with vertically slitted eyes, whose head jerked at the slightest sign of movement. A pair of feline tails twitched behind her, and the hand that wasn't holding onto Calder's shoulder sprouted short claws. Her partner loomed over her, a muscular giant with bony spikes growing out of his skin like ominous armor. He supported most of Calder's weight, propping Calder up with a forearm when the young man looked likely to fall. His spines jabbed into Calder's chest every time.

They both wore the red-and-black uniforms of the Imperial Guard, marked with the Aurelian Shield crest: a shield emblazoned with the moon-in-sun emblem of the Aurelian Empire. Like everyone else in their Guild, they had been alchemically imbued with the power of Kameira, forever changing their appearance and giving them a host of strange powers. None of them more frightening than their Guild Head, who could kill with little more than a touch.

Calder tried to drum up some anger at the Head of the Imperial Guard, but the image of the woman killing his father brought him nothing but grief. Jarelys Teach wasn't responsible for Rojric Marten's death.

The Emperor was.

And so was Calder.

May his soul fly free, Calder thought, and almost wept.

The pair of Guards dumped him out on the street as soon as they passed through the gate of the Imperial Palace, and he didn't bother to stand up.

The woman pointed with one claw. "An Imperial officer has been assigned to supervise you for the foreseeable future. He awaits aboard your ship, in the harbor. Do not attempt to leave the city by land, or you will be hunted down. At dawn tomorrow, if you have not departed on your ship, you will be hunted down. If for any reason your officer fails to make his regular report, you will be hunted down." She spoke as though she read from an especially boring shopping list.

Calder just nodded, still collapsed on the paving stones. He hadn't expected to be assigned an officer, but it made sense. He owed the crown for a ten-thousand-goldmark ship. They weren't simply going to turn him over to the Navigators without any supervision.

"Report to your ship by sundown at the latest," she continued. "If you do not, you will be hunted down. Do you know your way to Candle Bay?"

"I wish I didn't," he said.

Calder waited until the Guards were gone before pushing himself to his feet. There was no point in going anywhere except straight to the ship. His mother lived in the city, but she couldn't help him, and he dreaded telling her what he had done. His best chance at freedom lay in *The Testament*, his new ship, and in his job for the Navigator's Guild.

Maybe, once he cleared his debt, he could make the Emperor regret ever letting him live.

Jerri appeared at his shoulder, placing a feather-light hand on his arm. "Calder?" Her eyes were dark, warm, concerned. "Can you walk on your own?"

He demonstrated by marching a few steps down the road, scarcely paying attention to where he was going. "We have to get to the harbor."

"I heard," she said, hovering like she expected him to collapse.

He remembered the Emperor's face, cold and focused, with the crown gleaming gold on his dark, hairless head. It focused his willpower and his anger, propelling him through the crowd and down the crowded streets. "No one ever stops him," Calder said. "No one can." Jerri nodded as thought she understood perfectly.

"Someone should," she responded.

He had expected more of an argument. She drifted along beside him, apparently unconcerned, her eyes forward and her braid hanging down her back. Her eyes were red and half-lidded, as though she too had gone without sleep.

The sight sent a note of guilt thrumming through his gut. He had been focused on his own pain, his own tragedy. He'd forgotten about Jerri. She had been taken along on his plan, caught up in the summoning of an Elder and the destruction of Imperial property. While he was being tried by the Emperor, she must have been sick with worry, left with no idea what would happen to him.

"I'm sorry," he said at last. "This is my problem, not yours. You should go back to your family."

Jerri looked at him, eyes wide in evident surprise. "And miss the *Aion Sea?*"

That reminded him: she had been eager to attempt a jailbreak, delighted at the appearance of the Lyathatan, and just as angry at the Emperor as he was.

She, at least, didn't blame him for the disaster that had ruined their lives.

He couldn't have faked the smile that split his face in that moment. "I should have known better."

Waiting for them on the deck of *The Testament* was a dark-skinned Heartlander man in a pristine white suit. His white pants were freshly pressed, his white shoes polished, and his white hat round and wide-brimmed. A silver pendant gleamed around his neck: the White Sun, symbol of the Luminian Order.

Calder paused halfway up the ramp to his ship, staring. A Luminian? The Empire had sent a Luminian Pilgrim as his babysitter? He had already assumed that the Imperial officer would make all his decisions for him, but he had never imagined that they would come with a sermon on the side.

"Andel Petronus, pleased to meet you," the man said, unfolding a sheet of paper. "And you would be Calder Marten."

"What gave it away?" Calder asked, running his hand over his head. "Was it the hair?"

Andel ignored him, reading off the top of the page. "Calder Marten, in the name of the Aurelian Empire and with all the authority of the Emperor himself, you are hereby placed under my custody until your obligation to the crown is paid. Until such time, you are required to..."

The man in white stopped reading, folding the paper back up and slipping it into his pocket. "Essentially, I get to do whatever I like."

Jerri gave Andel a flattering smile. "And how much is that debt, exactly?"

"Five thousand goldmarks," Andel said, with no expression one way or another.

Jerri made a choking sound. "Five thousand? That's absurd!"

"You're right," Calder said, then he turned back to address Andel. "Why isn't it ten? The Emperor said this was a ten-thousand-goldmark ship."

"Apparently the Blackwatch declined to formally register charges against you," Andel said. "Leaving you burdened only with the cost of an Imperial prison."

That was more than he'd expected, and he likely had his mother's influence to thank. "Fair enough," Calder said, nodding.

Andel nodded back. "Anything the Emperor chooses to do is the definition of fair treatment." There may have been a taste of irony in those words, but it was hard to tell. Judging by his face, he seemed completely serious.

Jerri looked from one of them to the other. "That's more than all of us will make in a lifetime."

"Then I expect we'll get to know one another quite well," Andel said, adjusting his sleeves. "Think of me as part of the ship."

"I choose to think of you as the anchor," Jerri said lightly.

"I can see that," Calder agreed. "Over the side with you."

Unfazed, Andel pulled another paper from his other pocket. "Think of me as the part of the ship that tells you where to go and what to do at all times. Today, we are awaiting," he looked down at the paper, "a package of considerable size, to be delivered to a gladiatorial arena in Izyria."

Calder perked up at that. At least he would be performing actual duties as a Navigator, not simply being held prisoner on his own ship. Surely there was something on the Aion that could ensure his eventual freedom.

"How long does this trip take?" Jerri asked.

"Two months total, there and back again," Andel said. "For an experienced Navigator with a crew. For you, I would say four months. Maybe five."

For one trip? Calder had never done anything in his life for five straight months. He was afraid he'd go insane in a week. Besides which...

He glanced around him. He could feel the ship like an extension of his skin, feel the seamless dark green deck beneath him, the towering presence of the mast supporting a green-veined sail, the splash of water cradling the hull. He felt it, but he had very little idea how it was supposed to work. He'd be lucky to make it out of the harbor.

Then again, he was a Soulbound now. All Soulbound were supposedly capable of great feats. He would figure it out.

"What about the pay?" Calder asked, striking at the subject most near to his heart.

"Fifty goldmarks, on receipt of the package," Andel recited. "They were generous. At this rate, it will only take you thirty years to pay off your debt."

A crippling weight settled onto Calder's shoulders.

"Lighten up," Andel said, with a tone that suggested he was telling them to scrape barnacles. "There are worse fates than thirty years of arduous labor."

Calder looked around the deck in a daze. He had participated in the construction of *The Testament,* binding its pieces together into one cohesive whole, but the ship had never seemed so cramped as it did now. For the rest of his life, this would be his world.

From beneath them, a surge of timeless resentment boiled up into his mind. The Lyathatan, bound by invested chains and sworn into service, seemed incapable of contentment. So not only would he be trapped onboard a ship, he would be accompanied by a bound Elder whose loyalty would last only as long as its vaguely defined term of service.

Besides which, he had little idea how to actually work as a Navigator. What supplies would they need for a four-month journey? Would they be able to pick up food in Izyria? He could steer, but how would he find his way to the correct destination?

Calder wished he could keep up his conversation with the Imperial officer, to show this Andel Petronus that it was Calder's ship and *he* would give the orders.

Instead, he stood on the edge of the deck, lost.

It wasn't like him. He had always thought of himself as the one to take action, who was never at a loss for something to say or do. And now the sheer enormity of the future overwhelmed him.

Andel turned toward him, hat gleaming in the sun. He studied Calder's face with no apparent change in expression.

"While you were still sleeping in the palace, I had the ship loaded. We are now carrying twelve barrels of fresh water, two cauldrons, a set of pots, four canvas flags with the Navigator crest, two rifles with matching ammunition, three quicklamps, and almost a thousand pounds of food. Mostly beans, rice, cheese, and salted meat. There are three Navigator supply stations in the Aion, and we can stop and resupply at each of them, if necessary. I have their locations logged."

When he finished his speech, Andel tipped his hat. "It's in my own best interests to see to the success of this ship, after all."

Calder took what felt like his first full breath of air all day. The relief made him feel ten pounds lighter; he even smiled at the man in white. "Well done, Andel. I may have spoken too hastily with you earlier. Welcome aboard my ship."

Andel ran his hand along the railing and held it up, as though inspecting his fingers for dust. "Until your debt is cleared, Mister Marten, this is *my* ship."

Calder and Jerri spent the rest of the day preparing for their new life, under the direction of Andel Petronus. For one thing, they needed to retrieve clothing and personal effects from their family homes.

Alsa Grayweather, Calder's mother, was not in residence. The servants let Calder into the house, but they only had a vague idea what had happened to her, and the rumors were sending them into a panic. Calder had to convince one valet that he hadn't escaped from the Imperial Palace, as the man worried that Calder was on the run from the law.

He left his mother's home with a trunk of clothes in one hand and a shrouded birdcage in the other. The staff was only too eager to be rid of *that*.

The fate of his mother chewed at him, burdening him even more than his own future. He was sure she wouldn't be held legally complicit in his actions, as she was a Guild member in good standing, but he still didn't know what the Emperor would actually do to her.

But she wasn't at home. He needed to ask Andel; maybe he would know something.

Calder pushed through the crowd leading up to the harbor, Candle Bay stretching out behind *The Testament* like a deep green field. On the left shore, a pile of rubble spilled onto the rocks, as though an avalanche had swallowed up a hospital. Crews of workers scurried like beetles over the debris.

He tore his eyes away from the remnants of the Candle Bay Imperial Prison and back to his ship. Then he had to check the name on the hull, to be sure it actually *was* his ship.

There was a huge cage sitting on the deck, and two men standing around it.

Calder walked up the extra-wide, reinforced ramp that they must have built for the sole purpose of carrying the cage onboard. He supposed they had wheeled it up, considering the cage was big enough to hold a pair of grown lions. Its bars were rough steel, and its base and roof were both made of close-fitting planks of thick wood. No one would be strong enough to carry it.

Then again, if anyone could do so, it would be these two.

One of the men was sun-tanned and weathered as though he had spent his life aboard a ship, his dark hair worked into a hundred tiny braids. His right eye was covered by a rough leather eyepatch, and he carried a hammer at his belt.

At first glance, it looked like a craftsman's claw hammer, but it caught Calder's eye. He peered at it for a moment before he noticed the details that didn't quite fit: the metal was smooth, not nocked as a used hammer would have been, and the handle almost seemed to crawl with twisting shadows. When he recognized the flow of Intent, his eyes widened.

The boy's only friend is the hammer. When he sleeps, the hammer is clutched in his fist. When he is attacked—and he is always attacked—the hammer defends him. He smashes legs, arms, skulls with the hammer until it feels natural, until the crunch of shattered bones is the music of his life. A Kameira looms large among its victims, a slithering creature of liquid and shadow, but somehow it's not just a victim...it's one with the hammer, part of it, merged together...

Calder blinked his eyes free of the vision. If he wasn't mistaken, he'd just witnessed the intentional creation of an Awakened weapon. And, very possibly, a Soulbound.

The one-eyed man saw Calder looking at the hammer and grinned. He ran a thumb down the head of the hammer, preening.

His partner was utterly pale, as though he'd never spent a day outside, and had his hair cut short. This man didn't carry a weapon, but he had a broad shield strapped to his back. Calder didn't bother to focus on it; he could feel the Intent bound in the object clearly enough that he didn't need a closer look. Another Awakened weapon.

Both men bulged with muscle. Once, Calder had gone to see what the news-sheets called a "spectacle," a live performance with trained animals and talented performers with rare skills. A strongman had twisted an iron bar into a knot with nothing more than his bare hands, though Calder had suspected that someone had invested the bar beforehand.

Even that strongman would have fled from these two. They looked like they would have an easier time tearing another man's arm off than shaking his hand.

The one-eyed man stuck a hand out. Calder didn't hesitate before dropping his trunk of clothes and taking the hand; he was afraid that the man might take any reluctance as an insult.

"You must be the young Navigator," the man said, and broadened his grin. "Word is, you broke out of an Imperial prison and walked away with a brand-new ship."

Calder did his best to match the man's smile. "I wasn't breaking myself out."

He laughed like Calder had told a joke. "Well met, Navigator. We'll get along, I can tell. You can call me Nine."

Calder turned his attention to the man with the shield. "And you, sir?"

The pale man didn't seem to notice that Calder had spoken. He kept his eyes on the cage.

"You'll have to forgive Eight," Nine said. "He's picky."

Eight didn't clarify.

"Eight and Nine," Calder said. "There aren't seven more of you, are there?"

Nine chucked easily and rapped his knuckles on the bars. "We're not supposed to use our real names on this trip. Not sure what the point is. You may have noticed that we have a little trouble blending in."

It had been a busy, even catastrophic few days. That was how Calder justified it. There was no other explanation for why he hadn't noticed the gold crest that each man wore pinned on his shirt.

A small, golden pin marked with the image of a crown.

The Golden Crown: symbol of the Champion's Guild.

Calder couldn't stop his eyes from widening. How had he not noticed before? There were a pair of Champions on his deck. Real, living, Imperial Champions.

On *his* ship.

No Guild had made more of an impact on Imperial history than the Champions. All the ancient writers spoke of them. Loreli, the original strategist: *"If you may hire a Champion or persuade one to your cause, then victory is certain. Otherwise, heed my teaching."*

Heliora, the Witness who chronicled the Kings' War: *"I stood motionless from sunrise to sunset, watching the armies clash, recording every maneuver and every feint of one general against another. Then the Champions arrived, and I left, for the battle was over."*

Sadesthenes, the great historian and philosopher: *"If all men were Champions, there would be no war, for such a conflict would be too great and terrible to consider."*

Nazin, the hero of *A Tragedy of Sand and Tears*: *"I am not a Champion, my love. I am but a man."*

Everyone knew about Soulbound. They were impressive and even somewhat mystical beings, but as a Reader, Calder understood them. The birth of a Soulbound was simply one phenomenon of Reading and Intent, something that the Magisters were still studying to this day. They already understood *how* it worked, and someday they would understand *why*.

But Champions were not just Soulbound. They were the superhuman products of a secret process, trained from birth and raised to be unstoppable in battle. They were invincible warriors, the stuff of legends, the kinds of people who could tear giant Kameira apart with their bare hands and laugh while doing it.

And now, two of them were standing on his ship.

Calder couldn't seem to fit his bulging eyes back into his skull. He tried to speak, but his mind had frozen.

Nine either didn't notice his distress or didn't care. He looked aside from Calder, where Andel was climbing out of the hold. The Heartlander man's white suit was still pristine, somehow.

"The Captain has arrived, Pilgrim," Nine called. "Make ready to sail."

Andel didn't bother to look at the Champion. "I'm not a Luminian Pilgrim any longer. And we're still awaiting one more. A young lady."

Nine gave a low whistle and nudged Calder with his elbow.

Calder felt the Champion was misunderstanding something, but he couldn't find the words to explain.

Eight didn't react to anything, keeping his pale arms folded and his eyes locked on the cage. For the first time, Calder noticed the man behind the bars.

He was obviously a prisoner, manacled to a set of chains that were themselves bolted to the cage floor. He was naked but for a cloth tied around his waist, and built along the same lines as the two Champions; he looked as if he could uproot stone pillars with nothing more than the strength of his arms. Blond hair fell, loose and ragged, to frame his face, and his ribs were mottled with fresh bruises.

Calder gestured to the cage. "This is the package you wish delivered to Izyria?"

Nine cackled, slapping the bars with the flat of his hand. "Hear that? You're a package now. Special delivery to the Izyrian arenas. You're going home!"

The prisoner didn't respond. He simply smiled through the veil of his hair. His teeth were white and flawless.

Eight stayed quiet, watching as though he intended to stay in that position until the ship sank or the world ended, but Nine frowned for the first time. He slapped at the side of the cage. "Hey! Answer me. Do you hear me, Urzaia?"

The prisoner looked up, smile unbroken. "It will be good to see my home again."

He turned to Calder, his gaze making the young man shift uneasily. *What does he want? He has to know I can't set him free.*

Urzaia met Calder's eyes and winked.

CHAPTER SIX

Without the Guilds, the Aurelian Empire as we know it could not exist.

– ESTYR SIX

Calder had wondered how they would approach the Capital without inviting a greeting from the harbor-guns; after all, they were being led by a completely visible Lyathatan. If the Elder submerged itself, it would have to drop *The Eternal,* which would immediately sink. And thereby negate the entire reason for bringing it all this way in the first place. If it stayed above the waves, they'd cause a riot as soon as they passed within sight of shore.

Fortunately, Cheska had the answer. She wasn't quite back to her usual self—understandable, since she'd lost half her crew and half her ship in the mysterious attack from the Optasia, but she'd tied her hair back and found an impossibly tall hat. With that on her head, she'd taken charge, flying flags and flashing patterns with a hooded quicklamp at all hours of the day and night.

Finally, after a cannon barrage in a coded rhythm, her signals reached the right ears. Only a day out from the Capital, a Navigator's ship sailed into view, flags raised to indicate their assistance.

Though Calder had never seen the ship before, he found it easy to identify as belonging to the Guild. It had two masts and no sails, only two pairs of giant bat wings that spread wide enough to catch the wind. A pair of painted eyes graced the stern, so realistic that they seemed to follow Calder wherever he moved. It took a long conversation with Bliss to convince him that the eyes were actually painted, and not some bizarre Elder transplant.

With the combined effort of all the Readers on all three crews, they were able to rig up a contraption to let them haul *The Eternal* into harbor without the Lyathatan's assistance. It required every fishing-net and spare foot of line that Calder could draw out of storage, but they eventually had a gigantic net strung between both functional ships. The hastily-invested net, supported from beneath by a hidden Lyathatan, would drag the ruined ship over the water and safely to the dock.

To prevent *The Eternal* from twisting over and dragging everyone to a watery grave, supporting lines bound virtually every part to every other part—the wreck to both ships, the net to the wreckage, and every piece of the demolished ship to itself.

Together they looked like a floating shantytown, but Calder's Reading revealed the Intent to be surprisingly solid. Despite its appearance, everything should hold together.

Light and life, he hoped so. He would hate to sail into the Capital looking this ridiculous for no reason.

Cheska joined him at the wheel as he pretended to steer his ship toward Candle Bay. In reality, the Lyathatan and his Intent were doing most of the work, but he felt more in control with his hands on the wheel.

Captain Cheska Bennett looked almost exactly as she had the week before. Her pants were covered with patches of different colors, her jacket had been tailored to fit a man twice her size, and her hair billowed out behind her as she'd tied it without bothering to comb it. She could have hidden a pet dog under her hat, and she kept one hand resting on her cutlass as though she meant to draw at the slightest provocation.

Only in the smallest, most important ways was she different. She didn't wear a smile when she thought no one was looking, she moved more carefully, and she waited before beginning the conversation. Usually, she treated every exchange like a competition.

"Guild Head," Calder said, when the silence had become too much.

"Calder." The pause stretched longer, and for the first time, Calder got the uncomfortable impression that she didn't know what to say. "I'll be able to fix her, given time. If it takes half a forest's worth of time and I have to go in debt to an alchemist, I'll get it done."

"You won't shake the Reader's burn for months." It was an observation that meant nothing, a non-statement, simply to give her time to say whatever she needed to say.

"She's worth it. I called her eternal for a reason, and I won't give up on her until we both go down to Kelarac." Even when talking about the Emperor and the future of the Empire, Cheska had never looked so serious.

He gave her a grin she was supposed to share. "I wouldn't recognize you if you gave up. You wouldn't be the Head of the Navigator's Guild, that's for certain."

"I was out during the crash, you know. Hit my head or took too much of a shock when *The Eternal* was ripped apart, I don't know. But when I woke up, all I could think was, 'I lost my ship. I lost my ship. What kind of a captain loses her ship?'

"Then I saw your monster, and he had it. You kept it safe for me. That's... that was more than I expected. More than I had any right to expect."

Cheska was uncharacteristically somber, so he matched her tone. "I can only imagine what it would be like. If it was *The Testament*, I couldn't have left it there. How could I do less for you?"

She moved so that her hat shaded her face. Which, given that the hat was bigger than her head, didn't take much. "Just wanted you to know that I appreciate what you did. It'll take a while to get back up and running, but once we are...well, you just let me know what you need. I wouldn't be on the water if it weren't for you."

"I'll hold you to that," he said. She would feel more comfortable if she owed him.

She thumped him on the back with a fist, a little harder than necessary. "Keep it up, and I might decide you're not such a bad fit for the job." When he realized what she meant, he smiled all the way into Candle Bay.

Then they went ashore, and his pleasant mood stayed behind.

They were ambushed almost as soon as their feet hit dry land. Not because of anything he'd done, but because of his companions: three Guild Heads would certainly make a stir in the Capital. Cheska and Teach were swallowed up by a crowd of citizens pleading, demanding, or explaining one thing or another. Calder couldn't understand what they were so excited about, but he took the opportunity to gather his crew. *"A forgotten man is invisible,"* as Loreli once put it. With the people focused on the Guild Heads, he brought Andel, Foster, and even Petal together and started uphill toward the Imperial Palace. Whatever was going on, he didn't want to lose track of the crew.

He'd only taken a few steps when he noticed the one Guild Head who wasn't surrounded by a flock of petitioners. Bliss stood in the middle of the pack, frowning at a brown leaf she pinched between two fingers. People avoided her as though someone had traced an invisible ten-foot barrier around her.

Calder broke that barrier as if he hadn't noticed, though his crew stayed back with the crowd. Cowards or sages, he wasn't sure which.

"I'm needed urgently at the palace," Bliss said, in a voice that was anything but urgent. "But I need the Imperial Guard to admit me, which requires Jarelys Teach. And Teach is being distracted. Should I remove the distractions, so that she can focus on the greater good?" Her black coat wriggled, and she slid a hand closer to the buttons.

He spoke as quickly as he could, hoping to stop her from reaching inside. "No, I don't think that will be necessary, Guild Head. I'm sure she'll be along in a moment. Ah, people seem excited, don't they? What do you think has them so agitated?" With each word, he kept his eyes on her hand.

When her attention returned to the autumn leaf, he let out a breath of relief.

"We've lost control of the Imperial Palace," she said. "These people don't know it, because the Imperial Guards will have locked it all down, but they know the gates to the palace are locked. The last time that happened was the first night of the Long Mourning, when Elderspawn rose all over the world. I was very busy."

"We all were," Calder said dryly. So that was what drove them to ambush the first Guild Heads they saw? Worries born of bad memories? They were right to worry, if tonight was going to be anything like that night five years ago. He wasn't in the Capital on the day of the Emperor's death, but he'd lived through the aftermath. And he'd seen the results of a global Elder uprising.

And with the typical logic of frightened people, these good Capital citizens were stopping the few who could actually protect them. General Teach was wading grimly through the sea of men and women, constantly asking people to stand aside, and Cheska drifted along in her wake. Her grip on her cutlass was tight, as though she wished she could draw and cut her way through.

"Join the General, Bliss," Calder said. "Andel, Foster, and I will walk ahead of you and try to keep the streets clear. Don't hurt anyone, please."

Bliss treated him to the same suspicious scrutiny she had given the leaf, but just when he was planning on retracting his suggestion and throwing himself on her mercy, she nodded. "Very well. We should walk quickly."

With that, she moved over to Jarelys Teach. For two or three seconds, the crowd didn't recognize that Bliss wasn't one of them, but each person who finally noticed the girl in the long black coat staggered backward. In less than a minute, a space had cleared around Teach. The General placed a hand on Bliss' shoulder in thanks, and then ordered the crew of *The Eternal* to fall in behind her. The noise hadn't lessened—the people were shouting louder now, hungry for a reasonable explanation—but at least they had some space.

Calder muttered orders to Foster and Andel. Foster immediately agreed, drawing his pistol and ordering people away from Teach. He managed to clear his way up the street a little faster, and the speed of their tiny procession increased.

Andel didn't obey immediately. He adjusted his sleeves as he walked beside Calder, buying time to talk. At last, he said, "You're focusing on the wrong details."

Not a joke. Not a complaint. Not even a criticism, really, though it could be taken as one. Andel was serious.

"What do you mean?"

"Have you seen how desperate they are?"

The faces around them proved Andel right. The people around him weren't just pushy or demanding, they were *terrified*. They begged as though they were starving and only the Guild Heads had bread. But the street hadn't been this chaotic when he'd seen it from the ship; only the sight of Cheska and Teach, people who might have answers, had incited this kind of panic.

It didn't mean that they weren't afraid before, but that they'd pushed the fear down. There was nothing they could do about it, so they'd tried to live their lives as normal. Only, at the slightest hint of something they could do to save themselves, they snatched at it like wild dogs fighting over a scrap of meat.

"They didn't get this way because the Imperial Palace shut its doors," Calder said aloud.

"These people have seen something. If we don't know what it is, we risk running straight into it."

Andel joined Foster after that, moving people aside physically when necessary, but Calder fell back. This crowd didn't care about him; they only even noticed him when he blocked the way to Teach or Cheska.

He let himself drown in the mob.

It would have been a simple matter to open himself to their Intent, but Reading a situation rather than an object was risky. For one thing, the impression was more fleeting, and he often came up with nothing of use. For another, if the Intent of a crowd was focused enough, they could sweep him along with them. Instead of understanding the mob, he might join it.

Besides, his head was already lightly pounding from the previous days' exertions. He'd hardly had a chance to recover from the fight on the Gray Island before *The Eternal* was ripped to shreds, and since then he'd been Reading constantly: to communicate with the Lyathatan, to hold *The Testament* together, to rig up the net that dragged half a ship back home. He'd kept himself within his limits, but he was approaching them nonetheless. If he wanted to be of any use to anyone in the next few days, he needed to keep himself from Reader's burn now.

So he had to try more mundane methods of investigation.

Calder spoke to a shouting man beside him. "The Guild Heads came in on my ship," he yelled into the man's ear. "I'm with the Guild Heads."

Several people turned to him eagerly, babbling their questions one at a time. He held up a hand. "We've been at sea. What's happened here?"

Explanations came one on top of the other.

"The Luminians, they won't heal my son—"

"...doors of the palace shut! The last time they did that was when the Emperor died, may his soul fly free."

"...Greenwardens closed up their chapter house. I had an appointment, and now they're telling me you *Imperialists* drove them out of town!"

"...Magisters gathering together. They've sensed something coming, they know the end is here."

"...men in black, jumping from rooftop to rooftop."

"...these Independents want to tear the Empire down! You'll put them in their place for us, I know you will."

To each person, Calder responded as neutrally as he could, but the crowd wouldn't have let him leave if Cheska hadn't reached in and hauled him out by the elbow.

"Learn anything useful?" she asked him.

"*Something* is definitely happening in the Capital," he said. "It's not just the palace closing. Everyone has personally seen something that worries them."

"Uh-huh. And what do they say is happening?"

"Best I can tell, they've noticed the Guilds at each others throats."

Cheska clapped her hat to her head at a sudden gust of wind. "Yeah, I'd put that together too. Everybody wants me to take care of the other Guilds, like I can tell the Consultants how to do their jobs."

However long it actually took them to reach the Imperial Palace, it *felt* like all day, and the sun was beginning to sink as they arrived at the gate. The Guards crossed spears out of habit and training when they saw the party approach, but when they saw Jarelys Teach's scowling face and the hilt of her sword sticking out over the crowd, they hurried out to clear the way for their Guild Head.

It took a kind of slow-motion brawl to sort out everyone who was supposed to be inside the palace from the people who had to stay outside. Petal was trembling and clutching her bag to her chest, looking around wide-eyed like a mouse who had just survived a lightning strike. Calder made a mental note not to ask too much of her in the coming days.

Not that anyone else was in much better condition. Even Jarelys Teach, pillar of Imperial strength, had dark circles under her eyes, and she walked as though her armor had been weighted down with anvils. But as the gates crashed shut behind her, she issued an order.

"Report," she demanded. A woman in the uniform of an Imperial Guard, a blonde with orange cat eyes, saluted. She looked familiar enough that she sparked a memory in Calder.

Where's Meia?

He hadn't seen the Consultant for virtually the entire voyage to the Capital, nor on the longboat to shore, nor on the long hike up to the palace. If he believed in kind Fates, he would have thought she'd been lost at sea, swallowed up by one of the million hazards of the Aion.

But his luck wasn't that good, and he knew it. She would show up when she wanted, and likely at the worst possible time.

"We've engaged the enemy around the Emperor's quarters, ma'am," the orange-eyed Guard said. "Conventional arms seem ineffective, so we mobilized all Soulbound and combat-capable modifications. Each time we inflict enough damage, it grows back instantly."

"What is it?" Teach asked, marching down the hall as though she meant to plow straight through a brick wall. Calder and the others had no choice but to let themselves be dragged behind.

"A mass of what seems to be Elder flesh surrounding the complex. It seems to be growing out of the Emperor's room, ma'am. It rarely strikes back, and when it does, it's more disruptive than dangerous. We've sustained no real casualties."

"How long?" Teach asked. On her back, the black sword Tyrfang radiated such a hostile Intent that Calder actually fell a step back.

"This is the fifth day, ma'am."

The attack on *The Eternal* had come roughly three days before. Five days ago meant it had grown during the fight with the Dead Mother's Children, or soon after. A strange coincidence, that this should grow almost immediately after he threw Nakothi's Heart into the sea.

Calder edged closer to Bliss. "Is the Optasia inside the Emperor's rooms?"

"That's very classified information."

He was dealing with Bliss, so he was prepared for the conversation to take longer than necessary. "I'm the one who's supposed to be using it, so..." Hopefully, she'd get the hint.

She looked at him with wide eyes and an open mouth. "Oh, you're right!"

"You *forgot?*"

"I suppose since you are the one who needs to use the Optasia, you should have the clearance to know its location. Very well. I hereby grant you clearance."

Calder suddenly wished for the sweet embrace of Reader's burn. Even a pounding, unstoppable headache would be a relief from this. "Thank you, Bliss."

"Yes, the Optasia is in the Emperor's personal quarters."

So the Elderspawn in the courtyard outside was protecting whichever Reader had attacked them through the Emperor's throne. Or...the Elderspawn itself had done it. That was a disturbing thought; the Great Elders had broad enough power already without granting them access to a global net of devices that amplified Intent.

Calder knew they'd arrived when they crossed between two Guards, one with horns and one with the arms of a gorilla. Both of them were clutching halberds caked with rotten greenish blood. They struggled to their feet and saluted when Teach came into view.

She didn't wait for them to say anything, but pushed a pair of doors open.

The battle beyond was not what Calder had expected. In fact, if he hadn't already heard otherwise, he wouldn't have recognized it as a battle.

An open courtyard surrounded one building, which was big enough to swallow *The Testament* and *The Eternal* side-by-side, masts and all. The stone tiles of the courtyard were broken and spattered with inhuman blood, hosting a dozen Imperial Guards who all held long-hafted weapons.

But they weren't fighting. They were hacking away at the building.

The Emperor's quarters were covered in mounds of gray-green flesh that vaguely reminded Calder of Nakothi's Heart. Lumps of gristle oozed from the walls, covering any doors or windows completely. Only pieces of wall or roof showed through, and even those were crossed by tendons or patches of skin.

As the Imperial Guards struck with axe or spear, they gouged deeper wounds, revealing layers of pink, healthier-looking meat. Still not 'healthy,' exactly—nothing he would dare accept from a butcher—but deeper in it could actually pass for rotten meat rather than Elder flesh.

But as fast as the Guards chopped, the skin and muscle stitched itself together even faster. They had barely hacked away a few scars in what must have been five days of work.

"Stop!" Teach commanded, and they threw their weapons down gratefully, sucking in air. The stench was like Nakothi's dead island—sour wound and rotting flesh, but muted to tolerable levels.

"You've accomplished nothing," Teach said. "Why continue?"

The orange-eyed Guardswoman hesitated. "We tried stopping, ma'am, on the second day. The...substance...covered the whole courtyard in hours. In three days, we've just managed to cut it back to where it started."

Indeed, only seconds after the Guards had dropped their weapons, the greenish flab on the walls began to advance. Wounds sealed, slowly but visibly, and some of the patches of skin started to bulge outward.

The Guard with the orange eyes drew a sword and walked up to the wall. "We can't destroy it as fast as it grows. But as long as we do cut it—" She gave it a shallow slice, just to demonstrate. "—it stops."

The flesh froze in the wake of her cut, and even the healing stopped. After a few seconds of silence, the rapid growth resumed.

General Teach ran a hand over her head before allowing herself to reach back and grab Tyrfang's hilt. "Captain, get everyone back."

Calder was startled to hear Teach addressing him, and perhaps a little flattered. The Guild Head had never spoken to him with anything but hostility, and now she was trusting him enough to give him a responsibility. She would have to lose the habit of giving him orders if she wanted him to do anything useful as Emperor, but it was a start.

He had raised a hand to wave people back when the cat-eyed Guard spoke first. "Everyone ten steps back!" she bellowed, her voice filling the courtyard. "If you're not a Guard or a Guild Head, clear out. The General needs her space."

Ah, yes. Captain was a rank. That could get confusing, with Navigator captains and military captains all mixing together. If any captains of industry showed up, they'd have to start calling each other by name.

Calder lowered his hand, hoping no one noticed, and complied with the captain's order by retreating. Technically he wasn't a member of the Guard or the Head of a Guild, but he had every right to be here. He projected that confidence into his stance in the hopes that the Guards would overlook him. If he was dragged off like a willful child and he had to resist, that could be... awkward. If he knew one thing about governance, he knew that it was unwise to start a hostile relationship with one's own guards.

When everyone had backed away, Teach drew her sword. Nothing dramatic, nothing ostentatious, simply a woman pulling a weapon from its sheath.

The dramatic part came immediately afterward.

Light itself suffered as the blade seemed to wash everything in shadow. Calder's vision grew slightly fuzzy, as if everything shook, but the world *felt* deathly still. It was only to his eyes that even the stone of the courtyard buzzed in place. And to his Reader's senses...

Death, decay, execution, blood, carnage, war...

He pulled his mind back. Even the shallowest Reading revealed Tyrfang's deadly history, and if he looked any deeper, he wouldn't be able to focus on anything else. Instead, he focused on the appearance of the blade itself: rough black metal with veins of bright red crawling down the flat. As though the metal had absorbed some fraction of the blood it spilled.

Teach flicked the weapon at the Elder flesh surrounding the walls, drawing a thin black line the length of Calder's hand.

When Calder had fought the Children of the Dead Mother, Kelarac had given him an Awakened blade to use against Elderspawn. It had worked even better than Calder had ever expected; with a single cut, it reduced lesser Elders to nothing more than black sludge.

Tyrfang had a similar effect on this Elder fortification...but on a much greater scale.

No sooner had the black scratch appeared on the skin than the entire outer layer of the building blackened and sloughed off, filling the courtyard with piles of dead and rotten flesh. Foul liquid splattered everywhere, bringing with it a stench like corpses dissolved in acid.

Calder's shoes were splashed with black goo, and he kept his expression composed, as suited an Emperor. He would have all his clothes burned before dawn.

More of the structure was exposed now, surrounded by pieces of raw, pinkish flesh. Teach had drawn back her sword for another blow, stepping forward to drive the sword in, but an agonized shriek held her back.

It seemed to come from all around, from every bit of meat still living in the confines of the courtyard. A second later, the flesh attacked.

Ropes of muscle whipped out from the windows and the door, slapping at Teach. At the same time, smoking liquid sprayed from a bulb on the second floor, aimed to land on the General's head.

She slapped away one tendril with the flat of her weapon, blackening and killing it instantly, and backhanded another with her gauntlet. Teach side-stepped the fluid without looking up, taking a few casual steps back until the Elder thing couldn't reach her anymore.

When she was far enough away, the tentacles retracted, and the flesh ballooned out even faster than it had grown before.

"Bliss?" Teach asked, without turning around.

The Head of the Blackwatch leaned forward, squinting at the creature. "Hmmmm...I will examine it tonight. By morning, I'll know what to do."

"Very good." Teach turned to the Guard captain. "Rotating shifts, just as you had before. Don't let it grow any further before the Blackwatch are finished with their tests."

The orange-eyed captain saluted. "Ma'am."

As for the rest of them, that left the delightful proposition of finding rooms in a palace they *knew* was haunted by Elders. It was one thing to face Elder influence on the Aion, when you had your ship around you and your crew close at hand, but it was entirely worse to try and sleep in a bedroom where the building itself could be your enemy.

It will be clear in the morning, Calder told himself. Bliss would know what to do, and he could get on with being Emperor. It was strange; he was close to sitting on the throne, closer than he'd ever been since he'd first considered the possibility, but it had never seemed farther away. It was as though the Elders and the Fates were conspiring to throw every obstacle they could in his way.

He burned his clothes in a bonfire outside a palace window.

CHAPTER SEVEN

TEN YEARS AGO

Calder and Jerri sat on boxes, huddled over a table in *The Testament's* cabin. The room was so cramped it felt like a closet, and Calder sometimes found himself breathing too quickly, as though he were going to run out of air. The table was strewn with navigational charts, notes, and half-scribbled maps that Andel had provided.

For the last six weeks of their journey, Andel had plotted their course, and was even taking most of the burden of steering the ship. Calder helped with his Soulbound powers as best he could, but it was like trying to play the violin after having watched a genius musician. It *seemed* simple and intuitive, until you tried it. Calder felt that he should have been able to furl and unfurl the ship's sails with nothing more than a thought, but in practice, the green-veined stretch of skin had simply wrapped itself around the mast and refused to be dislodged. The two Champions had been forced to leap up to the crow's nest and untangle the sheet by hand.

Impressive, yes, but inconvenient.

Calder sensed *The Testament* like a second, simpler mind tucked away inside his own. It had a purpose, and it yearned to fulfill that purpose: to guide and protect them as they sailed the Aion. Somehow, it felt so eager that it almost fought Calder for control. He had never heard of a Soulbound Vessel wrestling its owner, but he had to admit that what he knew about Soulbound was largely academic. There was a stark difference between reading about Vessels and having one in his head.

His alliance with the ship may have started out uneasy, but they needed to smooth out that relationship if they wanted to survive the eldritch dangers of the Aion Sea.

Which brought them to the charts and maps on the table. They were a month into this journey, and Andel had guided them the entire way. At this rate, Calder would be relegated to a passenger on his own ship. He refused to let that happen, and Jerri seemed to agree with him.

If they were ever going to escape from the shadow of the Imperial officer, they had to chart their own course. Literally.

Jerri flipped her braid over her shoulder, running a finger along the map, tracing coordinates that Calder had provided. "And that would leave us... locked in ice, just south of the Fioran Reaches."

Calder frowned down at his own piece of paper, covered in calculations. At the moment, they looked like meaningless scribbles. "That's not right. If anything, it should abandon us on a stretch of shoreline outside the Izyrian jungle."

Jerri shrugged. "Looking at the tides, I thought it would come out somewhere in Erin. Maybe we're not moving as fast as we thought."

The ship pitched lightly to one side, and an inkwell slid away in a suicidal dive. Calder snatched it from the brink, leaving only a few drops of ink to splatter next to his shoes.

Jerri gripped the table with both hands, face a shade paler than usual. It had taken her a week or two to adjust to the movement of the ship, and she still wasn't fully accustomed to the constant rolling of the surf.

"We'll get used to it," she said for the hundredth time, giving him a tight smile. He returned it, feeling another wave of...not guilt, precisely. He had been an idiot, trying to break his father out in the way he did, but he regretted only his methods. And he hadn't forced Jerri into anything.

He didn't feel guilty, only responsible. The fact remained that she could have stayed back in the Capital, with a comfortable life and a family nearby, if not for him.

"Thank you," he said, after a few more seconds pause. "For coming with me. I don't know what...I'm glad I'm not alone."

She took a deep breath to settle her stomach, then smiled at him. "Anywhere's better than home."

Jerri had made comments like that before, which Calder didn't fully understand. As he'd heard it, her father had been a member of the Blackwatch who went missing in the course of his duties. Sometimes, she spoke of her father fondly, and other times as though she were glad to be rid of him. Likewise, when she mentioned her mother and the rest of her family at all, the very thought seemed to make her angry.

"You don't miss it?" Calder said.

Jerri rubbed her emerald earring, an absent gesture. "My family can be... demanding. They know exactly what they want me to do, and how they want me to do it, and that's the way it is. It takes dramatic gestures to get their attention, sometimes. They wanted to meet you, by the way."

Calder had never imagined meeting Jerri's family, taking his cue from her silence. She went home as seldom as possible, so he'd assumed he would never see where she lived or meet her mother. Now he felt a pang of regret that he might not get the chance.

"You told them about me?" he asked.

"Of course I did. I spent all my time at your house, obviously they would want to know everything about you. They were impressed when you joined the Blackwatch, though they were happier when you left." She raised one hand to her ear again. "It's something of a sore spot in my family."

Calder could imagine so. Jerri's father had died or vanished on duty as a Watchman, so it couldn't be comforting to picture Calder sharing the same fate.

"Hold on. They know I was kicked out of the Blackwatch?" Calder asked.

"I told them you'd *left*, obviously. I skirted past the 'why' of it."

"When did you have the chance?" Calder asked. They had boarded *The Testament* on the same day they were released from the Imperial Palace. Where had she found the time to fill her family in?

She looked at him as though it were obvious. "I went home to pick up my clothes. I had to explain where I was going, didn't I?"

"You told them the *truth?*" Calder asked, astonished. "You told your mother that you intended to run off with me, after I was booted out of the Blackwatch and destroyed an Imperial prison?"

"That wouldn't bother my mother," she said dryly. "She doesn't have the brightest view of the Empire. To her, that made you sound roguish."

Calder resolved to meet Jerri's mother.

"Besides," Jerri continued, "I didn't say that I'd 'run off' with you. That would have a different implication altogether, wouldn't it?"

She smiled at him and rested a hand on his arm, and his pulse picked up.

At that moment, Andel cleared his throat from the half-open door.

Calder spun to face him. The Imperial officer was standing with his hat in one hand and the door in the other. Sweat rolled down his face, and he fanned himself with the wide brim of his hat. His suit, usually pristine white, was damp with patches of sweat.

Still, he showed no expression. "We have a situation on deck, Marten. You should come take a look."

The more decisions Andel made for Calder, the tighter his authority would stick. Calder had to put a stop to that now. "I'll come when I've finished here, Andel."

"Suit yourself," Andel said. "You've got about ten minutes before the ship burns down around you. Spend it however you'd like."

He bowed his way out, pulling the door shut behind him.

Calder shared a look with Jerri. It was muggy and warm in the cabin, but not oppressively hot. Certainly nothing that suggested a fire.

Andel had been sweating.

In its cage, Shuffles began to laugh. It was covered up by a blanket, under which it slept most of the day, but it woke whenever danger was imminent. Its chuckles were deep and rich, the laughter of a cruel giant.

Together, Jerri and Calder rushed up onto the deck.

More than a month into the Aion, Calder had seen things he would never have imagined back at home. A finned monstrosity just beneath the waves, weaving its careful way around the Lyathatan, raising its spiky mouth above the water for long enough to hiss spitefully. A storm during which water rained up from the ocean and into thirsty clouds. An island that slid away, shy, whenever their ship got too close.

So when he opened the door to a faceful of oven-hot sunlight as bright as an alchemical flare, Calder felt a fresh round of familiar panic. Maybe this time, the Aion was revealing its full fury, and they would finally confront the wrath of something ancient and inhuman.

Jerri gasped next to him, clutching his arm with a hand edged in spidery tattoos. At her touch, he turned his gaze to the sky.

A constellation of flames danced over the ship, just out of reach of the mast, too bright and white to look like ordinary fire. They weren't traditional tongues of flame, either. Pyramids of fire drifted in stately laps overhead, spinning around cubes, spheres, twisted nests, and undulating snakes. This fire could take on any shape, it seemed, except the natural.

Calder stared for a few seconds before he noticed the pattern. The bright, geometric clouds of fire were not moving randomly, but cycling in some complex formation that kept them orbiting the ship. As *The Testament* moved, the flames followed effortlessly.

Calder extended his senses, Reading. He caught a whiff of Intent from the fire—alien, distant, curious, and almost joyful—but most of his attention was focused on the ship.

A ship did not experience emotions like a human being, not even an Awakened ship. Its understanding was slow and limited, more a sense of purpose than any actual thought.

But as far as it could, *The Testament* panicked. It did not like fire. Taut lines suddenly felt as though they quivered with tension, the seamless deck frozen in panic instead of calm and placid.

The ship wanted, more than anything, for Calder to make the fire *go away*.

In the cage, the prisoner—Urzaia—lay on his back with his arms folded under his head, apparently asleep. Eight, the grim man with the shield strapped to his back, alternated his gaze between Urzaia and the lights overhead. One-eyed Nine had stripped to the waist, his scarred back glistening with sweat, and he stood with his head tilted up to face the sky.

"Is this usual for the Aion, Navigator?" Nine called back, only seconds after Calder stepped out of the door.

Over the past few weeks, the Champions had learned the precise extent of Calder's inexperience. Namely, that he knew next to nothing about the Aion Sea. Eight seemed to trust that they would get where they were going, or else he didn't care where they ended up so long as Urzaia never escaped. But Nine blatantly pretended that Calder was an expert Navigator, asking his opinion on weather patterns or the mysterious behavior of the haunted sea.

The man may have been mocking him, but Calder got the impression that Nine was trying to extend him a measure of respect. To treat him as the man he would someday become, perhaps. It still made situations like this uncomfortable.

"The sea is full of surprises," Calder responded. He shot a glance over at Andel, but the man wasn't laughing; he was staring straight at the deadly fires.

Nine grunted, raising a hand to shade his eyes as one of the shapes dipped close to his face. He didn't flinch back from the heat, as Calder would have done. Perhaps Champions couldn't be burned.

Nine's braids swayed as he shook his head. "What do you think, Eight?"

"I'm watching the prisoner," Eight responded shortly.

"Fine," Nine said, "I'll take a turn, but we run into some sort of Elder-spawned sea serpent later, it's yours."

Eight said nothing. He continued standing with his arms folded, shield on his back, looking between Urzaia and the fire in the sky as though he thought his prisoner had engineered this somehow, as part of an escape attempt.

For his part, Urzaia began to snore.

Nine lowered one hand to pull the hammer from his belt, raising the other hand. He closed his eye for a moment, smiling a little.

And the hammer changed.

After only an instant, the Champion held more than just a tiny claw hammer. The steel seemed to stretch and swell, forming a blunt head of steel, its hilt becoming a shaft of solid shadow. In half a second, it was the size of a sledgehammer. He didn't raise the weapon, but left its head leaning against the deck.

That was impossible. No one fully understood Awakening or the powers of a Soulbound, but there were a few rules. For one thing, an Awakened object changed shape only once: during the Awakening process. Most Readers believed that the phenomenon had to do with the physical structure changing to align more closely with the invested Intent, but regardless, the Awakened object could not be reshaped afterwards. A claw hammer couldn't become a giant weapon of war any more than any hammer could spontaneously grow in a carpenter's hands. It was ridiculous, the kind of mysterious 'magic' that came from folk tales.

Yet if anyone could do the impossible, it ought to be the Champions.

Jerri's grip tightened on his arm, urging him to explain. "He shouldn't be able to do that," Calder said.

She shook her head. "Not that. Look." She nodded up at the geometric flames above the ship.

The grand orbital procession had practically frozen, each shape simply spinning in place instead of dancing and weaving around one another. The lights sat anchored, as though waiting.

The Intent in the air sharpened, like one giant, invisible eye had turned all of its scrutiny onto the Champion called Nine.

"He's drawn its attention," Calder said, fear bleeding into his voice.

Jerri managed to frown at him in confusion without taking her eyes from the spectacle in front of her. "Attention? Attention of what?"

Calder wished he knew.

But there was a second Intent, opposing the first, that emanated from Nine. Something edged, and cold, and a little morbid, like a condemned convict's manic laughter as the noose tightens around his neck.

The shadows on the haft of the hammer crawled like a nest of snakes.

Only a few seconds after he'd drawn his hammer, Nine let out a tightly controlled shout. And a hundred lashes of shadow whipped out from his upraised palm, each snapping into the center of a flame like frogs' tongues taking flies. The sky darkened noticeably under the canopy of shadow for a second, as though the sun had blinked, and then the shadows retracted. The hammer was just a hammer again, and Nine tucked it away into his belt.

Most of the flames had simply vanished. The temperature dropped into the sudden chill of a spring breeze, the light darkening from the white of a flare to typical afternoon brightness. Only five or six chunks of fire remained, bleeding sparks and wobbling drunkenly like an injured horse.

Nine scratched the stubble on his jaw, looking up at the fire. "Huh. Thought I got 'em all."

A silent shriek sounded in Calder's mind, desperate and pitiful at once, like a child with a papercut. He managed to shout a wordless warning before the unseen force retaliated.

The floating shapes of flame struck Nine like half a dozen bolts of orange-white lightning.

The Champion ignited. He roared, pain and anger and shock all mixed into one cry. The heat from his body flared again, sending another wave of heat passing over Calder.

Andel ran for the barrel of seawater they kept at hand for scrubbing the deck, but Calder had a faster plan. He dropped to one knee, pressing his hand against the deck.

A rope shot out from a coil nearby, wrapping itself around the burning Champion. He grabbed on, no doubt intending to tear the thick strand apart, but Calder was faster. With a mental effort, he used the rope to hurl Nine over the railing and into the sea.

The flames blazed brighter on Nine's body as he soared through the air, but he landed with a heavy splash. Calder had no way of telling if the man was alive or dead, or if he would have the presence of mind to stay afloat, but it was better than watching him burn to death.

Eight shouted at the sight, and for the first time, he took his gaze entirely off of his prisoner. He stared at the geometric flames in the sky, slowly removing the shield from his back.

The fiery lights returned to their dance, spiraling around one another in a slow orbit. Either they didn't see Eight as much of a threat compared to his partner, or he hadn't attracted their attention, but they seemed to ignore him.

Wind spiraled around the shield, carrying with it the icy bite of winter.

In seconds, frost coated the shield, and snow swirled around Eight's entire body. The few remaining flames froze in their tracks; once again, the hostile Intent in the atmosphere congealed. The invisible eye had returned, watching the Champion.

When the fires struck again, just as they had with Nine, Eight was ready for them.

The lights crashed down like orange lightning, but the bald, pale man was even faster. His shield blurred, and six sprays of campfire sparks shot out from him like geysers.

He'd swatted all of the flames from midair at the *same time*. Faster than Calder's eyes could process, he'd struck at least six times.

So this is a Champion, he thought. He wondered how much it would take to hire one for his crew, but quickly dismissed the thought. If he couldn't even afford to dig himself out of debt, how could he support a warrior like this?

The sparks fell to the deck, taking with them the heat and the unnaturally bright light. In fact, the air on deck was still being cooled by the blizzard Eight carried on his shield.

Before Calder, Jerri, or Andel could say a word, Eight had already stripped his Vessel off his arm and tossed it down. Without a second's hesitation, he ran to the railing, obviously prepared to vault over.

Calder couldn't help a certain sense of smug self-satisfaction, seeing that. He'd actually thought faster than the Champion.

Under Calder's control, the rope ladder drifted up the side of the ship, carrying Nine's body. The burned, one-eyed man smiled weakly. "Why'd you do that, Captain? I had 'em."

His head lolled as he passed out, and Eight grabbed him before he could fall back into the sea. He threw his partner over his shoulder like a sack of grain, turning to Calder.

"He needs rest," Eight said. Calder expected him to finish the statement, but he never did.

Jerri ushered him forward, toward the cabin where Andel usually slept. "Lay him down here. Andel won't mind sleeping below for a while, will you, Andel? We have two passenger cabins down there, though they're a little cramped at the moment."

"My ship is always open to you," Andel said, adjusting his collar. As frustrating as it was to hear Andel refer to *The Testament* as his ship, it was still gratifying to imagine him below, tucked in among the cargo.

Eight hadn't even waited for Jerri to finish speaking. He kicked the door open, laying Nine down on a bunk. Jerri rushed down the ladder for some wine, and Andel headed into the cabin to see to his belongings.

They left Calder on deck, which he didn't mind. He needed a moment.

His hands trembled with excitement, and he opened and closed his fists, trying to work out the excess energy. A strange expression had been carved onto his face, and he couldn't tell if it was a smile or a rictus of fear. His stomach roiled, almost as though he were seasick, and his thoughts moved too fast for him to catch up.

From the appearance of the dancing lights to Eight carrying Nine inside, not three minutes had passed. Calder had endured too many emotions in too short a time to even understand them all.

A voice rumbled up from the cage in the center of the deck. "That was well done."

Calder looked to the sixth passenger, whom he'd all but forgotten in the excitement. Urzaia still lay on his back, hands folded under his head like a pillow, eyes closed. He looked like a man enjoying a relaxing nap.

"Did we wake you?" Calder asked, voice dry.

Without opening his eyes, the prisoner grinned, flashing his perfect teeth. "The sparks are not Kameira or Elder, but something born of the Aion. They have order. Patterns. They like to...straighten things that are crooked. It is said they are drawn to lost ships, and they will guide you toward right paths."

Uneasy, Calder glanced at the seamless deck of his ship, where orange embers were still dying. "They were here to help us?"

The big man shrugged, shoulders brushing against the bottom of his cage. "Have seen ships they helped before. Burned, black skeletons of ships that drift on the water. If they could not protect themselves from the fire, they died. But hey! They are not lost anymore!"

He laughed, and Calder chuckled along with him. He couldn't help it; the bound man seemed to invite cheer.

As Sister Ulinda had once said, *"A smiling man is a friend to all."*

"But enough about the fires," Urzaia said, suddenly sitting up. He looked Calder in the eye, smile never fading. "I said you did well. You saved that man, the one who pretends his name is Nine. He may have survived the burns, but he would have spent a long time healing. It will not take so long, now. He owes you."

Even though it was coming from a man in a cage, at least *someone* noticed what Calder had done. "It's my ship, isn't it? I'm responsible for what happens here."

Urzaia tapped his knuckles against the inside of his cage bars. "You react quickly. That is good, on the Aion Sea. Make decisions quickly, act quickly, and you will be a good Captain. If you listen to your crew, and not to the Emperor." Urzaia made a disgusted face, as though he'd bitten into something sour. "He makes so many decisions for the Guilds, but he does not care about us."

Hurriedly, Calder glanced behind him, making sure that the other Champions weren't close enough to overhear. He wouldn't be surprised if they punished him for simply listening to treason like this.

And some part of him sensed an opportunity here. He never would have thought he'd find someone else who saw through the Emperor's façade. Certainly not so soon.

Calder leaned closer to the bars, lowering his voice. "How did you end up in a cage, Urzaia?"

The big man's eyes moved behind Calder to the open cabin door, then back. His smile widened a notch. "Come back tonight, second watch. There are no longer two of them, so they cannot keep eyes on me all night. You promise to watch me, and we will speak then."

He lay back again, resting his head on his hands. "For now, I will catch a little sleep. If we are attacked again, I don't want to miss it, yes?"

CHAPTER EIGHT

Each of the Great Elders has their own goals, and they are often in conflict. But why have they not destroyed each other? Why have they not destroyed us? On some level, toward some mutual objective, they must be working together.

— HEAD OF THE BLACKWATCH, FOUR HUNDRED YEARS AGO

Calder stood in the courtyard outside the Emperor's quarters, watching the Guards hack away at gray-green flesh. Bliss ran her hands along the skin like a child trying to find her way out of a cave.

The stars were still out, and Calder didn't remember getting out of bed.

"The bearer of Tyrfang has already given you her tour. I thought I'd give you mine." Kelarac turned to him, the steel over his eyes glinting silver in the moonlight, and smiled.

The Great Elder looked exactly the same as Calder had last seen him: metal blindfold, decked in jewelry, thin goatee, two gold-capped teeth. Maybe the Soul Collector appeared this way to everyone, as a sort of signature.

"If we keep meeting like this, people are going to talk," Calder said. He had already written this off as a dream when Kelarac appeared and Bliss didn't immediately notice and attack.

Although...the Guild Head had stopped running her hands along the bulbous skin surrounding the Emperor's quarters. She'd tilted her head as though listening for something.

Kelarac chuckled. "I have spoken with you more than anyone else this century. Some would say I favor you too heavily."

"You and Ach'magut both. If I didn't know better, I'd suspect I was being manipulated."

Kelarac wove his fingers together until his rings shone.

"You're a piece on a board, Reader of Memory. A card in the hand. You know it, too. But it's fortunate for you that you are a well-positioned piece, so that you may be lured into place rather than prodded. Your kind prefers sugar cubes to switches, don't they?"

Calder crushed any irritation before it could pollute his voice. Before one of the Great Elders, he had to keep his Intent on a tight leash. "I believe you're thinking of horses."

"No...no, I don't think so."

Kelarac waved a jeweled hand at the flesh-covered building. "I like to show my workers the result of their labor, it helps to support a grander vision. And this...without Nakothi's Heart, I could never have built this."

A chill ran down Calder's skin, as though he was wearing his real body and not just inhabiting a dream. "What have you built?"

"However imperfectly, however temporarily, I have created an organism that can control the Emperor's Optasia." He put his hands on his hips, smiling like a proud mother. "Without the attack on the other Navigator's ship, you wouldn't have ended up here. Not for a long time, at least, and by then certain windows would have passed."

It was growing harder and harder to control his Intent. "You have the power to destroy the world, and you used it to change my travel plans?"

"I told you before, Captain, I don't want to *destroy* the world. Only Urg'naut wants that, though Tharlos might accomplish it as an incidental by-product. I like the world the way it is now, only perhaps a tad more so. You'll understand. Bringing you here was one domino in a very long line, one note in a symphony that lasts millennia."

Whatever else the Great Elder was, he sounded very proud of himself.

"And you're telling me now out of a newfound spirit of fair play?" The Collector of Souls didn't give anything away for free.

Gold glinted in Kelarac's smile. "You can't steer the ship unless you turn the wheel. I need you where you are, doing exactly what you're going to—"

The Great Elder was interrupted by a girl's pale face, popping up and staring at him from an inch away. Bliss frowned into what, to her, should look like empty space.

"Dreams are like cobwebs," she said. "I don't like them in my hair."

When the Guild Head waved her hand, the courtyard vanished, and Calder woke upright in bed. Sunlight leaked in from the edges of his window, and Kelarac's dream was nothing but a memory.

Calder shivered as he dressed himself in the early morning light. These palace rooms were comfortable but drafty, and the autumn chill was starting to make itself known. But he shivered for more than just the cold.

Kelarac had come to him last night, either invading his dreams or dragging his mind away while he slept. He wasn't sure which possibility unnerved him more. He was sure their conversation had been real, and equally sure that Bliss had noticed them. Or at least noticed something wrong.

How much did she know? If she had seen him standing next to a figure she recognized as a Great Elder, he would be in the dangerous position of trying to explain to the Head of the Blackwatch why he was on first-name basis with Kelarac. If that didn't end with his body in the Aion Sea, it ended with seven spikes through him.

On top of the looming threat of death, an even greater fear loomed. Kelarac had spoken clearly last night. Too clearly. Before, the Soul Collector had doled out hints like a hunter baiting traps, careful not to give Calder too much information. Why had he changed?

Above all, why let Calder *know* he was being manipulated? It was one thing to know he was dancing to an Elder tune, and quite another to have Kelarac tell him to his face that he was nothing more than a piece on a gameboard.

Did Kelarac tell him because it wouldn't matter? Because Calder would play his role regardless, and he couldn't stop it? Or maybe Kelarac knew that Calder would resist, that he would do the exact opposite of whatever he thought the Elders wanted, which would itself play right into Kelarac's hands...

"If you find yourself thinking in circles, stop thinking." Not one of the great philosophers of history, obviously. Calder's father, Rojric. Calder had always found the words surprisingly wise: when thinking wasn't productive, he had to start acting.

Which was why he'd take the initiative. He'd go confront Bliss, find out what she knew, and try to enlist her help. If she killed him...well, there wasn't much he could do to stop her, and maybe his death would thwart Kelarac's plans.

Why do I even want to stop Kelarac? Calder had only interacted with two Great Elders in his life, and both of them had worked for Calder's benefit. Sure, maybe Calder was being used as part of an eons-long plot to devour the world, but it was working out for *him*. It wasn't his responsibility to protect the world from Elders.

The burning handprint on his forearm itched, and he absently scratched it. No one had carried his chest of clothes over from *The Testament,* so he was left with only a spare outfit that the palace servants had brought him: a set of shirt, pants, and jacket in red and gold. It looked suspiciously like a cross between the Imperial Guard uniform and a servant's livery, but at least he wouldn't be wandering the Emperor's palace in his skin.

He had just started pulling on the pants when his door swung open and Andel walked in, his white suit as pristine as ever. "Good morning, August and Illustrious Emperor. I'm here to dress you."

Calder looked from his servant clothes to the robes draped over Andel's arm. Fabric spilled over his arm in a waterfall of sunlight colors: yellow, white, and a bright, shimmering gold. Clothes like the Emperor would have worn.

"You're not really going to dress me, are you?"

Andel threw the bundle of cloth at him. "The palace staff seem to think I'm your manservant. They tried to get me to bring your tea."

"I could use some tea right now, actually."

"I'm sure Petal would brew it for you immediately."

Calder held up a smooth white garment, like a loose sleeved robe, and an identical yellow one next to it. "Which of these am I supposed to put on first?"

Andel folded his arms and leaned with his back to the door. "Whichever you decide, do it quickly. The Guild Heads want to meet with you."

Anxiety sparked in Calder's stomach as he pulled the white robe over his head. Was this Bliss confronting him about last night? "What for, did they say?"

"What did you do wrong?"

Calder froze with the yellow robe halfway over the white one. "I don't know what you're talking about."

Andel raised one eyebrow a fraction. "It's obvious why they want to talk to you. Same reason they sent you those clothes. You should start acting like the Emperor now, and they're going to guide you through it. You wouldn't have asked unless you were afraid it was something else, which means you did something wrong."

Calder relaxed, considering the gold robe that was probably his outer layer. Each layer was cut slightly differently, so that some of the previous colors would show through no matter how he wore them. "You have quite the imagination, Andel."

"If you get us executed after only one night in the Imperial Palace, I swear I'll make a deal with a Great Elder just to haunt you for eternity."

"Where's that tea?"

After looking over Calder's Imperial clothing and carefully not laughing, Andel led him through the palace hallways, over rare imported carpets and decorations that would cost more than a Navigator's entire journey. When they finally arrived at their destination, Calder was thoroughly lost.

Not only had they taken more turns that he felt were strictly necessary, this room looked exactly the same as fifty others they'd passed. It held a long, rectangular table in the center, chairs all around, and paintings on the wall. The only difference between this room and all the others in the palace was its inhabitants.

Servants stood around the perimeter, prepared to attend to any sudden requests. Jarelys Teach sat at one end of the table, holding her forehead in one gauntleted hand. Cheska Bennett had traded her hat for a bandana tying her hair back, and she was in the middle of an angry gesture with a rolled-up news-sheet. Mekendi Maxeus was the only one of them who looked somewhat calm, though that could have been the black mask that shrouded his features. His hands were laced together, his ash-gray staff leaning behind him.

A sudden disquiet rolled through Calder's gut. This was all too familiar. Andel leading him through the door, into a meeting of Guild Heads...just like aboard *The Eternal,* not long ago. How much had changed since then?

He supposed he'd find out.

"...have to move *now,*" Cheska insisted, not bothering to acknowledge Calder. "The longer we wait, the better it is for them."

Teach spoke without opening her eyes. "It sounds to me like we've already made our opening move."

"The remaining Regents will respond," Maxeus said confidently. "They will have to act, or else go back into hiding."

Rather than go stand against the wall with the servants and attendants, as he'd done last time, Andel simply walked out of the room. Calder understood. If he kept acting like a servant, people would keep treating him like one. Best to abandon ship while there was still a chance of keeping his dignity.

But Calder didn't like how alone he felt as Andel left.

Maxeus was the first to recognize his presence, giving Calder a shallow, seated bow. "The change of wardrobe suits you. Welcome. There's been some recent excitement here at home, as you may have heard."

"Did Bliss figure out how to get to the throne?" Surely there could be no more urgent cause than that.

"She's still working on it," Teach said. "Apparently the Elders sent something to spy on her last night, so she summoned a team of Watchmen to secure the courtyard. When she knows something, I'm sure she'll..." The Guild Head hesitated.

"Delay until she feels like it, tell us eventually, and leave out crucial details," Calder finished.

"I sometimes forget you used to work for her."

Cheska slapped the news-sheet down on the table. "Enough about the Elders! Light and life, we have enough *human* problems to last us until Urg'naut devours the planet."

At Calder's curious look, she slid the sheet over to him.

IZYRIA IN CHAOS, IMPERIALISTS TO BLAME, the headline declared. The article went on to describe the riots in the east, food shortages, and Guild-on-Guild violence. All precipitated by the 'Imperialists:' those Guilds who wanted to raise up a second Emperor after the first, may his soul fly free, was lost to an Elder attack. The writer even managed to insinuate that it may have been the Imperialists who engineered the Emperor's death in the first place.

The first thing Calder said when he'd finished was, "Imperialists?"

Maxeus inclined his masked head. "That's the charming moniker the news-sheets have given to our alliance, represented here. The Magisters, the Blackwatch, the Imperial Guard, and the Navigators are Imperialists, while the Consultants, Alchemists, Greenwardens, and Luminians are the Independents."

"The name isn't the problem," Cheska said. "The name is fine. If anything, calling us Imperialists reinforces that we're on the side of the Empire. The problem is that the news-sheets are all over us. Which means the people don't trust us. And if the people don't trust us, they won't trust whatever slack-jawed idiot we stick on the throne."

If Calder were a less generous man, that might have offended him. "Thank you, Cheska. If you wouldn't mind explaining something else to me, though, they claim that this was happening *yesterday.* Even the fastest Navigator couldn't travel here from Izyria in less than two weeks." Calder ought to know, as his ship was the fastest.

Cheska snorted. "Two weeks? With *fantastic* weather, clear sailing, an empty hold, and the Emperor's own luck. Maybe."

"That's what hurts the worst," Teach said, frustration bleeding into her voice. "There's no way they could have known. It's entirely fabricated."

There had to be something here he was missing. They were too upset for what amounted to little more than a slanderous lie. "Then what's the matter? We'll get the Witnesses to investigate, and they'll have to print a retraction. Instead of the villains, people will see us as the victims."

Maxeus steepled his hands again. "Unfortunately, despite their obvious deception, they're actually correct. Izyria *is* in chaos, their Regent is missing, and we are to blame. I received the news yesterday, through a method much faster than your ships."

"So how did they know?" Calder asked.

"They didn't," Cheska said, slapping her palm down on the table. "They just *guessed,* but they're right, and now we're sunk if we don't bail water."

There was still something Calder didn't know, some fact they were dancing around rather than addressing it directly. "It can't be that much of a disaster. What did we do?"

It was Maxeus who answered with a distinct note of pride. "We successfully assassinated Alagaeus, Regent of the East."

Calder stared at him, speechless.

"Possibly Jorin as well, though he was staying with the Consultants. As you know, the Gray Island is in somewhat of a mess right now, so news is scarce."

Calder still couldn't think of anything appropriate to say. The Regents were the four most powerful people in the world, on a level even higher than the Guild Heads. Contemporaries of the Emperor, they had come out of hiding—or, as some said it, hibernation—after the Emperor's death. They'd divided the world up between the four of them, and had prevented the Empire from falling to pieces.

If any one of them had been willing to accept the title of Emperor, Calder would never have gotten the job. Neither would Naberius, and likely the whole debacle surrounding the Heart of Nakothi would never have happened.

But they maintained that only the Emperor could rule the Empire. In a sense, they were the pillars on which the Independent Guilds rested.

And they were led by Estyr Six, the most terrifying woman in history. There were as many horror stories about her as myths, none of them comforting to her opponents.

"So you're telling me we're all going to die," Calder said. His senses tightened as he entered the state he always did before a fight. He was ready to run out of here and straight down to the dock, where he and his crew could board *The Testament* and stay on the Aion for as long as possible. Years, if necessary.

He'd been promised a position as Emperor, and he had no doubt that he'd make it to the throne eventually. But he would prefer it if his first act as the ruler of the world wasn't getting blasted to pieces.

Maxeus spread his hands. "Events have outpaced us, but this isn't a disaster. If we act now, we can salvage this. We can even turn it into an advantage. But we *must* act."

Calder realized he had half-risen from his seat, and slowly lowered himself back down. "What's the plan?"

Bliss couldn't wait for Alsa Grayweather to return. Well, she *could* wait, and she *would*, because there was no realistic alternative, but she didn't want to. As she stared at this Elder wall, as she'd come to think of it, she had begun to grow irritated. And with her irritation she became unpredictable. That was Tharlos' influence on her, and it couldn't be helped, but Alsa was the only one who could bring her back to reason.

She had sent Alsa away only six days ago, and she had been proud of that decision. At the time. It had been an attempt to keep Alsa both safe and busy while Bliss took care of her son, and it had worked beautifully. Bliss was pleased at her own foresight, and her tact in handling the situation.

Sadly, Alsa's absence left her alone with Tharlos.

What if those Watchmen behind you weren't Watchmen at all? What if they were dogs, dogs standing on their hind legs, wearing black coats and carrying spikes like they were people? Wouldn't that be hilarious? The thought from her Vessel didn't come in words, precisely, but in feelings. Like Bliss would be in for the joke of a lifetime if only she would let a Great Elder turn her subordinates into two-legged dogs.

She slapped the Spear through her coat, a quick reprimand, even though its idea did sound funny. And she could use a laugh—it was supposed to be good for your mood. The wall of Elder flesh surrounding the Emperor's quarters just would not cooperate, though she'd spent all night trying to expose its secrets.

After all this time, she'd learned only that there was someone trapped inside. But that knowledge came with its own problems.

Gray-green tendrils whipped out, suddenly aggressive, lashing her Watchmen and two of the Imperial Guards who were still cutting at the flesh with their weapons. A man scream, a woman pleaded, and all six of them backed off.

Bliss didn't. The Elder wall had never been so violent before, which provided interesting opportunities for observation. That was her purpose, after all: to observe the Elders and learn what she could from them. She could never stop their plans if she didn't know what they were.

None of the living whips struck at Bliss, even as she drew closer. They knew better.

She placed a bare hand against the sickly greenish skin of the growth. She wasn't a Reader, but she was a Soulbound, and she could sense a few things. For one, this Elder barrier wasn't just growing *around* the Emperor's quarters—it was a *part* of them. Shutters had turned into eyelids, plaster into meat, support beams into bones, and paint into skin. Not all of the building had been corrupted, but enough that she worried for the structure's stability if the Elder wall were removed.

The transformation excited Tharlos. *We could redecorate the entire Capital like this...but more! We'll go even further!* Bliss' mind filled with images of carpets like tongues, windows that bulged out into eyeballs, roof tiles sprouting hair.

That is neither positive nor constructive, Bliss chided herself. She didn't need to dwell on Elder imagination. That way lay madness, and Bliss could only tolerate a certain threshold of madness before she had to put her foot down.

Refocusing on the building, she confirmed once again that the inside of the Elder wall was hollow. The Emperor's quarters and all surrounding rooms should be intact, beyond the initial cocoon of growth. And there, in the belly of this newborn beast, a person was trapped.

And that was the core of Bliss' dilemma. Who was this person? Were they a prisoner, held hostage by an Elder? Were they the mastermind behind the Elder wall's creation? Maybe they were food, here to nourish the wall until it was no longer needed. She could be fairly certain that they weren't using the Optasia, because they rarely moved over to that side of the room. As Bliss understood it, accessing the global amplification relays should take quite a bit of time, and her mystery guest never spent long enough close to the Optasia.

Bliss didn't believe in luck, because whether chance outcomes were 'good' or 'bad' depended entirely on the opinions of the observer.

But in her opinion as an observer, what followed was extremely good luck.

She was just about to remove her hand from the skin of the Elder wall, her curiosity still unsatisfied, when a wave of energy passed through the air around her and entered into the Elder flesh. The wall absorbed a surge of nourishment, like a plant's thirsty roots being washed in fresh rainwater for the first time.

The lashing tendrils withdrew, the membrane bulged outward, and Elder muscles grew stronger.

Bliss wasn't quite delighted enough to smile, but she had to express her excitement somehow, so she clapped enthusiastically. Like a satisfied audience member at an excellent performance.

The Elder wall's vitality wasn't infinite, and it wasn't coming from within. It was being sustained from *without*, probably calling power from elsewhere with the Optasia. It was entirely possible that there was a circle of Elder cultists somewhere in the Aion even now, dying one by one to feed their lives into the growth of this wall. Well, as far as Bliss was concerned, the world would be better off with fewer Elder worshipers in it. Even though they had, entirely on accident, given her the clue she needed.

She didn't need to destroy the Elder wall; she had to drill through it, piercing a tunnel into its heart. It wouldn't rejuvenate until it received another influx of vitality, which it couldn't summon if they disconnected the Optasia. So all she had to do was pierce the hide while avoiding its attacks, bore through four or five yards of rubbery flesh, locate the Optasia in the darkness, kill the person protecting it, and remove the throne from Elder control without destroying the device itself.

Come to think of it, there were quite a lot of steps to this process. She should write them down.

No, wait! She should ask for help. That was what Alsa Grayweather would tell her to do. General Teach would probably appreciate it as well.

Pleased with herself, Bliss turned from the Elder wall and walked across the courtyard past her wounded Watchmen and Guards. Not only had she managed not to turn them into dogs, but she'd figured out the mystery of the unpleasant-looking Elder wall. It had been a good day.

She'd caught a Great Elder spying on her last night, which had been the first thing to spoil her mood. But even though it had tried to distract her, she'd managed to figure out the secret anyway.

That would show Kelarac. Him and his dreams.

"We provoked the Regents for a calculated reason," Maxeus said, addressing the room. "We did not expect to be exposed publicly, which is a setback, but I can still handle them. Plans are in place. Meanwhile, we must act like the Regents are not a factor."

"Then we should announce an Emperor as soon as possible," Teach said firmly. Her eyes on Calder were stern, but at least he didn't feel the murderous Intent that she'd shown him at every meeting in the past. That was progress.

Maxeus tightened his mask, as though adjusting it to fit a new expression. "We'll need to do more than that. We have the military power to match any Guild except the Champions, who have thankfully remained neutral. Or possibly disbanded. Kern has been vague. However, we do *not* have the economic base that the Independents do. Between the Consultant's Guild and the fortune of the alchemists, they will eventually sway the public to their side. But even if they cannot, time is still their ally. With the current lack of cooperation between Guilds, the Empire *will* fall apart. It's only a matter of time."

Cheska groaned loudly. "So we need...what? We have the better military, okay, so we attack. Scatter them. If there aren't any more Independent Guilds, then everyone's in favor of a new Emperor."

"Again, public opinion must stay on our side. We need a battle, but we can't strike first."

Calder and Teach saw Maxeus' point at virtually the same time, because they both sat up straight and looked at him.

"We force them to attack *us*," Teach said.

"I thought that was the point of assassinating Alagaeus," Calder said. He still couldn't talk about it without feeling a chill; however indirectly, he had been party to the murder of an Imperial Regent. If their side didn't win, he was going to die a traitor's death.

Maxeus rubbed gloved hands together like a man anticipating a fine meal. "We gained several advantages from the Regent's death, including the obvious benefits of his absence. We've reduced the battle capacity of the Regents by twenty-five percent, if nothing else. And I've proven the efficacy of a certain...pet project of mine. Besides which, even if we're blamed for instability in the east, the fact remains that Izyria was destabilized while under the command of Alagaeus. If that doesn't drive public opinion against the Regents, nothing will."

"But now we need to goad the other Guilds to action," Teach said, back on topic as usual. "Who will take the bait?"

Cheska ticked names off her fingers. "Kanatalia won't respond to anything but a blatant attack, which defeats the purpose. The Greenwardens are too weak and too quiet. In fact, I don't know the last time I saw a Greenwarden at all. The Consultants are too good. If they retaliated against us, no one would know. And besides, they're still dealing with that Elder attack on their island. Which leaves the Luminians."

Maxeus nodded as though that were the conclusion he'd wanted her to reach all along. "They're proud, they're strong, and their code makes them easy to provoke."

"It's done," Teach said. She turned to the blond, orange-eyed Guard captain standing behind her. "Take rotating squads and blockade the road leading to the Luminian headquarters at Hightower. Use whatever excuse you can to take a Pilgrim into custody, or get a Knight to challenge you. Hold the casualties to a minimum; we just need proof that they attacked us, I don't want you to waste men."

The captain hurried off, leaving Calder a little stunned. When the Head of the Imperial Guard wanted to act, she acted *fast*.

"Maybe you all discussed this when I wasn't looking, but why do we need them to attack us at all?" He tapped the news-sheet. "They made up a story about us, even though they got it right. Why can't we do the same? Trot out a few wounded Guards, and print up a story about how the Luminian Knights assaulted us because they were so against the idea of a unified Empire."

"Witnesses," Cheska answered simply. "Any story we put out can be verified or denied by the Witnesses. If we lie, they'll let everybody know it. That's what we would have done for *this* story, except that it just so happens to be true."

Which led Calder to wonder why the Independents had published the article in the first place. Was it really fabricated? If the Witnesses could verify anything, how would anyone dare to lie?

Short of asking the enemy Guild Heads, he would probably never know.

"And speaking of Witnesses…" Cheska continued. She reached under the table and hauled up a wooden case. A familiar one. She popped it open, revealing a set of white candles. "…we need to get a team on these *yesterday*. The alchemists and Consultants are better-funded than we are, so we might as well tap into what funds we can."

Calder's mouth worked silently for a moment before he objected. "Those are mine!"

She smirked at him. "Technically, they're the property of the Guild of Witnesses."

"I mean, I had them. They were in *my* room."

"That's right. Where my men found them and brought them to me." She waved a hand at him. "Oh settle down, we're not going to abandon you on the side of the road. We never needed you to Read these, just to carry them to us. We have other uses for you."

That was actually somewhat of a relief, but Teach took over by drumming armored fingertips on the table. "That brings us neatly to our *second* point of order: we must announce an Emperor immediately. Therefore, we can paint any enemy action as opposition to the Emperor instead of just a disagreement between Guilds."

There would be a lot of merit to that. Some philosophers painted disloyalty to the Emperor as morally equivalent to Elder worship. Even if Calder wasn't the original Emperor, the taboo would still work in their favor.

Maxeus shook his head. "There's an issue. If we simply raise some nobody to the position of Emperor, we can expect an outcry. However, I have a solution that I believe will smooth the transition."

Over the course of this meeting, Calder's biggest supporters had called him a nobody and a slack-jawed idiot. He was looking forward to a long and glorious reign.

The Head of the Magisters produced a sheet of paper, similar to a newssheet but printed on thicker paper. Calder could smell the ink, fresh from the printing presses, and the letters were bold and stylized. The palace sometimes put papers like these out in the Capital as Imperial announcements, and he could immediately see how they would lend him an air of legitimacy.

The contents of the paper were brief but poignant, starting with the seal of all four Imperialist Guilds on top...and the seal of the Witnesses at the bottom, verifying that the text was legitimately produced by the Imperial Palace.

Loyal citizens of the Empire,

In the wake of the Emperor's untimely and unholy death, may his soul fly forever free, we grieved together in the years known as the Long Mourning. As a people, we have been fragmented and leaderless, banding together under the banners of those who would divide rather than unite us.

But now, on behalf of all faithful Guilds of the Aurelian Empire, we will raise a new leader. A man who will bring us together, not drag us apart. A man who will once again protect us from the foul incursion of the Elders and their spawn.

In memory and honor of the original Emperor, the father of us all, we are hereby proud to announce the man who will lead us forward into the future, the Imperial Steward of the Aurelian Empire, Lord Calder Marten.

Calder's name was repeated in much larger, more flowery letters on the bottom of the sheet, as though he'd signed it. He'd never seen the signature before in his life.

"There are several versions of this declaration for various audiences," Maxeus went on. "This one is primarily aimed at Guild members and their families, but we have variants for laborers, nobility, and the educated classes. This also can't be our only announcement, of course; we'll have to send a coronation date along with it."

Teach scanned the paper and tossed it back onto the table. "It works. I can back it up. As long as you can keep the Regents under control."

Maxeus leaned back in his chair, folding his hands over his stomach. "If I've proved anything this week, it's that I know how to handle the Regents."

"But not the media," Cheska muttered, still reading. "Doesn't this seem a little...abrupt? The people have no Emperor, and then they read a piece of paper, and now they have one all of a sudden?"

"We have to strike quickly," Maxeus countered. "And we've done our best to acclimate the population of the Capital to the idea for years. If they're not ready for a leader now, they never will be."

Calder's stomach fluttered, and he was having trouble keeping the grin off his face. "Can I have this framed?"

Teach let out what might have been, in someone else, a laugh. "I suspect you can have whatever you want."

"If he can sit on the throne," Cheska reminded her.

"That's still a concern."

The door flew open, and Bliss hopped in. "No it's not! I figured it out."

Calder looked from her to the open door. "Have you been eavesdropping? Why didn't you just come in?"

Teach was beginning to look exhausted again. "You were invited to this meeting, Bliss."

"I was waiting for the appropriate moment," the girl replied, lifting her chin. "That was it. Now I need you all outside the Emperor's quarters with your weapons."

Maxeus stood up. "Not me. I have business to attend to at my estate, I'm sorry to say. Not that I would be much use against a wall of Elder flesh anyway." A Magister's greatest weapon was his Intent, and using Intent directly against an Elder creation was a particularly painful way to commit suicide.

Bliss waved him off. "I don't need him. The rest of you, follow me."

Teach and Cheska traded a look, but they followed without complaint. Calder took another look at the printed announcement.

Imperial Steward of the Aurelian Empire.

It was real. At last, he'd made it.

He folded the paper and slipped it into his pocket.

CHAPTER NINE

TEN YEARS AGO

The night was quiet, and only the slap of the waves and the throbbing hatred of the Lyathatan competed for Calder's attention. He was mostly focused on the caged man in front of him, who stood and stretched in the yellow light of a quicklamp.

Urzaia was too tall for his cage, his shoulders bunched against the ceiling, but he beamed at Calder. "I have to stand to tell a story," he explained. "It is not the same if I cannot use my hands."

"I am your captive audience," Calder said, his voice pitched low. He wasn't sure what the two Champions would do to him if they found the Navigator captain interrogating their prisoner, but he didn't want to find out.

"Are you sure? It has a sad ending, my story."

Calder raised his eyebrows. "It hasn't ended yet."

Urzaia was born in Axciss, the City of Champions. One of the bigger cities on the Izyrian continent, Axciss is known for two things: its gladiator arenas, always popular sport with the Izyrian crowd, and the Champion's Guild headquarters. Popular legend suggests that fighters are so common there because of the Guild presence, though some believe that the Guild only stays there because of the fights.

His father was a gladiator, a veteran of over two hundred fights that could fill the seats whenever his name appeared. Urzaia grew up in the stadium, sweeping seats and selling drinks as soon as he could walk on his own.

By the time he was big enough to drag bodies out of the sand, the Guild came for him.

His father had died only a few months before, killed by an infection after a victorious fight. When the Guild came through the arena, looking for hopefuls, his mother signed him up for testing. It would be the last time she ever saw him...but the last time she ever paid for his meals, either, so in her mind the scales were likely balanced.

The first test of the Champion's Guild is a simple one: you're paired up against another boy, and you have to beat him bloody before he beats you.

The strong win, the weak are eliminated. As the Guild only selects the biggest, strongest boys of their age, the fights can get vicious.

Urzaia never thought his initiation was fair; he knew how to fight, and the other boy didn't. He was pinning his opponent to the ground before the instructor's shout faded.

Most of the winners went to the Guild, while the losers—and the winners who had been injured too badly—were left in the street. Urzaia spent the next two years working for the Champion's Guild, doing mostly the same thing he'd done in the arena. He swept up, carried drinks, beat rugs, carried weapons, and dragged bodies either to the furnace or the graveyard. In the meantime, he learned the basics of combat.

He missed those days. There was a certain nostalgia in remembering the first time he drew an instructor's blood with the point of his sword.

The second test followed his working years. This time, it was a tournament, according to very specific rules. More like a gladiator's work than actual combat. This was practical, as Urzaia saw it; the bulk of a Champion's income in the modern age came from duels or exhibition matches meant to show off an employer's might.

Of the sixteen entrants in the tournament, Urzaia came in second. The final round was the first fight he had ever lost.

He and three others were selected for further testing, while the twelve who didn't make it were either expelled from the Guild or returned to another year of sweeping and hauling.

At the time, he'd expected a warm welcome from the older Guild members. Or at least an acknowledgement that he was one of them. Not so. They tended to ignore him, leaving him to train on his own unless he made a mistake. He didn't understand until later that the first two tests were nothing more than building a foundation. The true test came next.

They kept him in a room with a team of alchemists, forcing potions down his throat and syringes into his muscles. He still couldn't recall the memory without shuddering. He spent months in that room, alone at night and surrounded by faceless alchemists all day, living a nightmare. He saw things that weren't there, lost control of his body, and lived in *constant* pain. The agony was like nothing he'd experienced before or since, as though his own body had turned inward to tear itself to shreds.

After half a year of constant torment, he was released. His supervisors at the Guild seemed surprised to see him, but the ensuing barrage of tests were mild compared to the treatment that had damaged him in the first place.

When they finally concluded that he was in one piece, they released him into the Guild.

Years later, he found out that something had gone wrong during his test. He'd reacted badly to some of the alchemical processes, so while most candidates are kept at the agonizing stage for six weeks at the most, Urzaia spent six *months* feeling like his skin was stuffed with knives. They had expected him to emerge mad, if he survived at all.

But he was as sturdy on the inside as he was on the outside, and he left the care of the alchemists, as one of his supervisors put it, "Saner than when he went in."

After his release, the Champions finally treated him as—

"I'm sorry," Calder said, interrupting.

Urzaia lowered his hands mid-sentence. "Is something wrong?"

"They almost tortured you to *madness?*"

The former Champion shrugged one shoulder. "I am a very happy person. I have been, always. My mother once said that I was born with a smile on my face."

He smiled wider in demonstration.

Calder shook his head. "I start to wonder if we shouldn't just round up and execute all alchemists."

"Eh, it takes strong pain to make strong men. Injections into the bone are bad, and you do not want one. But the one giving you that injection, he is not always bad."

"That's...noble of you." Calder wouldn't have let the alchemists go, any more than he spared the ones who tormented his father.

"I am a noble man. Anyway, after my release, the Champions finally treated me as one of their own..."

Mental conditioning was a core part of Urzaia's Champion training. His trainers did not tear him down, but built him up. He was pitted against normal human opponents, with no enhancements or invested weapons, and made to feel invincible. Constantly, the older Champions would talk about how lucky he was to have joined their Guild, and how weak the others were.

After a year of this, Urzaia was ready to believe it. His wounds healed overnight, he was immune to most poisons, and even many Soulbound powers no longer affected him. His strength and reactions grew beyond anything he'd ever imagined, and his eyesight was as sharp as a hunting bird's.

He strode out into his first assignment feeling like he could take the world apart.

It was appropriate that he was sent straight to the arena. One of the fight masters, who owned an entire team of successful gladiators, had begun to monopolize the markets for new fighters. He'd bribed his way into all the prisons in the city, and as soon as they received a criminal with combat training, he snapped them up. None of the other masters could compete, and his team was milking the arenas dry.

So his opponents had pooled their earnings to hire a Champion.

For his first job as a member of the Guild, Urzaia had picked his weapons: a pair of hatchets crafted by an Izyrian master smith. Urzaia's father had used battle-axes in the arena, and he himself had gotten used to hatchets while chopping up firewood at the Guild. More than anything, the weapons simply felt right. He was no Reader, but he thought it must have something to do with their Intent.

He stood at the arena, sand under him and blue sky overhead, surrounded by a screaming crowd, and he felt invincible. The enemy had a team of eighteen, released to fight him in pairs. The first pair had spears and shields, while he carried only a hatchet in each hand.

He fought them two at a time until all eighteen lay dead or crippled, watching the fight master's face grow paler with each defeat. When he won the ninth fight in a row, the crowd stood to their feet and roared.

Urzaia had never enjoyed a fight more.

From then on, he expected similar fights every time. Odds stacked against him, fighting to correct someone who had twisted Imperial law to his own advantage, righting wrongs and defeating worthy opponents.

Instead, his second assignment shipped him north of the Dylian Basin. He was headed as far north as any man had ever been, where tribes had set up a chain of villages in the snow. Apparently, they no longer considered themselves part of the Aurelian Empire, and had formed their own society with their own rules. Urzaia was there to administer punishment on behalf of the Emperor himself, who had assigned this mission to the Guild. It was with a sense of pride that he set out, determined to hammer the primitive armies into the ice and return with documents of surrender inside a month.

The first year, he enjoyed his work. It was harder than he'd imagined to fight in the snow, so even when the villagers organized hunting parties of thirty or more, it was rare that he could kill even three or four before the others melted away. This was a challenge in itself, even though their warriors could not fight him evenly.

The second year, he wished for an enemy Soulbound. The ambushes had grown frustrating, and even when he flattened a village, the inhabitants would just pack up and move somewhere else.

The third year, he was beginning to question why he was there in the first place. Navigators seldom brought any news or orders for him, and when they did, it was only an order to stay where he was and continue working. Not that he was seeing any results. He had probably killed two or three hundred warriors, from various villages, but no single group took too many casualties. And none of them had even come close to surrendering.

By the fifth year, he had all but given up on performing his duties for the Empire. When he became bored, he would hike up the mountains and lure a Kameira—usually a Brightwolf, or an Icewinder, or a Hydra of some kind—down toward a village, where he would fight the warriors and the Kameira both. This was chaotic and often unsatisfying, but created a few interesting fights.

One day, everything went wrong. He couldn't remember exactly what led to it, but he woke at the bottom of an icy pit, a dead Brightwolf lying on his chest and slowly squeezing the life from his lungs. Both his legs were broken, his hatchets were missing, and the pit was surrounded by the corpses of fifty warriors from several local villages.

He fully expected to be flattened beneath the body of a Kameira, but a scouting party from a far-off village found him first. They dug him out, loaded him on a sled, and dragged him back home.

Stories of his violence had reached them, but none had seen him personally. They failed to recognize him, and so they let him live as one of them. While he was there, he realized they were living perfectly well without the Empire. Why did they need an Emperor anyway?

So he asked them why they had chosen to rebel, and they told him.

They paid taxes because their ancestors had always done so, but they never received anything in return. There were no roads. No one gave them food or shelter from the winter storms. No Guild came to defend them from the frequent Kameira attacks, and there were no chapter houses within a thousand miles. Quite simply, they had never been part of the Empire, except in name.

But the final blow came when an Elderspawn had invaded, years before. It moved from village to village, spreading a disease that slowly turned people into monsters. By the time the Blackwatch arrived, the whole region had been infected.

They offered no explanation, and taught the locals nothing. Instead, they killed everyone affected, and half of the seemingly uninfected children. Then they vanished during the night.

At that point, the villages had done something new: they called all their leaders together, from all over the region, and jointly decided to stop paying taxes.

That was when the Emperor finally took notice of them.

"When I heard that story," Urzaia said, "I decided that the Emperor must not know. If he knew the story, he would know this was not a rebellion, and he would not have sent me. By then, I had made enemies in many of the villages, as you might imagine. But those who would let me help, I helped. I built fences, fixed sleds, fought Kameira that attacked. I made a difference, I think. And I fell for a local woman, settled in, built myself a house. For two years I lived this way. It was boring, but sometimes boring is nice. And I could fight Kameira bare-handed, so that was exciting.

"After two years, another Navigator showed up with personal instructions from the Emperor. They had the Imperial Seal and everything. This paper told me that I had run out of time, that I needed to kill until there were few enough villagers to fit onto the Navigator's ship, and then to pack the holds with the rest. We would return to the Capital, where they would face trial.

"Not only did I tear up the order in his face, I was...not so kind to the Navigator. Or his crew. They sailed out much faster than they planned, I think. But now, I regret that I did not kill them and send their ship to Kelarac."

Urzaia looked to the distance and sighed, his smile fading completely for the first time. "Three months later, two of my brother Champions came to take me. It was the most interesting fight I'd had for seven years, so that's something to thank the Emperor for. But there were two of them, after all, and they were not weak. They are the ones who now call themselves Eight and Nine, actually." He nodded to the door of the cabin, beyond which Eight stood sentry while Nine recovered from his burns.

"They took me to the Capital, where my own Guild Head passed sentence on me in the name of the Emperor. I was stripped of my titles and rights as a Champion, and sentenced to death in the gladiator's arena of Axciss. This is not so rare, you understand. Criminals can continue making money for the Empire, even while they face the penalty of death. For me, I am happy to die where I was born."

Urzaia smiled again and settled back on his heels. Calder was sure his own face showed some combination of shock, anger, and horror, but Urzaia didn't seem to mind. "This is why you shouldn't trust the Emperor too much," Urzaia said. "He is not like they say he is. Maybe he cares about the Empire, but he does not care about its citizens very much."

The statement struck deep in Calder. It was exactly what he'd always said, based on his Reading of the Imperial relics.

He *had* to get this man on his crew. If only there was some way to get around his inconvenient death sentence.

Calder leaned forward and grasped the bars of the cage, staring intently into the Champion's eyes. "Urzaia. I can't do anything now, but I will come back for you."

The prisoner's eyebrows rose. "It would surprise me if you did."

"You just need to hold on. Stay alive. Do whatever you can. But some day, as soon as I *possibly* can, I will come back for you. I have reason not to trust the Emperor myself, and I can't let a man go who's smart enough to see things as they are."

Urzaia laughed, though he kept it quiet enough not to alarm Eight. "I don't consider myself a smart man. But if all I must do is keep winning, I can do that. I have not lost in the arena so far, and I don't see a reason to do so now."

He looked back at Calder, still grinning. "I will wait for you as long as I can, Captain. How long do you think it will take?"

Calder had no idea.

CHAPTER TEN

When the sky cracks, death can pass either way.

– THE RAMBLINGS OF AN ELDER-TOUCHED MADWOMAN
(FROM THE BLACKWATCH ARCHIVES)

The man in the steel blindfold could come and go as he wished, but Jerri was still a prisoner. That grated on her even worse than his attitude. More than once, she was prepared to leave, but he always said *something* to trick her into staying.

"Even the basest Elderspawn can wait in the darkness for a week. A servant of the Great Ones must be able to tolerate the dark."

"I can come and go because I am only a humble messenger. If I were fit to be the guardian of this room, I too would stay."

Each time he returned, she considered killing him. And each time, he managed to say exactly what would get her to stay. Even though she knew it was impossible, she started to wonder if he was Reading her mind.

That, and the Emperor's quarters had a full bathroom complete with a toilet and functional plumbing. Otherwise she would have burned her way to freedom days ago.

Now, on what she determined was her sixth day in the Emperor's Elder-sealed room, her self-proclaimed guide appeared again. He stepped out of the shadows as though he'd been there all along, gold teeth gleaming in the middle of his smile. "Good news, Mrs. Marten."

The name hit her hard, harder than she would have expected. She'd spent most of her married life on *The Testament*—and years prior to that, too—where everyone called her by her first name. On shore, no one knew them. Hearing it now, from a fellow member of the Sleepless in the belly of an Elder construct, felt...entirely wrong.

But he had likely said it just to see her squirm, and she wasn't about to give him the satisfaction. She threw her braid behind one shoulder and straightened her spine. "What is it?"

"They're *finally* coming in."

He had spent the last six days deftly dodging any question about what they were waiting for. Now...was this it? They'd waited for the Imperial Guard to stop poking at the Elder seal and finally wheel in the big guns?

But what did she care if the Imperial Guard made it in here?

"Are we going to wait here for them?" Jerri asked, finally. She hated to ask him, but she felt entirely out of her depth here. Whatever the cabal had this man doing, she didn't understand it.

Maybe it was a trick of the light, but her guide was a little harder to see than he had been a moment before. Even his brightly colored robes had dimmed to little more than shadow, and she could only pinpoint him clearly because of the reflections of gold in his jewelry. It was more than a little unnerving, which made her feel more at home. Dealing with Elders was *supposed* to be unsettling.

"Here's what I would like you to do, Jyrine," the man said, gently taking her by the shoulders. She didn't resist, allowing him to move her a few feet to the right. The soft organic light hanging from the ceiling hadn't gotten any dimmer, but he was still bathed in shadows, even inches from her face. As he moved, she sensed the movement of a vast bulk behind him, though she saw nothing more than a normal human silhouette. As though he were something massive cramming itself into the shape of a man.

He finally released her when she was standing with her back to the Optasia, facing the door. "Stand in this spot as long as you can, using the full extent of your power to defend yourself. That's all. When at last you feel like you cannot continue or you are about to lose your life, you can simply...stand aside."

Gold flickered in the darkness as he smiled.

The Elder seal around them trembled, and a beat of thunder shook the floor. The Guards had begun their attack. Her heart pounded and her breath quickened from a mix of fear, anticipation, and the sheer thrill of adventure. Her earring began to sparkle, gathering green light.

"Who are you?" she asked, not for the first time. He'd dodged her questions before, but now...now, she hoped, he would give her a real response.

"I am...a business partner of your husband's. I'm the one who arranged for your jailbreak and ensuing expedition through the void. I assigned you here, Jyrine Tessella Marten, and I sowed the seed of this moment long before you were born."

Jerri fell to her knees, pressing her forehead to the floorboards. "Kelarac, Great One," she whispered. Only in her most daring daydreams had she imagined that she would someday come face-to-face with one of the Great Ones. This was even better than she'd hoped; Kelarac was actively helping her. He had guided her wisdom closer to his own, so that she could continue serving the world.

"Do you wish to learn from me?" Kelarac asked, and his voice came from all around her.

"More than anything."

"I know the secrets of time, of the worlds, of the future and of human Intent. With a fraction of my knowledge, you could guide the Empire into a new golden age. Each man an Emperor, each woman an Empress."

She could picture it as he spoke, as though he were feeding her specific images. A man flexing his Intent to open a solid wall into a door; a woman climbing into a machine shaped like a winged Kameira, and soaring through the clouds; a little boy waving his hand and causing a thousand flowers to bloom in a field.

"The mysteries of this world are keys that can unlock any door," the Great Elder's voice went on. "And they will be yours…if you pay the price. And today, I take my price in *obedience*."

She stood, green power swirling around her fingertips and lighting the room. She'd never been so ready to fight.

With Kelarac's knowledge, she could shock the world. Prove to everyone, even Calder, that she'd been right. That she and her father were justified all along.

The Soul Collector laughed fondly, and the door tore open.

Jerri hurled fire.

At first, standing in the courtyard, Calder tried to take on a passive role in the defeat of the Elder wall. The mountain of flesh was not going down passively, lashing out at each of the Guards and Watchmen that dared approach. They were using their armor and weapons to clear the way for the Guild Heads—General Teach marched up with Tyrfang in one hand, keeping a healthy distance from the other humans so that the sheer aura of her weapon didn't strike them dead.

Bliss skipped along next to her, apparently immune to Tyrfang's power, the Spear of Tharlos leaning against one shoulder. When she and Teach struck together, it dwarfed anything Calder had seen before, exploding like an alchemist's charge and sending stinking flesh blasting fifty feet into the air. Calder had to stagger back and hold a hand up over his eyes to block a faceful of Elder gore. They stood in a tunnel slashed in the flesh, black-edged with death and corruption.

But the wall was still growing. They weren't getting closer to the heart.

Eventually, he knew, they would carve through. They *were* doing damage faster than the wall could heal, and they wouldn't stop until they broke through to the center. But at this rate, it could take hours. And Bliss had emphasized speed above all else. No matter what they had to do, they had to reach the inside of the Elder wall as quickly as possible.

Calder lifted the sheathed saber he'd carried from his room. He had wanted to avoid drawing the weapon in front of Bliss, in case she could somehow sense that it came from Kelarac. Besides, he was wearing clothes fit for the Emperor himself. He didn't want to ruin them with Elder blood on the first day.

But now, it seemed, he had no choice.

He pulled the sheath off with one hand, tossing it aside, and held the blade in the other. "If this doesn't work, I'll have ruined my clothes for no reason," he said to no one in particular.

"I hear you have to pay for the second set," Andel called from behind him. He hadn't known the man was here.

Calder stepped up to the Elder wall for the first time since his dream last night. In the daylight it loomed even higher, more menacing, a sheer cliff of rotting meat. The stench rolling from the freshly carved cave was indescribable, and he couldn't get too close to General Teach for fear that her sword would actually kill him where he stood.

But he did have one advantage.

Through the six-fingered mark on his right hand, he funneled his Intent and Read the simple Elderspawn wall. As he'd suspected, it was a simple creature, fashioned for the sole purpose of keeping them away from this room. It focused on him, preparing to lash out with its whips of muscle, and he moved his blade where the lashes would strike.

Raw Elder sinew met orange-and-black mottled steel. The orange of the Awakened blade flared, corrosive Intent surged in the weapon, and the tendril blackened.

A silent scream blasted out from the Elder wall, audible to Calder only through Kelarac's mark. The wall recoiled—not visibly, but through its Intent—and tried to attack around the blade. Each time, Calder intercepted the strike an instant before the whip actually landed.

He found himself grinning. Fighting like this made him feel like a swordmaster from legend, unbeatable and unstoppable, advancing against any number of opponents. His sword was always in the right place even before it was needed, and he fought on sheer instinct. Too bad it only worked on Elderspawn.

When he reached the cave that Bliss and Teach had opened, he dared not proceed any farther. If Teach happened to accidentally move the Intent of her Vessel backwards, he'd fall over dead.

Just as his father had, at the end of that same weapon.

Instead, experimentally, he drove his Awakened sword into the side of the tunnel. The simple Elder being let out another scream of Intent, and a massive chunk of the wall just *melted*. Odious black goo rolled like a tide over his shoes, and he knew he'd have to burn this pair too.

It was as he'd expected, remembering the fate of the Elderspawn on the Gray Island. Any lesser Elder that encountered this sword dissolved.

He would have to join the two Guild Heads, if they wanted to make it through the wall in any reasonable amount of time. Which left only the little inconvenience of figuring out how to fight next to Tyrfang without dying.

"Guild Heads!" Calder called. They were only a pace or two ahead of him, as their tunnel was incredibly shallow at this point, but they were both thoroughly engaged in digging through the Elder flesh. In fact, shovelfuls of carrion and rotting blood splattered him every time they moved. "Excuse me! General Teach!"

"Speak!" Teach ordered, without turning around.

More than the stench, more than the sickening sounds of blades in flesh, more than the reality of what they were doing, the Intent rolling off of her Vessel made him feel sick. "I believe I can speed us up, but I have to get closer."

Teach gave no acknowledgement that she'd heard, hacking away at the wall, but Tyrfang's Intent began to lessen. Her speed decreased in proportion, until the entire hall didn't *quite* blacken and die with every swing of her sword.

On the other side of the General, Bliss just held her Spear jammed into the end of the tunnel, humming an aimless tune. The wall's flesh actually fled from her blade, as if in fear.

Calder held his breath as he moved up, standing shoulder to armored shoulder. He immediately knew he'd been wrong; no matter how far Teach held herself back, the aura of the sword pressed against him like the edge of a blade. His vision blurred, and he could feel consciousness slipping.

He concentrated on his own sword, on the orange-spotted blade Kelarac had given him. Its power seemed to *push* around it, creating a little bubble where Teach's influence was weakened. It helped, but not enough. He needed something else.

In a last, desperate attempt to distract his Intent, he focused his attention through Kelarac's mark on his arm. The handprint grew warm and his Intent firmed, as though he'd braced himself against a solid foundation. That, finally, was enough. General Teach's corrosive power scraped at him, trying to find a foothold, but through the mark Calder could hold it at bay.

It was a little alarming that the mark of Kelarac could support his Intent, suggesting that the Great Elder was backing him directly in some way, but he chose not to focus on that. One job at a time.

Now that Tyrfang's nauseous power had lessened, Calder put his back into the work, swinging his own Awakened blade.

He was pleasantly surprised at how much his addition to the team actually helped. They soon fell into a rhythm: Teach slashed the wall, blackening the flesh for yards around. Then Calder impaled it with his glowing-ember blade, melting it to black sludge. Bliss finished by cleaning up, sweeping the dead matter away with the Spear of Tharlos.

They were through the Elder wall in minutes.

When they stumbled through a sudden hole and onto carpeted floor, it was all Calder could do to focus on catching his breath. He'd assumed there would be...more to it, somehow. They had gone from making slow progress to piercing through so quickly that he could hardly believe it.

He held his gore-caked blade over his head. "Victory!" he shouted, like an idiot. A few of the Guards outside took up a cheer.

"Not quite," Bliss said. She squinted up the hallway, to a room that looked just like half a dozen others. "There's someone waiting for us."

Calder couldn't sense anything other than Elders through Kelarac's mark, but he took Bliss' word for it.

Besides the sunlight spilling in from behind them, the hall was lit by dim organic bulbs hanging down from the ceiling. They cast a dirty, grayish light on their surroundings, like an Elder's attempt to devour all color.

"Here," General Teach said, striding up to a door and drawing her sword back, preparing to drive it completely into the room.

She didn't even try the doorknob, Calder thought, before Teach blasted her way inside. The doors blew inward as though she'd charged in with a sledgehammer.

A ball of green fire met her on the other side.

Teach jerked down and to the right, spinning to put her back against the wall to the right of the doorframe. She held Tyrfang up in both hands. She must have started to lose her grip on its Intent, because dirty white paint began to peel away from her as she knelt there.

Ordinarily, Calder would have felt the corruption of that murderous blade, but at the moment...he realized he was holding his breath again.

Green fire. It couldn't be. It couldn't be. That was a coincidence that strained all credibility; if he'd seen it in a play, he wouldn't have believed it.

"What we call coincidence is but the work of plans unknown." The philosopher Hestor's words struck dangerously close to home. If anything was the result of an Elder's plan, it would be Jerri's presence here.

But his wife hadn't died on that island after all.

Calder moved into the doorway and saw her, in the same red prison clothes she'd been wearing the last time. When he'd abandoned her to her fate. She'd launched a ball of flame even before he'd turned the corner, but he slapped it out of the air contemptuously with the flat of his sword.

That was something he would have never attempted, under other conditions; he didn't understand the Intent in those green fireballs, nor did he fully understand the power in his own sword. Instead of canceling each other out, the effects could just as easily have fed on one another and burned him alive. Besides, Soulbound blasts of fire were invariably *fast*. It was a stupid, unnecessary risk to try swatting one in midair.

This time, he hardly noticed. Jerri stood before him, fire gathering unnoticed in her left hand, eyes as wide as he knew his must be.

"Calder, what are you...what are you doing with the Imperial Guard?"

That actually made him smile, though he wasn't entirely sure he *felt* like smiling. "I thought you would have guessed. They're with me. I'm the Emperor now."

Jerri's right hand, the one not wreathed in emerald fire, came up to her mouth. Her eyes filled with tears. "You see? *He* told you the truth!"

Calder's feelings turned sour. Why had she brought *that* up? Now he was lost in the memory of slithering eyes on stalks, and the knowledge that he danced in the palm of an Elder's hand.

Bliss popped out from behind Calder. "Technically, he's the Imperial Steward. Sitting on the throne until someone, probably him, can be declared the true Emperor. For that, though, we're going to need the throne."

Everything seemed to happen at once.

Jerri focused her gaze on Bliss, anger burning through the lens of her unshed tears. Green fire glowed brighter.

The Head of the Blackwatch rolled out, extending the Spear of Tharlos to its full length. The spear of ancient yellowed bone radiated an Intent that swallowed the room, plucking at Calder with invisible fingers and urging him to change. He had to concentrate on Kelarac's mark, filling his mind with the borrowed authority of the Soul Collector, to face even that much Elder Intent without losing himself.

Armor clanked as General Teach launched herself into the room. Tyrfang's red-and-black blade rippled with dark power, and Calder found the breath snatched from his lungs. Utter despair rolled over him like a tide, as though he'd come face-to-face with his own executioner.

Whatever happened next, it happened so quickly that he saw it only in flashes.

Jerri released a flash of green fire and dove to the side, while the Spear of Tharlos struck straight at her. It would have missed the fire entirely, except it seemed to *twist* of its own accord, bending in violation of everything Calder knew about physical mass. It hit the fire straight on...just as Tyrfang's black edge arrived.

Soon after, when Calder tried to piece the moment together, he couldn't make it all fit. By rights, Teach should have been five steps farther away than Bliss. They should have been aiming at different points. The fireball should have passed both of them, and they all should have hit only air.

Instead, the power of Jerri's Vessel met Tyrfang, the Executioner's Blade and Bliss' Spear of Tharlos at the same time.

Inches above the flesh-shrouded cage of steel bars that men called the Optasia.

The Intent burned away the Elder flesh surrounding the Emperor's throne instantly; the heart-like muscle that had kept a grip on the metal dissolved into black powder. The force continued, tearing up floorboards and wall panels, rearranging and shattering furniture.

But the Optasia caught that blend of deadly Intent, accepted it, and sent it out to a thousand relays all around the world.

That was about as much as Calder's Reader senses caught before they were overwhelmed, and he collapsed on the floor of the Emperor's bedroom.

After the strange reaction of the Optasia, Bliss ran for the exit. She didn't prefer to run—running wasn't dignified—but sometimes the speed was worth it. Especially in cases of grave danger or medical injury.

There had been an injury here, she knew it. And very possibly some grave danger as well. Tharlos' spear was contorting in the pocket of her coat, twisting and writhing in silent laughter.

When she pushed open the bronze doors leading from the Emperor's chambers, she remembered that she didn't know what she was looking for. The courtyard was a scene from an Elderspawn slaughterhouse, with chunks of rotten grayish flesh lying everywhere. Wounded Imperial Guards limped here and there, gathering up the pieces and dumping them into buckets in case the creature pulled itself together again. She could have told them it wasn't necessary, but she approved of their cleaning efforts. Hygiene was important.

At first, she saw nothing wrong, and her heart sank even further. If she couldn't see the damage, that meant the Optasia's network had carried it somewhere else in the world. She might never discover what the Elders had done until it was too late.

One Guard, a woman with a tail like a peacock, was staring up at the clouds. Her bucket fell from a limp hand, spilling Elderspawn gore onto the ground.

This was what a mystery novel might call a *clue*. Bliss followed the woman's gaze up, expecting a six-winged Elder with a mouth like a shark's.

Instead, the sky itself was distorted. A long, winding stripe of twisted *wrongness*, like a river of heat haze or a transparent worm. The air fuzzed and twisted, high overhead, and Bliss almost thought she could hear a distant crackle.

She'd seen corruption like this before. This would only be visible from a certain angle; even as high as it was, no one outside the palace would notice anything wrong. And it would get much worse, very soon.

The sky was going to break.

When Calder came to, he had a moment of panic. The world was frozen around him, too still and too quiet. Something was wrong.

He tried to roll off his bed and grab the pistol that he knew would be next to him, but his wounds screamed in protest. His head pounded so badly that his vision actually dimmed for a second, and he was forced to lean back against his pillow.

Reader's burn, he realized, and as soon as he accepted the truth, reality came flooding back. There was nothing wrong—he was onshore. Aboard *The Testament*, the motion of the boat never stopped, and there was no such thing as silence.

He relaxed and let the pain fade away. Normally, if he'd rolled around like this, he would have woken Jerri immediately. She would be the one to reassure him, to make fun of him for worrying when everything was peaceful.

But she wasn't here. She would be locked in some secure corner of the palace by now.

So something was wrong after all, just nothing new.

Thoughts of Jerri shook up his memory, reminding him of the afternoon, and he once again tried to sit up. Again, pain convinced him to stay where he was.

What had happened? The Optasia had reacted strangely to the attack...an attack that shouldn't have landed in the first place. And why was Jerri there, in the Emperor's chambers, sealed in by an Elder wall that had been there since before she left the Gray Island?

None of that made any sense, so there was only one possibility. An Elder was pulling strings, shaping events directly instead of letting them fall out as they naturally would. Why? He had no idea, and his head hurt too badly for further speculation.

Soft light from a distant quicklamp filtered in around the edges of his window, so it must have been the dead of night. He surrendered himself to the pain, hoping sleep would take him quickly.

Just before he shut his eyes again, the window creaked open, and a man hopped in. He wore his hair long, and in one hand, he carried a dagger in a reverse grip. Fresh blood dripped from the weapon's tip.

Calder was so shocked that, for a moment, he refused to believe what he was seeing. Not that it was so unusual for someone to try and kill him—that was happening more and more, these days—but that the would-be assassin had come *exactly* when he woke up.

What were the odds? Seconds earlier or later, and he would have seen nothing. Heard nothing. This man would have cut him in half.

Calder gave up questioning his good fortune as his fight instincts kicked in. The killer turned to him, striding confidently over to the bed, flipping his knife in one hand. As he got closer, Calder realized he was humming a jaunty tune.

I have one shot, Calder thought. He didn't have time to waste struggling out of bed or fighting against his pain; he had to reach his weapon, and he had to do it in one movement. That was his only chance of survival.

When he'd gathered enough strength, he clenched his jaw against the pain and rolled off the bed.

His assailant caught him and tossed him back. "Whoops, there you go. Up up up."

The man didn't seem at all surprised or thrown off by Calder's escape attempt; in fact, he seemed not to care at all. He pressed lightly on Calder's chest with one hand, but no matter how Calder struggled, he couldn't raise his chest an inch. He tried to gather the breath for a scream, but the attacker pushed the air from his lungs. The attacker winked at him and raised the knife.

And a shadow slit his throat with a bronze blade.

Calder had never realized it before, having never seen an assassination from quite this close, but slicing a man's throat open took quite a bit of strength. The shadow ripped through his neck like a butcher slicing meat, and warm blood showered Calder's face. And most of the rest of his body too, he supposed. Not that he was in any condition to complain.

He scraped the blood from his eyes, ignoring the pain from his injuries and the insistent hammer-blows of his headache, desperate to see.

When his eyes cleared, he was in for a surprise: the man was still on his feet. His throat was split almost to the spine, but he held it together with one hand. The other smashed back against the black-clad figure behind him.

The killer with the bronze blade flew backward with the force of a cannonball, smashing a crater-sized dent into the wall and falling limply to the floor. Frowning as though the whole mess irritated him, the man with the slit throat collapsed a moment later.

Leaving a blood-soaked Calder alone in his bedroom with two corpses.

"What just happened?" His voice came out in a croak, and of course no one answered him. Gingerly, favoring his newly stressed wounds, he reached out for his cutlass. Whoever had brought him here was also considerate enough to leave his weapon within reach, so he was able to tug the hilt out of its sheath without much trouble.

A second later, he poked at his attacker's body with the tip of his sword. No movement. Surely he should be dead, given the amount of blood he'd lost, but Calder would have never expected him to continue standing with his head halfway severed. No point in taking chances.

Calder poked him again, harder this time, and almost shrieked as the *other* body groaned and lifted a hand to its head.

Not just one person who survived a blow that should have killed them, but two. He should take up gambling; clearly the laws of probability were meaningless around him.

The shadow pulled off the black cloth that had surrounded its head, revealing a mess of blond hair. Meia looked up at him, orange eyes flashing with reflected light. "Champions," she said, with a grimace of distaste. "I'm sorry. I should have been more thorough."

"I would have thought a slit throat was thorough enough." *A Champion.* His body chilled as he realized how close he'd come to death. If Meia hadn't been there...if it had been someone *other* than Meia, the Consultant who could fight Urzaia...

This was far too many coincidences for one day.

Meia hauled herself to her feet. "I've never met anyone that could survive that. But let's be sure, shall we?" She crept over to the man's body, pulling needles from her pouch.

A poisoned needle went into both thighs and both wrists before she sliced the tendons on the back of each ankle. Calder prided himself on a strong stomach, but he looked away. He'd seen enough for one night.

When she was done, she walked over to the door and opened it a crack, peering out. "The hallway is unguarded. That's a pity. He killed eight Guards, two Watchmen, and one Magister that I'm aware of."

Eleven people, killed just to reach a twelfth. This was all too much for Calder to take in at one time. He struggled out of bloody sheets, hobbling over to the wardrobe. He was practically naked in front of Meia, wearing only a pair of shorts, but he couldn't possibly have cared any less.

"I was going to ask how he got in, but I guess that explains it." His hands were shaking so badly that he couldn't open the wardrobe—fear, pain, exhaustion, and the rush of danger combined so that he was surprised his limbs didn't shake themselves off completely.

Meia moved to the window, closed and bolted it, and then returned to the door. "It's a good thing it *was* a Champion, in a way. They don't concern themselves with stealth, they just kill a straight line to their target. As soon as I noticed him, I followed. I would never have seen a Gardener."

And she wouldn't have stopped one either, he was sure, but that did bring up an interesting question. "How *did* you notice him? Where were you?"

She spared him a glance, saw that he was frozen in front of the wardrobe, and reached over to pull the door open for him. "I grew up in the palace for years. I could stay here for the rest of my life, and no one would see me if I didn't want them to."

Which didn't exactly answer his question, but it was likely the closest he would get. Calder removed the servant's uniform, the one that had been waiting for him earlier, and quickly pulled it on. His skin was tacky with blood, so these clothes would be ruined, but he didn't care. He felt too vulnerable without anything on.

This will be the third set of clothes I've destroyed since I arrived here. An idle thought, but almost enough to make him laugh.

"That explains how you were nearby, but you actually saw an intruder and saved my life. That's not your job." In fact, he wouldn't have been surprised if her job was the exact opposite.

She frowned at him. "Right now, my job is to keep the Optasia out of the hands of the Elders. That's what you're doing, isn't it?"

"Trust me, I don't want Elder tentacles on the throne any more than you do."

Meia turned back to survey the hallway through the cracked door. "Then we're on the same side."

As Calder finished buttoning up his red-and-gold jacket, he considered Meia. Over the last month or so, since he'd found out that Consultant assassins were after his life, he'd thought of the Consultant's Guild as heartless, bloodthirsty monsters who were only *pretending* to serve their clients.

Now, he was reminded of the Consultants as he'd always heard of them. The most loyal Guild in the Empire; the only one that had always, through the past two thousand years, had the Emperor's complete trust. Everyone knew a Consultant would guide you and help you, and would remain utterly dedicated to your cause...for the duration of their contract.

More than one of the great classical philosophers had words of praise for the Consultants. If he could get one on his side, even if the rest of their Guild opposed him, that could be a huge advantage.

A distant door slammed open, and booted feet pounded down the hallway, toward Calder's room. Meia eased the door shut, sliding away and over to the window. "Imperial Guards. They'll take you somewhere safe."

"Wait!" Calder called before she vanished. She froze, one foot on the open windowsill. "Why leave?"

She looked at him like he was asking why she sharpened her knives. "For the same reason I disappeared aboard your ship. Our Guilds are in conflict, and maybe soon open war. If they catch me here, they'll try to take me into custody, and I'll have to kill them."

The boots were closer to his door now, and raised voices had begun to call his name. He motioned for her to stay where she was. "Stay there. Don't leave."

She gave him a doubtful look.

"Trust me. Please."

He walked to the center of the room, casually putting himself between the door and Meia. If he wasn't mistaken, they would jump to conclusions any second now.

Sure enough, a Guard with massive lion paws for feet kicked the door in a second later, brandishing a musket and bayonet in his hands. He looked past Calder and gave a shout, leveling his gun.

Calder showed his empty palms. "Lower your weapon, Guardsman."

"Move out of the way, sir!" the man shouted, stepping forward as though to move Calder physically out of the way.

Calder walked into him voluntarily, so that the bayonet rested at the end of his chest. The Guard jerked the weapon away hastily. "This woman saved my life. *He* tried to kill me." He jerked his thumb toward the Champion's corpse.

More Guards poured into the room, and two immediately checked the body for vitals. "Slit throat," one said.

"Champion," the second responded.

"Good point."

Together, they drew swords and hacked the limbs from the man's body. Shivering, Calder turned away. "Excuse me, my friend and I would like to be taken somewhere else. I'm not feeling particularly safe in here, for some reason."

The Guard's gaze hardened when it moved over Calder's shoulder. "I'm sorry, sir, we need to ask her some questions. Standing orders."

"Why's that?"

"She's a Consultant, sir. One of the enemy."

"Ah, I can see your confusion." He stepped back, presenting Meia with one arm outstretched. "She's not a Consultant at all. She's a Navigator. A member of my crew, in fact, my new...cook."

Meia's eyes were back to a human blue, and she stared at him as though she could focus hard enough to Read his Intent. Maybe she could; was she a Reader? He had no idea. But if she was a Reader *and* a trained assassin *and* a warrior with enough enhancements to fight toe-to-toe with Urzaia Woodsman, that just wouldn't be fair.

The Guard looked uneasy. Calder took advantage, pressing him while he was uncomfortable. "Let's go, Guardsman. Lead me and my cook to safety."

He held a hand to his temple against a throb of sudden pain. "And a medical alchemist, as soon as possible. I'd like to kill this pain yesterday, if that can be arranged."

While the Guard was uncertain when faced with Meia, he knew exactly what to do with an injured ally. They practically carried him down the hall, sending for the palace alchemists, and Meia followed.

CHAPTER ELEVEN

Half a year after delivering Urzaia to the arena, Calder was finally start-ing to learn his way around the ship. He could furl the sail without tangling it nine times out of ten, and he could steer his way through a predatory coral reef without putting his hand on the wheel.

More importantly, Jerri had taken to the work of a pilot—she scanned the horizon, charted their course, studied their position by the stars, and logged whatever deadly creature or impossible phenomenon they encountered dur-ing the day. She enjoyed, as she called it, "planning a safe route through an endless maze of horror and death."

Calder had even grown used to the two monsters in his life: the Lyathatan and Andel. The Elderspawn, it turned out, existed in a perpetual state of mal-ice and burning frustration. It had very little to do with anything Calder did. So long as he allowed the creature to snag the occasional shark and otherwise let it sleep, he and the Lyathatan remained on good terms. He still got the impression that it was plotting something ominous at all times, and that its service to Calder was but one step in some insidious game, but he was begin-ning to realize that its game wouldn't end for another few centuries at least. He couldn't bring himself to care about that.

Andel was a little trickier to handle, in some ways. The problem was, he was just too *useful*. He tended to assume responsibility for every problem as soon as it arose, so he would often have fixed whatever-it-was before Calder was even aware. This undermined his authority in the eyes of the passengers, so Calder tried to take charge whenever possible.

But having a crew member who was *too* skilled was a good problem to have, especially when the total crew numbered precisely three. Calder con-ducted most everything related to the handling of the ship himself, but pas-sengers still ended up working for the duration of their journey.

Except this passenger.

Mr. Valette looked like a schoolteacher. He was thin as a fence post, with expensive spectacles and long gray sideburns, and he had a tendency to frown at Calder as though expressing deep, heartfelt disappointment. Only one thing ruined the impression: his long, black coat.

He refused to work, refused even to acknowledge it when Calder asked him to carry a box or tighten a line. He would simply frown and walk away.

The passenger seemed to spend most of his time scribbling in a journal, which he kept tucked away in the inner pocket of his coat.

Two weeks into the journey, Calder finally mustered up the courage to ask his passenger a question. "If you'll pardon me asking, Mr. Valette, what does the Blackwatch need in the town of, ah..." He had to glance down at the log to remember the name of their destination. "...Silverreach?"

Mr. Valette slapped his journal closed, glaring at him. "I would pardon you asking, Captain Marten, but I doubt my Guild Head would do the same. She would be irritated with you, in fact. If you had ever met her, you would know how terrifying a prospect that is. So let's keep our questions to ourselves, hm?"

Calder still had nightmares about his first meeting with Bliss, but he couldn't admit that to this Watchman. Valette wasn't the only one who preferred to avoid sensitive questions. "That's understandable, Mr. Valette, and thank you for the warning. But considering the nature of your business, this information could affect the safety of everyone onboard. I wouldn't want to run into any trouble with Elderspawn, after all."

The passenger scratched at one of his sideburns, considering this. "I do not anticipate trouble," he said at last. He slipped the journal into his coat, rising to his feet. "If you'll excuse me, I'll be in my cabin. The weather does not look like it will be kind to ink and paper."

Calder glanced up to the stormclouds, which rolled in a slow, spiraling whirlpool. There *was* a storm on its way, but it wouldn't be likely to harm his book. Clouds like those meant that the rain would come in reverse.

He headed over to Jerri, who was slumped over the ship's wheel, an expression of absolute boredom on her face.

"I've seen two fish today," she said, as he approached. "One of them ate the other."

"Looking for lives of excitement and adventure? Join the Navigators!"

She smiled out of the corner of her mouth. "At least it looks like rain today. That's the only difference from yesterday."

"And we won't even get wet." He leaned against the railing next to the wheel, watching her. "What do you think of Mr. Valette?" he asked, voice low.

"Reclusive and shady, like every other Watchman I've ever known. All of them. No exceptions."

"No wonder they kicked me out. So you don't want to know what's happening in Silverreach?"

Jerri looked out over the sea, her eyes narrowed. She began to tap her fingers, drumming a rhythm on the ship's wheel. Just when Calder was about to break the silence, she spoke. "I've...read about Silverreach before. Somewhere."

It wasn't too surprising that Jerri would have read something he hadn't, but he hadn't thought Silverreach was that significant of a town. "Is it famous?"

Her eyes flicked to him and then back to the horizon. "Not famous. But if I've heard about it, something must have happened there. We should do some research."

Calder thought about the pathetic four books they kept on the entire ship. "By 'research,' you mean..."

"We should steal Valette's journal."

That was more like Jerri. Rather than wasting time feigning surprise, he nodded. "How?"

"The easy way," she said, flipping her braid over one shoulder. "Wait until he's asleep, take the book out of his coat."

Andel thunked a barrel down onto the deck loudly, attracting their attention. "I thought you should know we had a beetle problem. Half of the barley will have to be thrown overboard, and we'll have to filter the quicklamp fluid."

Calder nodded to the barrel. "Is that the barley?"

"The beetles," he said. "They tried to mutiny, so I had to quell their rebellion. Show them who owns this ship." The lid of the barrel started to surge upwards, as though something inside was pushing its way out, until Andel sat on it. Seated comfortably on the barrel of beetles, Andel pulled his hat off and began fanning himself. "So what's this I hear about a theft?"

Calder and Jerri didn't look at each other before they spoke. They'd worked together long enough that they reacted immediately.

"We were planning to rob you," Jerri said.

Calder let out a sigh. "Wait until you were asleep, go through your coat, take away all your...valuables."

Andel looked at them calmly from his perch on the barrel, still fanning himself with the hat. "Not my precious valuables."

"Now that you've heard us, our plot has been foiled," Jerri said. "You've beaten us again."

Calder stared into the water, filling his gaze with regret. "We never should have opposed you to begin with."

"That's true," Andel said. "Without me around, you'd be face-to-face with Kelarac before we ever caught sight of shore."

It was common for sailors to reference Kelarac when referring to the bottom of the ocean, because everyone knew that was where the Soul Collector was sealed. But Calder couldn't help a shudder. Ever since he'd *actually* met Kelarac, the phrase had become more than just an expression.

"And it's good that you were planning to rob me, instead of our passenger," Andel went on. "As we wouldn't want the Blackwatch finding out we had any breaches of conduct. Not only would they feed us to Elderspawn, they wouldn't pay us."

The barrel under him shuddered, the beetles struggling to escape, but Andel didn't seem to notice.

Calder forced a smile, but his hands were clenching on the railing. Whenever he started to get used to having Andel Petronus around, the man had to get in his way. Where was the harm in a little book-snatching? He'd been brought to trial for worse.

Andel reached into his white jacket, pulling out a palm-sized, tightly bound book of his own. He waved it in the air, then tossed it to Calder. "Fortunately for you, I don't like sailing in the blind any more than you do."

Jerri leaned over the book as Calder opened it. The first line read, *"To my Guild Head, Bliss, from your servant Andrei Valette..."*

From a quick scan of the page, it went on to describe his plan of action when he reached Silverreach, including his predictions about what *The Testament*'s crew would do on shore.

"You copied his journal," Calder said. His forced smile had slipped away, replaced by naked shock.

"I used to work as a scribe for the Order. All I needed was a few minutes a day before and after I laundered his coat. He's fastidiously clean." Andel didn't even look proud of himself. He sat there with an expression of absolute calm, even as the beetles surged underneath him.

Calder held up the book. "Well done indeed, Mr. Petronus. Please take the wheel while we study this in my cabin."

"I've already read it," Andel said. "So I won't spoil the surprise. Surrender the helm, and I'll see if I can bring us back on course."

Walking past, Calder actually clapped him on the shoulder. "Thank you, Andel. Now toss that barrel overboard."

"And waste perfectly good beetles?"

Andel hadn't seemed panicked about the journal. He'd read it, and he hadn't come screaming out on deck, demanding that they change course. In fact, he seemed to accept the whole thing without complaint.

Calder couldn't understand why. They were sailing into a death-trap.

As it turned out, the journal wasn't *just* Valette's thoughts about his upcoming mission. It also included copies of his original orders, as well as the reports that led to those orders.

The reports, taken in tandem with Bliss' commands and Valette's notes, told a frightening story.

"Farmers in the region report sightings of what they describe as 'ten-legged spiders' running through their fields at night. These sightings are often accompanied by the usual signs: stolen livestock, missing books, strange signs cut into cornfields. When the community contacted the local Blackwatch chapter house, we responded with a standard investigation. However, it reached no conclusion..."

He flipped the page.

"In southern Izyria, we cornered a hive of Inquisitors. They had abducted the elderly and those of mental infirmity, taking them to a cave for a ritual preparation we believe was intended to invoke the void. Watchmen on scene were able to contain the Elderspawn, but this behavior suggests an uncharacteristic boldness. Inquisitors are usually content to watch."

Every entry was something like this. These ten-legged arachnid Elderspawn, these Inquisitors, had become active all over the Empire. There were sightings from Dylia, Vandenyas, the Nire, even the Capital. Overall, it painted a disturbing picture. As one entry put it, *"For Elderspawn to work with such coordination and precise timing suggests a greater intelligence at work. I think we all understand the nature of that intelligence."*

Most frightening of all were Bliss' thoughts on the matter.

"The town of Silverreach was built on Ach'magut's tomb. That seems like a silly place to build a town to me, so perhaps they deserve their fate. Except they didn't build the town, their ancestors did. Anyway, they should move.

"The Inquisitors only act together under the orders of their lord, Ach'magut, and he's dead. For now. If Ach'magut is alive again, it is quite possible that we are all moving according to a plan he laid more than two thousand years ago. You should travel to Silverreach and determine if the Great Elder has revived. You'll be able to tell.

"If he has, we'll have to schedule Silverreach for destruction. There is always the possibility that you will not return from this assignment, in which case I will assume that you have been captured and tortured by Ach'magut, and adjust my plans

accordingly. I hope that does not happen, because then I would have to send three hundred silvermarks to your widow, and that is expensive. Be safe."

Bliss' concern for the welfare of her Guild members aside, the news froze Calder's blood. They were sailing into the lair of a Great Elder who might be alive and waiting for them. In fact, their sailing to him could all be a part of his plan. Calder was having difficulty thinking of a more painful way to die.

By contrast, Jerri's dark eyes were sparkling. "What if he's *alive?* Can you imagine it? The Emperor is the only one who's ever seen Ach'magut directly!"

Sometimes, it was hard to tell when Jerri was joking. "That's exactly what I was thinking, except we're going to change course. I wouldn't drop anchor at Silverreach if there was a chest of gold buried every ten feet."

That was an exaggeration; he probably would go ashore in that case. Gold was gold, and the Elder *might* still be dead.

"It can't be too dangerous!" Jerri insisted. "Bliss is sending a man into the town, and she wouldn't have hired us if this was absolutely suicide."

Calder pointed at the journal page. "Even she's admitting there's a good chance he'll be heading straight to his death. I can't believe he accepted an assignment like this."

Jerri laid a hand on his arm, moving a little closer. She looked at him earnestly, speaking softly, and her voice sent a quiver through his stomach. "Calder, he agreed because it's worth the risk. That's the mission of the Blackwatch: studying the Elders in the service of humanity. You remember."

In another tone, that would have felt like a jab, but he did remember. He had already made a deal with one Great Elder for a cause he felt was worth it, and that hadn't worked out too badly. Not as badly as it could have, anyway.

Sensing her advantage, Jerri pressed forward. "Besides, you know your mother supervises everything the Guild Head does. Even if *Bliss* would have killed a man just to learn something, would *she?*"

That was a good point. Alsa Grayweather wouldn't have allowed this to proceed if there wasn't a good chance the man would return. And since Calder suspected it was his mother's recommendation that had landed him this job in the first place, he knew she wouldn't put him within a hundred miles of Silverreach if it wasn't *somewhat* safe.

"We don't have to change course," Calder said finally. Jerri beamed at him, so brightly that he found himself smiling back. He wasn't sure why she cared about this, but for some reason she did, so he'd enjoy her good mood.

Before he could say anything else, she leaned forward and gave him a quick kiss.

He froze for a moment, stunned. A smile leaked out, tugging one side of his mouth up. If he didn't know her so well, he would have thought she was *too* excited about going to town. But she had no reason to care, other than her boredom and her desire to go ashore. Maybe that was enough. For Jerri, the potential would just add some much needed spice.

Whatever the reason, she was happy to go to Silverreach. She was happy with *him*. And that was all the explanation he needed.

After learning that a Great Elder may be waiting for them in the town of Silverreach, Calder had lost himself imagining what else they might find.

It could be a town that seems normal, but at night, the townsfolk turn into bloodthirsty cannibals. Silverreach could have been wiped from the earth, covered by nothing but Elderspawn and squirming tentacles. They could literally sail straight into Ach'magut's mouth.

Maybe they would see nothing wrong, and would return to report that to the Blackwatch...but it would all be part of the Overseer's plan. He would sneak one of his Inquisitors into the belly of *The Testament*, and Calder himself would be the agent responsible for spreading an Elder infestation.

His speculation had run so wild that, when they arrived at Silverreach, he was not at all surprised to find it empty.

There were only three other ships docked, all of them smaller than Calder's. Fishing vessels, with their catch rotting onboard. Gulls screamed as they whirled around the harbor, gorging themselves on piles of rotten fish. The smell had everyone onboard the Navigator's ship wrapping rags around their faces, leaving only their eyes uncovered.

The town itself looked like a hundred others in the Empire—the houses were simple, mostly wood covered in plaster, with sloping tiled roofs and wide, cobbled streets. Silverreach moved uphill, watched over by a lighthouse that stood sentinel on the edge of the coast.

Everything was dark. Not only was the lighthouse unlit, but not a single window in the town winked. None of the chimneys blew smoke. A half-open door creaked as it swung in the breeze, audible over the wind and the shrieking of birds.

"I think we've seen enough of Silverreach," Calder said. With a brief thought, he Read the Lyathatan. For the first time, the Elder actually seemed...wary. It did not sleep, here in the shallows, but kept its eyes and its Intent fixed on the shores as though waiting for a threat. That, accompanied by the eerie absence of an entire town, was enough to persuade Calder that they needed to turn back out to sea as soon as physically possible.

Mr. Valette scratched at his sideburns, watching the shore. He was in full Blackwatch costume—black coat, iron spikes tucked into loops at his belt for easy access, with the squirming Elder Eyes badge of his Guild displayed proudly over his chest. A case of tools sat by his feet, ready to be carried onshore, though Calder couldn't imagine what tools the man would actually need. He was here to discover Elder activity, and obviously there had been some. He'd discovered it. The mission, in Calder's mind, was over.

"I may not have been entirely honest with you, Captain," Valette said. "There was indeed the...*remote* possibility of danger on this venture, aside from the usual. I don't mean to alarm you, but it seems that there has been a significant Elder presence here."

Calder tried to feign surprise, but his heart wasn't in it.

"I was expecting to question the locals," the Watchman went on. "However, I very much doubt there's anyone here in the shape to be questioned. If you could assist me, I'd be grateful. I would even be willing to pay an additional fee to you, out of my own pocket."

As interested as Calder was in making further progress toward his debt, he couldn't help but wonder what the man meant by assistance. "I don't see any reason for any of us to go ashore, Mr. Valette. You included. Nor can I determine what help I could possibly be to you; after all, I'm hardly a trained Watchman."

From her own position by the longboat, Jerri snorted. Behind the passenger, Andel raised an eyebrow at Calder. Calder ignored them both.

"Well, Captain Marten, I'm not a Reader. I have to do all my research the tedious way, and I don't think it likely that I will be able to do so here. If you could take a few Readings, get a sense of the Intent in the general area, that would be of great help to my task."

"I'm sensing something from here," Calder said. "I'm sensing danger, and a foolish risk that we don't need to take. If it helps you, sir, I'd be happy to swear in the Emperor's name that you overturned every rock in the town before leaving baffled."

Jerri frowned at him. "We can't just *leave* after coming all this way. The town is empty, so we can surely spare an hour or two to explore."

"I'm sure it's uninhabited," Calder said. "I'm not at all certain it's empty."

Andel scanned the shore from beneath his white hat, expression unreadable as usual. "This may surprise you, Mr. Marten, but I agree with the lady. All of us can go ashore together, as there's no chance of the ship drifting and no one could steal her. It's five o'clock now. If we leave before sunset, I don't anticipate too much risk."

Jerri held out a hand toward Andel, as though presenting him. "I'm seeing you in an entirely new light, Andel."

If the two of them had *not* read Valette's journal, Calder would have understood. Even he would have been tempted to investigate the empty town, if he didn't know there was a Great Elder underneath it. How could they have forgotten that?

"Tell me, what do we stand to gain from this risk?" Calder asked. "Because we have enough of a report to send to the Blackwatch. 'The town is empty, it seemed abandoned, and we thought it too dangerous to travel further.' Sounds reasonable to me."

Andel turned to him, face as clear as ever. "*We* won't gain anything. But the citizens of the Empire trust the Guilds to prevent things like this from happening. If we can learn anything here that prevents Elderspawn from emptying another village, that's worth some risk."

Mr. Valette nodded approvingly at Andel's words, his expression as close to smiling as Calder had ever seen it.

He could sense when he was beaten. Especially when he knew they were right. The smart thing to do from their own perspective was to leave, sail away and never look back. But something had happened to these people, and he had the chance to find out what. His mother risked her life for that every day.

Jerri slapped the side of the longboat. "Lower the boat, Mr. Marten. We're going ashore."

Another quote floated to mind, from the journals of Estyr Six: *"If you're not giving the orders, you're not the one in charge."*

Calder sighed. "Yes, Captain."

The air swirls with Intent, so thick that Calder could swear he's standing in a Capital crowd. Curiosity, terror, greed, and a strange, burning hunger blend and drift together so that Calder can scarcely tell one emotion from the other. There's

something strange about it, something that violates common sense; it feels as though the people of this town were passionate about research. Too much so. It's like a thousand people were so desperate for answers that their hearts might burst…

Calder took his hand from the beam of the house. He tried to shake away the lingering impressions hanging like cobwebs inside his mind; a thirst for knowledge, an inquisitive spirit desperate to be satisfied.

Jerri leaned over with her hands behind her back, smiling like a delighted child. "Well? Any *gruesome* deaths in the dockside house?"

He would have suspected that the unquenchable curiosity belonged to Jerri, if he didn't know better. She was entirely too enthusiastic about their trip to an abandoned, Elder-haunted village. "Nothing from the house," he said. That wasn't unusual; the structure of a house would usually contain, at most, the skills and memories of the carpenter who constructed it. "Everything I could read came from the air, which is unusual enough. Intent seeps into objects like a dye and stains them, it doesn't hang around like a fog. Except here."

It was hard to explain to someone who had never experienced a Reading, like explaining a chorus to a man who had never heard music.

Jerri lifted her eyebrows. "Any visions? Any idea what happened?"

"No visions, which is strange on its own. Normally I have to sort through pictures and impressions, but this was pure emotion. Like it pooled here."

She thumbed her earring, looking thoughtful. "What emotions?"

"Someone here, or everyone here, very much wanted answers to all their questions. But it was more than curiosity, it was…greed, it was hunger. I wouldn't be surprised to hear these people all stabbed each other over a riddle."

"Ach'magut," she said.

"That's what I was afraid of."

Ach'magut, the Overseer, was said to feast on the collected knowledge of humanity. Calder hadn't been a Watchman long, but he'd learned that much. He hadn't, unfortunately, learned where the Great Elder was buried.

Though circumstances now suggested that he was right under their feet.

Valette came walking out of a nearby home, carrying his travel-case in one hand like an itinerant alchemist. "Not what I expected," he said. "Whatever happened here, I thought it was sudden, but the evidence suggested these people packed up and left. There are no meals on the tables, no clothes strewn on the floor. Everything is tucked away so neatly I would almost expect that the town itself is a fake."

Andel followed the Watchman, keeping a pistol leveled on the surrounding streets. Shadows lengthened as the sun fell, and Andel was doing his best to keep a weapon on every patch of darkness at once.

"It's not a fake," Calder said. "They've left their Intent on everything."

Valette snorted. "Then they left of their own volition. No one *made* them sort their candlesticks in the middle of a kidnapping."

Calder still couldn't sweep the feeling of deadly curiosity from his head. The memory ate through his thoughts like acid. "I suspect their volition itself may have been compromised. What Elder do you know that feeds on knowledge and understanding?"

The Watchman gave him a sharp look. "You found something, I see."

"Enough to know we should be out of here before dark."

"I have what I need to bring back to my Guild Head," Valette said after a moment's hesitation. "Not what I'd hoped, but she'll be able to make something of this. I will need to take a full report from each of you."

Andel shoved his pistol into his belt and took off running.

Jerri's head jerked around, but she didn't move. Without stopping to think, Calder ran after him. He didn't know what had happened to the townsfolk of Silverreach...but he knew what it *felt* like, and that was almost as bad. If the same insane hunger had seized Andel, the man could easily be running to his death.

But in a second, even before Calder could catch him, Andel stopped. He was dragging someone out of a nearby doorway, someone that Calder had never seen. A boy, maybe a little older than ten, with hair like seaweed and several missing teeth. He was dressed like a Capital chimney-sweep, in ragged clothes covered in dust and dark stains, and he fought Andel as though he thought the former Pilgrim planned on feeding him to Urg'naut.

He did not scream.

"Let me go," the boy whispered. "I'm not going to make it!"

Andel's grip on his collar didn't falter. "Make it where?" In answer, the boy struggled harder.

With a sigh, Andel pulled the boy around and pushed his wrists together. "Well, if you don't have any information, then I guess I'll have to bind you and leave you in the street. We'll see if a night out in the open makes you more eager to answer any questions."

The boy frantically jerked away, trying to escape, but Andel made no move to actually tie his hands together. "Keep your voice down!" the boy hissed, and Calder could hear unshed tears. "The spiders are going to come back."

"What spiders?" Jerri asked, her voice low...and still excited.

He sagged in Andel's arms, face bleak. "The spiders took everyone away. I have to get food and things during the day, and hide myself at night. That's when the spiders come out."

"What do the spiders do?" Andel asked.

Valette didn't even wait for Andel to finish his question before trampling over him. "What do they look like?"

The boy was twisting his neck to try and keep an eye on every direction at once, but he did answer. "They're big, bigger than me, and they have eyes everywhere." He shuddered. "They take everything apart and put it back together. Everything."

Calder shuddered too.

The Watchman scribbled frantically in his journal. "Just as we feared. Inquisitors of Ach'magut."

"We're leaving," Calder said. "Bring him." To the boy, he added. "We have a ship, and we're getting as far away from here as we can."

The boy looked to the harbor, and his eyes widened as he noticed *The Testament* outlined against the setting sun.

Jerri grabbed Calder's arm as he'd begun to walk away. In a whisper softer than the boy's, she said, "Listen." At the sound, Andel and Valette froze. Even the boy stopped struggling, his eyes going wide.

Footsteps, coming closer. Not the rapid tapping he would have expected from giant spiders, but the ordinary slap of shoes against pavement. Calder looked back, waiting for the survivors to show themselves. There was plenty of room on *The Testament* for cargo, and they had enough supplies to carry a dozen refugees up the coast for another few weeks. Even if there were more, he could at least get them away from this haunted town.

But the boy struggled even more frantically against Andel's grip. "Run!"

The crew glanced at each other, but then didn't wait for any more instructions. They ran.

Calder had crossed the vast expanse of empty cobbles leading to the harbor, with only the dock in front of him. His ship was a black silhouette against an orange sky, and he was close enough that he could sense the perpetual fury of the Lyathatan beneath the waves. Even as he ran, he started to relax. Once they were onboard, nothing short of a Great Elder could catch them.

They didn't make it onboard.

From the water on either side of the dock, spiders the size of wolves splashed up and clambered over onto the dock. Two of them stood on the surface of the dock, giving Calder a clear look at them. For the first time, he wished the sun had set completely. Then he wouldn't have to see them.

It was difficult to tell the color of their chitin, but he thought it was dark blue, maybe a sort of slick purple. They had ten sharp, segmented legs, though two of them stayed bent up at all times, like arms. And they were covered in eyes. The segment he would dubiously term the 'head' was crammed full of eyes of every description: compound eyes, slitted reptilian eyes, even eyes that looked disturbingly human. Some of the eyes waved on stalks, which drifted toward the humans.

Looking at the two Elderspawn standing next to each other, he could see that neither of them had the same pattern of eyes or even distribution of limbs. One had eleven legs, four of which were pulled up and waving in the air. The other had ten legs, and three stalk-eyes to the two of its companion. It was as though they had been assembled from a child's kit instead of born.

Andel and Calder reacted in almost exactly the same fashion. Before Calder realized he had a gun in his hand, he felt the kick of a gunshot and the familiar peal of thunder. Smoke drifted up from him as well as from Andel, and both spiders staggered back a pace. One of them waved a shredded stalk that had once had an eye on it.

Like two bodies possessed of one mind, both Elderspawn cocked their heads. Neither seemed particularly inconvenienced by the shot.

Mr. Valette had dropped his case and now clutched an iron spike in each hand. "In the Emperor's name," he said, and it had the sound of ritual to it. "Mr. Petronus, Captain Marten, I'll thank you to take care of the one on the left. Drive it into the water, if you can. I will seal the limbs of the one on our right, that we may take it home for study."

Calder was still struggling with the idea of carrying another Elderspawn home on his ship when the decision was taken out of his hands. The footsteps from behind them caught up. He edged to the side, turning carefully to keep both the humans and the spiders in view.

Fifteen men and women spread out side to side, and so many of them wore robes that Calder almost thought they were Magisters. An older man stood in front, smiling, wearing over his robe a ragged coat that looked like it had spent countless nights on the streets. The old man stepped forward and raised his hands to the sky.

"Praise Ach'magut, in his endless bounty, for sending us new brothers and sisters! Friends, be welcome in Silverreach. You have come at the right time."

As if the stranger's calm around Elderspawn hadn't told him enough, Calder noticed the silver medallion that each member of the crowd wore hanging over their chests. The Open Eye. Not a Guild crest, that symbol, but it served much the same purpose. The Blackwatch watched for it in ancient documents.

More often than not, it stood for the Sleepless.

The old man laughed, and his people advanced. In Andel's arms, the boy had gone limp with defeat.

"It's not as bad as you think, friends," the old man said. "Don't despair!"

From past the end of the dock, a deep, male voice echoed over the water. "DESPAIR!" Shuffles shouted.

The sound reminded him of the presence of his ship. He stretched his mind out, a Soulbound calling for his Vessel. He could sense *The Testament* at this distance, but it was futile; while most Soulbound could draw power from their Vessels, his ship had no power to give. He could only control it, which was no help from so far away.

So he moved his Intent down, through the chains, to the place where the Lyathatan rested on the harbor floor. As clearly as he could, Calder called for aid.

The Elder gave no sign that it had heard Calder's call. It sat still, hunger and ambition and wariness and calculation all swirling in its ancient mind. As Calder and his crew were dragged away, it simply watched.

And waited.

CHAPTER TWELVE

An ordinary man could never perform the function of the Emperor, for his is not simply a 'job.' His importance lies in his existence, invaluable and eternal.

— JAMESON ALLBRIGHT, HEAD OF THE LUMINIAN ORDER,
FROM HIS ESSAY *OUR EMPIRE*

Calder lounged in a copper bathtub filled to bursting with noxious green sludge. Pain slid away from his wounds and muscles loosened as the alchemical substance healed damage he didn't even know he'd taken. Every breath burned the inside of his nose and made his eyes water, but the alchemists had insisted he breathe it in; even the fumes of this concoction played a vital role in his recovery.

He might have enjoyed it, if he wasn't using all of his attention to pretend that Jarelys Teach wasn't standing right next to him.

"We have been given some time. The Head of the Blackwatch reports that the damage to the sky shouldn't be visible for another two or three days, which gives us at least two days to craft an official response. We would like to have you use the Optasia immediately, but it's being inspected for damage by as many trustworthy experts as we could scrape up."

Calder had wondered. After the fight that had activated the Emperor's throne, he wouldn't have been surprised if the device was warped into scrap metal. "I could check it myself, if you're worried about confidentiality."

"Not Readers," Jarelys said sharply. She had been carrying a bundle of letters, which crumpled in her grip. "You activate the Optasia by Reading it, so we're forced to rely on ordinary alchemists, engineers, and historians. It's slow going."

It had never occurred to Calder to imagine how difficult it would be to investigate the history of an object without Reading. How would you even do it? Look for minute clues, he supposed, like the archived accounts of those who assembled the Optasia's network, maybe examine the structure of the throne for scuffs and scrapes. It sounded tedious.

"As for your *attacker...*" Her voice grew grim, and she shifted position on her stool as though she suspected an assassin to be sneaking past her at that moment. "We have confirmed that he was a Champion. As far as we can tell, he was in good standing with the Guild, though records have been spotty at best."

"Arrange a meeting with the Head of the Champion's Guild," Calder ordered. "He can answer for the actions of his men."

Teach's cold eyes slid over to him, disapproval written on her face. He slipped deeper into the opaque green fluid. He knew he shouldn't have used that tone with her, but if he was ever going to start being Emperor, shouldn't it be now?

With anyone else, he could have faked the authority and confidence he needed. He wasn't shy by nature, and taking command was largely a matter of self-assurance. But Teach was the woman who had killed his father.

No matter how he tried, he couldn't even make *himself* believe she would follow his orders.

She didn't release him from her icy gaze as she spoke. "As it happens, I have already arranged for a meeting with Baldesar Kern in a few days. It will be your first unofficial business as Imperial Steward."

Just hearing his newfound title pleased him, even if it wasn't quite as impressive as "Emperor." He'd get there.

"Thank you, General Teach." Should he still address her by title, or should he be calling her Jarelys, to emphasize his new social standing? He'd have to decide later.

She stood. "I must plan your security for the next week, but I have guards posted outside of every window and the door. They will respond if you need anything."

"I'm certain I'll survive my bath without assistance." The alchemists had prescribed a full morning of soaking in the tub, which he had already suffered since dawn.

Before leaving the room, Teach paused as though she'd forgotten something. "The Emperor never had a moment of privacy. Get used to it now."

Calder winced as she left. He had thought he'd covered up his discomfort nicely, but it seemed she'd noticed nonetheless.

"You kept sliding in deeper," Meia said. "It gives you away. If you wanted her to think you were comfortable, you should have feigned sleep."

Calder froze, very carefully not sliding any deeper into the sludge. His brief, panicked reaction was to scream for the Imperial Guards, but he stopped himself just in time. He'd decided to trust Meia, if only because she'd saved his life. Hopefully, if he showed her *enough* trust, she wouldn't kill him.

But how many people were going to barge in on his medical bath?

"Did Teach know you were here?"

She walked around in front of the tub, taking the Guild Head's stool.

Meia was dressed all in black, as always, with black cloth covering her mouth and nose. She didn't look at Calder as she spoke, her eyes flicking from entrance to entrance as though she expected another Champion to come barging through. "I'm afraid that she wouldn't welcome me back. She might not kill me if she recognized me, but she would likely have me detained."

She *had* said something about growing up in the Imperial Palace. He hadn't pried into it at the time, but now he was much more interested.

"Why would she recognize you?" Calder asked carefully.

Meia's eyes blinked orange for a fraction of a second, and just as he was starting to wonder if he was in danger, she answered. "This pertains to the security of the Imperial Palace, not to the Guild, so I suppose you're authorized to know. You would find out eventually. Either Teach would tell you, or someone else would get around to it."

Calder leaned forward, intrigued. "Don't worry. I won't repeat anything you say outside this room."

"If the information was so sensitive that it couldn't be leaked, I wouldn't tell you," she said, so matter-of-factly that it was a little insulting. "When I was young, I was assigned to the Emperor's security detail. We were a discreet unit protecting the Emperor from behind, just as the Imperial Guards protected him from the front."

Three figures in black had once tackled him during his audience with the Emperor. He had barely given them any thought at the time, but one had been a blond girl about his age.

"So we'd met before the dead island." He wasn't sure how he felt about that, but the memory of his father's execution dredged up a world of pain. If Meia hadn't held him back, he would have lunged at the Emperor. Maybe Calder would have gotten his revenge.

No, I would have been torn to pieces. From a certain point of view, Meia had unintentionally saved his life back then.

"We had."

"How many of you were there?" He'd seen three, but as far as he knew, there could have been a thousand young Consultants-in-training defending the Emperor in the shadows.

"Three. Myself, Lucan, and Shera."

Shera. The woman who had haunted him for months, who had directly or indirectly turned his life inside-out. If his Guilds won the current dispute, established him as the Emperor, and returned the Consultants to the fold, then Shera might be compelled to protect his life. He found some irony in that.

Another memory returned, more recent: on the Gray Island, as the ground crumbled far above them, three Consultants fought him. The battle that had ended in Urzaia's death. Meia, Shera, and one other: a Heartlander man dressed identically to the other two, except for the addition of black gloves. Lucan. The man who had been imprisoned in the Gray Island next to his wife.

"You three have made it a habit to get in my way."

Meia waited silently, undisturbed.

This isn't the way, he reminded himself. *I need her on my side.* He reached out a hand, shaking it free of green goop, and patted Meia on the knee. "Never mind. I appreciate that you're here, working with me. I know that you've always acted with loyalty to your Guild and to the Empire, and I'm certain that we'll continue to work more closely in the future."

He was proud of that little speech, but Meia's eyebrows raised. "I've already sent my report to the Architects. If they order me away, I'll disappear."

"*Or* you could join the crew of *The Testament.* I've registered you with the Guild as an honorary crew member." That was a lie, but he could make it the truth if she agreed. "When the Empire is whole again, you'll be on the side of the Emperor, defending the world from Elders."

He thought he saw the hint of a smile under her black veil, but it could have been wishful thinking. "The Empire will never be whole."

"How can you be sure?"

Her voice was suddenly sad, almost wistful. "Because the Consultants aren't holding it together. If we've given up, everyone should."

The words sent a shiver down his back in spite of the warm alchemical slop. Those were the words of someone who hadn't wanted to give up on the Empire...but who had been convinced that it was absolutely, irrevocably dead.

What did she know that he didn't?

"Besides," she continued, "We've fought against the Elders for years."

He was glad for another topic, and this allowed him to ask something that had fired his curiosity. "Speaking of which, how did you escape from Nakothi's Handmaiden?" He'd been sure the Consultants would only be able to distract it while he left on *The Testament,* but they'd apparently banished the Elder entirely.

"We killed it."

Calder let the silence stretch, waiting for the inevitable correction or qualification that was sure to follow. Even for the Blackwatch or the Luminian Order, it wasn't so easy to kill an Elder. Lesser Elderspawn were one thing; they were effectively the small, defenseless animals of the Elder world. But a Handmaiden was intelligent, vicious, and had lived for thousands of years. Even Kelarac had warned Calder not to use his Awakened blade against these servants of Nakothi. But the Consultants had managed it?

"How?" he asked, genuinely curious.

"The Consultant's Guild manages each client's issues with utmost efficiency," she recited. "In the event that the client is threatened while under the protection of the Guild, that threat will be removed."

The legendary Consultant secrecy. If he was honest with himself, he should admit that he was lucky to get even as much information as he had. But he decided to push for a little more. "Was it Shera?"

"It was the Consultant's Guild."

"She has an Awakened weapon now, and she didn't before. She might even be a Soulbound." With each word, he stared at Meia's face, gauging her reaction. "Did she destroy the Handmaiden?"

Meia might as well have been filling out paperwork back at the Guild. "The Consultants have resources beyond what you know."

"This is a matter of my personal security," he stressed. "Shera has tried to kill me...what, three or four times now?"

"No, she hasn't."

At last, a personal response. Calder leaped on it. "What do you mean by that?"

"If her primary assignment had been to kill you, you would be dead."

Now that he thought about it, Shera had been trying to accomplish something else each time she'd attacked him. Assassinating Naberius, securing the Heart, stopping Urzaia. But the fact remained that she *had* attempted to kill him, secondary though it may have been.

"But I have to be in danger now. Your Guild is working against me; wouldn't it be in Shera's best interests to have me removed? The more I know about her, the safer I am."

Meia flexed one hand, claws extending and retracting from her nails. He tried not to be intimidated by that. "I have no information from the Architects regarding you personally, so this is only my opinion. But I don't believe you are in direct danger from us at this time."

Of all the things she could have said on the topic, this surprised him the most. He'd thought she was working outside the interests of her Guild to support him, out of her lingering loyalty to the Empire. Not *against* her Guild, of course, but at least independent from it. He'd been sure that the Consultants as a whole would gladly murder him given the chance. "Why not? You're Independents, against the Emperor, and I'm the Emperor."

She placed a hand on his shoulder. "No," she said. "You're not."

Freed from the alchemical bath, Calder had his wounds wrapped in fresh bandages. His leg still ached and his shoulder was sore, but for the first time in days he could actually fight if he needed to. It was a reassuring feeling.

Palace servants dressed him in clothes that suited the Emperor: layers of blue from navy to aquamarine, draped around his body like a series of tents had artfully collapsed. He bore them with dignity as the Imperial Guard escorted him through the halls, though he felt like he stepped on his own hem every four or five yards. It was like learning to wear a dress.

More than anything, he focused on the clothes to distract himself from his destination. *"The educated man faces his problems, he does not turn his back."* Sadesthenes, though his wisdom was an unwelcome reminder just then.

The Guards led Calder past another courtyard, through a checkpoint complete with a pair of Witnesses, and into a building that outwardly looked little different from all the others in the palace complex. The walls were white, the tiled roof red, and Imperial Guards stood at every entrance. The differences were minor, but significant: there were no windows here, and the doors were heavy barred steel.

The Palace dungeon.

It's not underground, he thought. *Is it still a dungeon?* If it mattered, someone would correct him eventually.

The dungeon was fully occupied, and he could vaguely hear them behind their sealed doors, but not one of them could see out. So he passed through the hallways without incident, until his Guards stopped him at one particular door. A woman with eyes all over her arms twisted the key, and two Guards with combat-ready adaptations—one with a scorpion's giant tail, the other with savage claws on his hands—leaped inside. They scanned the room thoroughly and searched the prisoner before declaring it safe.

Only then did Calder step inside to see his wife.

Both times he'd spoken to Jerri since she'd left his ship, she'd been in a different prison. There was surely some sort of poetic justice in that fact, but it brought him no joy. Her hair was loose and messy, and they'd changed her last prisoner's outfit for a new one. This one was a dingy red compared to the last, with patches at the knees and loose threads on the sleeves. Strange, that the Consultant's Guild would dress its prisoners better than the Imperial Palace.

Otherwise, she was every inch the Jerri he'd known his whole life. Her dusky skin, the tattoo climbing from her left ankle up the side of her neck, even the way she brightened briefly when she caught sight of his face. Her eagerness to see him stabbed him through the heart, and the knife twisted when she lost that joy an instant later, lifting her chin and drawing up her shoulders to address him firmly.

"I'm pleased you weren't hurt, Calder," she said, professionally distant.

The Imperial Guards had retreated, giving them the illusion of a private space without actually allowing the prisoner any room to try anything.

"I was. The alchemists said that if I hadn't gotten treatment immediately, I would have suffered internal damage from your attack on the Optasia. And the Champion would have torn me apart. Was he one of yours?"

Calder doubted it—the Independent Guilds had plenty of money to hire the Champions, so they were the likely culprits. But her expression would tell him what he needed to know.

Her eyes widened. "We're not trying to *kill* you, Calder. I didn't even know you would be there at the Optasia, and the Champion...I had nothing to do with that. Nothing."

Under normal circumstances, she would have made a joke about him surviving a Champion's attack. She clearly wanted him to believe her.

And he did. No matter how many times she'd lied to him over the years, he believed her now.

"Then what are you doing here, Jerri?" His guilt at leaving her behind on the Gray Island had hardly faded, even though he'd known she had most likely survived, and now here she was in another cell.

She smiled, adding a twisted irony to her next words. "I'm here to help you save the world."

Calder glanced around at the tight walls, the low-slung cot. "From a hole?"

"From anywhere I can. I was told that I'd be able to put you on the throne if I followed along, and I see the wisdom in it now."

Put you on the throne. Even now, she claimed she was trying to help him. "I've done it without you. I'm *on* the throne, Jerri."

"But you haven't used it yet," she said quietly. "If you really want to be the Emperor, you need the Optasia. It's the only way humanity can speak to them."

A chill crawled up his arms. "What are you talking about?"

"What do you think?" Jerri leaned back against the wall, folding her arms, the way she always did when she lectured. "We need someone who can deal with the Great Elders on *their* terms, to represent all of mankind. The old Emperor refused to do that, but a *new* one, one whose reign was already arranged by the Great Ones..."

Calder stiffened. His reign had been arranged?

"Leave me alone with the prisoner," he said.

The man with the scorpion tail shook his head firmly. "We have strict orders—"

Calder met his eyes. "Now you have new ones."

Maybe it was the clothes, the ancient fashion that only the Emperor had maintained. Maybe it was the actual authority in Calder's newfound title, or his own projected confidence.

Whatever it was, the Guards left.

"The Great Elders did not *arrange* for me to be here," he said, giving into his anger even further now that the Guards had left. "They may have foreseen it, but they are *not* the reason I'm standing here today."

Jerri's mouth hung open, and she looked at him in a mixture of disbelief and disgust, as though he'd just announced that he was absolutely convinced the earth was flat. "How did you free your father from prison? With the Lyathatan, sent by Kelarac. Before that, how did your mother gain the support she did in the Guilds? She worked in the Blackwatch for *years*. Fighting Elders. Even your family's reputation is built on the Elders. Even the fights that drove your parents apart, all the Elders. You think the Great Ones had nothing to do with that?"

That was entirely different—they had been *fighting* the Elders, not accepting their help—but before Calder could protest, Jerri went on. "Most of your Navigator work had to do with the Elders. An Elder is pulling your ship, and another one sits on your shoulder. How did you survive the fight on the Gray Island? Kelarac stepped in, once again. Leaving aside the fact that the whole reason you were *there* was because of a fight to inherit Nakothi's power."

"I was there because of *you*," Calder insisted, but he could feel his self-righteous footing crack. "And how did you know about Kelarac?"

"And how did you know you were going to be the Emperor one day?" she asked, ignoring him. "How did the entire crew believe in you *so much* that they were willing to defy the Empire? You've been dancing to an Elder tune for half your life."

Calder's anger didn't fade, but he shut his mouth.

Jerri's voice softened as she went on. "I'm not accusing you, Calder. It would be an accusation coming from anyone else, but not from me. You of all people should understand that we *can* borrow the powers of Elders. It can be a good thing! They can be our partners, not our parasites."

He had to admit that, of all the people he knew who were not Elder-worshiping cultists, he'd relied on Elder powers the most. They worked to his benefit every time, and always for prices he could afford to pay. They were alien, menacing, and heartless, but most of them hadn't seemed to mean him any specific harm.

The thought didn't reassure him. It chilled him down to his bones.

Is this how the Sleepless make their recruits?

It had begun when he was a child, receiving Shuffles as a pet. Hearing his mother talk about Elderspawn in the same way you'd talk about wild lions; something to be respected, certainly, even feared in a healthy way. Even, perhaps, admired.

Somewhere along the way, he'd begun thinking of the Great Elders differently. Maybe some, like Urg'naut and Nakothi, were actively evil. Most weren't. They were simply alien, and indescribably powerful.

That was the crack in his defenses. That was where he'd gone wrong.

And he'd listened to Ach'magut.

Even now, he didn't think the Overseer had been *wrong*. It was impossible to imagine that any predictions of Ach'magut could be incorrect to the slightest degree; the Great Elder had spoken directly to him, and its words carried the weight of inescapable destiny.

But just because it was the truth didn't mean the Elder was being honest. Of course it wasn't. It was telling him the truth for its own complex, intricate reasons.

In his own way, he'd been trusting Elders all along.

Jerri watched him come to this realization, and her face softened in sympathy. "It's true, Calder. The sooner you accept that, the happier we can be."

We.

"If you still don't believe me, use the Optasia. Check for yourself. The Great Ones set up your attack so that it would scar the sky. Very soon, it will stretch and crack, opening a tunnel between our world and those beyond. That is when we will *need* a representative, Calder. Someone who can speak for us all."

The air over the Imperial Palace had been fuzzy and indistinct after the attack on the Optasia, though he'd heard it was only visible from the Imperial Palace. "General Teach says we have two or three days before that happens."

She laughed. "Significantly less than that."

"The Optasia might be damaged." He felt like a child, throwing up excuses to avoid a chore.

"A Great One intervened personally in this matter. He wouldn't leave the throne in a state where it couldn't be used."

"The *last* time I came face-to-face with an Elder, it was Nakothi's Handmaiden. She almost killed us both." Technically, the last time was his dream of Kelarac, but he could only hope that Jerri didn't know anything about that.

Jerri stepped closer to him. "Nakothi is...not the Great Elder you want to negotiate with. She's far beyond us, of course, and I'm certain that we could improve the world with her wisdom. But she's mad. Her Handmaiden was there to kill us all, and we're only lucky that it withdrew before it hunted us down and finished its task."

So Jerri thought it had fled. Maybe she was right. "The Consultants say they killed it."

"Did they? Are you sure they weren't lying to you? Trying to make themselves look better."

He wouldn't be surprised if Meia *had* lied, but then again... "She seemed fairly certain. And I suspect Shera was involved."

She was even closer now, and they were talking normally before he'd realized it. Close, intimate, friendly, the way they'd spoken ten thousand times. "Shera? How?"

Intentionally, Calder took two steps back toward the entrance. "She's a Soulbound now."

Jerri noticed what he'd done, and a flash of hurt crossed her face. She opened her mouth, and he could practically see the insult forming.

The door opened and a Guard stuck his head in. "Sir, we need you to see this. There's something..."

The floor, the walls, the entire building shook like a struck drum. The air seemed to buzz around him, and Calder and Jerri both staggered for balance. Without another word, Calder left.

When the world shook, Jerri recognized it for what it was: the plan of the Great Elders coming to fruition. The sky had cracked, and with it, the first gateway had opened between their world and...whatever else was out there.

Future generations would celebrate this day as a holiday; she should be filled with joy at her part in this momentous occasion.

Instead, she felt only frustration and anger. If the barrier had to crack, why did it have to be *now*? She was so close to persuading Calder, she could feel it. Even though he insisted on ignoring her, even though he was driving her insane with his refusal to listen to sense, she had still almost gotten through to him.

Now, though...now he would be listening to the Blackwatch's version of events instead of hers. She'd wasted her last, best chance to get through to him. Victory or not, she felt like screaming.

It was only after the first few seconds that she realized something was wrong.

The city had shaken with the force of the Great Elders' will. Perhaps the entire planet had. But that had died away in moments as the world stabilized. All this, Kelarac had led her to expect.

But in the corner of her cell, the shaking continued. The air trembled, a heat haze buzzing like a hummingbird's wing.

When the indistinct blur had reached a fever pitch, when the blur turned from dim color to absolute darkness, the Soul Collector stepped out from the void.

This time, he was not quite as human. His dark skin had the pattern of scales, his golden jewelry splattered against him as though it had been melted into patches. His clothes flickered and faded, as though they were on the verge of vanishing at any second, and the body beneath them was distinctly unnatural. It was a coil of shadows upon shadows with the occasional outline of a waving fin. Like a school of a thousand fish all feeding on each other at once.

She looked away from the eye-wrenching sight before she grew seasick. Nonetheless, she couldn't help the excitement growing inside her.

Unless she missed her guess, the Great Elder was *upset*. He had no reason to be so angry with her, and besides, she was fully within his control. Which meant that something else had happened...something important.

Maybe Jerri would get to help.

She had dropped to her knees as soon as Kelarac revealed himself, and he looked down on her with his steel blindfold bolted to his face. Only the blindfold remained as clear and distinct as ever, as though that was the only part of him that was *real*.

"The Killer survived," he said, and it was only half a question.

"I'm sorry, Great One. Who?" Was he talking about the Champion that had tried to kill Calder?

"*The* Killer. Your husband said her name: Shera. The latest of the Am'haranai."

Shera? What did the Soul Collector want with a Consultant assassin? "Calder says she survived. I haven't seen her since before the island collapsed." She snuck a glance up at Kelarac's face, but it was so distorted that she learned nothing. It looked like his cheeks had been stretched into a mask that was now stapled onto something else's head.

"When he mentioned her, I checked Bastion's island. She did survive. She was not meant to."

He flitted from one corner of the cell to another, moving with the grace of a spider. In someone else, she would have called it nervous pacing. "The Killer had *one* part to play, and she played it. Five years ago. She was supposed to die in obscurity, as she was born."

"Would you like me to kill her?" Jerri asked, suppressing her delight. If the Great Elders tasked her with killing Shera, she would go about her task with glee. The assassin had thrown her over the side of her own ship.

Kelarac froze. "Kill her? You would kill her? A woman who has bound her soul to an ancient weapon forged in the powers of the Emperor? A woman who destroyed a Handmaiden, drawing its essence inside her? Shera has made of herself a bridge between the Emperor's power and ours."

Something was wrong here beyond the obvious. The way Kelarac said it made Shera sound terrifying, but really, what she'd done wasn't terribly unusual. Even Jerri's Vessel contained a hybrid power of Kameira and Elder. "Pardon me, Great One. But what makes her more dangerous than any other Soulbound?"

Kelarac loomed over her, a mass of gold-flecked shadows that flickered and squirmed in the overshadowed light. "Her *place*," he said, and as he spoke she felt the echo of significance in the word. As though he referred to a force as broad as the universe itself.

"She should not have survived. It was impossible for her to die before her role had been fulfilled, but afterwards it should have been impossible for her to *live*." He looked down on Jerri, and seemed to consider his next words.

"You have chemical projectile weapons. Guns. When a bullet is loaded, it has not yet been born. It is born with the pull of a trigger. It lives only for a flash of light...and then it ends. The Killer was supposed to reach her end."

Jerri was beginning to see the problem. For whatever reason, the Great Elders had actually...made a mistake.

"Our plan, the vision we have for your world, ended with your kind in harmony with ours," Kelarac went on. "Now, every action the Killer takes is a disruption of that plan. She is what Ach'magut might call a *deviation*, but I am neither Ach'magut nor Tharlos. I do not enjoy deviating from perfection. More importantly to you, my plan saw Calder Marten ruling as King of this world. Now, our plan has changed."

Jerri's excitement turned to fear. If the Great Elders were changing their minds, or if their minds had been changed for them, then all the promises they'd made...everything she had come to expect...

Her entire life could have been for nothing.

The outline of Kelarac's body stretched, as though something within was bulging and trying to escape. "The last time our plans diverged this wildly, my brothers and sisters went to war. Engrave that into your heart, human. Another all-out war between the Elders with humanity at the center. You will be ground to *paste*."

"Let me out," Jerri said, desperate to find some hope. "Give me my Vessel, and I'll kill her myself."

Kelarac extended a hand, which for one mind-twisting instant seemed to have hundreds of fingers all overlapping each other. He reached into distorted space and pulled forth an emerald earring. "The deviation will be solved by greater minds than yours. You are in the proper place, for now, and you will play your role. There is only one thing that you can do for the greater good: you must not let the Killer meet the King."

He threw her earring over to her and, with a pop that left her ears ringing, abruptly vanished.

Jerri remained sitting on the floor of her cell—her second cell in as many weeks—trying in vain to catch her breath. She clutched her Vessel in a tight fist, relishing the feeling of being whole and powerful once more, but her mind was consumed by an overriding conviction.

I have to save Calder.

CHAPTER THIRTEEN

When the Shades of Urg'naut take a city, it vanishes entirely. When the Children of Nakothi take a city, it is defiled. When Ach'magut's Inquisitors take a city, it is depopulated.

– FROM THE ORIGINAL BLACKWATCH *BESTIARY OF ELDERS*

NINE YEARS AGO

Jerri was less than impressed with these Sleepless acolytes.

The group of robed men and women wearing the Open Eye medallions had dragged her crew through the streets of Silverreach, shoving them into a hollowed-out house that stank of fish. They acted like a gang of base kidnappers, and didn't even *try* to persuade the prisoners to their cause.

It would be hard to do, she had to admit, given that they were taking prisoners. But she wouldn't have made that mistake. She would have greeted any newcomers warmly, like guests, showing them that there was nothing to be afraid of.

Then again, there *was* something to be afraid of.

While the Sleepless were still pushing the crew of *The Testament* into the house, the spider-like Inquisitors caught up. They slid through the doorway, in the middle of the crowd of humans, and even the Elder cultists shied back. Jerri couldn't help a surge of contempt; she hadn't backed up a step.

The two Inquisitors circled Mr. Valette, making noises like the rapid click of a dozen knitting needles. The Watchman's captor stumbled away, leaving the man in the black coat to the Inquisitors.

To his credit, Valette didn't shy away. He held himself straight, chin up, and slid a black iron spike out of one pocket.

Jerri admired him. He stood against the Elders as an equal, unbowing. These acolytes could learn a thing or two from him about proper conduct.

At the sight of the Awakened nail, the Inquisitors got excited, waving their limbs and stalk-eyes and frantically circling him. He moved to keep both in view, but he wasn't fast enough.

One spider-leg flashed out, too quick to follow, and a spot of red bloomed on his calf. He cried out and fell to one knee, striking out with his spike. The second Inquisitor dodged, seizing his weapon between two surprisingly delicate limbs. Its partner seized Mr. Valette under the shoulders.

In one scuttling motion, they were gone, the door slamming shut behind them.

The old man in charge of the Sleepless shook his head sadly. "May his soul fly free. We must come to a closer understanding of our Elder neighbors. If we could communicate, we could have saved that poor man. Alas." He wasn't a member of the main cabal, the leadership of the cult, but he apparently had command of the other acolytes. If Jerri got the chance, she would see that he was 'demoted' to feed the worms of Kthanikahr.

The prisoners were separated by gender, as Calder and the others were prodded into a room full of male prisoners. Jerri was led across the hall, where a handful of women were kept.

As Calder saw her taken away, his eyes flashed with rage. He shot forward, breaking free of the first man holding him, but his weapons had already been confiscated. Three Sleepless piled on him, crushing him to the ground.

Hot rage boiled up, stoked by the fires of her Vessel. *How dare they treat us like this? We will rule them all someday.*

She was almost swallowed up by a daydream of sweeping this place with emerald fire, searing the flesh from their captors' bones and leading the imprisoned to freedom. Seeing Calder on the floor, struggling to fight for her, it was harder to resist than usual.

But she still had other goals. Instead of killing everyone, she forced a smile, reminding Calder that she was still all right. She allowed her captor to lead her across the hall, where she joined four other women with bound hands and feet.

When the Sleepless man pulled a stretch of cord from his pocket and moved forward to bind her, she gave him her most charming smile. His eyebrows raised, and she stepped in closer, leaning her chin on his shoulder.

She whispered straight into his ear, "If you touch me again, I will burn you from the inside."

His head bobbed back so he could look her in the eye. She tapped her Vessel so that her earring would spark ever so faintly.

Burn the disobedient to ash.

With greatest care, the Sleepless backed out of the room. He didn't take his eyes off her until the door was shut and bolted.

Jerri found a chair in the corner and pulled it around so that it was out of sight of the doorway. If the door swung open again, she didn't want Calder to see her free. She might have to come up with an explanation.

As she sat in the chair, unbound, and started to plan a way to use these developments to her advantage, she felt four sets of eyes on her. She looked up, and the other women gazed at her with expressions of awe.

"What did you say to him?" one of them whispered.

Looking at the four frightened women, Jerri realized her opportunity. "You have to know how to talk to these people," she said. "And to do that, you have to know a little about the Elders."

Calder's hands and feet were bound and he was bruised all over from being tackled to the ground, but frustration and anger choked him. Elderspawn, he could understand. They were evil and alien, and they viewed people as particularly stupid animals. But what were *humans* doing on the side of the Elders? How short-sighted or cruel did you have to be to take orders from a Great Elder?

More specifically, what were they doing to Jerri?

The boy who had tried to escape was shoved in a corner, wrists and ankles tied, just as Calder's were. He had a look of absolute despair on his face, as though he knew what was coming and it was too horrifying to think about. There were five other men in the room, besides Andel and himself. Four of them were in various stages of insensibility—either unconscious, dazed, or possibly dead. One, an old man with a wild mane of gray hair, watched Calder with a smirk.

"What are you squirming about? You think you can fight Elderspawn with both hands tied, do you?"

"I've seen worse," Calder said. He had. The Lyathatan looked like it was made out of sharks and nightmares, and made the Inquisitors seem like bizarre lobsters by comparison. As for their current situation...well, he'd been in tighter straits outside the Candle Bay prison. He'd been forced to bargain with a Great Elder to break out, true, but he *had* escaped. This was nothing.

The old man chuckled, raising both of his tied hands to lift a pair of glasses to his face. For the first time, Calder noticed two pairs of glasses hanging from a leather thong around the man's neck. Why would someone need two different sets of glasses?

He snorted when he saw Calder through the lenses. "What are you, eighteen?"

He was seventeen, but he didn't feel like saying so. "'Remember the wisdom of the blind man, who does not weigh the silver in another's hair.' Laius the Younger."

Gray eyebrows lifted. "Sounds like you've cracked a book. Must not be a local."

Calder smiled as broadly as he could, though his chin was bruised, and it came out more like a wince. "Calder Marten, Navigator Captain."

"Imperial prisoner," Andel corrected, "under the supervision and probation of the Navigator's Guild."

"Ah," the old man said, nodding as though the picture now fit perfectly. "And you are?"

Before Andel could introduce himself, Calder stepped in. "This is Andel Petronus, a barnacle that attached itself to my ship. Somehow, I can't seem to scrape him off."

Andel ignored Calder, focusing on the old man. "And you are?"

"...Duster," he eventually said.

Calder and Andel stared at him together.

"That was a strange pause just now," Andel said, just as Calder began, "If you don't want to tell us your real name..."

'Duster' grumbled, staring into his nest of a beard. Calder thought he saw the man's cheeks color. "If I say my name's Duster, it's Duster!"

Andel nodded to him, conceding a point. "Well, Mr. Duster, we've given you our professions."

"Don't tell me you're a valet," Calder said. "I won't be able to resist making a joke about dusting furniture."

Duster shot Calder a look, and addressed his response to Andel. "I used to be a gunsmith."

A light came on in Andel's eyes, and he stared at Duster's face as though he'd figured something out. Calder inspected the old man too, hoping to learn something. As far as he could tell, Duster was the same as every other man over seventy years old: craggy face, gray hair, scowl for anyone under thirty. Only his untamed hair and his two pairs of glasses set him apart.

But whatever Andel had figured out, Calder couldn't worry about it. He was too busy figuring out a way to escape.

"Were you any good?" Andel asked, his voice layered with implication.

Duster met his eyes. "Some would say so."

Calder jumped in before they could bore him with pointless reminiscing. "You don't have a gun, do you?"

From the way Andel and Duster looked at him, you would have thought it was the dumbest thing that had ever come out of his mouth. *It was an honest question.*

"Were you armed before you came in?" Duster asked, a little more harshly than Calder felt he deserved. "Are you armed now? What kind of kidnappers would they be if they let us keep our guns?"

"Not very good ones," Andel said, holding up a gun.

This time, the ensuing silence was shock, as everyone conscious in the room had their attention stolen by the sudden presence of a pistol.

Calder kept his voice calm. "Andel. Where did you get that?"

Andel gestured down to his white belt. "I tucked it into my pants while no one was looking. After they found my spare, they stopped searching. But don't get too excited. It's the one I fired earlier, so I have neither shot nor powder."

"Still, it's something. Good work, Andel." Calder's mind kept moving, piecing together a plan. They could at least threaten the guards with their weapon. That would be better than nothing, and it might slow the cultists down. First, they only had to get out of the room.

"All right, we can do this," he said at last. "It will only take me a day or two to Invest the latch enough that we can escape. Once we do, Andel—"

Duster snorted. "I'm a Reader, boy. Can't be done."

Calder stopped, a little stunned from the sudden interruption to his flow of thought. Before he'd collected himself, a question came out of his mouth. "You're a Reader, and you decided to be a gunsmith?"

He'd seen bad liars before, and 'Duster' was one of them. "Readers make good craftsmen! Anyway, if you *are* a Reader, why are you…" The old man hesitated, trailing off as he realized what he was about to say.

Calder finished for him. "…a high-ranking Guild member? Because it pays well, it's among the most respected positions in the Empire, and because it's what every Reader aspires to be. Not a gunsmith."

"Technically, it's because you were conscripted to pay off an *enormous* debt to the crown in reparation for your numerous, irresponsible, and destructive crimes." Andel's voice was as bland as his face.

"Thank you for volunteering, Andel. We needed to feed someone to the Elderspawn on the way out."

Duster must have been lost, because he returned the conversation to the previous track. "Anyway, I've only been in here three days. When it started, there were forty of us."

Calder looked at the room's eight total inhabitants: four unconscious or debilitated men, one little boy huddling in the corner, and the three of them. "Ah."

"Yeah. Those spiders pull a handful of us out at a time, and I'm not expecting any of them back, if you follow me."

Still, Calder couldn't imagine that a Reader had sat idly in a room for three full days. "You had to have found *something.*"

By way of demonstration, Duster pinched the cord between his wrists and pulled it apart. It tore like spun sugar. "Been working on this the whole time. Not that it will do me any good. First thing I did was try the door, and guess what? Too much Elder Intent. I barely Read it once without trying to swallow my toes. I do it again, or you do, and we'll likely kill everyone else in here."

The old man leaned back against the wall, eyes shut. His resignation frustrated Calder, but it seemed to intrigue Andel, who said, "You seem awfully cavalier for a man about to meet the Elders."

A smile touched the corner of Duster's mouth. "Nothing I can do about it, is there? Might as well wait my turn. And some things…well, not everybody fears dying quite so much as they maybe should."

Calder dismissed the gunsmith and his fatalism, chewing on their problem once again. They had two Readers and a gun; there *had* to be something they could do with those. And if the Inquisitors really took away groups of prisoners each day, then Jerri was in as much danger as they were. He needed to get everybody to safety, and he needed to do it immediately.

Andel only watched him think. At any second, Calder expected a sarcastic comment, and he was prepared to respond in kind. But Andel stayed silent, watching.

For the better part of the next two hours, Calder considered and rejected plan after plan. They didn't have enough time to invest anything substantial, and it would be foolish to rely too much on the gun. What if the cultists were willing to take a pistol round?

What it came down to, as always, was a lack of information. When did the Elderspawn Inquisitors come to take their prisoners? What would happen to them afterwards—might there be a chance to escape en route? Calder posed several small questions to Duster, but either the man didn't have the answers, or the answers were useless.

After two hours of collecting and sorting information, Calder finally asked, "Are you *certain* you have no idea where our other weapons are?"

"I was sure the last time, and I haven't come across any new information in the past ten minutes."

"Not a hint? Not a clue?"

Duster peered around, his eyes mockingly wide. "I can be fairly certain they're not in this room."

This time, Calder let himself be deterred. "We're going to have to fight someone or something, and we can't do that with an empty pistol. If we at least had some powder and ammunition, that would be *something*."

Absently, Duster pointed straight to the corner of the room.

Calder followed the end of his finger, but saw nothing there. "Are you trying to send me to sit in the corner, or…"

"My tools are in that direction. No weapons, but I could build a whole gun with the spare parts and tools I keep in there. Load it and fire it, too. We get to those, we could load the gun."

It was hard not to snatch the pistol from Andel and club Duster over the head with it. "You said you didn't know where the weapons are!"

"I don't. I know where my tools are. I always know."

Andel and Calder exchanged a look. "You're a *Soulbound?* And you're still in here?"

Duster let out a deep breath, ruffling the edge of his beard. "Not the kind of Soulbound you're thinking of, son. If you need somebody to assemble a working pistol in two hours, I'm your man. You want a musket that will strike in the damp and never jam, no problem. Can't throw much of a fireball, though."

"A Soulbound gunsmith should be the best," Calder said. "Why haven't I ever heard of you?"

Andel made a point of rolling his eyes. That was unusual for Andel; usually he understated his criticisms. And kept them less childish. Calder must have said something *really* stupid, but he couldn't figure out what it was.

"Be that as it may," Andel said, "I think we've strayed from the main point. Marten?"

"Good point. I'll get us out of the door. Duster, you'll take us to your tools. From there, we'll fight our way out."

Duster peered at him as though examining a jewel. "That's your plan, is it? Fight to my tools with an empty pistol, load it, and then fight the way out with *one shot?*"

"I wouldn't consider planning my strongest suit, but my plans have worked so far."

The gunsmith looked around, taking in the room where they were held prisoner. "Have they?"

Andel sighed, awkwardly lurching to his feet with his ankles tied together. "I hate to encourage him, but he's almost right. At least he's proactive, which I prefer to sitting here waiting to die."

Calder pointed to Andel. "See? He's onboard."

"I said following your lead was preferable to being eaten alive by Elderspawn. Don't let it go to your head."

But it was too late. Calder knew a compliment when he heard one, and he couldn't stop a slow smile. At this rate, Andel would trust him before the year was out. Then maybe he could work toward skipping out on his debt.

Duster reached down and pulled his ankle restraints off. They parted as easily as the bonds around his wrists. "Might as well face death like a man instead of lying here."

"The measure of a man is his attitude," Calder said brightly. Then he held out his bound hands to Andel. "Pistol, please."

With visible reluctance, Andel handed over the gun.

Andel Petronus gave Calder the gun on what one might call a whim.

While Andel didn't trust Calder Marten's character, he was starting to trust a few other things about the man. For one, Calder kept *trying*. Persistence was an admirable trait on the Aion, even when it resulted in the man trying the most ridiculous, least likely plans.

To get past the door, the Navigator took the pistol and hammered with the butt on the door. He pounded away in a rhythmic pattern, as though trying to tap out a code. Finally, when a robed man opened the door with a sword in hand, ready to subdue the prisoner, Calder broke his nose with the pistol.

It was quite possibly the worst plan Andel had ever seen in action.

What if the man opening the door had carried a pistol of his own? What if they hadn't opened the door at all? What if the Elderspawn had entered the room and simply eviscerated them all, unafraid of Calder's empty pistol?

But it had worked, and now—somehow—he and Calder and 'Duster' were crammed inside a dingy closet at the back of the house while cultists pounded on the door and shouted dire promises. Calder set his newly acquired cutlass down and pressed his untied hands against the door. "Everything coming along back there, Duster?"

The old gunsmith grumbled, his hands blurring over the upturned traveling trunk they were using as a table. He'd first loaded the pistol, faster than Andel had seen it done, and put it into Andel's hands only seconds after he'd received it. Now he was working on a more delicate project.

Duster—Andel already suspected the man's real name, though he couldn't be entirely certain—had a wide leather belt buckled around his middle. Every inch of the belt was covered in pockets and straps, and in each position, there rested a tiny handheld tool. If Andel didn't know differently, the belt would have convinced him that Duster was a leatherworker.

But now, knowing what he did, he understood that he was looking at the Vessel of a Soulbound craftsman. Even when Duster wasn't actively using his tools, their presence hung with dark gravity in Andel's mind. Soulbound made him uneasy.

Not that he would show it.

Duster continued rolling powder into tight cylinders, tying each end off so that a single cowlick of paper stuck out. As he placed one cylinder into a pile, his other hand was already rolling another.

"Make something that explodes," Calder had told him, and the gunsmith didn't question it. He'd simply begun wrapping powder in paper—it looked like a mixture of ordinary black powder and something else, a bluish dust that had doubtless come straight from an alchemist.

"How many?" Duster finally asked, now that he had a healthy pile of ten or so miniature explosives.

"As many as you can make," Calder said, just as a jagged pincer splintered through the door. The Elderspawn had arrived.

"...which is however many you have now," Andel continued. "We're out of time."

"Point taken," Calder responded. He released the door and steadied his hand on the hilt of his cutlass. "Duster, when this door collapses, light one of those things and throw it. Then...keep doing that."

Duster held one up, though Andel was the only one to see it. Calder was facing the door, which was steadily being shredded under the Inquisitor's assault. "Won't get much out of these, just a flash and a loud bang. Might light a fire, if we get lucky."

"That's all we need," Calder said, and at that moment the door burst inward.

The Navigator had to brace himself as a piece of the door slapped him, holding one arm to cover his face, but Andel was prepared. He was far enough back that none of the bigger debris hit him, and his eyes were narrowed to slits. When the Elderspawn scuttled inside the closet, Andel fired.

On the deck of a ship, a pistol was loud. Inside a closet, it was deafening.

A cloud of powder-smoke stole his vision even as the gun stole his hearing. His right ear felt as though a Watchman had driven one of those foot-long iron stakes through it, and his left was hardly better. But the ball had taken the lead Inquisitor in the head, popping one of its eyes. It flailed its ten spider-legs, backing up into the Elderspawn behind it. So the round had done its work.

Calder shouted something, probably trying to make himself heard over his own ringing ears, but a second explosion cut him off. It was the tiny bomb that Duster lobbed from the back, and it went off in a startling bloom of orange-white flame.

There were a number of Sleepless cultists behind the Inquisitors, but as soon as Andel had pulled his trigger, they'd gotten out of the way. Now the Elderspawn were fighting one another to back out of the doorway, flailing their spear-sharp legs as if they were blinded. They might have been screaming, though it would be impossible for Andel to tell.

Once the explosive had gone off, Calder charged forward. His lips were moving, which amused Andel in some small way. *He can't even hear himself, and he's still talking.*

Andel had decades of experience in combat, including several small skirmishes with Elderspawn. Never with Ach'magut's Inquisitors, unfortunately, but he had an idea how this should play out. Calder would strike quickly, hopefully drawing some blood or taking a leg from the Inquisitor, and then back up to avoid the counter-thrust. If he could disable the Elderspawn in the few seconds before the Sleepless regained their courage, then he would be able to regroup with Andel and Duster. The three of them would overpower one of the cultists, taking the man's weapon and turning it against the rest. In that way, they should be able to fight their way through the house. The narrow hallways helped them, preventing them from facing more than two or three at a time.

He was so convinced of this version of events, so absolutely swallowed by his vision, that he almost didn't notice when reality played out differently.

Calder struck with the cutlass once, and an Inquisitor's head slid off. Twice, and a crack appeared in the exoskeleton of the second. Though their heads held most of their eyes, they had at least a few sets covering every angle, and both struck at Calder as though they could see perfectly well—even the headless one.

But the young Navigator slid to the side, out of the doorway, and his blade flashed twice more. Chunks of Elder flesh fell to the floor in pools of inky purple blood, and the Inquisitors collapsed.

Then red blood sprayed against the walls.

One robed body fell down, two, three, and Calder lowered his cutlass. His chest heaved as he panted, though Andel still heard nothing over the bright ringing in his ears. Calder said something, gesturing to the dropped weapons, and then jogged away down the hall.

Before this moment, Andel hadn't realized that he had never seen Calder fight. Calder had mentioned something about his mother training him as a duelist, and Andel had taken it as a *joke*.

He looked at Duster, whose mouth was slightly open as though he couldn't figure out what to say. One of the cylinders blazed in his right hand, its paper fuse lit, and he absently extinguished the flame between two of his fingers.

Duster raised his eyebrows in a question to Andel, and Andel could only shrug. Then they remembered themselves and ran out.

Calder stood at the end of the hallway, facing an old man with a bayonet-fixed musket. The old man was visibly furious, his face red and his teeth bared in a snarl, as he thrust the bayonet toward Calder like a spear. Andel saw the problem immediately: Calder couldn't swing his sword to parry in the close confines of a hall, and couldn't get close enough to lunge under the superior range of the bayonet.

As Andel got closer, he simply lifted his empty pistol.

The old man jerked back at the sight of the gun, and Calder found his moment. The sword licked in, sliced the inside of the man's arm, and slipped out. He grabbed Calder on his way down, forcing the Navigator to waste time peeling him off.

Andel walked by them. He might have helped, but Calder could handle it.

Past Calder, Andel glanced to the right. Everything was as they'd left it there: door open, the little boy hunched in the corner, the four men in varying states of consciousness around the walls. So he looked to the left, where a locked door stood between him and the captive women.

It didn't take long to find a key; as luck would have it, the ring was tied to the belt of the old man clinging to Calder's shoulders. Andel delicately reached through Calder's straining arms to the old man's waist, snatching the keys and leaving.

As he did, Calder shouted something that Andel had no hope of catching. If his ears weren't ringing, he could have recognized a plea for help, but alas. He had no way of knowing what the boy wanted.

He turned back to the women's door—there were only three keys on the ring, so it took five seconds to figure out which was appropriate.

When the door swung open, he saw five women, just as he'd expected. But not in the way he'd expected them.

Jyrine knelt before them, arms spread. They crouched on the floor before her, nodding or weeping or both, and a strange green light filled the room like an echo of a quicklamp. Jyrine's head snapped around at the sound of the door opening, the light cutting off and her last words unfinished. Of course he'd caught none of it, but Andel would have given a hundred silvermarks to hear exactly what those words had been.

Maybe being in the headquarters of an Elder cult had gotten to him, but the scene before him looked exactly like the early stages of an initiation dedicated to Elder worship. He'd seen scenes like this before, in the Luminian Order; usually he'd kick the door down at about this point in the ritual, after which the room devolved into utter chaos.

Jyrine's eyes flashed with anger and irritation before snapping into a mask of happiness and relief. Tears even welled in her eyes, and she rushed up to him, saying something with a smile on her face.

Andel took a half-step back. It was how fast she'd covered herself, more than anything else, that told him something was actually wrong here. Only madmen or actors went from rage to tears of joy in a half-second.

But there were more important matters at the moment. He took his eyes off of Jyrine, waving to the others, leading them into the hallway. They hopped along after him until he used his stolen blade to cut free their hands and feet.

Calder had already gathered the men, and Duster was hurling fire at another Inquisitor who rushed down the hall toward them. Their crowd ran along together in a harrowing escape through the night-shrouded streets of Silverreach.

Swallowed up in their race for life, Andel pushed Jyrine to the back of his mind. He had worse to worry about, and he forgot what he'd seen.

For a while.

Thirteen people piled on *The Testament* and left Silverreach behind. To the sound of Elderspawn screeching impotently on the shore, Calder guided the ship out to sea.

Hours later, surrounded by black ocean, he sent his Intent down through his ship and urged the Lyathatan to stop. The monster halted its advance, the chains on its wrists tugging the human passengers to a comparatively gentle rest.

Nine of the ten passengers they'd picked up in town were asleep. Some of them rested in the spare cabins below his feet, others in his own cabin under the stern deck. *The Testament* had plenty of space for passengers and cargo both, and was intended to sail with a larger crew than this one. Though Calder could essentially operate the entire vessel alone, through his bond of Intent, there were a thousand tasks that no one could handle on their own. Magical powers aside.

They were anchored at the border of the zone most people called the 'deep Aion,' as opposed to the 'shallow Aion.' Here, they were unlikely to run into any of the unnatural hazards or monsters that plagued the deeps. Especially not with a giant pet Elderspawn of their own standing guard beneath.

Navigators had a different term for this area at the heart of the world: the Aion Sea. The shallows weren't the true ocean, with its unknowable terrors. They were something else entirely, something for lesser sailors.

Usually, Calder would have no problem setting the Lyathatan to anchor them even in the hazardous depths of the sea. The anger of their Elder or the agony of the ship itself would wake him if they were in danger.

But tonight, the perils of the Aion Sea loomed over him like a dark wave. His hands shook on the wheel, and his knees begged him to collapse onto the deck. If he did, he wasn't sure whether he would fall asleep as soon as his kneecaps hit wood or if he'd simply melt into tears.

The danger of Silverreach had come too close, and more than that, it was too personal. They'd grabbed him, taken his weapons, kept his crew. Locked Jerri away, where he had no idea what would happen to her. They'd threatened him with Elderspawn, and beneath it all, the oppressive presence of Ach'magut lurked as though he could split the earth at any second. Until they were two hours out of Silverreach, he'd still felt that silver tingle in his spine like he was being chased. He was having a hard time scrubbing the inhuman shrieks of the Inquisitors from his ears.

It was good that the fear didn't overcome him in combat; it never had. He felt clear and clean when facing danger, as though he could see farther and faster than normal. But afterwards, when he had a chance to think, the razor's edge he'd been walking finally sliced him.

He held himself together by sheer force of will, staring blankly into the night and trying not to think about what might have happened if they hadn't escaped. As he did, a bat-winged shape fluttered out of the darkness and a heavy weight landed on his shoulder.

Tentacles tickled his right cheek as Shuffles checked his expression. "DARK," the Elderspawn said, in its version of a whisper.

Inexplicably, even this presence—the presence of something that had just been giving him waking nightmares—settled him down. He reached up, letting the tendrils curl around his index finger. "Yeah, it's dark. But we're free, now. We've made it."

Shuffles grumbled, not caring for his optimism.

The tenth and final passenger of *The Testament* stomped over to Calder, eyeing the Elderspawn through one pair of spectacles. Duster had declined space in a cabin, choosing to sleep on deck.

"You seem to like Elders, for somebody who doesn't treat their worshipers so well."

"'Through understanding, we control the unknown,'" Calder said. "That's one of the Blackwatch creeds."

Duster grunted. "I've been checking your cannons."

"And?"

"Lend me your shoulder, and I'll push them into the water right now."

Calder was too tired to laugh, and his limbs felt hollow. Nonetheless, he managed a weak smile. "Only had to use them once, and it turns out we didn't need them."

"Not too many naval battles among Navigators, I'd guess."

"We don't need the cannons for ships," Calder said. "I'm more worried about other things of a similar size."

"THINGS," Shuffles rumbled.

Duster tugged on his beard before he spoke, avoiding Calder's eyes. "You know, I was just passing through Silverreach."

"Then you have Nakothi's own timing."

"Yeah, well, I don't have anywhere in particular to go. Give me meals, a bunk, a few silvermarks when we go ashore, and room to work, and I can take care of your cannon problem. Might be able to upgrade the rest of your equipment while I'm at it." He flicked his hand at the pistol Calder wore as though brushing away dirt.

Calder all but froze, like a man afraid to startle a deer back into the woods. "We could use a gunner, as long as you can hit an Elder the size of a whale at a hundred paces."

Duster snorted. "Son, at a hundred paces, I could shave you clean."

Shuffles chuckled into Calder's ear. "CLEEEEAAAANNN."

"That's a disturbing image, Duster, and I'll thank you not to repeat it. And I'll have to consult with the crew, such as they are, in the morning. That said..." He stuck out a hand for Duster to shake. "I expect nothing but a favorable response. Without you, we'd still be on dry land."

The older man hid a smile behind his beard, but it quickly vanished. He didn't take Calder's hand. "One more thing you ought to know. I don't intend to go into the hows and whys of it, so don't ask, but I've never trusted the Guilds. Nor the Empire, and I have my reasons. As for the Emperor...let's say that your Luminian wouldn't like what I have to say about him."

"Mr. Duster, believe me when I say that you are free to speak ill of the Emperor on this deck. Andel's asleep now, anyway."

"Keeping it polite, the Emperor is as distant and malicious as any Elder. Were it in my power, I'd see him stripped naked and quartered in the heart of the Capital at dawn tomorrow, and I'd take a saw to him with a smile on my face."

Duster had stone in his eyes, as though daring Calder to contradict him.

After a few seconds, Calder let out a laugh and extended his hand again. "Welcome aboard *The Testament*, Mr. Duster. I can see we'll get along."

The older man shook, bewilderment on his face. An instant later, he was the one to hesitate. "And about this 'Duster' business, well...that's not exactly my given name."

Calder staggered back in an exaggerated display of shock. *"What?* Off the plank with you!"

Unamused, Duster plowed on. "I'm trying not to spread it around, so keep it to yourself, but I used to be from the Capital."

"I'll tuck that away in my vest and hold it there. You can trust me never to divulge that you were from the most populous city in the world."

"...where I was a gunsmith," he continued, ignoring what Calder considered perfectly delivered humor. "Name of Dalton Foster."

Calder suddenly knew how his ship felt, snapped to a halt by the unbreakable grasp of the Lyathatan's chains. He stood speechless for a moment before saying, "Oh."

"Yeah."

"I see."

"Yep."

Of the dozen questions floating around in his mind, he only had the presence of mind to blurt out one. "Are you sure you want to work for *me?*"

CHAPTER FOURTEEN

Any Reader can investigate the truth of a crime, or the history of an artifact.
But the experience of a Reader is singular, and the rest of us must take their reports
on faith. It becomes vital, therefore, that an organization exists to vouch for the
veracity of its Readers and to keep those Readers under close scrutiny and control.

For with the exception of the Emperor himself, it should not be that Readers
rule over the rest of the populace by virtue of their extra-natural powers.

– FROM THE DOCUMENT RE-FOUNDING THE MAGISTER'S GUILD

"As your first official address as Imperial Steward," Teach said, "you'll be explaining to the upper crust of the Capital why there's a crack in the sky. Here are your notes."

Somewhat numb, Calder took the sheet of paper from Teach even as a flurry of servants draped layers of shimmering green cloth around him. Like this, he looked more like the Emperor than ever; they'd even found a thick silver chain to loop around his neck, a reminder of the jewelry that the original Emperor had always worn.

For the first time, he wished the Emperor was still around. Calder could use some advice, or at least some more information.

Looking up, he could see the crack. It was a jagged line in the center of the clear sky, like a black lightning bolt, making it look like they were all underneath a great sky-blue eggshell.

"You know, ancient scholars believed that the sky was a dome," Calder said, staring upward and ignoring the speech in his hands. "They determined that it spun around the earth, with the sun on one side and the stars on the other. Now, we know it's a layer of gas around our planet...and then it cracks."

Teach crashed her gauntleted hands together, glaring at him with ice-blue eyes. "Focus. These people are highly educated and influential, but they're as panicked as anyone else. It's your job to reassure them."

"I'm starting to wonder if the ancient superstitions were right. Would they find that reassuring, do you think?"

Mekendi Maxeus, Head of the Magisters, burst in the dressing-room, his gray staff in one hand. He turned from Teach to Calder. "They've gathered, sir Steward." No one was actually clear on the appropriate form of address for Calder, but Maxeus had apparently settled on 'sir Steward.'

Teach looked to the clock on a nearby mantle. "They're early."

"They're frightened. If there was just something sitting in the sky, we could pass it off as a rare astronomical phenomenon, but the entire city shook when it appeared. Perhaps more than just the city. They know it's Elders, and this is our opportunity to show them that *we* are the ones defending them, not the Regents."

Calder had never heard the man so animated. He was striding around the room, making broad, sweeping gestures with his staff, orating as though to an audience.

He glanced over his speech. It seemed heavy on reassurance, and light on any actual content. "The problem is, it seems like we caused the crack. Fighting near the Optasia. But I don't know what it is or how to fix it, so anything else I say is going to sound empty."

On its own, he didn't mind empty speeches. That was what people most often wanted: someone to feed them delicious lies. But today, Calder would be somewhat more reassured if he had *any idea* what was happening.

Maxeus gestured to the speech in Calder's hands. "We've written out everything you need to say. Stick to your notes, stay calm, and we'll be able to say we were the first to handle this crisis."

"I don't remember the Emperor ever holding any notes," Calder said.

Teach shrugged, which in her layers of armor sounded like an avalanche of steel. "More than you would think. He wrote the words himself, usually, but he managed to hide notes in his sleeves or on a desk."

It was Maxeus' turn to look at the clock. "And we have a podium for you, don't worry, but you should get to it. It's less about what you say, and more that you said *something*."

"But stick to the script," Teach added.

Cheska Bennett poked her head in, red hair tied back behind her. Unlike Calder, she hadn't been forced to dress up for the occasion, so she wore a patched-up jacket and pants that would have been at home on the deck of a ship. "Or don't. Scripts are more trouble than they're worth. Tell them not to worry, that we're handling it, then drop the curtain."

Teach started pushing Calder toward the door, Maxeus following along. "This isn't the time to make trouble, Captain Bennett," Teach said. "People are scared."

Cheska laughed, following Calder as he allowed the human tide to take him out into the hallway. "I noticed you didn't let me write him a speech."

"You weren't even invited to this event," Maxeus noted.

"Harbor's right next door, and so is my ship. Thought I'd pop in and give our new Steward some advice." She made sure she had his attention before continuing.

"Lose the script. Look confident, tell them you'll solve it."

Teach shouldered her out of the way as she herded Calder into the next room. "Thank you, Captain Bennett, please take your seat."

Never had Calder felt more like a sheep.

The building was a former opera house turned into a banquet hall. The seats had been removed, the floor leveled, and round tables filled the space. Around those tables now sat the great and powerful of the Capital; nobles, bankers, favorites of the Emperor, high-ranking Guild members—even a few from currently disgraced Guilds, like at least one Greenwarden—and people Calder didn't recognize but who were obviously rich. Their small talk was deafening, but as soon as Calder entered the room, silence followed him. Every eye took him in: his clothes, his bearing, the papers he had half-hidden in his sleeves, his two Guild Head companions.

And Calder recognized an opportunity when he saw one.

"Thank you, General Teach," he said, stepping out from her shadow. "Guild Head Maxeus." He walked on his own, unescorted, to the center of the former stage. The curved walls and the Intent of the building should carry every word he spoke to the farthest corners.

Cheska raised her fist to him, a gesture of support, and then leaned back in her newfound chair and propped her heels up on the table. A pair of Witnesses looked scandalized, but they couldn't say anything to the Head of the Navigators. From her grin, she'd been counting on it.

Calder glanced down at the script for a prompt. Briefly, he'd even considered actually reading it. He was acutely aware of everything—and everyone—that he didn't know, and a misstep here could haunt him for the rest of his life. The people in this room were frightened, no less than the average person on the street, and they needed answers for their own peace of mind. The script would give it to them.

Or he could do it himself.

Most of them would never know the difference, but he would. And he felt more comfortable improvising anyway.

"Ladies and gentlemen," he said, crumpling his prepared speech. "You may have noticed a new addition to the beautiful Capital skyline."

No one laughed. In the back of the room, Maxeus leaned more heavily on his staff. Teach put her head in her hands.

"I can promise you that the full resources of the Imperial Palace are currently dedicated to addressing this event and ensuring that it does not pose a threat to Capital citizens." That line was almost word-for-word from his speech, but the next wasn't. "It's no secret that the Guilds have not been fully cooperating with one another these last few years. But we have the absolute backing of the Blackwatch and the Magisters, both of whom are working tirelessly to protect you."

"So it *is* a threat?" someone shouted.

"Not to you," Calder said immediately. That didn't sound like something the Emperor would have said, but he was falling into a rhythm, so he forged ahead. "Let me tell you something about my history. I've spent the last ten years in the Navigators, crossing the deadliest parts of the Aion Sea hundreds of times, but I started in the Blackwatch. Whatever you know or think you know about the Blackwatch, you should remember that each and every Watchman is sworn to protect you from things that you would not believe. Things that you will never see. Are they a threat? Yes, they are. But not to you. To the people standing in front of you."

Calder scanned the audience, making eye contact with as many people as he could. "My address to you will be brief tonight, but I assure you that I'm not trying to replace the Emperor." *Yet*, he added silently. "A steward is a caretaker, a protector, and as Imperial Steward, I am trying to do one thing: to take care of you. To make sure that, when the Great Elders move, they're moving against *me*. Not you."

That was the job the Emperor should have done, before he lost sight of the value of a human life. Not that he could say that now. "So when I tell you not to worry, I'm not telling you there's nothing to be worried *about*. I'm telling you that there are people handling it. We, the loyal Guilds of the Empire, will protect you. That, you can rely on."

Then, amidst a growing wave of quiet whispers, he left the stage.

Calder heard all the opinions on his speech for the rest of the day, through the night, and into the next morning.

"It wasn't a *disaster*," Teach was saying. "You reassured them, you emphasized that it was the remaining Guilds who were protecting them and not the Independents. But you should have just read the script."

He took another bite of his fruit sandwich. It was a Vandenyas-style breakfast, which tended to be heavy on bread and fruit, but he'd been up most of the night fielding visitors. Apparently the highest levels of the Capital didn't feel like he was worth visiting until after he'd made his first public appearance.

In mid-sentence, Teach cut herself off and turned to face the door. Calder hadn't heard anything, but he still reached beneath his absurdly oversized robes for the hilt of his cutlass. Just in case. Teach had her hand on Tyrfang, so there must be at least some kind of threat.

An old man in an Imperial Guard uniform burst through the door an instant later, gills flapping on the sides of his throat. He didn't wheeze or pant with exhaustion, though he leaned his hands on bent knees. "Guild Head. We've just confirmed the report. Mekendi Maxeus is dead, and one of his properties has been burned to the ground."

Calder dropped his breakfast, his drowsiness and Teach's lectures forgotten. He'd thought the most important thing he had to deal with today was the aftermath of his speech, but this news would completely overshadow his performance.

Which was good; he thought he could have done better, given another chance.

As soon as he recognized the direction of his own thoughts, he was disgusted with himself. *What's wrong with me? A man is dead.* A man who had supported him, though they certainly hadn't been friends.

He wasn't exactly grieving, any more than he would cry for the death of a stranger. But he had known Maxeus, had seen him just last night at the banquet hall, and now the man was gone. It was a heavy weight, and the loss of any life should deserve mourning.

But he let himself move on after only an instant. Someone had killed the Head of an Imperialist Guild, and there was work to be done.

"Did we capture anyone?" Teach asked, already walking for the door. Calder followed her.

"All enemies withdrew," the old man said, falling into step with them. "So far, eight Magisters have made witness statements. They all agree that it was a pair of Consultants, one of whom looked like she may have had Kameira modifications, and one Soulbound."

Teach slammed the door open one-handed without pausing her stride. "Do we have any former Guards who defected to the Consultants?"

"None that I'm aware of, but we're still looking into it. The statements conflict, and there are Witnesses looking over the scene now, but a few points are very clear. The Guild Head offered the Consultants a chance to leave in peace, but they responded by attacking him. This is clearly an act of aggression on the part of the Consultant's Guild."

Calder thought back to his own experiences with the Consultants, from Shera fighting him on the deck of his ship to Meia coming out of nowhere to defend him. Aggressively confronting a Guild Head was well in character for them. Doing it openly, where there were witnesses around and Readers could investigate...

That didn't sound like an official action of the Consultant's Guild.

Mekendi Maxeus' mansion was on the fringes of the Capital, with just enough space between it and the surrounding houses that it didn't feel like it was on a busy street. Rather than one building, it looked like a complex of simple, square houses all stacked like blocks around and on top of one another, as though the mansion had grown from a small township all fused together. The grounds made the word "mansion" appropriate: they were immaculately tailored, with rows of shrubberies giving way to a pair of massive tiger statues by the main entrance.

Across from the mansion was the still-smoldering skeleton of a building. It sat in a pile of ash, its burnt and cracked innards exposed, a tower of smoke reaching to the clouds.

When Calder's carriage rolled up to the wreckage, a crowd awaited him. Teach dismounted first, scanned the crowd, and forced everyone three steps back before she would allow Calder to exit the carriage.

He left with as much dignity and solemnity as he could muster, considering that he felt like tripping over his voluminous robes. Everyone bowed to him, but they were speaking to Teach: giving her their rendition of events, asking for support, demanding justice, simply trying to get her attention. Judging by the staves they carried, they were all Magisters.

The mighty Emperor descends, and no one notices, Calder thought. He considered doing something to capture their attention, but it would no doubt seem like the petty action of a boy. He didn't need to do anything to make him seem even younger.

So, instead, he slipped off to examine the burned building. It seemed to be a warehouse, considering the large open space and the remnants of crates and barrels, which led him to immediately wonder why the Head of the Magister's Guild needed a warehouse across from his home. Did he expect to need eighteen pounds of salted tuna in the middle of the night?

Calder tried to get a sense of the Intent, but it was far too weak and muddled to give him any useful picture. That was normal. A building wasn't like a small tool; it gained Intent only slowly, over years of use. No one focused on a warehouse as they used it, no one noticed it, and as a result its investment was weak. The fire hadn't done it any favors either. The destruction of its form would also lose much of its Intent, leaving very little for Calder to see.

As he moved around one still-standing patch of wall, he came face-to-face with Meia. She was dressed all in black, as usual, and had knelt to inspect something she'd found on the floor. A needle.

"This wasn't a Consultant assignment," she said, without looking up.

"Were you riding in the carriage with me? I know you're good, but if I didn't see you from six inches away, I'll be *really* impressed."

"A Consultant is always where the job requires her."

He hadn't expected an explanation. "You're sure that your Architects didn't authorize this?"

"I checked at the chapter house. According to the official story, the team was only approved for Shepherd work. Reconnaissance, tracking, observation. No direct aggressive action."

Calder looked around at the smoking ruins of the Magisters' building. "Well, *someone* took some aggressive action. And the Magisters say it was you."

When Meia didn't respond, he looked over to her, only to see that she'd vanished. Seconds later, he found out why: Jarelys Teach was marching up to him, trailing men and women in robes and staves.

"It's not appropriate for you to be alone out here, sir," she said. She didn't look straight at him, keeping her eyes on the crowd, but he heard the rebuke for what it was.

Calder didn't acknowledge it. "The Consultant's Guild didn't officially sanction this."

"The Guild also doesn't openly recognize that they employ assassins," Teach responded. "But that doesn't stop them from doing so." She didn't ask where his information came from.

"We have to respond to this." He wanted her opinion, but he couldn't be seen asking for it. Not with all these strangers around.

"Yes sir, we do." She gestured with one hand, and a handful of nearby Imperial Guards began moving Magisters back. When they were out of earshot, she continued, her voice low. "Our course of action is obvious, and I'm sure my fellow Guild Heads would agree with me. We have full justification for an attack on the Gray Island. The Consultants attacked and killed an allied leader without provocation, and the Witnesses will corroborate that. It's exactly what we wanted: an excuse to attack them as soon as possible, but keep the public opinion on our side."

Calder nodded absently as he thought. There was still something strange about all this.

"I've already sent a messenger to Captain Bennett. The hour *The Eternal* is seaworthy, I want to load up the entire Navigator's Guild with as many soldiers and Guards as we can and head straight for the Gray Island. The longer we delay, the more likely that Estyr Six herself will get involved."

Still, Calder didn't speak.

"If we act immediately, we can remove one of our strongest enemies before the Regents even know we're moving. The situation is very clear."

"Except that it's a trap," Calder said, finally.

Teach's hand twitched up toward her shoulder at the mention of a trap, seemingly on reflex. "All our information suggests that it was a mistake on the part of the Consultants. A botched mission combined with a Soulbound who lost control."

"There's only so much coincidence I'm willing to accept," he said. "First, the Independents find out about Alagaeus' death *weeks* before they should have, and they publish it in the news-sheets. It forces us to hunt for an excuse to attack. Then, only a few days later, the perfect excuse drops out of the sky and lands in our laps."

"If you're suggesting the Consultants manipulated events to that degree… if they were capable of coordinated action on that scale, they'd rule the world."

"I don't think it was the Consultants that set the trap."

The Elders had a plan. Their actions with the Optasia, the Emperor's death, the steadily growing conflict between the Guilds…If the Great Elders weren't pulling the strings, they were at least enjoying the show.

Teach stepped closer, lowering her voice even further. "It's fine for you to express these doubts to me privately, but keep them away from the public. We need to make sure that people see you and the Imperialist Guilds as one and the same."

"I understand, but the confidence of the people isn't our biggest problem. The Elders are involved here."

"The Great Elders have a plan. They *always* have a plan. We fight back by facing them head-on, and not hanging back in fear because they might—"

Teach snapped around, staring at the section of wall. Her hand was already on Tyrfang's hilt, though Calder hadn't seen it move. She seemed transformed, like a lion poised to pounce, her Intent sharp and focused.

With hardly a second's hesitation, she lashed out with Tyrfang's power.

A lash of dark power flickered out, like a whip-crack of shadow. It blasted the top half of the wall to rubble, striking the figure that had been crouched on the other side. Calder had managed to deaden his senses before the attack, because he'd seen it before: the corrosive Intent would have left him with nightmares for days.

Teach leaped, clearing the remaining wall in one bound, and slammed into the ground. She stood over the crouching figure with her blade ready to draw.

"Remain on the ground. If you attempt to stand, you will be executed. If you speak without permission, you will be executed. If you draw a weapon, you will be executed."

The injured woman coughed and started to crawl out, so Calder caught a glimpse of blond hair and orange eyes. Meia.

"Stop!" he ordered, walking forward to make sure that Teach didn't strike again, but one look at her face told him it wasn't necessary. The Guild Head was even more shocked than he was, her face going pale.

"Meia?" Teach asked.

Meia raised her head and tried to speak, even as blue scales popped up irregularly over her skin. She finally hacked out a breath and collapsed, breathing heavily, her muscles squirming on their own beneath her black uniform.

"She's been working with me," Calder said hurriedly. "She protected me from the Champion, and I suspect she'll soon join my crew. She's on our side."

Teach looked at Meia as though staring through a window into the past. "Could be she is. But the last time I saw her, she…"

The general let the thought trail off. When Imperial Guards came rushing over to tend to their Guild Head, she ordered them to load Meia back into a carriage and take her to the palace. "Full alchemical recovery," Teach instructed. "The palace staff knows her, they should know how to deal with her enhancements. Three sets of eyes on her at all times. Any mistakes will be personally addressed by me."

Teach and Calder rode back in the carriage behind Meia. They'd seen what they needed to see in Maxeus' warehouse, and now they were faced with a decision.

Namely, whether to declare war on the oldest Imperial Guild.

General Teach was totally certain of her opinion. "Decisive action here could prevent a full-scale war. If we destroy the Consultants, we destroy the capacity of the Independent Guilds to organize. In the best-case scenario, we may even be able to get the Architects on our side."

Cheska Bennett seemed to agree. "Once *The Eternal* is back in the water, I'll lead the attack myself. This is what we needed."

As for Bliss… "I have supervised the repair of the Optasia. As far as we are capable of determining, it has sustained no permanent damage. It's in swib-swab shape, as you sea captains say."

Calder exchanged a look with Cheska. "No one says that, Bliss."

"I see the books have misled me. I will be rid of them."

Bliss didn't have much to contribute to the ongoing discussion, but her presence gave Calder an excuse to leave. While Cheska and Teach discussed the logistics involved in a coordinated assault on the Gray Island, with Bliss providing the occasional observation, Calder slipped away.

The Optasia was unharmed.

He hadn't gone back to see Jerri again, but the last time he did, she had insisted that he *needed* to use the throne. Since the device was the only reason the Imperialist Guild Heads had allowed him to assume the role of Imperial Steward in the first place, he could reasonable assume that they wanted him to use it. So one way or another, he was going to end up using the Optasia. He might as well get a look at it first.

On the second day since the sky cracked, Calder changed back into his old clothes—pants, jacket, sword, pistol, and *at last* a hat—and met with Andel and Foster. Together, they would go test the Optasia for the first time.

"Why us?" Andel asked, as they moved toward the Emperor's old quarters. Life in the Imperial Palace hadn't changed him at all: he was still wearing the pure white of a Luminian Pilgrim, the silver sun emblem hanging on his chest.

"I've asked myself that question every day for almost ten years, Andel," Calder responded, adjusting his hat.

"You want to get killed messing around with Imperial relics, that's your business," Foster grumbled. "You can leave me out of it." He didn't actually leave, though. He wore his shooting glasses on the tip of his nose, his reading glasses hanging down against his broad beard. He carried guns everywhere that he could fit one, as though he felt the Capital was more dangerous than the depths of the Aion.

"I don't have a reason in particular," Calder said, finally answering Andel's question. "I have to go inspect the Optasia, so I might as well feel like myself while I do it. None of the Emperor's clothes, no one following me, no official escort."

While he was still speaking, his official escort arrived.

She was the blond Guard captain with orange eyes, the one he'd seen before. She saluted as he passed, falling into step behind him. "Sir. With the number of recent attacks on the Imperial Palace, General Teach thought it would be wiser for you to have an attendant."

"So long as you feel like yourself, sir," Andel said.

The building that housed the Emperor's chambers was looking somewhat worn, after the battle with the fleshy Elderspawn that had occurred in its courtyard. Several shutters had been ripped off, the walls were scarred, spots of dead flesh still lingered everywhere, and the stench of half-burned flesh hung in the air like smoke.

Calder pushed open the great bronze doors that led inside, following the red carpet. It had been torn almost to shreds. The paintings hung askew, and inside the Emperor's chambers themselves, the destruction was worse. Here was where Teach and Jerri had clashed directly, with Bliss' Spear of Tharlos thrown in for good measure. The floorboards were peeled up, the walls cracked, and palace workmen hadn't had long to repair the damage. Tarps and bare plaster covered the worst of it.

The Optasia stood exposed, a cage of steel bars like the skeleton of a great chair.

Foster moved forward, and Calder grabbed his arm. "Don't Read it," he warned.

"How else are you going to check it for anything?"

Calder didn't really have an answer for that. "If you Read it, you activate it. And if there *is* still a problem, it would pass to you."

Foster grumbled something into his beard, but didn't keep moving forward.

If he was honest with himself, Calder was here for a break more than anything else. There was nothing he could do with the Optasia unless he was willing to use it fully, which still frightened him. Anything the Great Elders wanted him to do deserved serious consideration first.

All in all, they stood staring at the throne for a full ten minutes before Andel politely suggested they stop wasting their time and leave.

On their way out, they passed a goat-legged Imperial Guard shuffling a sheaf of papers in his hands. He didn't even know to bow when Calder passed, muttering to himself and scribbling on the topmost page.

"What's the worst that could happen to you?" Foster asked Calder.

"I could go insane and die."

"*Besides* that."

"It works perfectly, but I don't know how to use it, so I end up cursing an Erinin orphanage and everyone inside it dies."

Andel held the great bronze door of the building open so everyone could pass. While they did, he asked a question of his own. "How likely is that, do you think? The Guild Heads all verified that the Optasia should be in working condition."

Calder relaxed, letting his Intent drift back through the building to the Emperor's chambers. He wouldn't be able to Read anything properly at this distance, but he was surprised by a flicker of something strange.

He paused as the door slid shut, trying to figure out the wisp of unusual Intent he'd just picked up. He couldn't quite place it, but it felt like something...hidden.

After a minute or two of quiet Reading, he finally placed the feeling.

"Someone's in there," he said.

CHAPTER FIFTEEN

Eventually, the arena killed everyone.

The contests of duelists and gladiators were governed by centuries of tradition, and here in northern Izyria, tradition weighed heavier than Imperial law. The Emperor himself, as the story went, gave in to the tradition of the ancient Izyrian tribes by dueling one by one for their support. Here, that story was told to reinforce one simple point: even the Emperor bowed to the rules of the ring.

So when Urzaia was condemned to the arena to die, they couldn't just lop of his head and be done with it. There were procedures to follow, spectators to satisfy. Fathers who couldn't feed their children bought tickets to the fights, and roared more loudly than the rest. As long as they were happy, the arena's administrators made money. The more money the administrators made, the more trickled down to the Patrons whose fighters cut and bled on the sand. It was in everyone's best interest to keep the drunken, unruly mob in the stands happy.

And Urzaia did.

The rough iron gate rattled as it rose, and he marched up the stairs of yellow stone like the Emperor on his way to a coronation. He wore his trademark mismatched armor: leather straps over his chest and one arm, a patch of chain mesh over his heart, and thick gauntlets on both hands. The haphazard mix of protection made the gold-scaled hide wrapped around his left arm seem almost commonplace. If anyone was looking for a Vessel, their eyes would first turn to his hatchets, his gauntlets, or perhaps his ornate belt-buckle carved in the image of a snake eating its own tail. His captors had delivered his Vessel to him only after ensuring he was wrapped in invested chains.

That was another rule of the arena: the fighter had to walk onto the sands at his best.

When his feet left stone and crunched on sunlit sand, the crowd roared. He beamed at them, basking in their cheers and in the sun on his flesh, and lifted his black hatchets to the sky. The sound swelled. Not a seat was empty on this fine summer's day; it was a healthy crowd even for a blood match. Two sides would enter the arena, and only one would walk away. At most.

Urzaia fought once every three days, which was all his Patron would allow.

Every three days, excluding emergencies and Imperial holidays, he fought. His life was the wager, without exception—the Emperor's command insisted that he die on the sands.

He had defied that command for three years.

Urzaia walked with a hatchet in either hand, the power of his Vessel flowing from the upper half of his arm to the rest of his body, the song of the crowd surrounding him. His blood thrummed with life, until he felt drawn tight like a new bowstring. An opponent had cut his little toe off in the last match, but he'd taken an even trade out of the man's skull. His wounds had healed by now, and he was back in fighting shape, though he'd have to watch his balance.

Thoughts like those flew through the back of his mind so that he was hardly aware of them. He was enjoying the moment too much to dwell on the future.

He may have been sentenced to die here, but the arena gave him a reason to live.

His opponent met him on the sand, a man whose scars twisted his face into an eternal snarl. He wore a wolf pelt with the beast's head over his own like a hood, and he carried a sickle in each hand. He must have been trying to make a signature for himself, like Urzaia's hatchets. It would help the audience to remember him.

The man might already be famous; Urzaia only remembered those who stood in the ring against him, and those were all dead men. He *did* know that the audience applause was significantly cooler than it had been for Urzaia, and there were a few jeers thrown in for good measure. This stretched Urzaia's smile even wider.

"Only one of you?" Urzaia gestured to his opponent with one hatchet. "It is good to see a man in the arena at last!"

The crier's voice boomed throughout the arena, enhanced by invested acoustics. "Once again, Imperial citizens, we have a blood match to slake your endless thirst!" He waited for the cheers to die down before continuing. "Clearly, you all know the man who splits his foes like logs for winter, the undefeated WOODSMAN!"

Wild cheers accompanied this announcement, as they always did the introduction of fighters. Urzaia simply couldn't believe they were putting him up against a lone opponent. Every match thus far had been tilted against him in some way, designed to end in his death. He didn't blame the administrators; that was how the arena should be. But for this man to pose a threat to him alone...was he some sort of legendary Soulbound? Perhaps a Guild Head had come in disguise.

"And against him, the tamer of beasts, the victor of a hundred contests under Patron Gametti, the man who is a full team unto himself...HOUND-MASTER!"

And Urzaia felt the heavy weight of disappointment once again. Of course they would send more teams against him, and he was foolish to expect otherwise. For his three hundredth match, they had surprised him by matching him against *two* teams. He shouldn't have allowed himself to hope for one man who could threaten him.

He looked at the other iron grates behind the Houndmaster. Based on the man's name, he was assuming there were some dogs or Kameira back there, but none of the gates moved. Were there invisible Kameira wolves surrounding him even now?

The thought cheered him a bit, and he swept a hatchet to one side experimentally. No sudden squeals suggested he'd bitten into invisible dog flesh.

When the crier finished his lines—a few more sentences about the glory of the Empire and the history of this arena in particular—and the bell at the top of the tower rang, Urzaia was still waiting for the hounds to show up.

Before the ringing faded away, the Houndmaster dropped one sickle and pulled up a yellowed horn that had hung against his chest. It looked like a ram's horn, and Urzaia had assumed it was another decoration to go along with the man's wolf cloak.

Why draw the sickle at all, if he meant to drop it? Urzaia wondered. *Did he want me to believe he'd close with me?* Urzaia was forced to conclude the man was merely foolish.

He did stand back and let the Houndmaster blow his horn. The man was an experienced fighter, so he would certainly have a way to counter a straight-forward strike. Besides, Urzaia wanted to see what the horn would do.

The sand shimmered with heat, and seconds after the cry of the Hound-master's horn echoed through the arena, the sand began to swirl. It gathered into four densely packed shapes, each the detailed outline of a hound. Urzaia spotted individual teeth and snarls of unruly fur, all sculpted on bodies of packed sand. The sand-hounds bared their teeth at Urzaia and snapped their jaws open in a bark, but they made no sound. Still, they looked so realistic that Urzaia practically heard their growls and cries in his head.

He whistled, impressed. This Houndmaster was a Soulbound, obviously, and his Vessel must be the horn from some Kameira that controlled sand.

Sloppy of him, to reveal his Vessel so clearly, but at least the man had a flair for the dramatic.

The Houndmaster snapped a command, and all four dogs sprinted toward Urzaia. He leveled his axes, still smiling.

If this was to be his last fight, he wanted to give the crowd a good show. Just because this was a death sentence didn't mean he couldn't milk a little joy out of it while he lasted.

Eventually, the arena killed everyone.

Calder and Jerri sat in the highest, cheapest seats of the arena where they wouldn't be recognized. Not that they had many acquaintances in Axciss, nor enemies for that matter, there was still one man whose notice he'd rather avoid. Until he could fulfill his promise.

He wouldn't raise Urzaia's hopes before he could break the man free.

Pushing the three-cornered hat lower on his head, where it would conceal the bright flame of his hair, Calder turned his attention from the fight to the stack of papers in front of him. "Six exits from the arena floor."

"Covered in iron bars while any match is in progress," Jerri said. "And leading straight into the dungeons." She leaned forward, gripping her braid in both hands, dark eyes gleaming.

Calder looked at the outer edge of the arena. The whole building was constructed like a yellow stone bowl, with seats up the edges of the bowl and a flat plane on top. Guards sat in the shade of stubby towers, muskets in hand. "Gunners on the walls," he said, scribbling the information down. "They're here for the crowd's protection, but they'll be in the way if anything happens during a match."

Urzaia smashed one dog into a spray of sand, which splashed into the Houndmaster's eyes. Jerri and the rest of the crowd erupted in cheers.

"The Patrons, arena administrators, and Imperial guests stay in the private box," Calder said, looking to one end of the arena. Two fat men, one woman with tall hair, and a robed Magister were sitting within, along with a handful of standing attendants. "Do they have their own exit, do you think?"

Jerri screamed for Urzaia once more and then turned to him. "They'd have to. I can't imagine a little Heartlander lady squeezing her silk skirts through the common crowds. Can we get him up there?"

"We might be able to get *ourselves* up there," Calder said. The crest of a Guild member opened doors, very often in a literal sense. "I doubt we could take a gladiator straight from the arena, up through the common seats, into the box, and past the arena's guards."

Still, he wrote it down as a possibility.

Jerri turned to the side of the arena opposite the box, where perhaps fifty seats had been removed and the slope of the walls leveled. It was a flat square of stone like a miniature arena. "What's that?"

"I don't know. Executions?"

"I think they like to save executions for the main floor," Jerri said, wincing as Urzaia took a slice to the face from the Houndmaster's sickle. The crowd groaned along with her.

Could it be for announcements? No, most announcements were made from the arena floor or the Imperial box seats. Why, then, were they keeping that clear platform in the middle of the seats?

He needed a closer look.

The crowd of an arena was a totally different species from the audience in an opera house or theater. Pushing down a row was more like forcing his way through a mob; no one was seated, most people were shouting and waving their arms around as though to imitate the fighters. One woman smacked Calder so hard with her elbow that his head rang, and she followed it up by screaming in his ear and shoving him farther down the row.

At this rate, he would be beaten to death by the spectators before he reached the end of the arena. Calder shot a glance at the guards in their towers overhead, hoping they wouldn't react, and pulled his pistol from his jacket. He held it overhead like a banner as he advanced.

The crowd glared at him, and a few even spat at his feet, but at least no one pushed him anymore. Finally clear of the press of bodies, he took a deep breath, and immediately wished he hadn't. The air was hot and thick with salt, and sweat, and blood, and almost ten thousand unwashed bodies.

"A man shows his weakness when he casts shame on his ancestors." A contemporary of Sadesthenes had written those words, though his name escaped Calder at the moment. He supposed he was showing his weakness right now, because he was suddenly ashamed of his Izyrian ancestors who had built this arena and those like it. It celebrated the opposite of civilization: the brutal, unfettered rule of blood and steel. Writhing in the seats, crying for blood, these looked like Elders rather than men.

Then again, he'd been raised in the Capital. The people here would probably say that keeping bloodshed confined to the arena was the very definition of civilized, keeping aggression out of the streets.

His philosophical musing kept him occupied as he slid past the grubby Izyrians filling the seats, his pistol still outstretched. At last, he reached the square platform.

It was exactly as it seemed: a section of seats flattened and raised to create an even surface that could be viewed from anywhere in the arena. Since the platform interrupted what would normally be a flight of stairs, there were exits built underneath. He peeked through one wooden door, which opened onto a spiral staircase that seemed to lead outside.

Calder tucked his pistol back into his jacket and unfolded his piece of paper and a stub of paper-wrapped charcoal. He made a quick, crude note of the exit positions. If they could get Urzaia up to this platform, they would have a straight run out of the arena.

A voiceless roar slammed into his ears like a crashing wave, and his head jerked of its own accord to the heart of the arena. There, a bloody Urzaia stood with one black hatchet lifted to the sky. The other was embedded in the center of the Houndmaster's chest, splitting his horn Vessel in two. The man's body sagged around the hatchet blade, which was the only thing keeping the corpse aloft.

Urzaia didn't seem to care that he was holding the weight of a man with one hand. He smiled broadly at the crowd, the blood running down his face highlighting each of his teeth in red. The audience went wild, shouting for the Woodsman.

Calder couldn't help thinking back to three years ago. The last time he'd seen the former Champion, the man had a smile that could blind an eagle at a thousand paces. Now, there were two black gaps where teeth had been knocked out in fights. The man showed more scars than armor, and several deep wounds showed that he'd have new scars when he next entered the arena.

If Calder had been faster, perhaps he could have helped Urzaia leave whole. Three years was already too long, and he would have to wait even longer.

The crier shouted something that was swallowed up by the shouts of the crowd, and then walked onstage himself. He gestured to Urzaia, who flicked the Houndmaster's corpse off the end of his hatchet and followed, still smiling and waving to the crowd.

Led by the arena crier, Urzaia walked out of the sand and below...only to emerge a minute later in the arena seats. Right by Calder.

The fighter was so close that Calder could smell the blood on him. He tipped his hat lower, trying to squeeze back into the crowd—he couldn't take it if he saw a look of hope on Urzaia's face, hope that Calder would have to disappoint.

But the spectators weren't content to let Calder leave. This close to the Champion gladiator, they screamed and pushed forward, shoving Calder up to the rough edge of the stone platform. Only by bracing his boot against the wall and flailing his pistol around did he earn a pocket of air, and by the time he looked back up, the crier and the Champion were standing above him.

On the platform.

The crier's first statement was lost in the crowd, but his second was just barely audible: "...almost five hundred lives taken in the arena, with no signs of giving up!"

"None can make me surrender!" Urzaia shouted, raising his fists. His hatchets were missing, Calder noted—he must have given them up before he was allowed to get within reach of the paying spectators.

The crier waited for the furious cheers to die before he continued. "Are you here for glory, Woodsman? Or do you live to take lives?"

Urzaia laughed, a booming laugh that Calder was sure would have filled the arena even without invested Intent. "A man once promised to return my freedom," he said. Calder felt as though his bones had turned to ice. "I must live so I can collect on that promise. And while I wait, I might as well have a little fun!"

The audience screamed, even as Calder forced his way through them and back to Jerri.

Urzaia would have to wait a while longer. There was nothing he could do about that. But the next time Calder visited this arena, he wouldn't leave alone.

CHAPTER SIXTEEN

"Someone's in there," Calder said.

No one wasted his time with questions or complaints. Andel looked at Foster, who shrugged and pulled open the door to the Emperor's quarters.

A goat-legged Imperial Guard lay sprawled on the carpet inside, papers strewn all about him where he'd dropped them. He'd been conscious only a minute before, and there was little chance he'd taken that instant to pass out on his own. Someone else *was* inside.

Nothing beats the satisfaction of being right. Together, Calder and Andel rushed in quietly, hauling the Imperial Guard out the door and back into the courtyard. The blond captain looked likely to shout, so Calder shook his head.

According to Calder's silent, frantic signals, his crew shut the doors.

"What's the security like in this building?" Calder whispered.

"It's usually a death-trap for anyone inside," the Guard captain responded, her eyes locked on the door. "But it's been uninhabited for years. I need men."

"Go get them. Capture, not kill. And send someone to inform Teach."

She saluted and ran off, shouting before she was *quite* out of earshot.

"Who do you think it is, sir?" Andel asked, folding his arms and watching the door.

"Consultants," Calder said. Someone had already hired a Champion to take a crack at him. Why not a real assassin? "They killed Maxeus a couple of days ago, and now they're working up the ladder."

Foster drew a weapon, holding it low in both hands. "You're not real humble, are you?"

"'Humility is the death-knell of the soul,'" Calder quoted. "Enterius, I think."

"Loreli had some views of her own on the matter," Andel said. He didn't sound particularly alarmed by the idea of a Consultant waiting for them in the Emperor's chambers. "'Humility is the perfection that we should always seek, but can never truly achieve.'"

"You were a Luminian; obviously you'd take *her* side."

"I wasn't aware you'd been in a dispute with the Regent, sir."

That actually raised an interesting point. He'd always thought of Loreli as a strategist and scholar from the ancient past, not a contemporary. But she hadn't ever died, not really, and she was currently awake and serving the Empire as a Regent.

She didn't want another Emperor. What did that say about—

His unproductive train of thought was broken by the Guard captain's return. "They're taking up position," she said. "I suggest we remove you to a safe location."

"Thank you, Captain, but I decline." Calder pulled off his hat and swept her a bow. "I'm wearing my own clothes today, I'm hanging out with my own friends—"

Foster coughed pointedly.

"—my own colleagues, and I'll handle this the way I usually would."

"Foolishly, but directly," Andel said.

"I would have said 'bravely.'"

"I'm sure you would have, sir."

Honestly, Calder was in a better mood than he'd been in for…weeks, probably. His wounds were starting to improve, though they were also starting to *itch*, he was finally feeling at home in the Imperial Palace, he thought he was making headway in his identity as Imperial Steward, and for the first time he was faced with an assassin that he'd outwitted and overmatched from the very beginning.

"I have to insist," the Guard captain was saying. "We have no idea who the enemy is, what he wants, or what he can—"

She was interrupted by the deafening shriek of tearing metal, which filled the courtyard as one of the Emperor's bronze doors crumpled like a used handkerchief.

Calder was still trying to figure out how to react to the sight of a balled-up door when it began to roll, with ponderous force and surprising speed, away from its housing and straight toward him.

He dove to the side as Andel and Foster did likewise, the three of them separated by a loose ball of bronze. Something exploded—a gunshot, he realized, close to his ear—and then a dark-skinned man in the black of a Consultant Gardener was slashing a bronze knife toward his waist.

Calder staggered back, grasping at his sword, but he knew he wouldn't make it. The assassin was too close, too fast, his approach too unexpected.

Andel moved first.

He slammed into the Gardener with a running shoulder-tackle that sent the man rolling over the tiles, bronze blades clattering away from his hands.

Calder looked at Andel with relief and more than a little astonishment. "You saved me, Andel."

The quartermaster was still on his knees, unbalanced after the tackle, but his eyes were on the Consultant. "Not quite yet, sir."

Both of the Gardener's hands came up, and a pair of tiny silver knives flashed out. One flew toward Andel, one toward Calder.

This time, Calder was ready.

His Awakened cutlass was in his hand, blade glowing with irregular orange spots like the pattern on a live coal. He slapped the throwing knife from the air, though the sudden motion pulled on his wounded shoulder. At least he hadn't put too much weight on his injured leg; if it collapsed on him again, that would be the opening the Consultant needed.

Calder recognized Meia's friend Lucan. They'd met once, in the depths of the Gray Island, though Calder hadn't recalled the man's name until Meia repeated it.

He started to speak, but the Gardener had pressed his palms against the stone tiles of the courtyard as though Reading. *He's welcome to it,* Calder thought. He looked up at the Guard captain, motioning to surround the attacker.

Then the ground of the Imperial courtyard surged to life like a sea in storm, thrashing and throwing men around. Calder slammed to his back, which didn't do his wounded shoulder any favors, and saw that Foster's body was being tossed around like a rag doll.

He only had a brief second to wonder about Foster. When had the gunner gone down? Was he immobilized by one of those Gardener paralyzing needles, or was he dead? Then the rock beneath Calder shook any sense from his head.

Calder woke seconds later, to Andel's soft laughter and the feel of his wrists tightly bound behind his back. He squirmed around for a better look, and saw Lucan only a few feet away, sitting cross-legged on the now motionless stone.

It was with relief that he noted ropes on Foster's hands—no one would bother to tie a dead man.

"That's kind of you," Calder said. If he could make conversation, maybe he could point out some common ground. Just knowing Meia might take him out of this. "Tying us up, I mean. I thought you'd be more likely to slit our throats."

He almost winced. Why give the man any ideas?

"I like to make sure my victims deserve it," Lucan said, calm as a soft breeze.

Yet you still call them 'victims,' Calder noticed, but he didn't say it. He raised one eyebrow at Lucan instead. "And you thought *we* didn't deserve it? You're a generous man. Besides, mercy is a quality I never thought I'd see in an assassin."

"You know many hired killers, do you?"

More and more every day, it seems, he thought. Out loud, he said, "'The quality of mercy is among the rarest of virtues, and rarest of all in killers and kings.' Sadesthenes. You should read him sometime. Timeless wisdom in the classics."

"You're assuming I haven't read him already," Lucan said, unperturbed.

Calder brightened a little. If he'd read Sadesthenes, that might make for more common ground. More reason for him to let them go. "Have you?"

"No."

A dead end. Calder cast around for a change of subject.

"I can't help but notice you're not making a hasty getaway." Around the edges of the courtyard, Imperial Guards were pulling themselves to their feet and calling for backup. Lucan had to notice, but he didn't move or point them out.

"And you're chatty for someone with his hands tied. I can still make a gag."

As long as Lucan kept responding, Calder could keep the exchange going. And the longer their chat stretched, the more chance for an escape. "I enjoy getting to know interesting people. A Consultant saboteur who attacks the Imperial Palace, fights three men singlehandedly, and then lingers on the scene of the crime is an interesting man indeed." Not to mention the way that he apparently used Reading to temporarily Awaken stone; Calder would have to get the Magisters to explain that one.

"Your flattery is indeed the most powerful weapon in your arsenal, sir," Andel piped in. He was weighing in to help the conversation along, the same as Calder, and humor would lighten any situation. "Thank the God we have you to defend us."

"Shut up, Andel!" Calder said, as he'd said a thousand times on the ship.

"Mmmphmphmmm!" Foster said. Joining in the banter, just as he would on *The Testament*…and, not coincidentally, letting them know he was conscious and alive.

"Shut up, Foster," Calder said, and he'd never put more affection into the phrase. "Now, stranger, I'm sure you know my name. I've learned to assume the Consultants know everything."

And of course he knew the Consultant's name as well…or he thought he did. He wouldn't want to use the man's name and then get it *wrong.* He'd look like an idiot.

Lucan stared up into the crack at the sky, seemingly undisturbed. "Calder Marten, twenty-six years old. Tried before the Emperor for counts of sabotage, theft, destruction of Imperial property, instituting a jailbreak, and conspiracy to commit fraud. Sentenced to forced labor in the service of the Navigator's Guild."

Calder didn't think he'd actually been *tried* for half of those crimes, but that didn't make them any less accurate. "That's…not exactly the list I remember, but it's impressively comprehensive nonetheless."

"You tried to attack the Emperor, and I helped to hold you back. It was a test of our reaction speed."

Calder whistled through his teeth, as though he'd just placed a memory. "That *was* you. I'd thought…you know what? It's not important. Serving the Emperor at such a young age. You must be even better than I thought you were, Lucan."

The effect was as good as he'd hoped. Lucan went stiff, staring at Calder with eyes slightly wide, surprised at the sudden use of his name. A second later he regained control of himself—no doubt remembering that he'd introduced *himself* only days before—but even that much was enough of a crack in the façade. It reminded Calder that the man was more than an assassin and a Gardener. He was human…and all humans could be beaten.

Even, in the end, the Emperor.

Out of what Calder could only imagine was petty spite, Lucan didn't respond. He only watched as the orange-eyed captain gathered a group of Guards and surrounded the Consultant, leveling crossbows at him.

She knelt behind Calder, sawing at his bonds with a knife. Calder made a mental note to see what he could do about promoting her. "Are you hurt, sir?

"I think Foster's poisoned," he responded. "Get him to an alchemist as quickly as you can. Any casualties?" Lucan's attack had been focused on Calder and his crew, but it had bruised half a dozen nearby Guards.

"No dead," the captain responded, to which Calder let out a breath of relief.

"Admirable restraint." When the ropes left his arms, the blood started to flow, leaving an irritation like an itch just beneath the skin. Calder rubbed at his wrists. "So, Lucan, would you mind telling me why you decided to linger?"

Lucan looked from one Imperial Guard to another, half his face covered, seemingly deciding which to kill first. "Curiosity. I thought I'd have a word with the Guild Head in charge."

Anger and frustration flickered through Calder before he would suppress them. He'd thought he was past people overlooking his authority, at least here in the palace. "And what makes you think I'm not in charge?"

Lucan answered immediately and with brutal honesty. "Ex-criminals and Navigators don't get set up as the next Emperor. No offense intended, but I expect the Guild Heads proposed you as a disposable alternative. Bait for the Elders, and something to keep the common people happy."

Disturbingly true, and Calder realized he'd been half-squatting to face the sitting man at a more even level. He straightened, feeling a flash of pain in his injured leg. "That's true enough, but no one holds my leash at the moment."

"Trust me," Andel said, from the floor nearby. "It's not a job anyone would want."

Calder wasn't sure if the quartermaster was trying to irritate him, or trying to defuse a dangerous situation with levity. Either way, he could play his part. He turned to the Guard captain.

"You can feel free to leave him tied up a little longer. Good for discipline." To Lucan, he added, "So you can tell me what was so important that you risked execution or capture for the chance to say it."

Lucan met his eyes calmly, and Calder caught a brief impression of the man's Intent. He was absolutely at peace, ready to die if he accomplished his mission.

Calder shivered.

"My life is the least of what's at stake," the Consultant said. "I've already inspected the Optasia, with every intention to sabotage it so you couldn't use it. Now, I've changed my mind."

And I've got Nakothi in my bathtub, Calder thought. "Have you?" he said.

"Yes. You have to destroy it."

Calder spotted his hat where it had fallen to the ground, picked it up, and placed it on his head. If nothing else, the gesture gave him time to think.

Lucan could easily be lying, but the timing was too good. Jerri had spent significant effort trying to persuade him to sit in the Optasia, and all the Guild Heads seemed to agree. The only argument he had against it was a vague unease, along with the desire to prove he wasn't dancing to some Elder's tune.

Now, it seemed like the Consultant was offering him exactly what he wanted: a reason not to trust the Emperor's ancient artifact.

"Consultant Lucan, we might have something to discuss after all."

Before taking Lucan into the Emperor's chambers, Calder had a quick, quiet discussion with the Guard captain.

"He's not going to attack us," Calder insisted. Not only did the Consultant's Intent suggest that he was perfectly content helping, but he'd had a chance to kill Calder in cold blood. He hadn't taken it. Lucan had earned a measure of trust.

"We're at war with his Guild," the captain said stubbornly. Her orange eyes flared. "We were encouraged to ignore even the Emperor's orders in the interest of keeping him safe, and as far as I'm concerned, this is directly relevant to your security."

From what Calder had read of the man, the Emperor was not used to being ignored. "Did you ever actually ignore him?"

"Of course not. He was the Emperor."

With that, the captain proceeded to disregard Calder's wishes and have Lucan searched and bound. The Guards took his shears, the veil over his mouth, and an impressive array of smaller weapons secreted all around his person. Everything from his handkerchief to the lint in his pockets was confiscated, in case it might possibly be invested; which, in normal circumstances, Calder would have applauded. In this case, he insisted they hurry.

He wanted to find the truth about the Optasia as soon as possible.

Finally Lucan was ready, absolutely unarmed and hands bound. Before taking him into the Emperor's old room, Calder pulled the Guard captain aside once again. "Please send someone to retrieve my wife. Don't bring her in yet, but keep her close. I may have some questions for her."

This time, he was thankful that she didn't raise any objection. She only nodded and passed the orders on to a lesser Guard.

Together, Calder and Lucan stood before the Optasia. Though the room around them had been ruined in the confrontation between Teach and Jerri, the throne itself was spotless. Its matrix of steel bars sat polished and gleaming, and Calder felt a vague sense of readiness radiating from the device. As though its Intent was receptive and eager, ready to be used.

"It enhances your perception," Lucan said. "The Emperor had a network of relays built all around the world, statues that look like him. When you connect to the Optasia, it's like your own Intent separates from you, but magnified a thousandfold. Sitting on this throne, you can Read a building on the other side of the planet."

"No wonder he controlled the world," Calder muttered. He couldn't help a little flash of jealousy. He understood better than most how powerful the Emperor actually was, but the man also had access to *this?* It was a wonder he'd ever died.

"Well, he didn't rely on this. He sealed it away from himself. *Rumor* has it that he even employed...watchers, to make sure he never used it. And if he did, to kill him if it drove him insane."

Calder stared at Lucan, sure he'd caught the Consultant in a lie. "He had this device, but he never *used* it?"

Lucan faced the Optasia while emitting sadness and regret, as though remembering his own execution. "One time, that I know of. I gathered that he used it more often when it was built."

"Because of the Great Elders?" If there was one weapon the Elders would have feared, it was this throne.

"Have you tried Reading it?" Lucan asked.

Calder thought back to Jyrine, insisting that he join his Intent with the device as soon as possible. "You might say I was warned not to." Anything Jerri wanted that badly, the Great Elders must want as well. And it pained him even to think that.

"I did," Lucan said grimly. "It's like staring into the eyes of Kelarac himself."

"Kelarac doesn't have any eyes," Calder responded, deliberately casual. Out of the corner of his eye, he watched Lucan's reaction.

Between the Consultant's Intent and minor flickers in his expression, Calder was able to piece together his emotions. He was confused at first, and then suspicious. Not the reaction of someone who had met Kelarac before.

It was good to be sure.

"It's common knowledge," Calder explained. "Haven't you read Fisher's *Treatment of the Aion Sea?*" He wouldn't have, as Calder had made up the title on the spot, but Lucan brought the conversation back to business.

"Feel free to Read this for yourself. It's a conduit straight to the Great Elders. The Emperor was afraid to use the device, lest he draw too much attention, but now...anyone who sits in that thing might as well feed themselves to Kthanikahr."

Might as well feed themselves to Kthanikahr. Kthanikahr, the Worm Lord, was a monster even by the standards of the Great Elders. His body could be seen even now, a miles-long worm half-exposed where it had burrowed in and around a towering mountain. Myth held that Kthanikahr digested his victims alive over a thousand years.

And Jerri had tried to get him to sit on the throne.

Calder forced his anger back when he noticed the wince on Lucan's face. If the man was a strong enough Reader to rock the stone outside like storm-tossed waves, he would certainly pick up on Calder's anger. He was probably causing the Consultant a nasty headache.

"Thank you," Calder said. "I don't believe I need to do that. Let's say I have every reason to believe you're correct."

Calder leaned over to the Guard captain. "Bring me the Consultant the alchemists have in recovery. Meia." The captain saluted and left.

"Consultant Lucan," Calder continued, "I would like your opinion of a small personal matter. Please observe, after which I have a few requests to make of you."

Lucan glanced back at the mesh of silvery bars. "Will you destroy the Optasia?"

"I think you'll find this discussion very relevant," Calder said. Whether he destroyed it or not depended largely on Jerri's behavior. Lucan didn't seem satisfied with that, understandably, so Calder gave him a friendly smile. "As a show of our good faith, I'd like to introduce the newest addition to my crew. I believe you've met."

The Guard captain returned in seconds, perfectly on time. Calder once again reminded himself that the woman deserved some kind of reward. Meia hung over her shoulders, clearly unable to support her own weight, and so close the two women really did look like sisters. Both blond, and if Meia turned her eyes orange, it would have been impossible to think they weren't related.

Lucan showed more emotion than he had since he'd first appeared: pure astonishment. "Meia?"

Meia didn't meet his eyes, for reasons Calder couldn't quite figure out. "I was careless," she said.

She's embarrassed, Calder realized. He forced back a budding smile. That was...cute, really, was the only word for it, but Meia wouldn't appreciate the observation. Even weakened, she could probably tear his arms out of their sockets, so he should probably—

Even his thoughts were interrupted by the surge of frozen hostility radiating from Lucan. On the outside, he didn't look any different, but his eyes were fixed on Calder and his Intent said that he was three seconds away from a bloody murder.

Calder put a hand to his sword, taking a healthy step back. "Meia, please convince your friend. Hurry." If anything, the hostile Intent sharpened. "Hurry, please."

Lucan pulled his wrists apart, passing through the ropes binding his arms together as though they'd rotted off. Calder couldn't believe his eyes. He wouldn't have been able to tear ropes like that without *days* of Intent and focus, while Lucan had seemingly done so in minutes.

The Imperial Guards reacted appropriately, seizing Lucan by the shoulders and slamming him to his knees even as they leveled weapons. Two grabbed Calder and pulled him back.

Then Meia limped up to her Guild-mate, shouldering aside the Guards, and smacked Lucan on the back of the head. "Calm down. If I wanted to escape, I could have done it anytime."

Calder took a deep breath as Lucan's Intent dissipated. *Escape? She's not a prisoner.* He might have said something indignant if he wasn't still worried about Lucan killing everyone in the room.

"He's not keeping you captive?" Lucan asked Meia.

Meia shook her head. "He couldn't. And I'm not a member of his crew, either."

"*Provisional* member," Calder put in. If he could recruit Meia fully to his side, that would be a coup for his authority as Emperor. Imperial Steward. Whatever they called it.

"I already have a Guild, thank you," Meia said, but her attention was still fixed on Lucan.

A Guard pushed Lucan farther toward the ground, but he didn't seem inconvenienced. "So what's wrong with you?"

"More carelessness," Meia said, which was better than saying she'd gotten on the bad side of Jarelys Teach. "When we get back, I'll have to report myself to the Architects."

When Calder saw Lucan's answering smile, he realized that Meia had done exactly what he'd wanted: defused the man's hostility. It had taken a little longer than he'd hoped, but had worked in the end. That was what counted. "You can let him up now."

The Guards looked to the captain, but Calder outranked her. "Release him," he repeated.

They did, taking a step back from Lucan but keeping hands on their weapons. That was probably wise, he had to admit. Lucan remained on his knees out of his own will. "What's the assignment, Meia?" he asked.

"Stop the Elders. They're the highest priority for all of us. The Imperialists can't keep an Emperor on the throne if he's constantly under threat of Elder possession, and the Independents can't successfully establish a new world order if they're only serving the world up to the Elders piece by piece. We should be working together, not against each other."

Not precisely how Calder would have said it, but it was a good answer. If she believed it, and he thought she did, then she should keep working with him. He just had to phrase it the right way...

"Did the Architects order you to do this?" Lucan asked.

Meia's answering pause didn't make her following words sound very persuasive. "They would."

Nonetheless, Lucan seemed pleased. "Maybe they would." He turned to Calder. "Captain, I'm still here because I agree with Meia. Whatever else we do, the Guilds can't dance to an Elder's tune."

You've been dancing to an Elder tune for half your life. Jerri's words. Now suddenly, disturbingly, echoed. He had some soul-searching to do later, but for now, he needed Lucan and Meia both on his side. "That's well said, and your loyalty to the Empire is why I kept you here, Consultant Lucan. Anyone who can look past our current Guild rivalry is someone I can work with. And your personal knowledge of the Optasia will come in handy for our next guest."

Calder waved to the Guard captain, indicating that she should bring Jerri forward.

There was a moment of awkward silence.

Calder cleared his throat and made his intentions more obvious. "Could you bring the next guest in, please?"

Her orange eyes moved around, like she was looking for the next guest somewhere in the room. "I wasn't aware we had another guest, sir."

She was excellent at her job, Calder was sure, but she wasn't a member of his crew. They hadn't worked together long enough to read each other's minds. "My wife, Captain."

She looked as though he'd asked her to haul in the garbage, but she did bow and leave.

Calder turned back to Lucan, who looked somewhat amused. "That would have worked better if I hadn't been forced to explain. More dramatic."

"Are you still in frequent contact with the Sleepless, Captain Marten?"

More than I want to be. He turned to face the door, prepared for his wife's arrival. "Too frequent, Consultant Lucan."

When the door opened, the captain brought Jerri into the room.

She looked much as Calder had last seen her, messy and unkempt in her secondhand prisoner's uniform, though she seemed angrier. She probably hadn't appreciated it when he'd walked out on her, even though the sky was literally cracking apart. She was shackled with enough chains to restrain an Imperial Guard, and Calder almost had them removed before he reconsidered the anger in her eyes. *No. Let her wear them.*

"You just drag me out of my hole whenever you wish, now?" she asked.

Calder gave a flippant response, knowing it would annoy her. "That's one of the perks of being Emperor. I get to drag whomever I like wherever I like."

Jerri barked out a sound too ugly to be a laugh. "You're not the Emperor, but you *could* be, if you would just *listen* to me!"

The same argument as before, but more heated. Well, so be it. He had temper enough to match both of them today, after knowing she'd tried to trick him into killing himself on the Optasia. "In point of fact, that's exactly why I've brought you here. I'm going to ask you a question, and I'd be very interested in listening to the answer."

He gestured to the Optasia, which sat alone and almost forgotten in the corner of the room. "What exactly should I do with this, Jerri?"

"It's a relic of the Emperor," Jerri answered, in a tone that suggested he was an idiot. "You sit in it."

"And then what will happen to me?"

"Calder, I'm not a Reader."

"No, you're a *Soulbound.*" *Something else you lied to me about.* "But I have every faith in your ability to answer the question."

She sighed, as though giving into a child's demands. "As I understand it, the device will expand your awareness. Thanks to a network of relays, you'll be able to Read practically anything on the planet from this spot."

Almost word-for-word how Lucan had explained it. So she understood the Optasia perfectly. "Including the Great Elders," he prompted, waiting for her to admit it.

"Of *course* including the Great Elders. That's the whole point. This is the only way for you to understand them, and to negotiate with them on an equal level. With you on the throne, humanity will finally have someone to speak to the Elders on our behalf. You'll have a seat among the immortals, Calder. It's something we all desperately need."

Once again, she was trying to convince him he would be saving the world. Not handing his body over as a husk for the Elders. Finally, he'd caught her in an outright lie. He turned to Lucan.

"We've heard from the crazed Elder cultist, and now let's hear from a neutral party. Jerri, Lucan here is a Consultant who came here to sabotage the Optasia. He Read the throne for himself, and instead of leaving, he stayed here to warn me."

"And you call him a neutral party?" Jerri asked, but quickly latched on to a different detail. She turned away from Calder to Lucan. "Consultant Lucan, did you say?"

"Jyrine," Lucan said, shocking Calder. "I'm glad you made it out alive."

Of course. They were practically cellmates. Next door in the Consultant dungeon, they must have gotten to know each other. For an instant, a suspicion bloomed: if they knew each other already, how could he possibly trust anything Lucan said? Maybe he was Sleepless himself.

But if this was all part of their plan, they would have concealed their connection. He would never have found out. In fact, this could be an advantage: if Jerri knew Lucan, then she knew he was a Reader. She'd know he was telling the truth.

"Lucan, what would happen to me if I tried to use the Optasia?"

The Consultant didn't hesitate. "You would go insane in minutes. Perhaps seconds. The Great Elders would core you like an apple and put whatever they wanted in your place." No member of the Sleepless would warn him like this; they would leave him to walk blindly into danger.

"That's some compelling imagery," Calder said. "Jerri, your rebuttal?"

But he could see that his wife's mind was elsewhere.

As soon as she heard the Consultant's name, Jerri recalled a vivid memory. Crouched in her cold cell on the Gray Island, she listened as Lucan spoke to his ally. To Shera.

She almost shivered at the unnatural timing of this 'coincidence.' Kelarac was controlling the game now, and he had placed her within reach of Shera's allies. "Lucan," she said. "The Consultant named Shera visited you while you were in prison. Do you know her well?"

Lucan's response was absolutely calm. "We've worked together."

That was confirmation enough for Jerri. She turned to his blond partner. Meia? Maia? Something like that. "How about you? Do you know Shera?"

"I don't believe I'm required to answer you, madam," Meia said, but Jerri knew the truth. Kelarac had delivered two of Shera's closest allies into her hands.

She nodded, turning back to Calder. "You've met Shera before. She's tried to kill both of us. She *did* kill Urzaia. Would you trust her companions?"

"Consultant Shera and I have a separate account to balance," Calder said. "If I refused to do business with any Guild whose members have attempted to execute me in the past, I'd be working alone. Or maybe with the Greenwardens," he added.

He was being intentionally obstinate; ignoring her logic and making a point to say the opposite of whatever she did. In other circumstances, she could try and get him alone, make him engage her argument.

But she had to take this opportunity, whatever it cost her. *You must not let the Killer meet the King.*

"I've been warned about Shera quite recently," Jerri said, hoping he would sense sincerity in her Intent. "However little you know of her, let me assure you: she is the greatest threat to you and to the future of humanity, not any Guild."

Calder's brow furrowed, and his hand began crawling for his pistol. "*Recently?* Who warned you, Jerri?"

"She's your enemy, Calder, whether you believe it or not," Jerri said. She was close to him now, the Guards closing in on her from every direction. "And whether you *like* it or not, I'm still your ally."

She spun to face Meia, drawing power from her earring. The Vessel, the source of her power, delivered to her by Kelarac himself.

There were two targets here, two allies of the Killer, but she knew she would only get one shot. And if she could eliminate only one target, she'd prefer to remove Meia; the blond Consultant was a stranger, while Lucan had listened to her stories while they were both captives of his Guild. If she had to kill one and spare the other, she would prefer it if Lucan walked away.

"Stop her!" Calder shouted, drawing his sword instead of his gun. The Guards shoved her to the ground, but she had already released a shot of green flame. It blasted over Calder's shoulder, tearing through the air with palpable hunger.

Meia stood with orange eyes wide, staring at her approaching death. In the instant before the blast struck, Jerri knew she had succeeded. Meia couldn't escape.

Calder twisted, trying to get his orange-spotted blade between Meia and the fire, but he was too slow. He couldn't stop it.

But Lucan threw out a hand.

Meia collapsed as though weighted down, like every inch of her clothing was suddenly anchored to the floor. Jerri's attack tore through the wall of the Emperor's room, leaving a smoldering hole the size of a bullet.

I've failed. The Guards piled on top of her, practically smothering her with their weight, and she knew she had only seconds before they pried her earring away. She couldn't even see Meia, so her only option was to burn her way free of the Guards if she wanted to try again.

Her Vessel raged inside her, begging her to incinerate the bodies in her way, but she forced it down. Calder would never trust her again

"Her earring!" Calder shouted. "The earring is the Vessel!"

She was surrounded in a cage of limbs, both human and otherwise. The Kameira enhancements of the Imperial Guards blocked her in a menagerie of tentacles, talons, claws, and scales. But through the chaos, she caught a glimpse of another face; pressed, like hers, against the floor.

Lucan's dark skin was a shade too pale, and his eyelids fluttered as though he hovered on the verge of passing out, but he looked as though he recognized her. And Jerri saw Kelarac's will.

She wished it didn't have to be Lucan, but this was one last Elder-sent chance to remove one of Shera's greatest allies. The moment was here, she had her earring, and she didn't even have to kill anyone else. Truly, the Great Elders had set the stage.

Though she knew Lucan wouldn't hear her over the chaos, she felt she had to say something. "I'm sorry," she said.

Her Vessel wasn't sorry. It crowed triumph.

Calder shouted louder, reaching closer, trying to grab her ear.

A wave of dry heat blasted up as a single bolt of green flame flashed out from Jerri's hand. It drilled into Lucan's stomach.

The Guards saw the flash of light on her face, tearing out the earring and leaving a bloody hole in her ear. But it was too late. Jerri let them drag her off back to her cell, knowing that her task was over. She had already won.

Lucan was dead.

The Guards were still shackling her to the walls, growling threats about her execution, when Calder marched in. He still held his sword, as though he'd forgotten its existence, and he stared at her in undisguised horror.

Even now, that still hurt.

"Why?" Calder asked. "Why him?"

Jerri spoke simply, knowing he would recognize honesty. "That might be the last chance I get to strike a blow against Shera. I had to make it count."

"Because *she's* the greatest threat." He pointed to Jerri with the tip of his sword. "Who told you that, Jerri?"

"Who do you think?"

He nodded as though she'd confirmed his every suspicion, then gestured to the Guard nearest the door. An instant later the door slammed shut, leaving Jerri once again in darkness.

CHAPTER SEVENTEEN

No two Kanatalia workshops look the same—just in the Capital, Calder had seen some covered in quicklamps like trees with glowing fruit, some with huge glass tanks on the roof, and others that were built like round domes instead of square boxes. He supposed it had to do with the types of experiments they ran in there, but no one got inside a workshop without strict Guild approval.

They didn't look alike, but they all smelled identical. It was what he imagined acid would smell like, mixed liberally with soap and something coppery. His imagination told him it must be blood, and his logic told him it was probably copper.

But just in case the alchemists needed to top off their blood-tank today, he tried to stay inconspicuous as he lurked behind their workshop. He wanted to catch one alchemist alone, not a group of guards changing shifts.

On every other side of the building except this one, the workshop had ten yards or so of clearance. Here, in the back, it was little more than an alley: a few feet of street separating a back exit and the brick wall of a cannery. An aluminum box the size of a carriage took up the entire space, and the copper-acid-soap smell wafted most strongly from that direction. It made Calder's hours of waiting all the more unpleasant, but it also took up every inch of space between the alchemical workshop and the cannery. It was wedged in so tightly that the mice had to scamper over the top of the box to get past.

Which meant that Calder only had to huddle next to the metal box when the guards came by. They would unshutter their quicklamp, shine a quick flash of light down the alley to make sure the box was still intact and unopened, and walk away.

A broken half of a bottle and a scrap of coat told him that some homeless Capital citizens had used this tactic before to steal a good night's sleep. It was to his good fortune that none of them had tried it tonight. At least, not on his side of the box.

A glimpse of motion, the sound of furtive shuffling, and the sight of a ragged shadow made him convinced that someone was rummaging through something on the other side. He didn't begrudge this mysterious person their space, though he did wonder how they avoided being spotted. The patrols always came from that side, so the guards had to see this figure every time they opened their quicklamp. But they never said a word, simply walking away.

Kanatalia was more generous to squatters than he would have expected.

It was well after midnight before the rear door opened. By this time, Calder was more irritated at the work habits of alchemists than anything else. Who worked past midnight? Why couldn't they leave promptly at sunset, like everyone else? They could have been considerate enough to spare him over six hours of waiting in the ice-cold dark as the winter wind froze his coat to his body.

Alchemists. Always thinking of themselves.

But he pasted a big smile on his face as the opening exit almost crushed him against the brick wall. The man walking out of the workshop wore thick gloves, a leather apron that hung down past his knees, and a pair of goggles currently pushed up onto his forehead. The skin around his eyes was a shade paler than elsewhere, showing where the goggles usually rested.

The man had a shock of pure black hair, but lines at the corners of his eyes showed that he was at least twenty years older than Calder. He was carrying a sealed glass cylinder in both gloved hands, and something that looked like a six-legged cat floated within, suspended in a bluish fluid. He moved as though he were hauling something heavy, but he stopped when he saw Calder.

"Charity is three days away. If you have a medical issue, I'm afraid I can't help you. I'm not that kind of alchemist."

Calder pointedly adjusted his hat. He'd worn the three-cornered hat and his dark blue coat because he thought it made him look more like a Navigator. Each of his coat buttons had the Navigator crest on them. What more did he have to do?

"I'm not looking for charity, sir, but if you're feeling charitable you could spare a moment to hear me out."

The alchemist grunted as he pushed past Calder toward the metal box. "Give me a second. If I keep holding this thing, it might come back to life."

He did something to the side of the box, Calder couldn't see what, and the entire metal top lifted straight off. It was supported at each corner by a metal pole, which together raised the top panel of the box a few feet up. The smell of burning blood and soap grew stronger as the alchemist shoved his glass cylinder inside. The sound of shattering glass followed him, as well as something that sounded suspiciously like the yowl of a cat.

The alchemist turned back to Calder as the box slowly hissed shut behind him. "Now then, what can I help you with?" His tone made it sound more like, "Go die in a hole."

There was no sense in antagonizing someone while asking for a favor, so Calder did his best to radiate pleasant contentment. "My name is Captain Calder Marten, of the Guild of Navigators." He extended a hand.

The alchemist actually leaned over and inspected the hand, sniffing at Calder's palm, before pulling his own glove off and shaking. Calder had known dogs that were more discreet.

"Lampson," the alchemist said. That was all.

"An honor to meet you, Mr. Lampson. Now, I apologize for approaching you in this manner, but I was looking to purchase some alchemicals, and I was wondering if you might help me."

Lampson squinted at him. "The chapter house will sell to you, if you're a Navigator. Guild members get thirty percent off the street price."

Calder knew about the discount, which the honorable Guild of Alchemists was only inclined to offer because they originally marked each of their potions up eighty percent. "Thank you for your recommendation, but I've already been to the chapter house. I'm afraid they weren't able to satisfy my specific needs."

The alchemist glanced him up and down once. "As I said, I'm not the sort of medical alchemist you're looking for. I deal primarily in organ processing and storage, so unless you'd care to make a donation..."

"I like all my organs where they are, though I appreciate the offer. It's less of a service that I'd like to purchase from you, and more a selection of your stock. You see, I have a wall in my home that I would like to demolish."

Lampson's mouth opened in a silent 'ah.' "There's a crew of workmen I can recommend, if you'll give me a few moments to retrieve their information. They're highly rated by the Guild in their use of munitions."

Calder clapped the man on the shoulder and chuckled, as though he'd made a joke. "No, no, that won't be necessary. I'd not want to trouble them."

"Navigators. Can't say I'm surprised. What are you looking for?"

"What do you sell to the army?"

Lampson passed a hand over his face. "Look. Listen. I...look. If this wall is in the Capital..."

"It's a continent away."

"...if it's in the Capital, this will get back to me. The Guild understands if we do some business on our own initiative, as long as the workshop gets its fair cut, but if this draws the Imperial Guard down on me, I'll paint them a picture of you if I have to. I'll even give them your alias, if that will help them somehow."

An alias. That would have been a good idea. He'd been trying to add a sense of credibility by giving his name, in case Lampson checked with the Navigator's Guild, but in hindsight that was stupid. The alchemist wouldn't be bothered to check his name, and an alias could save him trouble down the road. It was amazing how quickly you forgot the basics.

"It's *not* in the Capital," Calder assured him. "I'm setting sail for Vandenyas before the sun rises, if all goes right." It was probably too late, but he'd decided to start throwing a few lies into the mix. Better now than never.

"Well, either way, I'm going to need to spread the marks around if we want to get this done. And as I don't see a valise packed with paper anywhere, you should make a visit to the bank. While you're doing that, I can take inventory and see what we have, but I'll warn you now, it would be better if you had a real alchemist along. On your own, you're more likely to blow your ship to splinters than to demolish your...wall."

If Calder had an alchemist aboard, as many Navigators did, then he wouldn't be begging in an alley behind a workshop. But at the moment, there was a more pressing issue in play. "That's a reasonable concern, and I thank you for it. But on the matter of payment, I was thinking of something less formal."

The alchemist's eyebrows climbed so high that they vanished into his messy black hair. "You want me to give you a barrel of Othaghor's Fire on faith and favors?"

It wasn't as unreasonable as he was making it sound, Calder was sure. Favors were a common currency between the different Guilds, and typically considered a denomination higher than goldmarks. No amount of money would call the Blackwatch to your side when you wanted them; only a direct investigation followed by an official Guild action could do that. But if a Watchman owed you a favor, then you had someone to tell you if that shadow tapping your window is a rogue tree branch or a soul-eating minion of Urg'naut.

And among the Guilds, favors from the Navigators were prime quality. Navigators were required for any business on, in, or through the Aion Sea, so space on a Navigator's vessel—at least, on the vessel of any Navigator not currently shackled by an Imperial debt—was worth an appropriate pile of gold. If Calder owed Lampson a favor, the alchemist could exchange it for rare Kameira corpses from Aion islands, for a free delivery to Izyria, or even for passage to virtually any coastal city in the Empire. It was practically a priceless coin, and one that Calder didn't spend lightly. If he'd had any silvermarks to spare, he would have begun by negotiating a price.

But Andel kept a miser's grip on the purse-strings, and anything that trickled to Calder was soaked up by the normal expense of a Navigator mission or by his endless debt.

It was a good deal for Lampson, which was why Calder didn't entirely expect the man's suddenly slumped shoulders or his dejected sigh. "I might have known. Well, I'm not your man, Captain. Try the next one of my colleagues who takes a visit to the dump."

Calder glanced around, half-expecting to see some reason for the man's sudden refusal. Maybe an Imperial Guard watching from the end of the alley, or the Kanatalia Guild Head on a sudden inspection. "I'm sure you're aware, the service of a Navigator can be very valuable."

"Sure, yes. But there's two problems with that. First, you're too young to be a Navigator Captain."

Calder reached beneath his coat and into his jacket to withdraw his Guild crest, but Lampson held up a hand to stop him. "I don't doubt you're a member of the Guild, because you wouldn't come this far without some kind of proof, but there's no way in the Emperor's good name that they've given you your own ship. So what good is your favor to me? That's one problem, and the *second* is that you're a Navigator."

He spread his hands helplessly. "I've heard too many stories to trust Navigators in the bright light of day. And here you are in Urg'naut's shadow, lurking in an alley to ambush me. I don't think your captain knows anything about this, and I think once he does, you'll already have a ship full of munitions for free."

Despite his every effort, Calder had misplaced his business smile. "I'd be happy to draft up a contract, if you'd like."

"I'm sure, but who would we get to enforce such a contract? This isn't exactly a Guild-approved transaction. They'll let me go my way as long as they don't get involved, but if I have to have a Guild representative to witness a contract, they'll want to know everything's fair. All the more so if we hire a Witness. And if we don't go that far, well, who's going to defend my rights if you decide to drop anchor on the back end of Vandenyas?"

Calder did his best to salvage the situation, but it was clear that this ship had sunk. That was one prospect down, and Lampson would likely tell the guards to check more carefully behind the workshop tomorrow. But there were other workshops in the Capital, and he wasn't willing to give up yet.

He'd crawl through freezing alleys every night, if it meant keeping his promise to Urzaia Woodsman.

Lampson finally escaped his grasp, slamming and bolting the door behind him as he returned to the workshop. Which left Calder standing in the wind next to a box of alchemical garbage.

Five years in a Guild, and look how glamorous his life had become.

Metallic thunder rolled out, like someone drumming on a steel can. At first he thought it was coming from inside the workshop, but he still reacted to the noise by glancing around the alley.

So he saw a dark, ragged shape clambering over the giant metal box toward him. It was a shadow surrounded by enough torn edges to completely obscure its shape, so in the split second he saw it, Calder jumped like he'd seen an Elderspawn wildcat.

His body was shocked into motion with a lightning bolt of panic, and he scrambled to pull his cutlass from its sheath. He had it in his hand, his training keeping the tip steady even though his hand *felt* like it was shaking, even as he cursed his own instincts. He should have gone for his gun. Why hadn't he? Basic sword training from his father, advanced instruction from his mother, solo dueling drills on the deck of *The Testament,* and it all added up to him relying on a length of mundane metal instead of the miracle of modern weapons technology he kept inside his coat.

Since Dalton Foster had joined his crew, the man had done a complete upgrade on the ship's small armory. If Calder ever decided to sell his sidearm, he could somewhat accurately bill it as a 'Dalton Foster original,' which he estimated would increase the value by at least a hundred goldmarks. But here, when he might actually need the carefully crafted weapon of a master gun-smith, he'd drawn his sword instead.

All this self-recrimination flitted through his mind in the beat of a hum-mingbird's wing, while the creature of hazy darkness came to perch on the edge of the alchemists' dump.

Tilting its head, it spoke.

"Um...hello," it said.

She said. Judging by the voice alone, she sounded like a little girl.

A younger Calder would have immediately sheathed his sword for fear of scaring her, but he'd spent the past five years sailing the Aion Sea and most of the preceding two in the Blackwatch. He had enough experience with Elders to know that they could imitate human voices better than human shapes.

"Hello," he said, cautiously. Whether it was an Elderspawn monstrosity in that shadow or a girl in a stiff and ragged cloak, a greeting couldn't hurt.

"I'm not..." she kept speaking, but her voice dropped too low for him to hear it. "...okay?" she finished.

Calder peered closer into the shadows. Now that he was paying attention, he could read the darkness to some degree—the storm of chaos around her head was just hair, frizzy and wild as though it had never been combed. The shroud on her body meant she was wrapped in clothes too big for her, and her face...as he looked, he could see that her pale skin had been smudged with grime.

So one of the residents of this street had come to sleep here after all. He felt a surge of guilt, and finally sheathed his sword. It was pitiful enough that a little girl should have to spend the night in an alley behind an alchemical workshop; he didn't have to threaten her as well.

And if she was an Elderspawn who had perfected her disguise to this degree, then as the great strategist Loreli had once said, *"Sometimes one is simply beaten."*

"I beg your pardon," he said, holding his hands out to demonstrate that he'd left his weapon behind. Very slowly, he rummaged around in his coat pockets. He hadn't taken a billfold with him, having not expected a cash transaction tonight, but he should have *something*. He came up a few seconds later with four crumpled marks, six copper bits, and a tired silvermark. He presented them to her in both palms, as though offering seed to a sparrow. "I'm afraid this is all I have on me." A sudden idea struck him, and he added, "Though if you need a place to stay tonight, I have a ship in the harbor. We're anchored through morning."

The girl's entire outline shook briefly as she shivered. "Ah. That's not. I have..." She held up a wine bottle and shook it. The liquid within sloshed, and as it did, it glowed a pale orange.

He was no alchemist, but he suspected that wasn't actually wine.

"You needed." She didn't finish the sentence, but instead made an explosion noise and moved her hands apart, demonstrating a blast.

Calder eyed the bottle. "That's not going to explode, is it?"

She shook her head vigorously, and then jerked her head at the big metal box beneath her. Reaching her hand down, she gave the side a slap.

Just as before, the top lifted with a steady hiss, this time carrying her along with it.

"Look," she said, now from overhead.

With a hesitant glance up at the lid—if he leaned in to look and the top crashed back into place, he was afraid it would smash his head like a grape—he peeked inside.

It wasn't the dump he'd expected. Only one corner was walled off to contain garbage, with about the same capacity as a trash-bin. The shattered remnants of Lampson's cylinder lay in that section, liquid pooling at the bottom but not spreading to the rest of the box. The six-legged cat was nowhere to be seen.

Outside of that partition, the space looked like a miniature alchemist's workshop.

Rows of colorful potions were displayed on a short rack against the far wall, and a pair of goggles sat next to a pair of gloves on a folded apron next to them. A stack of books bore titles like, *Effusions of the Various Kameira in the Southwest* and *A Lexicon of Philters,* while a miniature table and stool dominated the remainder of the floor. The table was covered in notes, diagrams, and sketches, while the stool was padded with a small cushion. A half-eaten sandwich rested on a plate.

Of all the things Calder had imagined might be inside the mysterious metal box, he had never considered this.

His attention turned back to the desk. With the lid closed, even someone six inches shorter than Calder would have to work with their neck bent. Calder himself would have had to lie halfway over the table, if he were seated on the stool. It would be worse than working in a closet.

He glanced up at the girl, and this close, he could tell that the complex alchemical scent was coming from *her*, not from her lab. He could also see her face in much more detail, and she was looking at him with a childlike expression of apprehension. Waiting for his opinion.

"Are you an alchemist?" he asked as steadily as he could.

She smiled a little, nodded, then reconsidered. After another few seconds, she shook her head. "Not Guild," she whispered. "I was an apprentice."

He wouldn't ordinarily ask for the personal history of this strange back-alley alchemist, but she'd already shown him her home. He could use a few more details. "What happened?"

She fidgeted, avoiding his gaze. "Delivery to the palace. I messed it up. Imperial Guard didn't want me..." she trailed off again before picking the sentence back up. "...back here. The alchemists let me use what they don't need."

Calder still wasn't sure how she'd ended up in a sealed mechanical box, but he could piece the rest of the story together well enough. She'd continued her alchemical studies, obviously, but she couldn't work for the Guild if the Imperial Guards were after her. He couldn't imagine how she did any business in the Capital at all, in a situation like that.

"...quicklamps?" she asked. He missed the first half of the question.

"Do I *have* quicklamps? Yes, on the ship." Quicklamps were effectively glass jars of glowing liquid, and they could be brightened or dimmed to almost nothing by adjusting an alchemical valve. They were much safer than traditional lanterns on a ship, for two reasons: first, quicklamp glass was tempered by alchemists, and could withstand impact that most lanterns could not. Second, quicklamp fluid on its own was difficult to ignite and put out very little heat. So no one could be burned by a quicklamp, and if it *did* break, it wouldn't light the ship on fire. There would just be some luminescent paint on the boards for a while. It would only go up in flames if they were struck by lightning or attacked by some sort of fire-breathing Kameira—a dropped match wouldn't do it—and in those cases, the ship was in danger anyway.

You could buy fifty lanterns, a cask of oil, and a crate of candles for the price of one quicklamp, but no solution was perfect.

"Fuse?" she asked. "Powder? Alphidalious extract? Black amber resin?"

"Fuses and powder, but extract...can you spell that for me?"

She shrugged and slid off the lid of her box, slipping inside with the fluid motion of a stage performer. "Okay. I have it. With all that, I can make a bomb."

Calder had been waiting at the bottom of a cold, black hole, and now he was watching a rope ladder slowly drift down from the heavens. "You're willing to make explosives for me?"

By this time, she was scuttling around her little cabin, packing everything she could into a cloth pack. She carefully slipped a pack of sealed tubes into a pocket, buttoned the pocket shut, and looked up at him. "Favor," she said firmly.

So she'd heard him already, and she was ready to take the deal. He would have preferred a skilled Guild alchemist, but anyone who would work without deepening his debt was a miracle to him. "Of course, yes! I'll have a contract drafted up, if you like."

She pushed a book into her pack before looking back up at him. "Take me with you."

He hesitated. Except in the unbelievably unlikely coincidence that she wanted to go to the city of Axciss in Izyria, anywhere he could take her would be out of the way. "I have urgent business in Izyria," he said. "I need to put your explosives to work. But if it's somewhere close...where would you like to go?"

"Somewhere," she whispered, then shook her head as though correcting herself. "Anywhere."

She hugged her pack to her chest, looking at him like she expected him to object.

On the contrary, while it was out of his expectations, this was better than he could have hoped. He could take her, she could do her alchemist's work on the journey, thus saving them time in the Capital. And then he could dump her in Axciss and be done.

Well, maybe not in Axciss. There would be a hunt for unregistered alchemists in Axciss after an explosion at the arena. Somewhere else on the Izyrian coast, then.

"I'm certain we can find you somewhere. My...a woman of my close acquaintance is from Vandenyas." At this point, he wasn't sure how to describe his relationship with Jerri, so he skipped past it. "We can set you up there, where it's warm, after we're done in Izyria. Unless you'd prefer—"

She cut him off by spearing him with her eyes. This was the most resolute he'd seen her, and suddenly she looked years older. "Take me with you. On your ship. I don't want to be here anymore."

That should have required a little more deliberation, and he certainly should consult with his crew. Jerri might enjoy having another woman onboard, or she might not. And Andel wouldn't appreciate having to spread their already-meager income around further. He was already being surprisingly agreeable about this daring plan to rescue Urzaia, considering that a daring rescue plan is what had led to Calder's debt to the throne in the first place. Foster...Foster would grumble about anything, but he was actually the least likely to raise a real objection.

But the one asking him was a young girl dressed in rags who was forced to practice alchemy in what amounted to a giant garbage bin. Sympathy made the decision for him.

"What's your name?" he asked softly.

"Petal."

There was one other thing he had to know, just to make sure he didn't add kidnapping and endangerment of a child to his growing list of Imperial crimes. "And how old are you, Petal?"

She cast her gaze down to the street as though embarrassed. "Twenty-three," she said.

Calder stared at her. Light and life. She was older than he was.

CHAPTER EIGHTEEN

*From the moment Guild Head Kern joined the battle, our troops were no longer
required. I would call the destruction 'absolute.'*

— FROM THE OFFICIAL REPORT OF THE SOUTH SEA REBELLION

In the last week, Calder had spent more time in carriages than in the
entire rest of his life combined. They weren't nearly as comfortable as he
thought they should be.

He paused with his pen halfway to the page, looking to Andel. "How do
you say, 'I'm sorry my wife killed your assassin?'"

"Not like that."

Calder, Andel, and General Teach were all riding together, and even
though this carriage had been constructed to the Emperor's specifications,
it was still crowded with that much armor. Teach took up more space than
Calder and Andel combined, her armor filling the space with the smell of
iron and oil.

These two were not the first people he'd ask for advice regarding a diplo-
matic letter, but they were all he had. He'd wanted a Consultant's touch, but
Meia was gone. The medical alchemists in charge of her care had come in to
an empty bed, and the Imperial Guards outside the doors never saw a thing.
A thorough search of the Imperial Palace afterward had revealed no trace of
her. Once again, Meia had disappeared.

Though if she chose to pop up in the middle of this very carriage, he still
wouldn't be entirely surprised.

"An official apology would be a mistake," Teach put in. She was watching
the streets through a crack in the window, presumably looking for threats, but
she had enough spare attention to criticize his letter. "It implies that you are
in some way responsible. You can express your condolences, since you did not
officially execute the Consultant, but it might ring hollow. Given that we're
preparing to attack their headquarters."

That the Imperialist Guilds were gathering for an attack was common
knowledge, even if their target was a secret. A secret to most, at any rate.
Calder was certain that the Consultants would know exactly what they were
planning, and would be coming up with some way to counter them.

"I'm still not certain I *want* to attack the Consultant's Guild," Calder said,
though it was mostly an empty protest. The Navigators were recalling to the

Capital and stocking up on supplies, the Imperial Guards had begun training for naval warfare, and the Magisters were bringing up what weapons they could. The Witnesses had published an article in the news-sheets exonerating the Imperialist Guilds for "any attacks they may conduct in the pursuit of justice." The tide was going out, and Calder could see it.

But he couldn't fight the feeling that he was playing straight into someone else's hands.

Teach didn't respond to his words, but she shook her head faintly as she kept watch out the window. Andel was the one to speak up, and surprisingly, he did so without a trace of mockery. "You should recognize when a battle is lost, Captain."

"If the battle's already lost, I can't imagine why we're still sending our troops."

Andel didn't rise to the bait. "Not that battle. Yours. The Guilds are moving out, and your only hope of maintaining your position is to move with them."

Calder turned to him, and out of respect for the man's forthright honesty, he responded in kind. "Even if this is an Elder plot? Even if this is Othaghor dividing us up piece by piece, to be devoured one at a time?"

Andel leaned forward, the White Sun of the Luminians swinging at the end of its silver chain. "'The educated man embraces the inevitable.' Sadesthenes, I believe."

"I hate it when you use Sadesthenes against me," Calder said.

"Imagine how the rest of us feel."

He was right. Calder was still trying to fight yesterday's battle, something most of the ancient scholars would have counseled him against. "So I should just give up, then?"

Predictably, Andel had an answer for that, too. "We're fighting them, whether you like it or not. So if there's going to be a battle, we may as well figure out how to win."

Kelarac's gold-capped smile appeared in Calder's mind. He was sure that the Great Elder would have been delighted with the way events were proceeding. But that didn't mean Andel was wrong; if they really were cornered by the Elders, the only way out was through.

The only thing worse than getting forced into a battle was getting forced into a *losing* battle.

"Very well," Calder said, nodding to Andel to concede the point. "Then we've already taken our first step toward victory. We're heading to see Kern."

Teach sighed. "Which will either lead to victory or to your gruesome death." She had been very much against Calder personally coming on this little carriage ride, and had agreed only on the premise that she accompany him.

"If you're worried that it will be too dangerous, you could have brought more Guards."

"They wouldn't help. Baldesar Kern is loyal and stable enough, but if he decides to kill you, I'm the only one that can hold him back long enough for you to escape." She didn't claim that she could kill him, Calder noticed. Only that she could temporarily keep him in check. That said everything he needed to know about Kern's ability.

"I'm sorry to worry you," Calder said. "But while I'm at it, I should tell you that I'll be leading the attack on the Gray Island."

Teach turned from the window at last to glare at him, and her attention carried the baleful, deadly aura of Tyrfang's Intent. It was hard not to shrink back. "Absolutely not. Two minutes ago you didn't want the attack at all."

"I can change my mind quickly, when necessary. I'm decisive."

"That's a flattering word for it," Andel said.

"As long as we're trying to win, then I need to be there. I captain the fastest ship in the Navigator fleet, I can use the Emperor's crown, and I need a reputation as someone who handles my problems personally. I won't fight if I can help it at all—"

"I was worried for a moment there," Andel murmured.

"—but I have to be there. If only to show the people that I can do something myself."

"If you want to do something, then find a way to use the Optasia," Teach insisted. After Lucan's testimony, Calder had demanded a more thorough investigation into the state of the Emperor's throne. Finally, they had taken a volunteer Reader from one of the Imperial Prisons and allowed him to briefly use the Optasia—under careful supervision—in exchange for a commuted sentence.

After five minutes, the man had clawed out his own eyes. He would spend the rest of his days in a Luminian sanatorium.

The carriage slowed, clattering to a halt, and Calder opened the door without waiting for Teach. "Yes, well, at the moment I'm somewhat attached to my eyes."

When they'd boarded the carriage, Teach had said only that it would take them "to Baldesar Kern." Calder had assumed they would end up at a chapter house, or a mansion, or maybe a fortress of some kind.

He'd never expected the Head of the Champion's Guild to live in a quaint little townhouse, with a yard and a white-painted fence. Patches of flowers grew in front of the porch, where a pair of rocking chairs sat side-by-side. The door was bright blue and the roof tiles a matching shade; it looked like the home of a grandmother. He half-expected to see a pie cooling on the windowsill.

Guild Head Kern himself knelt by a section of wooden fence. He wasn't much taller than Calder, but he was broad, with enough solid muscle to suggest that his skin was packed with rocks. His black hair was winged with silver, and he squinted at the fence in utter concentration. He'd rolled his sleeves up so that only his bare forearms were splattered with paint.

Very delicately, he dipped his paintbrush into the can at his side. When it came up dripping white, he brushed it lightly against the fencepost, as though afraid that he might break the wooden plank if he pressed any harder.

As Calder dismounted from the carriage, he examined the full length of the fence. Only the segment in the middle was new, unpainted wood; the rest of the posts in the row were white and somewhat weathered; they might have stood there for years.

It was so mundane that Calder almost couldn't believe this was the Head of the Champions. The man who had singlehandedly sent a rebel fleet down to Kelarac. The series of novels about his legend were labeled "Not Suitable For Children," due to their expressions of extreme violence.

"I hope you don't mind if I keep working as we talk," Kern said, squinting at the fence as he applied another stripe of paint. "It's almost lunchtime, and I have to take my roast out of the oven."

Calder was standing in the man's yard, wearing the Emperor's old clothes, and Kern obviously knew who he was. Yet he didn't seem to care.

In a way, that made things easier.

Teach stood by the carriage, keeping watch over Calder, and Andel started to walk over. Calder motioned for him to stop. "Of course I don't mind. Would you like some help?"

Kern flashed him a smile. "Promised I'd do it myself, or I'd take you up on that. It would do you good to get some stains on those clothes."

Calder glanced down at the layers of dark purple, violet, and lavender that he'd been forced to wear today. "I assure you, they're not mine."

"I know."

Silence stretched as Kern kept painting, moving as though he expected his paintbrush to shatter. He was waiting for Calder to make the first move, and he seemed like a man who appreciated the blunt approach, so Calder dove right in.

"I want the support of the Champions."

"I'm sure you do," Kern said. He sounded gentle, without the edge of sarcasm Calder might have expected.

"We're currently planning a major military action, and having the Champions along would go a long way toward ensuring a decisive victory."

Kern's brush paused. "A major military action. I don't mean to seem hostile, Captain Marten, but have you ever served in the Imperial Army?"

"I've drawn my sword before," Calder said, the words dry. "I've fought Elderspawn, cultists, rebels, Consultant assassins, Imperial Guards, Kameira... you name it, I've crossed swords with it."

"I would expect no less from a Navigator Captain. But I'm asking you if you've ever been a part of an army."

Calder thought back to the clash between the Blackwatch and the Consultants. That might count as a battle, but hardly as an army. "I have not."

"It's nothing to be ashamed of. Most people haven't. We've been an Empire so long that precious few of us have ever been soldiers. Even if you had, the Imperial Army is effectively a standing police force." He returned to his work, moving his paintbrush carefully up the fence. "I may have lost my point somewhere in there. Forgive me."

Calder had been waiting for the Guild Head's argument so that he could counter it, but now he'd lost his balance. He tried to regain the initiative. "Your experience alone would be invaluable. And I know the Champions are more loyal to the Empire than any other Guild."

"Hmmmm. The Empire. That's tricky." He tucked paint into the last few corners of a fencepost, sat back on his heels, and examined his handiwork.

"What's tricky?" Calder prompted.

"Is there an Empire without the Emperor?" He waved a hand before Calder could respond. "I suspect you're tired of people calling you a figurehead. I know you didn't take the job unless you had the hope of real power someday, so I won't hammer on that. But the fact remains that my loyalty was not to the idea of a united Aurelian Empire, it was to one man. Now that the man is gone, who am I fighting for?"

He was trying to mire Calder in an argument. Whether he'd been doing it intentionally or not, he was keeping the focus on the intangible aspects of Calder's position, taking the subject away from the Champions. If Calder couldn't keep the conversation grounded, it would go nowhere.

"Will the Champions commit to fight for the Empire, or not?" Calder spoke firmly, holding the man's gaze, hoping he would be impressed rather than offended by blunt speech.

Kern tapped excess paint off his brush, watching Calder. "I will not commit the Champions to your cause. First, we don't believe in it. Some of us think your Guilds are crazy for trying to hold the Empire together, some of us agree with the Regents that we'd be better off governing each region separately, and many of us just don't care much. Second, we don't believe in *you*. You're young, you're no one, and you've come out of nowhere. You're clearly just a puppet for the Guild Heads, but we don't understand why they need you at all."

He nodded to someone over Calder's shoulder. "No disrespect intended to General Teach. But that's why I *will* not call up an army of Champions to your rescue. There's a more pressing issue: I *can't*." Kern's brush glided smoothly over the wood.

"There is no Champion's Guild anymore. There are only Champions. I'm the Guild Head no longer, and I expect the Witnesses will issue our public declaration of complete dissolution within the month."

Teach made a choking sound back by the carriage, and Calder felt like the man had punched him in the gut. The Champions were the second oldest Imperial Guild, behind the Consultants. Half the stories of Imperial unification began or ended with the legendary powers of the Champions. If there was no Champion's Guild, then how could Calder pretend there was still an Empire?

"What happened?" Calder managed to ask, even though he felt like a child faced with the death of a hero.

Kern sighed. "The Emperor died. Without him, there was no one to tell us what to fight for. Or what *not* to fight for. Champions started to take contracts at their own discretion, all over the world, until eventually most of them stopped reporting to me altogether. I only know one way to make people do what I want them to, and sometimes force doesn't work. Sometimes the tide goes out, and you can't stop it."

A snap cracked the air, and for a second Calder thought he'd heard a gunshot. But it was the half-painted fencepost, broken in two under Kern's brush. The bristles had actually *stiffened* somehow, temporarily frozen like they'd been made of steel, and a casual push of Kern's hand had snapped the thick plank of wood in half.

His shoulders drooped, and he tore both halves of the broken fencepost away. Casually he hurled them over his house, where they landed with the clatter of wood on wood. As though these two pieces had landed on a pile of many others.

Kern walked over to the porch, where a stack of spare boards waited. "This always takes twice as long as it should, but it's my own fault. Accidentally threw a stove through the fence in the first place."

There was nothing else Calder could get from him, so he might as well leave. His first meeting with a legend had gone much worse than he'd hoped. "It may be futile, Guild Head, but I have to try one last time. Will you support us?"

"The only Champion I can speak for is myself," Kern said. He picked up the board with one hand and a hammer with the other. "As for me, I don't trust you enough to risk my life for you. That's nothing to take offense about. You haven't proven yourself yet. And I *will* be risking my life, if you're asking me to go up against Regents and Gardeners." He propped the plank carefully in place, lining up a nail. "That's about all there is to say on the matter. Now if you'll excuse me, I'm trying not to break this one."

Calder left Baldesar Kern gently hammering his broken fence back together.

Back in the Imperial Palace, Calder dropped Andel off at his rooms. He'd intended to return to his own, but Teach stopped him.

"Without the Champions, this battle becomes even more dangerous," she said.

As though Calder needed another reminder of his failure. "If you think you can persuade him, please do."

"He won't change his mind for me. Nor for anyone else we know, I think. You went to see him in person, and that shows respect. In a year or two we'll try again."

"In the first month of his reign as Imperial Steward, Calder Marten oversaw the dissolution of the Champion's Guild and led an attack on the Consultants," Calder said bitterly. "He was driven insane shortly thereafter by the throne he inherited from the Emperor."

Teach tapped him in the chest with the back of her fist. She didn't seem to put much power into it, but he gasped for breath and staggered backward two paces. His wounds forcibly reminded him that they still ached. "Self-pity is a bad habit, and you should lose it as soon as possible. The attack on the Gray Island is going forward, so as I see it, you have two options. You can support us with the Optasia, which is by far the better choice, except that we can't prepare you to use it safely. Otherwise, you can accompany us."

Calder set his emotions aside, focusing on the conversation. "I've already made my decision clear. You need me."

Teach worked her jaw as though chewing on something. Finally, she said, "For that, I *can* prepare you."

Then she led him on an exhausting path through the Imperial Palace. Calder had always known the complex was huge, but seeing it on the map didn't have nearly the same impact. As they walked deeper and deeper, mile after mile, Calder's wounded leg started to throb. Even his healthy leg ached, and he wondered how Teach could even stand walking this distance in her armor.

All the while, they never left the palace grounds. It was like a city unto itself, and Calder was seeing its underbelly for the first time. *I'll be spending the rest of my life here,* he realized, and it was a strange thought. He'd grown up in the Capital, but the Imperial Palace was a totally separate world.

Each time Teach passed a group of Imperial Guards, they offered to join her, but one and all she turned them down and instructed them to forget her passage. "You did not see us," she said, more than a dozen times.

She's going to kill me and hide the body. When the thought first came to him, it was a joke, but as more time passed he wondered. Maybe she actually intended to lock him away until the battle was over; that could be what she meant by "preparing" him.

At last they came to a stone building the size of an outhouse. It was completely out of style for the rest of the Imperial Palace, sticking out like a gravestone in the middle of a kitchen. The tiny building was little more than a rectangle of rough stone and a steel door, which was guarded by two Imperial Guards. They both had mouths filled with the pointed teeth of crocodiles, as well as absurdly muscled arms and six-fingered hands. They could have been brothers.

For Teach, they stepped aside, though they eyed Calder suspiciously.

"I haven't opened this door in more than five years," Teach said, taking a heavy steel key from a cord around her neck. "What you're about to see is highly privileged, and there are fewer people allowed in here than in the Imperial treasury."

Calder's expectations rose with each word. Now, if there were anything less than a dragon on a hoard of gold inside, he would be disappointed. "What is it?"

"The Emperor's personal armory."

CHAPTER NINETEEN

With Petal aboard *The Testament*, all of Calder's plans for freeing Urzaia advanced easily. Almost too easily. He distrusted any plan that wasn't full of danger and fraught with unnecessary risk.

She manufactured explosives so quickly and cheaply that Foster had become suspicious. He knew something about alchemy from somewhere in that past he refused to discuss, and he complained loudly that there was no way she could put together a functional charge without...a list of ingredients that Calder never bothered to remember.

So they'd tested one. Each of Petal's charges was a rectangular wooden container the size of a cigar box. In fact, they *were* cigar boxes, filled with alchemical solutions in several independent chambers and sealed with resin. Andel lit the fuse and launched the charge with the force of his arm, aiming at the whale-sized shadow that had been following them for days. The creature occasionally poked an eye-stalk out of the water to take a look at them, and Calder had gotten sick of it. He'd originally planned to let the Lyathatan deal with it.

When the charge flew straight for the underwater shadow and detonated, sending a plume of water up like a missed cannon-shot, Calder knew he wouldn't have to bother his pet Elderspawn. And the charges worked.

After that, Foster went from calling Petal a "waste of bilge-space" to "genius."

Upon reaching Axciss, the entire crew went on a visit to the arena. Petal seemed terrified of the crowds and Andel was surprisingly absorbed in the fights, but they all came to the same conclusion.

The exits behind the victor's stage were the easiest place to smuggle Urzaia out. There, Petal only had to blow up one wall. Anywhere else, there were at least two walls that required destruction. And Jerri was quick to point out that the section of wall behind the victor's stage could be removed without affecting any load-bearing columns, while the other exits came with a risk of partially collapsing the arena.

That was a risk Calder might be willing to take, but not with a coliseum full of spectators. And he wasn't sure where Jerri had learned anything about architecture or demolition, but she *sounded* certain.

So they began their clandestine operations. Two charges packed under a rain-barrel outside the arena, leaning against their target wall. Foster and Petal both assured him that the charges were shaped appropriately for their needs, though Calder neither knew nor cared what a shaped explosion looked like. All he needed to know was whether it would work when they needed it to.

"Absolutely," Foster said, looking him in the eye and daring him to doubt.

"I think so," Petal mumbled into her hair.

Good enough for him.

For redundancy's sake, there were two other charges hidden in the stairwell leading out. It would be more difficult to leave without stairs, and more dangerous to any bystanders caught in the blast, but that was their only plan in case the rain barrel was moved or emptied during the blast.

Besides that, they carried six other charges for a potential manual detonation. As Foster had said, "When you're dealing with explosions, you need backups for your backups."

Now, the night before Urzaia's scheduled fight, there was one more step. Calder and Petal would bribe their way underneath the arena for a few minutes with the Champion. Urzaia deserved to know the plan.

And if there were any other problems, it would be better to find them out now.

Petal had finished hiding half a dozen cigar boxes in various places around her coat and skirts—their backups, if some of the charges needed to be replaced. She was along to make sure all their equipment was working. It was Calder's job to get them into the arena.

Not that he had any idea how to do that, but he found that a smile, a Guild crest, and five goldmarks would work as well as a key in most places.

They were heading out of their room at a nearby inn when they ran into Andel. He stood in their way like a white-clad wall, hat perfectly in place, face impassive as he watched them.

Calder faced him with a carefully calculated puzzled expression. "Andel? Is something wrong?"

Inside, he was seething. This was exactly what he'd been afraid of all along.

Never, at any point, had Andel questioned their plan to rescue Urzaia. At first, Calder and Jerri had gone to great pains to hide it from him, but eventually it was inevitable that he would find out. When he did, he'd said nothing. Not a word. He accepted it and continued doing his duties about the ship.

The closer they got to the actual execution of the plan, the more helpful he'd been: putting advice in here and there, accompanying them to the arena, doling out correction or encouragement or sheer cynicism.

He'd helped too much. For at least a year, Calder had been waiting for the man to stand in their way.

And now here he was, actually blocking the hallway so they couldn't pass. He'd known it wouldn't last.

"What's your plan?" Andel asked.

"Get inside, check the charges, compare notes with Urzaia. Tonight is our only chance." They'd planned on speaking with him two nights before, but it seemed he only fought every three days. They could certainly wait for his next fight, later in the week, but Calder had rejected that idea.

He'd made the man wait four years. There was no way he was going to show up now and say, "Here I am to rescue you, Urzaia! Now, keep risking your life and wait until I'm ready."

No, he'd waited until absolutely everything else was in place to speak with the Champion. And now that the time had come, Andel had a problem.

"That's not a plan," Andel said. "That's a series of goals."

"I'd be happy to fight a semantics duel with you another time, Andel. To-morrow evening, perhaps, while we're making full speed away from this city." Hopefully with Urzaia onboard and a minimum of fuss behind.

Andel adjusted his hat. "I'll get you into the arena," he said. Calder immediately tried to figure out how those words could possibly be a trick. "Under tradition and Imperial law, gladiators have the right to invite a member of the Order to give them death-rites on the night before a match. I may have parted ways with my Guild, but I am still a Pilgrim."

Calder leaned closer to Andel, trying to pierce the shapeshifting Elder-spawn's clever disguise. "You'd like to help us violate Imperial law? That would make you an accomplice."

"From a legal standpoint, I'm quite certain we'd be tried separately. Rather than your accomplice, which is what I'd be in the Heartlands, an Izyrian court would likely find me a separate offender and hang me."

Petal shuffled uncomfortably at the mention of hanging, but Calder was still waiting for an explanation.

"...this may come as a surprise to you, Marten, but I had a look at Urzaia's charges on the way over from the Capital. He doesn't deserve to be where he is, and even if he did, he's paid the price by now. I have a great respect for Imperial law, but I am not a slave to it."

He spoke so succinctly, so matter-of-factly, that Calder almost forgot the man was speaking nonsense. Until this point, Calder would have called An-del Petronus *passionately* devoted to the law.

But here he was, ushering them out the door to detonate some Imperial property.

Clearly, Calder had missed something somewhere.

Andel's White Sun medallion got them through the arena guards faster than Calder would have thought possible. In fact, one of the guards pulled the former Pilgrim aside for a few private words before they entered.

Then they were allowed inside the arena, directed to Urzaia's room outside the sand, and given full run of the facility. Just like that.

"Either the security here is much more forgiving than I would have expected, or having you along has made things significantly easier," Calder said.

"I'm twice your age," Andel said, without slowing his pace or turning around. "I give the commands, because I know what I'm talking about, and you execute them with energy and enthusiasm. That's how it works."

Not long ago, that reminder of Andel's authority would have stuck Calder's lips together like some of Petal's alchemical resin. No way he would say anything to encourage the man after a comment like that. Now, though, Calder was used to it. "You were right this time. Edge case. Take your praise, beggar, and begone."

"I've had to beg before," Petal said softly, and that killed the conversation.

Urzaia was waiting where any gladiator would the night before a match—in a small room just outside of the arena. The only difference between Urzaia and his fellow fighters was that Urzaia got his own room.

Either he was too dangerous for company, or no one wanted to share a room with the Woodsman. Both ways worked for Calder.

They used the key Andel had been given by the guard, and then again on a second, inner door. Before Andel opened the second one, Calder stopped him.

"We have the keys. Let's take him now." He was getting excited the more he thought of it. "Why not? No need to blow anything up. We take him and just walk out. The worst we'll have to face is a few guards."

Without a word, Andel pulled open the door and showed him why.

The room was small and made entirely of the same yellow stone that shaped the arena. They could see the arena through two iron gates, and a cold breeze wafted in from the night, stirring the grit and straw on the floor. On a bunk set against the wall lay Urzaia, laying back with his head pillowed on his hands, just as he'd slept on the deck of *The Testament*.

Both wrists and both ankles were manacled, their thick chains leading to the stone wall. Without even checking, Calder knew they'd been invested. Even if they hadn't been invested before they were brought to this chamber, they would be by now; the Intent of hundreds of captors and prisoners in this cell over the years. If the chains had held so far, they'd hold tonight.

Besides which, Calder glanced around the room and couldn't find Urzaia's black hatchets. They must arm him only before the match, which made sense. He wouldn't leave without his Awakened blades, especially since one of them was likely his Vessel. Calder and his crew had been disarmed at the door, though fortunately Petal hadn't been thoroughly searched.

Just in case, Calder took the key from Andel and headed over to Urzaia's manacles. He knelt down to try the circlet of iron on the man's ankle. The key wouldn't even fit in the lock.

He'd known it was a long shot, but he was ready for a break of good luck. He pressed his fingertips against the cold metal and Read...nothing useful. A muddle of Intent with the clear purpose of keeping the latch *closed*.

Maybe with one of Petal's charges—

Calder was cut off by bands of warm steel wrapping around his throat, choking his air. He clawed at his waist, looking for his saber, but his belt was empty. He slapped in utter futility at whatever was strangling him, but he might as well have saved his strength. It was worse than steel; it was Urzaia Woodsman's arm.

"Hello, who are you?" came the Champion's cheery voice. After another few seconds, his grip on Calder relaxed, and Calder's vision swam as he tried to keep his breathing under control.

"The Navigator Captain!" Urzaia boomed, and his voice carried surprise and delight. "You made it! Four years is a long time in the arena, but I am fortunate. They only started *really* trying to kill me last year."

Calder turned to face the gap-toothed Champion's smile. Rubbing at his neck, he asked hoarsely, "What were they doing before?"

"Before, the fights were almost fair. I did not think so at the time. But when it suddenly became difficult, I asked why. My Patron told me they could not find anyone to fight me when it was only me against an opposing team. So I have been fighting *all* of the other teams."

He laughed when he was finished, but Calder thought back to Urzaia's fight with the Houndmaster. A Soulbound with the power to create four hounds to fight for him had been considered one full team. He had been enough to give Urzaia some new scars. Picturing the Woodsman fighting an arena full of enemies like that...

His memories were interrupted as he noticed a strange gleam from Urzaia's eye. He leaned closer, inspecting it, and the Champion noticed. He chuckled, tapping his finger on the eyeball. "It is hard to notice, is it not? I lost the real one…oh, who remembers? But I do not want to ruin my beautiful face with a patch, so I paid an alchemist for a replacement. Worth every mark!"

Calder should have gotten here sooner.

"How long have you been fighting…like that?" he asked. It wasn't the question he *should* be asking, but he needed to know.

Urzaia frowned, considering. "More than a year now. Fourteen, fifteen months, I would say."

Calder gripped the man's shoulder, which felt like grabbing leather armor. "I know it's been longer than I wanted. But trust me a little more. Tomorrow, we're getting you out."

The Champion patted him on the arm reassuringly. "Don't worry. If I trust a man one day, I will trust him the next, until he gives me reason not to. And here you are! I was right to trust you, yes?"

Calder had to look away, his throat choked with emotion. All this time… all this time, and Urzaia still trusted him.

In the meantime, Andel explained the plan.

"I have to win one more time, yes?" Urzaia grinned. "No problem! If this is the last fight of the Woodsman, I will give them a real show!"

Behind them, the door opened.

Calder straightened immediately, stepping behind Andel. Their previous arrangement may have looked suspicious: Calder the closest, obviously speaking to Urzaia, the Champion grinning like a fool, with Andel standing deferentially behind and Petal huddling in the back. It would be clear that Calder was the one talking with the gladiator, not Andel the Pilgrim. That wouldn't be enough to get a guard to draw steel, but it might spark some questions.

Into the room came the guard they'd met earlier, the one at the door. And with him, he brought his supervisor.

The man's rank was obvious. His hair was solid silver, his uniform pristine. He had a four-pointed star on his chest, where a Guild member might wear their crest, and he looked at them like a man deciding which variety of acid to spray on a bunch of sewer rats.

"Who are these two?" he asked his subordinate, gesturing sharply to Calder and Petal.

The guard didn't have an answer, so Andel stepped in. "Guests of the

Order and friends of the supplicant. They're here to provide a measure of comfort before Urzaia's last moments. Should they come."

The supervisor squinted at Andel as though trying to see through his words with sheer force of will. For once, Calder was glad for the man's mask of a face.

"We do not allow unsupervised access to the arena," he said, evidently forgetting that his guard had done just that. He extended a hand, palm-up. "The key, if you please."

Wincing, Calder handed it over. The guard paled, and the supervisor's face tightened as he gathered his obvious anger. Clearly, Andel wasn't supposed to relinquish control of their arena key.

"Search them," the supervisor commanded. "Search the prisoner. And then get them out."

Urzaia was still smiling, but now it made him look more dangerous than ever. He could snap a man's neck without losing that smile. "I am not a prisoner. I am a gladiator of the arena."

"You're chained to a wall, is what you are. Search him first, see if they slipped him anything." The man's gaze stayed locked on Andel, as though he suspected the Luminian Pilgrim would try passing Urzaia something *now*.

Which gave Calder enough space to step to one side, out of the man's view, and gesture to Petal. He mimed scooping something out of his pocket and throwing it away.

Her eyes grew wide.

During their first encounter with the guards, they hadn't been inspected. They had willingly divested themselves of weapons and moved along. Now, based on the search the guard was giving Urzaia, they wouldn't have the room to hide a needle. Which meant that Petal needed to rid herself of six alchemical charges in a way that didn't see anyone detained or detonated.

Petal started edging closer to the edge of Urzaia's bunk, behind the supervisor's back. The guard had finished patting Urzaia down, and was glancing up to check for his next target.

Before the man had a chance to notice Petal was gone, Andel spread his arms. "I didn't smuggle weapons in to a gladiator who requested death-rites," he said, and Calder was certain he only spoke to keep the men focused on him. He was better at this than he had any right to be, as a representative of the Imperial court.

For his part, Calder kept his eyes on the supervisor. Out of the corner of his vision, he saw Petal producing cigar boxes and sliding them under Urzaia's bunk.

One of the boxes scraped over the stone floor, and Calder spoke up, desperate to cover the noise. "Ah! It's...so...so great to see you, Urzaia, I'm sure you'll make it out alive tomorrow."

Urzaia chuckled, and Calder couldn't tell if he was playing along or if the man was really just that relaxed. "I always have so far. I don't see why tomorrow should be any different."

Petal tossed one more charge under Urzaia's bed, and then raised both of her small fists triumphantly.

A second later, the supervisor turned to her. "Get away from him. Over here." He knelt to pat her down, businesslike and professional. "I hope you took the Pilgrim up on his rites, Woodsman. Tomorrow's a big day."

Calder had no idea who this man was, but he spoke as though he knew something Urzaia didn't. In the meantime, his subordinate had finished with Andel and moved on to Calder. He was in for a disappointment, as Calder had nothing suspicious on him.

His shoelaces were invested weapons, and he could kill a man with them given enough time. But nothing suspicious.

Urzaia raised his eyebrows at the supervisors words. "If it is twelve men and I must fight without my hatchets, that is not a surprise. I have done that already."

The supervisor snorted, but said nothing else. Seconds later, he stood. "We're done. Woodsman, we'll see you on the sand."

The two guards marched the crew into the hall, leaving Urzaia alone.

With half a dozen alchemical munitions under his bed.

The crew had to rise before dawn to make it to the arena in time to ensure seats, which meant that Calder had a grand total of three hours sleep. None of the others were much better off, except for Jerri, who for some reason was looking forward to the day with endless enthusiasm.

"Jerri, since you're chipper this morning, sound us off."

"With pleasure! Petal, you're first up."

"Checking the charges," Petal whispered.

"Foster?"

"Oversight," he grunted. "I'm on the closest guard."

"Andel?"

"Backup. I have a seat on the opposite side of the arena, and I will signal Foster if I notice something wrong."

"Cheer up, Andel, all you have to do is watch the fight! I, on the other hand, will close off the staircase as soon as the match begins." Calder pointed to himself and said, "And then what, Calder? Why, thank you for asking. Once the fight is over, I will be the one to detonate the charges." Technically, Foster or Petal should be covering this job, but he didn't feel right leaving it to someone else. In the worst-case scenario, he could take full blame for the plan.

The Emperor needed him alive, or the thousands of goldmarks he'd sunk into *The Testament's* construction would go to waste. If Calder went before an Imperial court, he'd likely get off with nothing more than a swollen debt.

Which would be painful enough, but anyone else would be executed or imprisoned for life.

"And if something goes wrong?" Jerri asked, as though delighted by the prospect. She could roll out of bed bristling with energy. Calder, on the other hand, currently wanted to knife someone.

"Andel signals Foster, Foster signals Petal and me, I tell you," Calder said. "Or we all notice and run."

"What about the charges?" Petal asked, then shook her head. "The extra charges." The ones they'd left with Urzaia.

"The arena can keep them," Calder said. He and Andel had considered and discarded half a dozen different plans for retrieving them, but in the end, it was less dangerous to leave them where they were. They wouldn't spontaneously explode, and unless someone was stupid enough to light them on fire just to see what would happen, they were no danger to anyone. The risk was that some guard would stumble on them and call off the fight, or increase security. So long as that didn't happen, they were clear.

As soon as they bought their tickets and headed into the arena, Calder could tell something was wrong.

Seven Magisters waited in the arena—one for each section of spectator seating, and one in the Imperial box. They were in the process of attaching small bronze shields to the outside of each section, facing the arena.

"What are *those?*" Jerri whispered to him.

"Invested protections," Calder whispered back. "They might be Awakened. If they think they have to protect the audience in addition to all the Intent already invested into the arena, then they're preparing for something big."

"What is it?"

"I'd need to get closer to be sure, which means we'd have to wait until the Magisters are gone."

Only the Magisters didn't leave. Petal scurried down the far staircase, checked both of the primary charges and the two backup charges, and then settled into a nearby seat. Andel grabbed his own seat at the end of the arena, Foster sat directly underneath a guard tower, and Calder and Jerri found seats together next to the victor's stage.

When they first arrived, there were only a scattering of other spectators. Two hours later, the stadium looked full. Two hours after *that*, and Calder realized he'd been wrong before; only now did he understand what 'full' really meant. It was somehow even more crowded than it had been the last time he was here, as though they'd squeezed out all the air and replaced it with people.

At least it wasn't as hot as it had been last summer, so he didn't have to bake in the scent of sweat.

Jerri shot Calder a parting smile as she squeezed past him and a small family to slide into the staircase. The match would start soon, and when it did, she needed to clear the stairs as soon as possible.

If she didn't, anyone in the way would die in their explosion.

Finally, after what felt like a night and a day of waiting, the crier made his way onto the arena sand. At the mere sight of him, the crowd lost all reason, and the coliseum shook with a sound like a berserk beast.

"LADIES, GENTLEMEN, AND GOOD CITIZENS OF AXCISS!" This time, the crier didn't only rely on the acoustics of the stadium, but raised an invested horn to his lips. His words boomed out, easily cutting through the noise. "TODAY, WE HAVE A TREAT INDEED FOR YOU! ALL THESE YEARS, YOU'VE SEEN ONE MAN TRIUMPH AGAIN AND AGAIN OVER STAGGERING ODDS! ONE MAN—IZYRIA'S VERY OWN WOODSMAN!"

At the mention of Urzaia's name, the crowd erupted again, until it sounded as though Calder stood in the middle of a great battlefield. It did nothing but give him a throbbing headache on top of a night's worth of exhaustion.

"BUT I'M AFRAID, GOOD CITIZENS, THAT THE ODDS TODAY ARE TRULY IMPOSSIBLE. FOR TODAY THE WOODSMAN FACES NOT MEN, BUT A CREATURE FROM MYTH AND THE NIGHTMARES OF THE ELDERS THEMSELVES! A TERROR OF THE AION SEA! THE DREADED...CINDERBEAST!"

As his speech reached a crescendo, the biggest gate onto the sand slid open. Two Greenwardens, robed entirely in verdant leaves, marched out. They each hauled on a leash...attached to a massive Kameira. The Cinderbeast was coal-black, shaped like a hairless bear or a misshapen wolf, with two spiraling onyx horns above its eyes. Its tail, longer than one would expect, lashed like a whip.

Its eyes were red, swollen orbs, and even from here Calder could practically taste its mad Intent. It growled, scratching at the sand, but its collar was obviously invested. It did not strike at the Greenwardens holding its pair of leashes.

The crier shouted again, embellishing an entry for Urzaia, but Calder didn't hear it. Even as Urzaia marched into the light, black axes held high, Calder's mind was whirling.

What now?

The plan called for them to wait for Urzaia's victory, because after more than five hundred victories in a row, only a fool would bet against one more. Then again, he wasn't fighting men. He fought some sort of...horned bear creature four times his size. And if it was a Kameira, as Calder was certain it was, then it would have some power over nature. Judging from its name, it might be able to set Urzaia on fire. Waiting for the fight would be ridiculous; they had to rescue Urzaia as soon as possible. So what was the plan? Detonate an extra charge somewhere else, as a distraction, and then get Urzaia up to the victory stage?

He was still considering his options as the Greenwardens unclipped the Cinderbeast's collar and hurriedly withdrew. The Kameira glanced from one side to the other, as though trying to figure out if it were really free, and then sniffed at the air. Smoke rose from its nostrils.

Finally, Calder put the clues together, and the bottom dropped out of his stomach. He'd never felt as stupid as he did in that moment.

Copper shields in front of the spectators. Magisters standing ready. Smoke drifting from its nostrils. Light and life, they'd called it the *Cinder*beast.

It was going to breathe fire.

Kameira could use their powers in a thousand different ways; it might summon fire from the heavens, or throw fireballs somehow, but the point was that it set things on fire with its Intent. He was no alchemist, but he knew he didn't want fire involved in a plan that relied on explosives.

He shot to his feet, shoving a bigger man down into his seat as he ran forward. He actually punched a boy five years younger in the jaw, feeling terrible about it, but the boy wouldn't *get out of the way*. By the time anyone realized what he'd done and got upset about it, he'd already moved on.

Calder had started out ten yards from the stairs, but he still wasn't fast enough. The Cinderbeast drew in a deep breath of air, filling its lungs, and exhaled a stream of pure flame.

The copper shields at the front of the seats lit up as they absorbed excess heat, and the crowd gasped in unison. So the Magisters had done their jobs, and the people were safe. The Greenwardens had done their jobs, and the Cinderbeast hadn't gone on a berserk rampage. And Urzaia had done his job, because he'd obviously anticipated the fire and had somehow leaped completely *over* it, in an inhuman jump that would have shocked Calder at any other moment.

In fact, the only one who had failed to do his job was Calder.

Because those spare charges, those half a dozen alchemical charges with their unlit fuses, were still below in the arena waiting room. Only two iron grates away from the fire.

The flame flowed through the grates and into the room like a river, then faded. There was a bare instant, a frozen portrait of time, in which nothing happened. Calder almost started to believe that they were safe, and that he had time to figure out a way to stop this.

Then the coliseum echoed like a struck drum the size of a city, and smoke billowed out from the grate. It was all the way on the other side of the stadium, but Calder still trembled and lost his balance. The stone cracked all around, a black line racing up the stands.

And people scurried out of the way like an evacuating anthill as the arena seats slowly, ever so slowly, began to crumble.

On Calder's side of the arena, he was in more danger of being crushed as panicked people desperately sought the closest escape—which, in his case, meant straight past him and toward the stairs. But, as the first woman to reach the door to the stairway found out, the entrance was locked. Jerri had sealed it with alchemical resin as soon as she'd managed to clear people out of the stairway.

So Calder found himself mashed against the base of the victor's stage, losing breath by the second, as people struggled to smash in the door. The iron-banded wood bowed, and he prayed it would break so that the people behind him would stop pushing.

Something almost as good happened—the stone against his face suddenly slammed against him, and a deafening sound set his ears ringing.

Jerri had detonated the charges.

He wasn't sure how she'd done it—he held the matches, and Petal had the backup set—but he almost wept with relief. The people backed off, leaving his lungs room to expand, as they fled from the door as though expecting it to explode.

In that brief moment of freedom, he glanced at the arena.

The Cinderbeast was in the stands.

As half of the arena slowly fell apart, the invested shields had fallen as well. Streams of fire chased spectators away, though they fell well short of the nearest—people had stampeded on instinct after the first explosion.

Through the fire and crumbling stone, Urzaia Woodsman ran toward the monster. Calder couldn't see the man's expression, and certainly couldn't hear him, but he was sure the Champion was laughing.

Calder pushed his way back through the crowd, meeting surprisingly little resistance. People were fighting this way, but if he clambered over the seats, no one cared enough to stop him going the wrong way. It was his life to waste.

When he caught sight of Urzaia again, the gladiator was riding the Cinderbeast's back like a horseman on an unruly mount. He struck with one of his hatchets, and the impact slammed the Kameira into the stone seats.

In the back of his mind, Calder wondered at that. When Urzaia fought the Houndmaster, his hatchet had sunk into the man's chest. Now it was striking with enough impact to drive a giant Kameira into stone. If it could hit that hard before, wouldn't it have blown the man's corpse into the stands? And how did Urzaia's body withstand the opposing force?

It wasn't worth considering just now, but as a Reader, Calder was still curious.

He finally started to slow when he got close to Urzaia. He needed to be nearby when Urzaia was finished to lead the man out before he was recaptured, but Calder wasn't foolish enough to interfere in a Champion's fight.

Which was just as well, because there was nothing he could have done to help.

The Cinderbeast built up momentum, loping across the back of the stone seats and bucking its head to try and gore the Woodsman. It didn't come close. When that failed, it swatted at Urzaia with its claws, but the Champion swung around its neck like a monkey on a branch, laughing the entire time.

When the Kameira blew a burst of fire at nothing in particular, Calder knew it had given up. Urzaia must have sensed the same thing, because he swung himself down and to the Cinderbeast's side. He steadied himself on the ground, drawing his hatchets back.

Stone cracked under his feet, and Calder stared. No matter how fast the coliseum was tearing itself apart, the stone shouldn't have softened. Could the fire have done something? Or maybe the Intent of thousands of desperate people...

As Urzaia slammed his weapons forward, Calder realized the truth. A handful of separate pieces clicked together in his mind.

The stone wasn't that weak, Urzaia was *just that heavy.*

Rumor had it that the Sandborn Hydra, a Kameira actually native to the Izyrian desert around this very city, had the Intent to increase or decrease its own weight. The Blackwatch had commissioned some research into its unique properties as part of their work on *The Testament,* in the hopes of making the ship lighter without compromising hull strength. The research had come to nothing, as no one could locate a Sandborn Hydra for testing.

But according to legend, the Kameira's hide was made of gold scales. Urzaia wore a golden hide around his upper arm.

Come to think of it, the black hatchets were a little obvious for a Soulbound Vessel.

In the time it took Calder to realize what was happening, Urzaia had slammed both Awakened weapons into the side of the Cinderbeast with the full force of his Soulbound powers. The Kameira's ribs caved in as though they'd been struck by a falling star, and its huge body blasted away from Urzaia. It scraped rows of stone seats away in its flight, finally slamming against the top section of the arena wall in a spray of dark blood.

Seconds after its impact, as the dust billowed up and Urzaia calmly walked over to Calder, the entire half of the arena collapsed completely.

Urzaia said something to Calder and then laughed, but the sound was washed out by the avalanche of crashing stone. Instead of responding, Calder jerked his head and ran for the exits.

As they got closer and the noise died away, Calder shouted back to him. "Urzaia. How would you like a job? I could use a ship's guard?"

The Woodsman made a show of thinking about it for a few seconds, even as he ran. There was a thin sheen of sweat and blood on his skin, but he wasn't even close to running out of breath. *Champions are just...unfair.*

"Guard is boring," he said at last. "But I am a very good cook."

CHAPTER TWENTY

The Bellowing Horror is meant to unnerve the minds of men, for it repeats only the most vile and disturbing bits of our conversation. Yet in the end, the men and I grew fond of the creature, as it caused us no harm and fed on the rats that plagued our vessel.

– FROM THE ORIGINAL BLACKWATCH *BESTIARY OF ELDERS*

The Emperor's armor was white and smooth, so that it looked like Calder's chest and limbs were protected by giant eggshells. The plates were joined by chain at the joints, and the entire suit was invested to weigh practically nothing, so at times Calder forgot he was wearing it.

He extended his senses down into *The Testament*, steering his ship after the Navigator fleet that carried the army of the Imperialist Guilds. Navigator ships stretched out over the oceans for miles to his left and right, covering the shallow Aion in colored sails and Imperial banners. But every time Calder Read his ship, he had to forcibly ignore his armor. The Emperor had left a mountain of Intent in the suit; this was the same armor he'd worn in the Elder War. As a result, Calder almost lost himself in the armor's depths each time he Read.

It was an inconvenience, and one that he was quickly growing sick of. But since he suspected the armor was impenetrable, he would manage. He could withstand a little inconvenience for the sake of invincibility.

The armor was one of the treasures he'd taken from the Emperor's armory, over a week ago now. It was the primary reason that General Teach had allowed him to lead the assault on the Gray Island.

Although "lead" was perhaps too strong of a word. *The Testament* was lagging behind the rest of the fleet as the Consultants' island loomed in the distance. The Lyathatan drifted along sluggishly beneath him, barely keeping up with the ship instead of pulling it forward.

That was one of Teach's requirements. She'd made him promise to stay in the back, as far from danger as reasonably possible.

Even if he wasn't technically in charge of his own mission, at least he *looked* like an Emperor. Between his armor, the Awakened sword on his hip, the golden crown on his head, and the Imperial flag he was flying, he struck an impressive figure.

The Gray Island, on the other hand, wasn't living up to its name. Rather than the towering wall of fog that he'd seen on his last visit, the island was only a little hazy. That meant something significant, he was sure, but he had no idea what. It could mean that the Consultants had abandoned their headquarters, or that they needed to see clearly to aim their cannons. Maybe they'd decided to surrender.

A harsh cry, like the dying of a violin, sounded from high overhead. A brown lizard twice the size of a horse began to descend on his ship, flapping wings like an oversized bat. Through Kelarac's mark on his arm, Calder sent his Intent down and into the ship, ordering the Lyathatan to a halt.

Minutes later, *The Testament* finally settled, and the Kameira—a replacement for Teach's dead Windwatcher—came to land on the deck. Jarelys Teach leaped off its back, saluting when she saw Calder.

Secretly, it alarmed him every time she did that. Some part of him felt like the Emperor was standing just behind him.

"We have a problem," she said, and immediately Calder's crew gathered to listen. Foster leaned on a cannon as though he weren't paying attention, though Andel walked up boldly. Even Petal peeked her head up from below deck, staring from a nest of her frizzy hair.

At first, Calder glanced around for Jerri and Urzaia before he remembered the truth. It hurt like a fishbone stuck in his throat.

There were too few of them left.

"The Consultants have a visitor," Teach said, as she handed the winged lizard's reins to Andel. "The Regent of the South."

Calder's blood chilled. Jorin Maze-walker, who some texts called Cursebreaker, didn't show up in war stories as often as his companions Estyr Six and Loreli. Instead, he had left his marks in other fields: architecture, exploration, cartography, linguistics, and the advancement of Reading as a discipline. He wasn't credited with the founding of the Magister's Guild, but his philosophies were instrumental in its creation.

The legends didn't say much about his combat potential, but he had lived through the Elder War. He couldn't be easy to kill. More importantly, he would have been one of the strongest Readers of his day, carrying invested weapons with thousands of years of Intent.

"You saw him from the air?" Calder had been on the Gray Island not long ago, and the place was a maze. If she'd spotted him from the back of her Kameira, she'd gotten lucky.

Teach shook her head. "I only had to get close enough. Tyrfang recognizes its creator."

Its creator? That confirmed one of Calder's worst fears about the man. If Jorin had been the one to Awaken Tyrfang in the first place, he would understand everything about it. He'd have some way of matching Teach in battle. "I guess we should count ourselves lucky it wasn't Estyr Six."

Teach neither agreed nor disagreed. "I don't know Jorin personally, though I've met him briefly twice. If he's not quite Estyr Six or the Emperor, he's still on their level. I wouldn't like our odds if we were ambushing him in his sleep, and he's hardly sleeping."

Calder's breathing quickened. Only a moment ago, it had seemed like the ships were barely crawling toward the Gray Island, but now he felt like everyone else in the fleet was speeding toward their doom. "What are our options?"

"We have to go after him immediately," Teach responded. She reached into a saddlebag, strapped to the side of her mount, and pulled out a black-and-red helmet that matched her armor. As far as he could remember, he'd never seen her with her head covered before. "I can only stall him on my own, but together, we have a chance of removing him."

"Together? Me and you?" Calder was flattered that she thought him capable of fighting alongside her, but the sudden surge in confidence seemed out of place.

From underneath her newly donned helmet, Teach gave him a look that told him to stop being an idiot. "Not me and you. Me and *her*."

She pointed behind him.

Without much surprise, Calder turned around to see Bliss standing there. Her Blackwatch coat reached down to the deck, and her pale hair blew behind her in the ocean breeze. She stood perfectly straight, her face serious. "Hello, Calder Marten. You should pay closer attention to your surroundings."

"Hello, Bliss. I don't see how that would help."

The Head of the Blackwatch would likely have spent ten minutes telling him about all the reasons he should pay more attention, but Teach was kind enough to cut her off. "Bliss, can you back me up? If we can remove Jorin immediately, we'll have practically disarmed the Guild."

While that wasn't true from Calder's perspective, he could see how it might seem so for Teach. The Consultants didn't have a Guild Head; without Jorin, there was no one else who could fight on the same level as Bliss or the General.

An uncomfortable memory surfaced from a week or two before. Somehow, a Consultant Soulbound and her partner had managed to kill Mekendi Maxeus. He'd been a Guild Head, a powerful Magister, awake and alert. If they could kill him, why couldn't they do it again?

But Bliss cocked her head, thinking. "Someone has been considerate and removed Bastion's Veil. If it stays gone, I can release the full extent of my ability. I can remove the island, if you like."

Calder shivered.

"But if the Veil comes back, they will restrict me almost completely. I still do not think I will be in danger from the ordinary Consultants, but under those conditions, I will not be an opponent fit for Jorin Curse-breaker."

Andel cleared his throat. "Excuse me. Bastion's Veil?"

"The wall of mist that's usually around the island," Calder replied. He'd learned some things this past few months, after all. He had no idea what the Veil could do, but he at least knew what it was called.

Teach looked troubled, and her Kameira croaked at her from behind. She reached back to calm it, stroking the glittering scales crowning its head. "I was not aware of that. More reason to strike quickly."

An explosion rang out from the island, followed by a splash next to *The Eternal.* The front of the Navigator fleet had gotten into range of the Consultants' cannons.

General Teach's gaze moved to Calder. "You have the crown?"

"Yes," Calder said, resisting the urge to add *'ma'am.'*

"Try to use it on the Consultants. If it works on them from a distance, then you'll conquer the island yourself. If Bliss and I can kill Jorin or force him to retreat quickly enough, we'll force the Architects to surrender on our own."

"And if they have countermeasures for both?" Calder asked, knowing the answer.

"Then we do it the hard way," Teach said. She swung up onto the back of her winged Kameira, a legend in crimson-and-black armor. Tyrfang hung behind her in its sheath, radiating deadly Intent.

Bliss joined her a moment later, hopping straight from the deck onto the lizard's back. "Good-bye, Calder Marten. I will see you again tonight, if we both survive. Perhaps also if we both die, assuming common beliefs about the afterlife are—"

The rushing wind of the Kameira's takeoff swallowed her last words.

The cannons from the island were firing in earnest now, a distant and irregular drumbeat. No Navigators had returned fire, likely because none of them were within range of a valuable target.

Calder looked at what remained of his crew. Dalton Foster, the gunsmith, sitting on a cannon. Andel Petronus, the quartermaster, standing calmly with his hands behind his back. Petal, the alchemist, quivering with her head peeking up from below.

It was the first time he'd been alone with them in weeks.

"Five years," he said quietly. "I've known some of you for longer, but it's been five years since we knew I'd end up here. I was hoping that more of us would make it, but...we're here, and we're together." He had more to say, but he concluded with a simple, "Thank you."

Foster nodded. "Captain."

Andel bowed. "For better or worse, you've made my life much more interesting."

Petal popped her head up. "I still like it here," she said.

Something snapped in the air like a leather flag flapping, and Shuffles bowled past Petal and flew up to Calder. Its claws dug into Calder's shoulder, its tentacles tickled his cheek, and its black eyes scowled. "FOR BETTER OR WORSE," it shouted.

Calder rubbed its head, though he couldn't tell if it liked that or hated it. "That was almost heartwarming, coming from you." With another effort of Intent, Calder once again Read the Lyathatan.

Move, he ordered.

Even as *The Testament* jerked forward, the Elder's resentment came through clearly. *The human orders me, he borrows the power of the Great Ones, but he will see. In only ten thousand years, I will rule a piece of this ocean floor, and my domain will be absolute.*

In ten thousand years, maybe it would hunt down Calder's distant descendants, but that was their problem. For now, he needed the ship to move.

Before long, he'd caught up to the rest of the fleet.

Two Navigator Vessels were obviously taking on water, having taken too many hits, their crew floating on longboats or simply swimming away. Several others sported damage, but most of the Guild reached the dock of the Gray Island largely unharmed.

The first ships pulled up to the edge of the dock or to the rocky shores of the island, Imperial Guards leaping off the decks and onto dry land.

They faced no enemy.

Silently, the Consultants were allowing the Navigators to settle in, delivering their payloads of soldiers. Other than the cannons, which had now gone quiet, there was no sign that the island was even inhabited.

Under the cracked sky, all was peaceful.

Calder pulled out his captain's horn, a hollow tin cone that magnified his voice. It had been invested to amplify its effect, and as he spoke, his voice boomed out over the island.

"Friends of the Consultant's Guild, this is the Imperial Steward, speaking with the authority of the Emperor himself. Lay down your weapons and come out of hiding. You will not be harmed. I repeat, lay down your weapons and come out of hiding. You will not be harmed."

Calder had been somewhat worried that he wouldn't be able to tell if the Consultants countered the power of the crown or if they simply couldn't hear him, but he could *feel* the Intent flowing from the Emperor's crown and infusing his words. If any Consultants were within earshot, and still felt any loyalty to the Empire, they would obey.

But at his words, a thin cloud of mist rolled down out of the trees. Not a thick bank of fog, but hazy wisps like smoke. The cloud got thicker deeper in the island, and he thought he heard crashes in the distance, but it could be the waves playing tricks on his ears.

Not one Consultant showed up.

Cheska called over to him, a captain's horn of her own in hand. "The crown's a misfire. We're heading in."

Calder waved back, acknowledging her point, as Cheska signaled the Imperial Guards, soldiers, and various members of the Navigator's Guild to advance up the slopes of the Gray Island. Every ship had come packed with combatants except *The Testament*; Teach had insisted that he should never come closer to shore than the sound of his horn would carry.

The sturdiest Imperial Guards marched in the front, those with thick skin or rigid carapace that would make them tough to kill. So they were the first to run into the traps.

Tiny alchemical explosives popped into flares of light all across the face of the island at the same time, sending chunks of rock rolling back into the advancing forces. Some Guards stood firm against the assault, while others bowled over into the men behind them.

After the miniature avalanche, the advance froze for a few minutes, while the Guards got their bearings. Calder didn't see any deaths and surprisingly few injuries, but the armored Guards had taken the brunt of the trap. As they gathered themselves, the Imperial Guards advanced once again.

This time, Calder didn't see what struck them down. It might have been darts, or a poison gas, or even bees, as far as he knew. But the front ranks started slapping at themselves, waving crazily in the air, and collapsing. Some of the toughest members withstood the traps, continuing forward, but many others stayed on the ground. Now, there were corpses.

But after the first wave, no one behind them suffered the same symptoms. Either the traps had run out of darts, or the Consultants were preparing a different surprise. It was hard to see details in the chaos, even through a spyglass.

Seconds later, the ground erupted in enemies. Black-clad Consultants burst from behind boulders, from under camouflaged trap doors, and from the trees. As one, they each discharged pistols, stabbed with spears, or struck with their daggers. They seemed to come out of nowhere, at least three attackers for each victim, and then they faded back into their territory.

Of course, they weren't without casualties. One Imperial Guard with clawed hands seized a Consultant by the neck, pulling the man's head off. A woman, a Navigator, managed to shoot one Consultant in the chest and stab another before the third killed her.

Those enemies that had encountered resistance remained, dead or locked in hopeless combat. The majority of the Consultants had disappeared, fading back into the landscape.

Unable to watch quietly any longer, Calder signaled the Lyathatan. It pulled the ship forward, easing it toward the battle in progress.

The Consultants had found a way to resist his crown since his last visit, as he'd feared they would. But maybe it wouldn't work at close range. Maybe it only worked once. Either way, he needed to try something else.

As he got closer, he realized he wasn't alone. *The Eternal* was off to their port, which wasn't unusual; Cheska had just repaired her ship and wouldn't want to see it damaged so early, and she needed a vantage from which to call orders. But to starboard was another Navigator's ship, one that seemed to be edged in gold. Empty golden snakeskins the size of blankets hung from the railings and virtually every surface, streaming in the wind like flags.

He'd never seen the ship before. That in itself wasn't particularly suspicious, as new Navigators joined the Guild every month or two, but it was hanging back just as he was. He looked over to Cheska and jerked his thumb in the direction of the other ship.

She understood. They were close enough to communicate without use of a captain's horn, so she called over. "Scavengers. Don't worry about them. They'll hang around any battle to see if they can get something out of it."

Calder was still somewhat curious, but he put the other ship out of his mind. He was no tactician, but he could tell the battle was not going well. The Imperial Guards had stalled, unable to press forward in the face of traps and potential ambush.

He shouted through the captain's horn as he approached, demanding that any Consultants reveal and surrender themselves immediately. Not one complied. The closer he got, the clearer it became that the crown simply wasn't going to work. Whether the distance was stopping him, or the thin layer of mist, or whether Jorin had come up with some countermeasure, it was clear that he couldn't order the Consultants to give up.

Which left one chance for a quick and easy victory: eliminating Jorin. If Bliss and Teach succeeded in removing Jorin from the fight, the rest of the Guild would have little choice but to give up. Whether he died, fled, or gave up, it would result in victory for the Imperialist forces. Calder just had to leave it to the Guild Heads.

He wasn't prepared to do that.

The Testament drifted closer to the island as he kept shouting orders to the hidden Consultants. Maybe something about the Intent of the captain's horn interfered with that of the crown. If he descended in person, he might be able to break the stalemate.

Besides his futile commands and Cheska's periodic orders, the day was largely quiet once more. For a handful of minutes, the Imperial Guards on the shore simply milled about where they were, searching for hidden bolt-holes or traps. There was no sense advancing into more traps, while Calder and Cheska waited for news from the other Guild Heads.

Each minute that scraped by felt like hours, with the sun seemingly frozen overhead. Finally, as he could take it no more, Calder decided to have the Lyathatan carry him over to *The Eternal* so that he could confer with Cheska more closely.

Then General Teach smashed through the treeline as though blasted from a cannon, her armored form crashing through a stray pine. She trailed dark power like a smoky comet, and as she landed, the grass crisped up and died around her.

"Withdraw!" she shouted as she pushed herself to her knees, propped up by Tyrfang's naked length. The blade was a pure, almost haunting black, with an irregular vein of throbbing red up the center. Even at this distance, Calder felt its Intent press against his mind. He had to focus through Kelarac's mark, bracing himself, in order to stay conscious.

Consultants scurried away from their hiding places like wasps from a kicked hive, scrambling to escape Tyrfang's radius. Not all of them made it; a few black-clad figures lost strength mid-stride, tumbling to a halt on the dying grass. Half a dozen of the Imperial combatants met the same fate, keeling over in silence if they were too close to Teach's landing site. The rest of the Imperialists on the beach retreated in a panicked wave.

A man jogged out down from the island, another dark sword in his hand, and trees blackened around him. He wore a wide-brimmed hat and a pair of dark-tinted spectacles, as well as a billowing brown coat that looked as though it was *made* of pockets. But even that wasn't enough storage for him; through the spyglass, Calder saw a ring of keys on one hip, something like a shriveled head on the other, and a variety of other packs and pouches that he would expect from any Reader in the field.

Jorin Curse-breaker followed the line of dead grass like a road straight to Teach, but the deadly power of his weapon pulsed outward like a wave. If her Intent was a headsman's blade, his was a tide, killing and corrupting everything around him. If grass died under Teach's influence, under his, it dissolved to black ash.

When the bodies began to crumble and blow away, the Imperial Guards fled back to the ships. Calder added his own orders to Cheska's: "Retreat. Regroup. Back to the ships." None of them could resist the power of the Awakened blades, and it was foolish to try.

The Regent of the South tipped his hat back, scratching at his hairline. "My oath to eternity, it's not so large a request. Pack up your dancing monkeys and take your show back on the road. We have no bare axes between us, and as I see it, we'll be a family again before year's end."

Calder took a second to puzzle over the man's speech, but apparently Teach understood him. "Please withdraw to your territory, Regent. This is a Guild enforcement matter."

Jorin replaced his hat, shrugged his shoulders, and ran forward. Faster than he had any right to—he must have some sort of enhancements, like Teach herself. In a blink, he was before the Guild Head, slamming his blade down.

The Regent's sword met Tyrfang, and the explosion of shadow and deadly Intent was so strong that it blacked them out for a moment. A few of the slowest Guards died, struck down before they could reach the longboats.

Calder didn't have a quarter the combat experience Teach did, but he could tell that she was losing. Jorin's assault was vicious, his power overwhelming, and with each defense Teach lost ground. In the few clear glimpses Calder caught of her through his spyglass, she was breathing like a bellows. Her armor showed several clear cuts, and Jorin's coat was seemingly unharmed.

The crown wouldn't even distract Jorin; he was one of the Emperor's original companions, so the crown had never meant much to him. Calder cast about for something else, anything else, he could do to tilt the battle in Teach's favor. He could have Foster fire on the Regent, but the two fighters would have to separate first. And if they failed to kill him, if he had some protection against cannonballs or musket-fire, then Jorin's attention would turn to them. He'd sink *The Testament* from where he stood.

Finally, Calder's thoughts returned to something he'd realized only a moment ago. *None of them could resist the power of the Awakened blades, and it was foolish to try.*

None of *them* could do it, but *he* could. He had once before, against the Elderspawn wall outside the Emperor's quarters.

He tightened his sword-belt and grabbed a pistol. "Andel, take me ashore. I'm about to keep Jorin from killing Teach."

Shuffles chuckled from the rigging, where he was gnawing on a fishbone. "KILLING."

Calder pointed up. "He gets it."

Andel looked at Shuffles. "He's delighted because he thinks you'll be murdered."

"If it makes him feel any better," Calder said, dropping the longboat, "he's probably right."

CHAPTER TWENTY-ONE

FIVE YEARS AGO

Calder had once imagined sailing as a tedious chore, but in years of travel-ing the Aion, he'd never felt that way. Either the sky was raining acid, or they were fleeing from some monster large enough to eat the ship, or they were trying to figure out how to avoid stepping in the next deadly trap. Even when days passed by bringing nothing but endless blue, the tension never abated. There was always the understanding that certain death could emerge from the depths at any moment.

Until the last six months. *This* was boring.

After escaping with Urzaia, they'd loaded him up on *The Testament* with the intention to follow the coast south for a few weeks. If anyone had some-how caught their trail, they would expect a Navigator ship to head straight into the Aion, not to stay close to the shore where lesser vessels could tread.

It had been a good plan. Calder still thought so. But sometimes even good plans went awry.

There was one thing they hadn't counted on: that every ship in the Empire would be in the water looking for them.

Calder couldn't understand it. He hadn't expected anyone to know who had destroyed the arena and taken Urzaia, but just in case someone remem-bered who'd given the Champion a ride over from the Capital, he'd decided to act as though he was being pursued. He'd been sure it wouldn't happen.

But they were only three days out from Axciss when they'd run into the first vessel flying the Imperial flag. The captain of the enemy ship had de-manded that they drop anchor and prepare to be boarded, so Calder had taken advantage of *The Testament's* superior speed. The Lyathatan had dragged them away and into the deep Aion, where no one but a Navigator could fol-low.

Except they ran *straight* into Navigators. A pair of them, one with a ship made entirely out of a giant crab carapace, and another that was bone-white from stem to stern. These, too, had insisted that Calder stop.

This time, Calder had asked for an explanation. They told him only that they were on orders straight from the Emperor, and that any suspicious ves-sels were to be detained and searched.

"For what?" he'd asked.

"Prepare to be boarded," he'd been told.

They couldn't take the chance. They had to assume that the Emperor was searching for his fugitive Champion, so they outran the Navigators and returned to the coastline, where they continued south as fast as the Lyathatan could take them. When the giant Elder threatened to capsize them, they switched to their sails for a while.

And when weeks stretched into months, Calder realized that he was spending every day with nothing more than water in his sights, keeping watch for merely human pursuers. The difference between this and the true Aion Sea was painfully dull, and he finally began to understand the stories of sailors gone mad on long voyages. Before this, he'd assumed they were captured by a sanity-devouring Elder. Now, he knew, silence and solitude had an Elder power all their own.

Even Jerri was crabby and irritable after half a year at sea, and Petal never emerged from her quarters. Andel hadn't said a word in days, and Foster... Foster tested his weapons twice a day. And each time, he got closer and closer to putting a round into Calder's head.

He still wasn't sure if that was supposed to be a warning, or if the man was unconsciously fighting a desire to kill him.

Only two inhabitants of *The Testament* had kept their spirits: Urzaia and Shuffles.

"It is time for lunch!" the Champion declared, ringing a bell for no apparent reason. They could all hear him. "And today we have fresh-caught barberfin, delicately seasoned in the Dylian style with a side of mild beans and a half-ration of Moscarelli wine!"

Fish. That's what he was saying. They were eating fish again.

Calder glared at the platter in his hands as though he could turn the fish to beef with the sheer force of his Intent. "Do we have *anything* left in the stores besides fish, Urzaia?"

Urzaia beamed at him. "These did not come from the stores. I caught them myself, just this morning! There are no fresher! Also, I left the heads on them. Delicious delicacy."

He held one up, putting its empty black eyes and gaping mouth next to his face. "Look at him. Look how surprised he looks!" Urzaia imitated the barberfin's slack, dead expression and let out a booming laugh.

There was a gun in Foster's hand, and it looked like he was physically restraining himself from discharging the weapon into Urzaia's face.

Something fluttered like a flag caught in the breeze, and a familiar weight settled onto Calder's shoulder. Tendrils brushed his cheek. "LEFT THE

HEADS ON," Shuffles said, in what was practically a whisper. Relative to its normal volume.

Urzaia pointed his fish at the Elderspawn. "You see? The tiny monster has better taste than the rest of you."

Shuffles launched itself from Calder's shoulder and fluttered over to land on Urzaia's. Its tentacles quested toward the fish.

Calder marched to the wheel, swiveling to keep an eye on the entire horizon.

Urzaia noticed. "What's wrong, Captain? You should eat your fish."

The tension that ran through Calder was a novelty, and he savored it. If this ended up as another false alarm, he'd...he didn't know what he'd do. He would probably just eat his fish and cry on the inside. "It's the middle of the day. If Shuffles woke up before nightfall, that means it expects something interesting to happen."

Jerri ran on deck, hurriedly smoothing her hair. Her braid was loose and sloppy today, but she tugged it into a semblance of order as she raced up. "Are we in danger?" she asked, in tones of desperate hope. For once, Calder agreed with her. Danger would be a welcome break.

"We can only hope," Calder muttered, then he caught a glimpse of something on the horizon. Fumbling at his vest, he finally grabbed a spyglass and held it up to his eye.

He let out a breath. Five Imperial ships, coming straight for them. They were heading away from the Aion Sea, which was strange; they couldn't have actually traveled through the deep Aion, as none of them were Navigators, which meant they must have looped around.

There could be no mistake: they were headed here for *The Testament*.

"We only have a few hours before they reach us," Calder said, and he hated how excited he sounded. "Jerri, Andel, find us somewhere to dock and drop Urzaia. They're between us and the Aion, so we can't slip away and hide. Foster, ready the ship's guns. Petal, prepare to receive wounded." That wasn't likely to be necessary, but he had to give her something to do. "Urzaia...bring me that fish."

Urzaia was only too happy to comply, Shuffles chuckling on his shoulder. Andel had dragged a barrel on deck, onto which he placed a map. He and Jerri pored over it together, already in a lively discussion. Petal crept up to Urzaia, snatched a fish, and then scurried away. Her hair followed her like storm-cloud, and as she climbed down the ladder, it was the last part of her to vanish.

Foster, meanwhile, had tucked his pistol away without moving toward the cannons. He stared at the coast, scratching at his beard.

"What's itching you, Foster?" Calder asked, as Urzaia prepared him a meal.

"I think I know somewhere to dock without trouble," Foster said. His voice carried a weight of reluctance that Calder couldn't miss.

"Where?"

"We're probably three hours from the town where you found me. Silver-reach. We've passed it four or five times over the last couple weeks, only I didn't want to mention it."

Calder remembered a silent town, ten-legged Elder Inquisitors, a batch of crazy cultists, and the dingy room where they kept their captives. He remembered Silverreach.

But it had been a long time, and memories lost their edge. Besides which, he had years of experience on the Aion since then. Elder cults weren't quite as terrifying when you'd come face-to-face with their masters enough time.

Then again...there was that rumor that the Great Elder Ach'magut was imprisoned beneath Silverreach. He might not have the same respect for cultists or lesser Elderspawn, but he maintained a healthy respect for the Great Ones.

His gaze turned to Jerri. She would know exactly what he was thinking, and she'd have an opinion.

She met his gaze, and she didn't look excited. Rather, she seemed resolute, as though she'd come to a decision on her own. "Andel," she said loudly, "let's plot a course for Silverreach."

Beneath his white hat, Andel turned from her to Calder to Foster. After deliberating for a second, he nodded.

Urzaia smiled over them all, like a benevolent statue of the Emperor. "So," he said. "Where are we going?"

The town of Silverreach actually looked significantly better than Calder remembered it. Its harbor was clean and clear, the few boats having long since been cleared away. The lighthouse on the cliffs over the town had a new coat of paint, and its glass sparkled in the sunlight like a beacon all its own.

From the harbor, where the Lyathatan grudgingly held them in place, Calder could see straight down the central street of the town. On either side, the houses were in good repair: here a fresh coat of paint, there a new door. One sloped roof nearby had most of its tiles recently replaced.

But there were still no people. No smoke rose from the chimneys, no dogs barked, no voices whispered behind closed shutters. In fact, it was even quiet compared to their previous visit; this time, not even gulls called.

Urzaia wasn't smiling. He had his hands on his hatchets, and he faced the town with more respect than he had shown his opponents in the arena. "What happened here?" he asked, his tone demanding an answer.

Even as Calder sent a pulse of Intent into the ship, furling the sail overhead, he answered. "The spawn of Ach'magut."

Urzaia nodded once. "Lower the boat, please, Captain."

Calder did so, and the longboat landed in the water with a splash. The Champion moved over to it. "I will hide in the closest of the houses, and I will stay near the doorway. If the Emperor's men search for me, I will kill them rather than travel deeper into the town. When you come to retrieve me, do not enter the house. Instead, call to me from the street. If I do not answer your third call, leave me behind."

With that, he swung over the side of the ship and into the waiting longboat. Seconds later, Calder saw him rowing toward the shore. Each time he hauled on the oars, his boat launched closer as though he had his own personal Lyathatan pulling him forward.

"I don't think I've ever heard him speak seriously before," Andel said. "I'm impressed."

"Pull out some cargo," Calder ordered. "We're receiving guests, and we need to be ready to explain why we're here." He glanced over at Foster, whose eyes were locked to the shore. "Foster? Do you need to inspect the equipment?"

Foster shook himself, snatching his shooting-glasses down from the bridge of his nose. "No, I'm...no, Captain. Bad memories, is all. I'll have everything laid out for inspection when our guests arrive."

The five white sails and five red Imperial flags were almost upon them. The crew of *The Testament* scurried over the deck, setting out their weapons and cargo for inspection.

Calder even laid his cutlass and pistol on the deck, once he saw the longboat deploy from the nearest ship. He was making a show of being unarmed, which would demonstrate his cooperation and goodwill toward the boarding soldiers.

But he was a Navigator aboard his ship, and the Lyathatan was restless beneath them. He was anything but unarmed.

It took Jerri and Foster both to wrestle Shuffles back into its cage. Its deep voice kept booming, demanding and angry at once, but they eventually got the Elderspawn back under control. When the resonant voice vanished, Calder knew they had finally gotten Shuffles' blanket over its cage. He'd invested the blanket to lull creatures to sleep, though it didn't seem to work reliably on Elders.

But it had worked this time, and with only minutes to spare; the Imperial longboat was close enough that Calder could make out the individual faces of its passengers.

He squared his hat, unfurled a ladder over the side of the boat, summoned a welcoming smile, and waited.

The first aboard was a man Urzaia's size, with slabs of thick muscle that made him look as though he could put his fist through *The Testament*'s mast. His skin was darker than Andel's, so he must have been a pure-blooded Heartlander. Far from home, then.

He scanned the deck with a hand on the butt of his pistol and, finding nothing amiss, he bowed to Calder. Then he stood aside. Two smaller men climbed aboard next, followed by a Heartlander woman. They all wore the deep red uniforms of Imperial officers; similar to those worn by Imperial Guards, but different in style and trim. These were not Guild members, just soldiers. But in this case, they outranked him.

The woman was Calder's age, perhaps a little older, and she had no badges of rank on her chest. Even so, the others stepped aside as she walked forward.

When she was ten paces from Calder, she saluted crisply. "Second Under-lieutenant Mora Belyard, sir. Permission to come aboard?"

Calder wasn't sure where a "second under-lieutenant" ranked, but he doubted it was very high. And he couldn't ignore the irony of a potential enemy asking to come aboard after she was already standing on his deck.

But then, he had very little idea what to do with the Imperial army. In the Capital, virtually everything was controlled by the Imperial Guard, with whom he had entirely too much experience. He knew the Guilds had less of a direct presence outside of the major cities, but he'd never learned the proper etiquette for greeting a second-under lieutenant as she stood on his deck.

He let none of his uncertainty show on his face. Instead, he returned a haphazard version of her salute—he tried his best, but he couldn't do any-thing about a lack of practice—and nodded to her. "Welcome aboard, Under-lieutenant Belyard. I admit, I was surprised to see your flag, but we've moved all our weapons and most of our cargo up for your inspection. If you'd like to see the rest, I'd be happy to show you our hold."

Not 'happy,' exactly, because Shuffles was currently in the hold. If they removed the blanket from the cage and came upon an unexpected Elderspawn, he would have some quick talking to do.

A smile flickered over Belyard's face. "That won't be necessary, Captain. Give me a moment, and I'll be off your ship and we can leave you to...whatever you were doing in an empty, condemned town. To which the Emperor has restricted access."

Calder winced. He hadn't known Silverreach was restricted, though in hindsight it made perfect sense. The Emperor would have learned about the Elder presence by now, and had doubtless issued the restriction to keep ordinary vessels from stopping here. As a Navigator, he wouldn't have been expected to dock here at all—Navigators only traveled where they were requested, and who would put in a request for an empty town? Besides, Calder contacted the Guild as little as possible. Even if his Guild Head tried to keep all her ships out of the area, *The Testament* might never have gotten word.

But that couldn't be the reason Under-lieutenant Belyard was here. The five ships had been on him before he'd decided to set course for Silverreach.

Why, then?

Belyard pulled the glove off her right hand and knelt, pressing her bare palm against the deck.

Of course. He'd been afraid of a Reader coming aboard ever since they'd picked up Urzaia, but for some reason he hadn't considered it today. *Stupid.* It was possible that, with a little luck, she might be able to pick up a remnant of Urzaia's Intent.

And it was absolutely impossible for her to miss the presence of the Lyathatan, chained beneath their ship. The Elder's presence was permitted by the Navigator's Guild, but if she didn't know that, she might take Calder into custody and turn him over to the Blackwatch. Which would have its own set of complications.

One of which included being forced to abandon Urzaia ashore in an Elder-haunted and abandoned town.

He shivered as he felt her Intent pass through the ship, questing and insistent. After almost fifteen minutes, she steadied herself on the rail and pulled herself to her feet. "I apologize for the inconvenience, Captain. Nothing out of the ordinary here."

He couldn't conceal his surprise. She had scanned his ship and found *nothing* unusual?

"Really?" he asked.

Another quarter-second smile flashed across her expression. "Nothing out of the ordinary for a Navigator's ship. We'll take our leave immediately, and I apologize once again for the inconvenience."

She started to turn, but Calder needed more information. If they were looking for Urzaia, why hadn't they thought to look ashore? If they weren't, then why had they chased him into the shallows?

He began hesitantly. "If I may ask, what *were* you looking for?"

She turned back to him, tightening the glove onto her hand. "These past few months, reports of Elder activity have increased weekly. The Emperor has the entire army, both the Luminian Order and the Blackwatch, and half the Navigators on containment duty. Every city and town supervised, every vessel inspected. It's hard enough on us, but the alternative is leaving Imperial citizens to the Elders. And the Emperor would never allow that."

No, the Emperor would never *abandon his citizens to danger when he had the power to save them,* Calder thought, and he could taste the cynicism. But he had one more question. "I'm sorry. Increased Elder activity...all along the Izyrian coast? Surely there's somewhere we can safely make port. They can't be everywhere."

She eyed him with an expression he couldn't read. "Not everywhere along the Izyrian coast, Captain. Everywhere. We've received emergency reports from all over the Empire."

His heart began to pound like a war-drum.

"When I said the Blackwatch and the Luminian Order had been mobilized, I meant all of them. The entire Guilds. Every chapter, everywhere."

Calder nodded acknowledgement to the Under-lieutenant, giving her one of the shallow half-bows that polite society favored in the Heartlands. "Thank you for your concern and your prompt response, Under-lieutenant."

"Take my advice, and bring your crew elsewhere. I know the Navigators are exceptions to most rules, but this town was quarantined for a reason. There's no sense taking chances, especially now."

Under-lieutenant Belyard saluted one more time and left the ship, taking her men with her.

When she left, Calder let out a deep breath. "All hands on deck," he said quietly, and Andel opened the hatch to shout down for Petal. Technically, he should have brought Petal up on deck for the officer's inspection, but that would have shaken Petal's nerves for days. As she was an alchemist, he'd planned on saying she was in the middle of a delicate project that could not be abandoned without risk to the safety of all onboard. In the end, it hadn't mattered.

Petal emerged a few seconds after her hair, quivering and looking around for soldiers. When she saw none, she scurried up to the stern deck to join the rest of the crew.

Andel stood as dispassionately as ever, hands behind his back, the silver crest of the sun gleaming on his chest. Foster grumbled into his beard and fiddled with a musket. Petal glanced up at him through the veil of her hair. Jerri stood in the center, in a simple green dress totally unsuited for the deck of a ship. Her emerald earrings flickered in the sun, her braid hung down behind her, and she gave him a brilliant smile.

He winked at Jerri but watched the whole crew, minus Urzaia, fixing them into his mind. For once, the Aion Sea was the direction *away* from the Elders, which showed that everything in the world had gone wrong. And here they were in Silverreach, where they more than expected a Great Elder was buried. If he'd heard the reports of Elder activity before, he would never have stopped here.

But here they were, and Urzaia was ashore alone. Granted, he was the one most likely to survive an Elderspawn assault by himself, but he still wasn't safe.

In case the worst happened—and in this case, he couldn't even imagine how bad the worst possibility was—he wanted to remember the crew like this. As they were now.

From beneath his feet, a male voice boomed out in rumbling laughter. Shuffles was joining in.

So they *were* headed into lethal danger. Strangely, that made Calder feel better. At least he knew.

"We're going to get Urzaia," Calder said. "Jerri and Foster, stay with the ship. Andel and Petal, with me."

There was a moment of communal confusion as everyone worked out what he'd said. Jerri's eyes flashed. "Petal can stay, *I'll* go." Petal shivered like a leaf in the wind, and even Andel looked confused.

Calder met Jerri's eyes. "If we don't make it back, we need people aboard who can actually sail out of here. That means someone who can navigate and a Reader who *might* be able to persuade the Lyathatan to move. That's you and Foster. I need someone with me who can fight, and that's Andel. He can also potentially help me carry Urzaia out of there, if Urzaia is...immobilized. For the same reason, Petal is coming along for potential first aid."

Andel moved to the second longboat, which was actually salvage from another Navigator's wreckage. It was three feet shorter and a little wider than the first longboat, so they had taken to calling it the 'shortboat.'

"That makes just enough sense that I won't reject it out of hand," Andel said. "Personally, I would rather take a few potions than Petal herself. I'm afraid she'll freeze up if we're in danger."

Petal raised a hand. "Me too," she said softly.

Calder placed a hand on her head, feeling as though he was comforting a child. "I have every faith in you, Petal." The thought came to him that she was *still* almost five years older than he was, but it was too late to change his attitude now. "You've never run before."

"I usually hide," she whispered, but he ignored that too.

"All ashore that's going ashore," Calder called, dropping the shortboat and spinning out the ladder. Jerri was still glaring at him, but she did wave to him as he left. Foster was loading one of the port guns, leveling it at Silverreach. Calder appreciated the caution.

In the shortboat, Calder and Andel took one oar each—the first longboat wasn't wide enough for two, but this one was. They began pulling for shore, and Calder couldn't help but notice how much longer it took them together than it had Urzaia alone.

As they drew closer, Calder extended his Intent. If he remembered correctly, he should be able to get a sense of the same strange, Elder Intent he had detected last time. It had hung in the air, thick as spring fog.

This time he sensed...nothing. Just as he might have expected in a normal town.

They tied up to the dock and walked ashore; other than the boards creaking under their weight, the town was absolutely silent. When they got closer, Calder leaned a hand against the closest building.

The Intent was calm, almost welcoming. As though a happy family had lived within for years, investing the house around them with their peace.

For once, there's less *danger than I expected,* Calder thought, pleased with himself. He'd over-prepared this time, and that was a good state to be in.

Then his memory died.

It was impossible to put into words, that sensation. It was as though someone had reached up and pulled a chain, switching his awareness off like a quicklamp. The world didn't go black, it just...vanished, as though he'd forgotten to pay attention to anything.

When he came back to himself, blinking and looking around, the crew was gathered together in the pool of light cast by a single candle. The *whole* crew.

Urzaia, looking around grimly with a hatchet in each hand. Jerri, her mouth half open in awe. Andel, clutching his White Sun medallion with his eyes closed. Foster, sputtering and jumping to his feet. Petal, quivering and holding a tiny quicklamp out for light. And him. He realized he had his sword in hand, but didn't remember drawing it.

As he adjusted to the gloom surrounding the dim light, he realized they were standing on smooth tile, not the rough cobblestones of Silverreach's streets. Dark shapes loomed over them, the silhouettes of a hundred towers.

No. He squinted closer. *Not towers. Bookshelves.*

Books lined the towers in shelf after shelf, stretching up to the distant ceiling. They were shadowed and difficult to make out, but he caught a glimpse of a dozen different colors and styles of cover. More books than he had ever imagined.

They were in an enormous library.

CHAPTER TWENTY-TWO

When we speak of 'the void,' we mean that vast and empty realm we occasionally observe as powerful Elders travel or communicate. Some ancient scholars believed that this void connects us to other worlds, but none could ever prove it. Who would lightly step into the realm where Elders tread?

—NOTES FROM THE BLACKWATCH ARCHIVES

The battle between Jarelys Teach and Jorin Maze-walker had been terrifying enough through a spyglass from a safe distance away. As Calder stood on the Gray Island docks, amidst the scattered bodies of those who hadn't run fast enough, he found that the experience close-up was far worse.

Teach, clad in red-and-black armor, carried a matching sword. Tyrfang's Intent was the macabre madness of a slaughterhouse, the sharp edge of an executioner's axe, the fear of the condemned facing obliteration. It pressed against Calder's mind with visions of blood and inescapable death, even as its aura actually darkened the ground around her. As Teach fought, desperate and defensive, the earth died with each of her retreating steps.

And Jorin advanced, following her, his own sword a twisted mirror of hers. Up close, Calder saw its defects: patches like rust or bloodstains that mired the surface of the blade. They seemed to crawl, like patches of worms, and its Intent was a knot he couldn't begin to untangle. Like every spiteful, hateful, murderous Intent he'd ever felt, all trapped inside one weapon. Its power wasn't as focused as Tyrfang, but it was heavier, the weight of two thousand years crashing down around Teach's defenses. Jorin moved forward almost casually, hacking his way closer to a lethal stroke, his dark-tinted glasses flashing in the sunlight.

Mist played around their legs as they fought, and with every clash of Awakened blades, darkness and crazed Intent swallowed them. Rings of dirt blasted out whenever their swords met, as though even the dirt couldn't bear to be so close.

And Calder was planning on walking into *that*.

Surely I'd be better off shooting him. He'd considered it before, but back on the ship, he hadn't wanted to draw Jorin's attention to *The Testament* for nothing more than a distant chance. Now, though...

Calder pulled the pistol from his belt and fired.

It wasn't likely to be a lethal shot. At thirty yards, even someone much more skilled would need their share of luck to kill someone with a single bullet. Foster was always mocking his abilities, trying to goad him into practice, but today it seemed his luck was good. Jorin staggered back, struck in one arm, and for an instant Teach was able to push *him* back.

A pink light shone within the wound, as though Jorin hid a quicklamp in his coat, and an instant later he was as strong as ever. The light continued to shine, giving Calder hope that he'd at least inflicted some injury.

Then the Regent flicked his gaze over to Calder, just for an instant, and a river of dark Intent whipped out. That was all the attention Calder warranted, and it would be more than enough to kill him and dissolve his body. But Calder had prepared a defense.

He hoped.

As he'd done once before, Calder drew his own Awakened sword and braced his Intent through Kelarac's mark. His Intent seemed to solidify, as though propped up by a bigger, more permanent force. He felt himself steady, and as Jorin's power struck him, it was first lessened by the aura of Calder's orange-spotted blade. The strange energy invested in this weapon seemed to be toxic to Elderspawn, and it did an admirable job of reducing Jorin's attack.

So when the wave of shadow struck him, slamming up against his Intent fortified by Kelarac's mark, Calder expected to survive. He didn't expect to push through it so easily. It felt like pushing against a freezing wind blowing off of a graveyard, stinking and repulsive; it wasn't pleasant, but it certainly wasn't difficult. Resisting Tyrfang's aura had been much harder back in the Imperial Palace, and judging by the way Teach had been repeatedly pushed back, Jorin's weapon couldn't be weaker.

Calder opened himself up to Read the atmosphere around him, and instantly understood. The Emperor's white armor. He was wrapped in protective Intent so ancient and solid that it defended even his essence, letting him march forward even under Jorin's attack.

That worked, he realized, with no small measure of disbelief. *Now, can I take a direct hit?* He decided not to test that.

Jorin still wasn't watching him as he jogged closer, evidently having dismissed him with the single attack. Calder's heart pounded. He only had to distract the Regent, to occupy him long enough to give Teach a chance to kill him.

Calder was close enough to begin his strike, stepping forward to drive his

Awakened cutlass into Jorin's side, before the Regent saw him. Jorin's head jerked back in disbelief, and he barely managed to avoid a cut from Teach as he back-stepped away from Calder.

Together, Calder and the Guild Head forced Jorin onto the defensive. It wasn't pleasant, fighting within both corrosive auras—it was like forcing his way through a lake of raw sewage—but it was bearable. Between his own sword, Kelarac's mark, and the Emperor's armor, he could stand among two of the greatest fighters in Imperial history.

For about five seconds, Calder had never felt more powerful.

Then Jorin blasted him with Intent, another gust of freezing wind, staggering him in his tracks. The Regent followed up with a slash to Calder's face, making him jerk his cutlass up, but it was a feint. Jorin reversed the strike to land on Teach.

And it did land. Teach had thrown herself out of position to protect Calder, only to take the cut on her armored left arm.

The sound of the strike was a satisfying clang of metal-on-metal, and for a second Calder believed that her armor had saved her. Then he saw the dark scratch on its surface and heard her agonized scream.

He had to shoulder-tackle her out of the way to protect her from Jorin's follow-up. She never lost her grip on Tyrfang, even as she tumbled to the ground and rolled away.

"You're the seedling Emperor, then," Jorin said, panting. "Let's have you go a round or two."

Calder attacked first. As Loreli, another Regent, had once put it: *"In a duel, the defender is losing."* Jorin swept his black blade in a lazy arc, as though he meant to slice the orange-spotted cutlass in half.

When Calder turned the hit, Jorin's eyebrows climbed up into his hat. "Here now, where'd you get that sword?"

Instead of responding, Calder attacked the man from the left, opening up some space, trying to force him away from Teach's body. If he gave her some time, she might recover, though her low, pained moans didn't give him much hope.

The Regent tolerated that for a few exchanges, then he lost patience. He reversed the sword in both hands, driving his blade into the ground.

All around Calder, the earth blasted away into loose black grit. He lost his footing, tumbling to the ground, shielding his mouth and eyes with his arm. Even when the air cleared he couldn't find purchase, coughing in the rising dust-cloud, trying to clear the dirt from his eyes.

Jorin walked up, a hazy figure, calm and unhurried. "If you survive, we'll have a chat about your sword. But I don't mean to pressure you. Life is such a brief candle." He raised his blade.

And, as Calder had experienced several times before, he was suddenly somewhere else. The world shifted around him, as quick as a vanishing stage curtain.

Now, he stood on a floor of polished white marble, and he was feeling remarkably better: he was warm, and clean, and not at all covered in blackened grit. He stood in a shrine of some kind, though where there would usually be a statue of the Emperor was instead a towering marble figure of some kind of warped fish-creature. There were no walls, only rows of columns looking out onto the sea.

The sea stretched all around him. This shrine must have been on some tiny island on the Aion, because he didn't see any other land, only black storm-tossed waves. The wind outside was wicked, stirring up wild surf, as black clouds danced and lightning lit the night.

Other than the lightning, the scene was illuminated only by a smoky torch dimly flickering over the statue's head. Calder felt that he should have been freezing, but somehow the wind stayed a perfectly comfortable temperature.

"I once intended to have this built," Kelarac said. "It's in the center of what you now call the Aion Sea." He stood looking up at the statue, just as Calder remembered him: a fashionable Heartlander, his thin beard neatly trimmed, clothes just as the Emperor would have worn them, rings on every finger and waves of jewels on his neck. A few of his teeth gleamed gold as he smiled, and his most prominent feature—the polished band of steel over his eyes—reflected the strikes of lightning.

"Why didn't you?" Calder asked politely. He was still trying to be considerate, out of respect for a massively powerful being, but in truth his frustration had grown. Kelarac was behind Jerri's actions somehow, but he still pretended to be Calder's friend.

"Timing. It's all about the proper place, isn't it? The right time, the precise location. Temporal or spatial, if the *place* is off even slightly, then it might as well have never existed at all…"

Calder let the Great Elder muse privately. In their previous meetings, he had never waxed philosophical, instead sticking close to business. It could mean he was ready to give Calder a gift, or to eat him alive.

"You didn't destroy the Optasia," Kelarac noted.

"Yet."

"You believe it would destroy you."

"Would it?" Not that Calder would take the word of the Soul Collector, but a straight answer would be nice.

Kelarac's golden teeth flashed. "That depends on a number of shifting factors. Place, as I said. However, I can assure you that even though the throne might be unsuitable, the rest of the network is very much intact. I can find a use for it."

"Of that, sir, I have no doubt." Calder made the words sound respectful instead of wry.

"In exchange for your word that you will deliver the Optasia to me, I can deliver some immediate help. Allies that can save you from your current situation."

Calder's mind flashed to the strange Navigator ship, the one decorated in gold. "Those were your people waiting outside the Gray Island?"

Kelarac folded ringed fingers together. "They're nearby."

"And they can actually save me from the Regent?"

"Oh yes."

Calder had been trying to stretch the time as much as possible, but he only had one answer. "I'm sorry. I can't." The price was too high.

Delivering the Heart of Nakothi was one thing; he'd given a piece of one Elder to another. If Kelarac had been willing to dig a little, he could have excavated a heart on his own. But as far as Calder was concerned, that had been an equitable trade...and even now, it didn't weigh easily on him. He often wondered what horrors Kelarac could perpetrate with a piece of the Dead Mother's power.

But instead of flying into a rage, as Calder had half expected, Kelarac nodded. "Too high a price. I think you estimate the value of the Emperor's device too favorably. Soon, it may not be worth the metal from which it was cast. But I wouldn't be much of a collector if I didn't know how to haggle, would I?"

Kelarac's smile was friendly, but Calder reminded himself that it came from a Great Elder. "Did you have another price in mind?"

"Always, Reader of Memory. Always. You recall, I'm sure, the Consultant called Shera."

There were a few scenes in his life that Calder would never forget. They were burned into his brain as if by acid. One of them, to his eternal regret, was the image of Shera pushing Jerri over *The Testament's* railing and into the ocean. He could still see Jerri's eyes as she fell; they were locked on his, still carrying shame and terror.

"I do," he said.

"Then perhaps you'll find this price more palatable. I will send you my allies. In exchange, you and they will cut your way through the Consultant's Guild and execute Shera without mercy or compunction." His calm had slipped briefly, his voice vicious. "Afterwards, if her body were to find its way down to me, I would be...even more generous."

Calder watched the Elder, chewing on what he'd just heard. What did it mean that Kelarac valued Shera only slightly less than the Emperor's throne? That he would give up possession of a worldwide network of Intent amplification that could turn any Reader into an army, in exchange for guaranteeing Shera's death?

What did the Elders care about one Consultant?

"The last time I saw Jerri," Calder said quietly, "she asked me much the same thing."

"In some ways, she is a wise woman. In others, she is still foolish, but here she is wise."

What had Jerri said? That someone had *warned* her how dangerous Shera was. Someone who had gotten to her in her cell, and who had returned her Soulbound Vessel to her.

Kelarac. It had been Kelarac all along. Calder wasn't surprised, but he felt as though his eyes had been opened for the first time. He broadened his smile until it was almost painful.

"I think...not. I think I'll take my chances against Jorin."

The Great Elder's own smile had faded, until he looked regretful. "There are wiser courses, Calder Marten."

"If your allies are nearby, tell them to stay *away*. I have no use for you, you Elder-spawned filth, and you can shove yourself back into the hole you came from." His anger built with every word. "I'm tired of dancing like a puppet for you, so I'm cutting the strings. If you show yourself in front of me again, we'll see if the Emperor's armory might, by chance, have something that can make a Great Elder bleed. You turned my wife against me, and light and life, I'll make sure you pay for it."

His voice was ringing out by the end, until his shouts filled the storm-lit shrine, and he was panting as he finished. The dream didn't go away. The marble under his feet remained as solid as ever.

"You'll be the one to pay the price, little King," Kelarac said quietly. "Yours is a sad defiance, because defiance requires a choice, and you have none. You are an actor on a stage, speaking lines that have been said a thousand, thousand times before."

Calder tried to respond, but his throat was stuck. The shrine and the storm faded into darkness, until all that remained was the gleam of the Great Elder's blindfold. And the echo of his voice:

"Dance on your string, little puppet. Dance..."

Calder returned to reality caked in dust, with Jorin advancing, raising his sword for a strike. He scrambled backwards with hands and feet, trying to stand, knowing that it was all but hopeless.

Still, he'd defied one of the Great Elders to its face. The stories were filled with noble fools who tried that. They usually died horribly, but Calder found the feeling strangely liberating. He might die, but at least he wouldn't die a slave.

He raised his sword to block the oncoming blow, hoping desperately that the Emperor's armor would be able to take a hit. When Jorin struck, Calder had no choice but to meet the edge of the Regent's blade with his own. The clash of Intent seared into his mind, and he slid backwards another few feet.

The dust had cleared away, leaving the sky shockingly blue...except for the dark crack spreading through it. An opening into the void. A fingerhold for the Elders, probably. And below that, the Aion Sea, with a Navigator's ship just beside him. It loomed over them, so that he was about to die in its shadow.

Perfect. I'm going to die under a Navigator's ship, and it's not even mine. Those gold-edged sails were too gaudy for his taste.

Jorin walked forward to finish Calder, but his expression changed. He snapped his head up, looking at the ship, and then leaped backwards. Something—someone—enormous slammed into the ground where he'd been standing. A man in slate-gray armor, with a pair of maces strapped to his belt. He carried a helmet under one arm, leaving his head bare. His hair was black, with wings of silver at the edges.

Baldesar Kern, Head of the Champion's Guild.

"I see you changed your mind," Calder said, as soon as he'd caught his breath. The relief was flooding his mind, filling him with elation.

Kern shrugged one shoulder without turning around. "Not quite. I told you, I wouldn't fight for someone I didn't trust. If you're willing to stand up to a Regent, I'll trust you."

Jorin had taken out a roll of bandages and had begun wrapping the black blade of his sword. "Baldesar Kern, if I may presume."

Kern inclined his head.

"I can still make a rousing fight if it's just the two of us, so I can only assume..." Four more silhouettes stepped up to the edge of the ship, outlined in sunlight. "More Champions, yes, as I thought. Well, that's just clear as a winter spring, isn't it? I admit I am overmatched."

"You'll come with us," Kern said. It didn't sound like a question at all.

Jorin tilted his hat back to look at the Champions on deck. "I doubt it. Unless you happen to have some Harrowing wine onboard, which I can't imagine you do. You'd have to be five hundred years older than you look."

Kern shifted his helmet to one hand, still not wearing it, and drew a dark, heavy mace with the other. "If you make me use my Vessel, this doesn't end well for anyone."

"Particularly not for *you*, if I grasp the—"

The Champion shot forward, slamming his mace into Jorin's chest. Or what should have been Jorin's chest. Instead, the Regent managed to get his half-bandaged sword between him and the weapon. The force still blasted him backwards as though he'd been fired from a catapult, and when he hit the ground, a cloud of black dust and ash billowed up.

Kern slipped his mace back into his belt, watching the cloud rise. "Too dangerous to chase him. Let him run."

Calder thought the words were meant for him until the Champions on deck saluted and returned. Gingerly, Calder walked forward. The fight had done no favors for his still-healing leg. "Thank you, Guild Head. If not for you, I'd be one more pile of dust."

"Oh, I don't know," Kern said, giving him a once-over. "That's some fine armor you're wearing."

"Still, I owe you."

Kern shook his head. "The debt's not to you. I was hired."

A chill seeped back into Calder's bones. "Hired?"

"Shortly after you spoke with me. A Heartlander man, I imagine a Reader, said he had a good feeling about you. He hired me and as many others from the Guild as we could round up. Paid in goldmarks."

"He told you to save me?"

"Told me to give you a chance," Kern said. His face cracked into a small smile. "Said he was confident you'd prove yourself. I didn't believe him, but I do now."

Calder didn't want to ask, but he had to know. "You said he was a Reader. How did you know?"

Kern hung his helmet from a loop on his belt. "Some places, Readers have strange customs. They believe blinding yourself helps you sense Intent more clearly. This man, he seemed like the polite, civilized, educated type, but it looked like he'd blinded himself. He wore a metal blindfold over his eyes."

CHAPTER TWENTY-THREE

Upon realizing that they had been mysteriously transported to a towering library that most likely had connections to a Great Elder, Calder's first reaction was not fear. It was irritation.

He'd tried to leave a few people behind to protect them, but the entire crew had ended up off the ship anyway. If he'd known it would turn out like this, he wouldn't have wasted his time worrying.

Petal's tiny quicklamp expanded the circle of candlelight, allowing everyone to see the surrounding bookshelves in more detail. Each structure stood as tall as any building in the Capital; ten stories or more of endless books stacked to the cavernous ceiling.

After staring into the darkness for any sign of movement, Calder carefully slid a little closer to the books.

On the bottom shelf, dusty scrolls were surrounded by glass cases. On the next, the books were bound by wood and hide—he knelt to examine the spine of one tome bound in polished blackwood, and found that he couldn't read it.

That fact alone confirmed what he'd already suspected: there were Elders involved. And not the lesser Elderspawn, like Shuffles, who seemed to have little more intelligence than animals, but the higher Elders. Maybe even a Great Elder.

It had been over a thousand years since any language except Imperial was heard among humans. That left two possibilities: either these words did not originate with humans, or they were over a thousand years old.

Either way, that meant Elders.

His memory whispered to him the name of the one sealed underneath Silverreach: *Ach'magut.*

Without inspecting that thought any further, he turned back to his crew. They had shown their training and experience by standing with their backs to the candlelight, weapons in hand. Even Jerri looked fierce and ready for battle, though she only held a dagger. If Elderspawn attacked, she'd last even less time than Petal, who held a stoppered bottle of acid ready to throw.

And that was a cheery thought, wasn't it?

They were still comparing notes. "...I was on the wheel. I didn't lose consciousness, I didn't even *blink*, but I found myself here with no warning." Jerri.

Foster had a pistol pointed off into the gloom as he scanned the shadows. "Doesn't matter how we got here, we've got to go. Now. I've been imprisoned by crazy Elder worshipers more than enough in my life."

"If you'd like to be the first to run off into the dark, Mr. Foster, be my guest." Andel sounded calm, but he had one hand on his pistol and the other around his White Sun medallion.

"Might as well die out *there!*" Foster shouted. "It's better than standing around here, waiting to die!"

Urzaia's voice was even louder than Foster's. "You will not die here! I will protect you!"

Whatever they decided to do, Calder was certain that shouting wasn't the way to go about it. Foster started to reply, and Andel opened his mouth to cut him off, but they both froze when Calder's cutlass cut down the middle of the group. His blade came to rest inches above the candle's flame.

"That's enough of that," Calder said, his voice little more than a whisper. "Urzaia, lead the way. Foster, take the rear. Andel on the left, I'll take the right. Walk straight down the row of bookcases. Petal, leave a mark on every row we pass."

"Walk *straight down the aisle?*" Foster choked out, though at least he stayed quiet. "If they're waiting for us, that's right where they'll be!"

"Or they're waiting for us to go back the other way, or waiting for us to stay here, or waiting for the light to go out so they can take us one by one." Calder kept his eyes locked on Foster's as he spoke. "We might be playing into their hands no matter what we do, so we may as well try to escape while we're at it."

Foster grumbled under his breath, but Urzaia had already taken up his position and started a slow march. The rest of them followed.

Every few yards, Petal carefully let a drop of acid fall from her stoppered bottle. It scarred the floor with a hiss and a little wisp of smoke, leaving a mark the size of a breadcrumb in the smooth floor.

They had traveled for the better part of an hour, according to Andel's pocket-watch, when Jerri gently rested her fingers on his arm. "Don't look up. There's something moving between the bookcases above us. Do *not* look up."

Calder resisted the urge to throw his head back and stare straight up, keeping his movement natural. He continued to scan the shadows around them, as he had the entire time, but this time he allowed his eyes to flow a little higher.

For the first minute or two he spotted nothing, which was agonizing in its own way. The only thing more frightening than Elderspawn he *could* see were Elderspawn he *couldn't* see, and his imagination told him that they were right behind him, descending to the back of his neck on silent threads.

But he kept his calm, and finally he caught something—a flicker of movement at the corner of one of the bookshelves, like an insectoid leg being withdrawn.

His heart pounded, his breath came faster, and he feigned a stumble to grab onto Urzaia's shoulder. When the Champion looked at him, surprised, Calder whispered the situation to him.

Urzaia's face darkened, and his hands tightened around his hatchets, but otherwise he gave no sign that Calder had spoken. He continued marching down the hall as Calder and Jerri conveyed the information to the others.

Even as he whispered to Andel, Calder's thoughts buzzed frantically. The position of the Elderspawn left them with very few helpful options. *They're above us, so they're tracking us. They'll see everything we do. We have to reach the end of this room at some point, so will they drop down on us then? Will they wait so long?*

They had seen enough curve of the ceiling at this point to realize that the room did in fact have an end; they weren't sealed in some sort of Elder-generated dream world. The room had walls, though they were unbelievably far apart. In the back of Calder's mind, he wondered if the bookcases acted as columns, helping to support the weight of the chamber.

If they stood and fought, the terrain didn't favor them. How could it, against an enemy capable of leaping down on their backs from above?

Since they couldn't stop, that left only one option: move forward as fast as they could.

Calder increased his pace, and as soon as the others realized, they matched him. Within ten more minutes, the crew had effectively doubled their speed, and was all but running down the library aisle. They maintained complete silence, so only the pounding of their shoes and their harsh panting breaths cut through the quiet.

Overhead, the flickering movement of the Elderspawn hurried to match them. Calder began to catch them more often, even when he wasn't focusing, as they hurried from case to case. With enough fragmented pictures—jointed, alien legs and eyes that waved on flexible stalks—he confirmed what he'd already suspected. These were the spawn of Ach'magut, the ten-legged spiders with innumerable eyes. The same ones that had haunted Silverreach four years before. The Inquisitors.

But this time, they were keeping their distance, watching. Observing. Calder was forcibly reminded of Ach'magut's title: the Overseer. It made sense that any minions of his would keep their distance and watch before engaging, but if that was the case...

Why hadn't they done so last time?

On the crew's last visit to Silverreach, the Elderspawn had attacked outright, forcing them into the hands of the cultists. They were acting differently now, more cautiously. What had changed?

It was sheer madness to try and guess the mind of an Elder, but Calder had a disturbing thought. What if they *had* acted this way, four years ago? What if the two Inquisitors they saw were just the Imperial Guard of their kind, sent to take them into custody, while hundreds more watched?

An image formed in Calder's mind, of Silverreach above with its streets of "empty" buildings. He was beginning to see the town differently now.

Not a town at all. A hive.

But ultimately this was all just speculation, and in reality, the Inquisitors hadn't attacked yet. The sooner they reached the end of the room, the sooner they could find an exit. The ceiling had curved down low enough now that they should come upon the end any second.

No sooner did the thought come to him than they reached the end of the library, the ceiling flowing down to meet the floor in a polished gray wall. The light of Petal's quicklamp spilled onto the wall in front of them, illuminating a vast door of bronze.

He wasn't sure it *was* a door, at first. There were no hinges he could see, and the bronze was almost a perfect circle. It only made contact with the floor at one point. Its surface was covered in symbols and diagrams, interacting in a way that reminded Calder of ancient astronomy texts. Like someone had charted the movements of the stars on this ancient panel of bronze.

It was only when he extended a hand, intending to Read the panel for instructions, that he became certain it was a door. Its Intent flooded his mind, hammered his awareness, as though this was the very *picture* of a door and anything that he had once recognized as a doorway was only a feeble delusion of his pitiful mind. *This* was a door, and all else was but a pale copy.

He trembled at the overwhelming gut-punch of Intent, sucking in a deep breath.

The others had begun to quietly debate what this bronze circle was, and what the diagrams on its surface meant. Maybe they were a map, maybe directions, maybe a dire warning to travelers.

"It's a door," Calder said, walking up to it.

"Are you sure?" Urzaia asked doubtfully.

Calder's nose tingled, as though it was about to bleed, but he put two fingers to his face and they came back dry. The aftermath of his attempt at Reading. "I have never been more sure of anything in my entire life," he said.

He quested around the edges of the bronze doorway until he found three symbols in a row—like human thumbprints, though the lines were too twisted and irregular. Calder pushed on them, only the slightest application of force, and the door began to slide upwards into the wall.

"Wait," Andel said, as the door began to move, but it was too late.

If Calder had thought his impressions of the entrance were overwhelming, if he thought the previous wave of Intent was too much for his senses, they were *nothing* compared to the seething ocean of information that violated his mind now.

On the other side was a writhing, pulsing, squirming mass of limbs, eyes, tendrils, ears, appendages without name and without number.

On the other side was a vast book of endless pages, containing all the knowledge of countless years, such an unknowable repository of truth that a thousand humans could not hear it all with a thousand lifetimes of study.

On the other side was a world unto itself, a complex and ancient dream more real than waking.

On the other side was Ach'magut.

Calder stood frozen, all his senses consumed in the Overseer, but in many ways he was more aware than before. He knew when Foster broke free of the spell binding him, turning to flee from the Great Elder, only to come face-to-face with an army of Inquisitors.

He knew that Petal's fear was crystallizing into the knowledge that she could not fight Ach'magut, which brought with it a measure of relief.

He knew Andel's revulsion, which was matched only by a bizarre knowledge. The former Pilgrim was disgusted by Ach'magut's existence, but he was still on the lookout for something to gain from this. As though he could turn Ach'magut's knowledge against the rest of its kind.

He knew Urzaia's grim resignation, as the Champion realized that some things could not be fought.

And he knew Jerri was terrified and excited all at once, as though she'd come face to face with everything she'd ever wanted...and it could kill her at any second.

All this, Calder knew in an instant.

The Great Elder's tentacles slithered between them and among them, analyzing their emotions, their pasts, their physical compositions. He knew them, weighed them, factored them into his plans.

And within Ach'magut, at the nexus where all the tentacles originated, a single eye opened. It was human in shape, but bigger than Calder's head, with an iris of hypnotic, poisonous blue.

INTERESTING.

The voice scoured Calder's mind like a desert wind, carrying with it all the meaning one word could possibly have.

YOU ARE THE RESULT OF A DEVIATION.

From that sentence, Calder learned more than he wanted to know about how he'd ended up in Silverreach.

Centuries ago, Ach'magut had allowed an alteration to his grand, cosmic plan. He'd been willing to risk a small change that might disturb the future, in the hopes of opening up new facts and new results. That deviation had resulted in everything in Calder's past, from the personal to the very distant—everything from the death of the Great Elders to the formation of the Empire, and everything from the meeting of Calder's specific parents to his birth to his expulsion from the Blackwatch. Everything, as moment toppled into moment, was the inevitable result of Ach'magut's action in the distant past.

The Elder could see it, could read the potential paths of his choices as easily as Calder could predict how a ball would roll across the floor. But the world was more interesting when it was unpredictable, as the Overseer knew well.

And Calder had ended up in this room, at this moment, with this precise group of people. Which Ach'magut had *not* predicted.

All this and more, Calder learned from what was essentially a single sentence. He didn't feel like part of a conversation, he felt like a student desperately trying to keep up with a ferocious lecture from an ancient Witness.

THIS OPENS NEW PATHS. NEW DOORS. NEW ANOMALIES.

Calder tried to respond, to barter for his life, but this was nothing at all like bantering with Kelarac. This had more in common with being flattened underneath a collapsing building.

He could feel it when the Great Elder turned his attention from Calder to the others, as though the point of a sword had been taken away from Calder's throat. To each of them, Ach'magut spoke.

Petal trembled, facing something that was so much *more* than her that she felt like a grain of sand that would soon blow away. She clutched her quicklamp to her chest as though it might protect her somehow, and the subtle warmth on her fingers was only a distant comfort.

Her one hope, which she clung to even more desperately than her light, was that she was too far beneath Ach'magut's notice. Maybe the Great Elder would overlook her entirely, as she deserved, and allow her to go on her way. Even if his Inquisitors killed her, it would be better than what the Overseer could do to her.

Then his attention fixed on her, spearing her through the middle, and she knew with a bone-deep certainty that he spoke to no one else but her.

YOU HAVE FOUND YOUR HOME.

That was all, but she read volumes into that single sentence. Her body shook with an involuntary sob.

When the Great Elder said it, she could more easily doubt her own name. Her home wasn't in the streets, where she'd spent her childhood. It wasn't in the Guild that had rejected her, or in the box where she'd hidden for years.

She'd found it on a Navigator's ship.

Somewhere in her mind, Petal had planned to leave once they made port at a place that felt right. She still wondered if the rest of the crew wanted her around, if they even needed her for anything.

With the Elder's words, that possibility died.

Foster had his eyes squeezed shut, with his Reader's senses even more tightly closed. He didn't want even a *hint* of this monster's Intent leaking through, because it would crush him to dust.

Then Ach'magut spoke to him, and Foster knew he might as well have saved his effort. He couldn't shut out the Elder's Intent any more than he could shut his ears against the sound of an erupting volcano.

THEY ARE GONE, Ach'magut said, and Foster's eyes opened wide.

He stared into the Great Elder's single, gigantic eye as though he sought clarity there. But the Overseer had been perfectly clear.

His family, his former wife and his children whom he hadn't seen for years, were gone. He should abandon them. He may as well give up, because the future did not allow them to survive.

Foster's heart clenched, but sheer stubbornness took over his mind. He would throw himself into the Aion Sea before he let an Elder tell him what to do. Now, he'd have to find his family again if it killed him. He would prove to himself that the future could be controlled, could be denied, and that Dalton Foster would be the one to do it. But in his soul, he knew the truth.

Ach'magut had predicted this.

Urzaia had put up his hatchets. There was no point in resisting, any more than he could resist a crashing wave with the power to capsize *The Testament*. Sometimes, a man faced forces so far beyond him that defiance became an absurdity.

But laughter bubbled up inside him, and he let it show on his face. The Great Elder could do what he wanted, but he could not make Urzaia Woodsman despair.

The eye focused on him, a strange bulb on a stalk rattled next to Urzaia's ear, and Ach'magut spoke to him.

YOU WILL DIE BEFORE YOU SEE DEFEAT.

At that, Urzaia did laugh.

Andel grabbed his medallion in his fist so hard that he wondered if his palm would bleed. The Luminian Order encouraged hatred of the Elders, but he knew the truth: the Elders were not manifestations of pure evil, but so chaotic and foreign that they might as well have been. Each of the Great Elders was unique in purpose, and they would be true to that purpose.

Everything Ach'magut said would be factually correct, and Andel could rely on its predictions of the future. He knew that as surely as he knew up from down.

Ach'magut's words would be correct. But they would not be the truth.

WHAT CAUSE DO YOU SERVE? For a moment, Andel couldn't take a breath.

He'd given up the cause of the Luminian Order, but he had never abandoned the teachings of the Unknown God. Even this job, as an aide and supervisor to Calder Marten, gave him the opportunity to guide a young man forward. Without support, Calder would be headed for a future more destructive than Andel could imagine.

Still, Andel's Imperial supervisors intended him to guide the young Navigator back into the folds of the Empire, and Andel wasn't sure he wanted to. He'd seen enough in his life to know that even the Emperor couldn't be trusted, not fully.

If the Guild couldn't be trusted, and the Empire couldn't be trusted, what did the God want him to do?

Jerri trembled before the Overseer, one of the two Great Elders her father had always sought to meet. Anyone in the Sleepless would give their left leg for this chance, but now that she was here, she saw how futile all her plans were. She'd dreamed of this moment before, had actually charted out the questions she'd ask and how she would interpret the potential responses.

But she was nothing more than a tiny longboat on a storm-tossed sea. She did not chart her course, she merely tried to survive until the ocean stopped.

YOUR FATHER WOULD BE PROUD, the Great One said, and every nuance of meaning flowed into her mind. Her father *was* dead, as she'd suspected for years. *May his soul fly free.* Ach'magut's words told her that, if he were alive, he'd be proud of what she'd done. Proud of her.

And in the future, he would be proud of the woman she'd become. She would accomplish more than her father had ever dreamed.

Seconds had passed as Ach'magut turned his gaze from one member of his crew to the other, and though Calder heard the words, they meant nothing to him. The Great Elder did not speak through vibrations in the air, but through a language of Intent so subtle and complex that Calder couldn't catch a glimpse of its mechanisms. If the Overseer did not want Calder to know his words, that was how it would be.

But now, the strange wave of Intent broadened. Ach'magut addressed them all as a crew, as he had at the beginning. His words were for Calder, but every living thing in the great library—from the human crew to the innumerable Inquisitors—served as a witness.

THE THRONE WILL SOON BE EMPTY.

Calder didn't need the volumes of explanation that came along with the Elder's voice to tell him what those words meant. The Emperor was going to die. Soon.

And Ach'magut was telling *him.*

Hope and feverish expectation surged up in equal measure, as Calder dared to resurrect a foolish dream that he had carried since childhood.

A rustle came from behind him, as of a thousand sticks falling to the floor. He turned to look, as he was sure he was supposed to, and saw fields of Inquisitors bending forward. They'd folded their first legs and pressed their jaws to the floor.

It took him a moment to realize what the hordes of Elderspawn were doing, and when he did, his breath died in his lungs.

They were kneeling.

To him.

HAIL THE EMPEROR OF THE WORLD, Ach'magut said, and Calder stared incredulously into the Elder's one giant eye. Never, in his most distant dreams, had he ever dared to imagine this.

The crew was looking at him now, and he could feel their reactions as easily as his own. Awe, fear, disbelief, hope, and sheer, mind-numbing shock.

But Ach'magut had one more thing to say, and he delivered it with a finality that made Calder wonder if the Great Elder would ever speak again.

SHOW ME THE FUTURE.

Calder's return to *The Testament* felt like his first trip to Ach'magut's library—that is, it felt like nothing at all. It wasn't as though he'd fallen asleep, but as though he'd forgotten the journey.

He returned to awareness seated on a sack of beans with his back leaning up against the railing. He had traveled there from the library, he was sure, but no matter how he searched his memory he couldn't recall the slightest detail of the time between.

The last thing he remembered were the words of Ach'magut. Those, he couldn't forget.

The rest of the crew was strewn around the deck as though they'd been dropped there out of the sky, and they started to stir at the same time he did. Urzaia was on his feet and inspecting his armor, maybe checking himself for injuries, before Calder managed to stand up.

As soon as he did, he stumbled to the wheel and sent his Intent into the ship. He'd woken with an inexplicable certainty: that they should leave Silverreach as soon as possible. Not that he needed any supernatural urging to do that; he had already planned to show this town the back of his sails and never return.

The trick would be convincing the Lyathatan to stir. Calder had worked the Elder unusually hard over the past few months, and it had begun to let him know that it deserved a rest. Typically, it did so by sending him images of a broken ship littered with human bodies.

Today, the impression he received from the Lyathatan was very different.

The servant of Kelarac strains at its chains, eager to haul its cargo into the ocean. If it were allowed, it would depart without the human passengers, but a greater will consumes it. Not the will of the Lyathatan, nor the will of Kelarac, but the will of another Great One.

The Lyathatan knows it is in danger, that all the plans it has laid for the future will come to nothing if they cross the plans of Ach'magut.

With the closest thing to fear that Calder had ever sensed from the creature, the Lyathatan hauled *The Testament* out to sea. The acceleration made him clutch the wheel and sent Petal tumbling shoes-over-shoulders across the deck until Urzaia caught her. The Champion stood with his feet planted on the deck as though a hurricane couldn't budge him.

In minutes, they left Silverreach behind. The town and its unlit lighthouse were swallowed up by the night, until the whole world was nothing more than the starlit waves, *The Testament*, and the submerged shadow pulling them forward.

That was when the ocean trembled.

A ripple shot across the surface of the water, like someone had dropped a pebble into a bathtub. Seconds after that, Calder heard a great roar, and sudden waves blasted them from behind. The aft half of the ship lifted up and slammed down, sending a creak of pain through Calder's Vessel.

Petal started to tumble the other way, but Urzaia grabbed her out of the air and tossed her onto his shoulder.

The ocean shook with the wrath of a storm, but the Lyathatan neither faltered nor fumbled, dragging them forth as a team of dogs drags a sled. Calder mustered enough focus to wrap ropes around the entire crew, steadying them and ensuring he wouldn't lose them overboard.

While he did, he considered the explosion behind them. At first, he wished he could extend his senses far enough to pick up some Intent, but he had to admit the truth to himself. He knew what had happened. Silverreach had been destroyed.

Whether Ach'magut had blown the town to pieces for secret reasons known only to the Elders, or whether something they'd done had led to the town's collapse, Calder had no idea. But the Overseer had sent them away with an urge to flee only minutes before an explosion came from the direction of Silverreach. Either the town was gone, or they'd been deceived by the most coincidental earthquake of all time.

Calder knew which way he'd bet.

The night passed before the Lyathatan started to slow down, and Calder had enjoyed no sleep at all. He doubted anyone else had either. His bunk remained steady enough, though it was pitched at a fifteen degree angle thanks to the ship's speed, and he was certainly exhausted. But the Great Elder's words haunted him, prodding his consciousness like red-hot needles.

The throne will soon be empty, he'd said. And, *Hail the Emperor of the world.*

If there was ever anything to be excited about, inheriting the entire Empire would count. Calder spent the entire night turning the Elder's intentions over in his mind, trying to find the angle. The hidden agenda. He knew beyond a doubt that Ach'magut had a plan, and a Great Elder wouldn't care if that plan involved exalting Calder or crucifying him. One human life was simply irrelevant, on the Overseer's scale.

So there was every possibility that the prophecy might doom him, which was how every folk tale of Elder prophecy usually ended. But one thing Calder never doubted: the Great Elder wouldn't be wrong.

He might be playing Calder for the benefits of a game millennia in the playing, but he wouldn't be wrong.

Which meant that Calder would get revenge for his father after all.

At the first glimmer of dawn, the Lyathatan finally slowed to a crawl, and Calder bolted from his bunk. He threw on some clothes, replaced his hat, and shot outside.

The crew was already waiting for him, and they looked worse than he did. Foster's hair and beard had escaped his control entirely, hanging around him like an angry stormcloud. Petal leaned against the railing, holding her knees to her chest. Jerri paced back and forth, muttering, and Andel stared into the distance with his hat in his hand.

Urzaia, by contrast, beamed at the rest of them. "How wonderful is sleep after an adventure!" he said, and Foster glared.

When Calder emerged, they all turned to him. For a second, no one spoke, so Calder cleared his throat to break the silence. "So. I suspect we have a few things to talk about."

Foster turned his glare to the Captain. "You think so? About what?"

Calder looked from him to Petal to Urzaia. "Jerri and Andel know my story already, and I'm sure you've picked up pieces of it. But in light of recent events, you deserve some...context."

So Calder told them. He told them about his childhood, the sale of Imperial relics, his father's arrest, his time with his mother and with the Blackwatch, and his own mistakes that had led to his banishment to the Navigators. To his father's execution.

"I know the Emperor as well as anyone alive," Calder said. "I've tracked his movements to get to relics, I've Read a relic or two myself, and I've even met the man. He doesn't care about us. He's so far distant he might as well be an Elder himself."

He kept an eye on their faces as he spoke, looking for disgust or rejection. He was speaking blasphemy, essentially, but he had to know they could handle this much. What he saw pleased him. Andel's face was a mask, Foster looked like he agreed, and Petal stared wide-eyed like a child hearing a story.

"When I was a child, I realized that the Empire needed to change. And it wouldn't, as long as the Emperor remained in charge. Well...it looks like he won't be there much longer. Now's our chance to steer the Empire where *we* want to go, and if I get a chance, I intend to take the wheel."

Foster snorted. "You can't do a worse job than the old man."

Urzaia, unsurprisingly, laughed. "Wherever you go, Captain, I will stand in front of you. You keep your promises, and the Emperor does not."

"I want to stay here," Petal whispered.

Jerri practically danced over to him, where she threw her arms around him. "This is *perfect!* Oh, light and life, I could never have imagined it...The Emperor has no official duties, the government works without him. He's a figurehead with the absolute power to indulge his whims, so you won't even have to *do* anything. Just...whatever you want!"

"I appreciate your faith in my ability to do nothing," Calder said dryly, but he had to force back a smile.

It wasn't time for celebration yet; the biggest obstacle of the day stood in front of him. One person had yet to respond.

Andel replaced his hat. "Don't plan your coronation yet. Until the Emperor dies, if that can even happen, you're just a young man past his ears in debt. And even if he *does* die, I doubt he considers Ach'magut's recommendation reason enough to name you his heir."

Calder deflated a little. Andel was essentially right; there was a long road between him and the throne.

But he'd get there. That, he never doubted.

CHAPTER TWENTY-FOUR

I found allies in the void, but enemies too. I was not surprised. There are enemies everywhere. But strangest of all were those that were neither hostile nor friendly: the guardians in white.

— THE UNKNOWN WANDERER, FROM *OBSERVATIONS OF THE UNKNOWN WANDERER* (HELD IN THE BLACKWATCH ARCHIVES)

The Consultants had lost the battle, no one disputed that. After they spent the rest of the day scouring the Gray Island, shaking as many Consultants as they could out of their holes, the Imperialist Guilds took to their ships flush with victory.

Even if the attack hadn't worked out quite as they'd hoped, even if General Teach was wounded and in dire condition, even if many of the Consultants were still on the run, they'd won. The Gray Island was theirs.

And now the Consultants were fleeing.

They'd come out of a hidden harbor on a black ship with a twisting eye where the crow's nest should be. Calder didn't recognize the ship, but he recognized its kind: it was a Navigator's Vessel, and not one belonging to the Guild. The Consultants had their own pet Navigator.

Not the first secret they'd kept from the other Guilds, he was sure.

The ship led them on a spirited chase, but in the end it was only one vessel, and they were more experienced on the Aion. Calder cornered it himself, and took it upon himself to address the Consultant refugees onboard.

Including, he was sure, the Gardener Shera.

Calder stepped up to the railing, raising the captain's horn to his lips. "Ladies and gentlemen of the Consultant's Guild, you may notice that we have you surrounded. We're going to escort you back to the Capital, where—"

He'd intended to say, *"Where you'll be treated with all respect and courtesy,"* but a pudgy green monster fluttered down from the rigging and interrupted him, in a resonant masculine voice that boomed out over the ocean. "SURROUNDED!"

Calder lowered the horn and muttered to Andel. "Cage it or shoot it, I don't care which."

He gathered himself before addressing the Consultants again. He'd lost his place, so he simply made it up. "...where representatives of loyal Guilds will gather to determine your treatment." That sounded appropriately vague, if not as friendly as he'd intended. Shuffles' appearance had tainted his mood. "I can say that, if you cooperate, we would be delighted to have an organization with your expertise on the side of the Empire. We only wish for humankind to stand united, as the Elders wish to consume us all—"

He knew it was a mistake as soon as he said it.

"CONSUME US ALL!" Shuffles declared, even as Andel chased it across the bridge.

"Andel, Foster, I'm shoving *something* into a cage as soon as this is over. I'd rather it be Shuffles."

After another moment to clear his mind, he picked up the captain's horn again. "I assure you, we have only your best interests at heart."

"BEST INTERESTS," Shuffles said with a laugh, making it sound like the threatening declaration of a demented murderer. Calder gave up, tossing the horn to the deck. If the Consultants didn't get the point by now, they never would.

For a few seconds they didn't respond, and Calder wondered if they might not have a captain's horn of their own. He was planning on moving closer before a cloud of mist exploded into being around the enemy ship.

Bastion's Veil. Only instead of surrounding the Consultant's island, it shrouded their vessel, rapidly expanding into a solid bank of fog. Calder stared into the cloud, anger and hopelessness warring within him.

They'd gotten away.

Even now, Cheska was organizing a search, shouting her orders to the other Navigators, but he knew they wouldn't catch up. The majority of the remaining Consultants were aboard that ship, not counting the thousands of Guild members on assignment all over the world. They'd taken Consultant headquarters away, but what had they really gained?

He slumped down to the deck, leaning his back against the wheel, and closed his eyes.

Someone sat down next to him.

He looked over to see Bliss staring at him from two inches away. "In pets, sudden listlessness and lack of energy can indicate that they are sick," she said.

"I'm not an animal."

"Then you're distressed." She reached into her coat and pulled out a folded-up blanket. It was big enough that it should have made a noticeable bulge in her coat, leading him to wonder irrationally if she'd created it out of nothing. She reached around him, tucking the blanket over his shoulders.

There was nothing wrong with him that a blanket could possibly solve, but it was nice to have someone worry about him for once. He leaned his head back, looking into the sky. "Thanks," he said.

"You're welcome."

She joined him in looking up, even as all around him the Navigators searched frantically for the vanishing ship.

"The crack in the sky," he said suddenly. "What is it really?"

Bliss pondered for a moment. "There's nothing wrong with the sky. What we're seeing is a rift, such as the Elders use for transportation to and from the void. It is simply very high above us."

For Bliss, that was a surprisingly coherent answer. He decided to push a little further. "What's on the other side?"

"Popular belief says it's where the Elders come from. That's likely to be true. We can verify that most of the Great Elders use the void for transportation and communication."

Calder digested that, but Bliss wasn't through. "You've seen Ach'magut's library, haven't you?"

He would very much like to know where she'd heard that, but there was no point in lying now. "Yes."

"While Ach'magut was dead, we liberated our share of books from that library. Stole. Liberated. Liberated or stole? Either way, once we'd decoded the languages, we learned a few relevant facts. First, ours is not the only world out there."

"I know that, Bliss," Calder said. "My tutors showed me the planets through a telescope."

"I didn't say planets," she said. "And don't interrupt. Each Elder pursues something, and they move from world to world through the void in pursuit of it. Ach'magut pursues knowledge. Nakothi pursues the perfect balance of life and death. Urg'naut pursues absolute nothingness. Tharlos…" she paused to push down on her coat, "…pursues *change*. But wherever they go, they work apart. Against humanity, but neither with nor against one another. As we understand it, it was very rare for one Great Elder to ever encounter another."

"Then how did we end up with *seven*?"

"That part of the books is very clear," Bliss said softly. He found that he couldn't tell what color her eyes were, besides 'pale.' "They were lured here. Lured and trapped. For untold thousands of years, the Great Elders have bickered and jockeyed with one another, but in the end they all have the same goal. To be free of this prison."

Calder looked into the cracked sky. If that were true, all they would have to do is hold the door open, and all the Great Elders would leave. It sounded too good to be true.

But one detail stood out, and he had to ask the question. "They're trapped here...then who trapped them?"

Bliss sighed. "That," she said, "is a very good question."

FIVE YEARS AGO

Only four weeks after their encounter with the Great Elder, *The Testament* arrived at the Capital. Either luck or the foresight of Ach'magut had been with them, because they'd sailed straight through the center of the Aion Sea with no more trouble than a vanishing island and a stray wormcloud. Not even the most optimistic Navigator would promise a trip from Aurelia to Izyria in one month, but they'd done it.

They were still miles away from the Capital when Calder saw that something was wrong. Ships, Navigator and otherwise, fled from the direction of the mainland like startled birds. Some of them were on fire. A few headed back toward the Capital, but it was a trickle compared to a flood. And not one of them responded to Calder's request for information.

The Capital was so vast that it practically swallowed the coastline; once land was in sight, everything Calder could see stretching north and south was all part of the city. And all of it hung under a cloud of smoke, as though every chimney everywhere had started belching non-stop. Over the water drifted a constant sound that Calder only identified when they got closer: bells. Hundreds if not thousands of bells, all ringing in constant chaos.

The Testament was even closer before they could see the third sign of disaster. The red flags, bearing their moon-in-sun Imperial Seal, had all been defiled. A legion of Imperial flags always flapped above the Capital, ranging in size from those no bigger than a hand to the ones over the palace, which were broader than *The Testament's* sails.

All of them had been scarred with a new addition: a thick black line slashing diagonally down the middle.

Calder's eyes turned to Andel.

The former Pilgrim removed his hat once more, staring at the shoreline. He pressed the hat over his heart, one final gesture of respect.

"What will it be, Andel?" Calder asked quietly. He couldn't deny a trembling of his own heart; as much as he'd hoped for this, the Emperor had always seemed constant. Eternal. Even when he'd finally believed that the Emperor would die, there was a difference between *knowing* it and seeing the evidence.

Andel shook his head. "I'm still trying to make excuses. Maybe the Capital came under attack, maybe there was a rebellion, maybe this is some game by the Elders and we're still back in Silverreach. But I'm neither a fool nor a coward. I know the Emperor is dead, may his soul fly free."

That was a first step, but anyone with the knowledge they had would have come to the same conclusion. Calder waited for the rest, but Andel didn't say anything.

He carefully placed his broad white hat on his head, adjusted it, and walked away.

"Where are you going, Andel?"

"To do my job," Andel called back. "You all have reasons to be glad the Emperor's dead. Who says I don't?"

Not daring to believe it, Calder watched Andel as he climbed up and took the wheel.

"The Capital's in turmoil, Captain," he shouted down. "Making port would be a dangerous gamble. I suggest we plot another course."

That was the first time Andel had ever called him "Captain."

"Sounds wise to me, Andel." He stepped away, where he could see the man in white standing over the wheel.

Andel executed a shallow bow. "Then we sail at your command, sir."

THE END

OF THE ELDER EMPIRE: SECOND SEA

NEXT TIME, FOLLOW CALDER IN…

⊙F KINGS & KILLERS

THE ELDER EMPIRE : THIRD SEA

For updates, visit *www.WillWight.com*

TURN THE PAGE FOR A GLOSSARY AND
EXCERPTS FROM THE GUILD GUIDE

GLOSSARY OF TERMS

AM'HARANAI The ancient order of spies and assassins that would eventually become the Consultant's Guild. Some formal documents still refer to the Consultant's Guild in this way.

ARCHITECT One type of Consultant. The Architects mostly stay in one place, ruling over Guild business and deciding general strategy. They include alchemists, surgeons, Readers, strategists, and specialists of all types.

AWAKEN A Reader can Awaken an object by bringing out its latent powers of Intent. An Awakened object is very powerful, but it gains a measure of self-awareness. Also, it can never be invested again.

Jarelys Teach, the Head of the Imperial Guard, carries an ancient executioner's blade that has been Awakened. It now bears the power of all the lives it took, and is lethal even at a distance.

All Soulbound Vessels are Awakened.

CHILDREN OF THE DEAD MOTHER Elderspawn created by the power of Nakothi out of human corpses.

CONSULTANT A member of the Consultants Guild, also known as the Am'haranai. Mercenary spies and covert agents that specialize in gathering and manipulating information for their clients.

Consultants come in five basic varieties: Architects, Gardeners, Masons, Miners, and Shepherds.

For more, see the Guild Guide.

DEAD MOTHER, THE *See: Nakothi.*

ELDER Any member of the various races that ruled the world in ancient days, keeping humanity as slaves. The most powerful among them are known as Great Elders, and their lesser are often called Elderspawn.

GARDENER One type of Consultant. The Gardeners kill people for hire.

INTENT The power of focused will that all humans possess. Whenever you use an object *intentionally*, for a *specific purpose*, you are investing your Intent into that object. The power of your Intent builds up in that object over time, making it better at a given task.

Every human being uses their Intent, but most people do so blindly; only Readers can sense what they're doing.

See also: Invest, Reader.

INVEST Besides its usual financial implications, to "invest" means to imbue an object with one's Intent. By intentionally using an object, you *invest* that object with a measure of your Intent, which makes it better at performing that specific task.

So a pair of scissors used by a barber every day for years become progressively better and better at cutting hair. After a few years, the scissors will cut cleanly through even the thickest strands of tangled hair, slicing through with practically no effort. A razor used by a serial killer will become more and more lethal with time. A razor used by a serial-killing barber will be very confused.

KAMEIRA A collective term for any natural creature with unexplainable powers. Cloudseeker Hydras can move objects without touching them, Windwatchers can change and detect air currents, and Deepstriders control water. There are many different types of Kameira...though, seemingly, not as many as in the past. The Guild of Greenwardens is dedicated to studying and restoring Kameira populations.

Humans can borrow the miraculous powers of Kameira by creating Vessels from their body parts, and then bonding with those Vessels to become Soulbound.

MASON One type of Consultant. Masons are craftsmen and professionals in a particular trade, covertly sending back information to their Guild. There are Masons undercover in every industry and business throughout the Empire.

MINER One type of Consultant. This secretive order is in charge of the Consultants' vast library, sorting and disseminating information to serve the Guild's various clients.

NAKOTHI, THE DEAD MOTHER A Great Elder who died in the Aion Sea. Her power kills humans and remakes their bodies into hideous servants.

NAVIGATOR A member of the Navigator's Guild. The Navigators are the only ones capable of sailing the deadly Aion Sea, delivering goods and passengers from one continent to the other.

For more, see the Guild Guide.

READER A person who can read and manipulate the Intent of objects. Every human being invests their Intent subconsciously, simply by using ordinary objects. However, Readers can do so with a greater degree of focus and clarity, thanks to their special senses.

Readers often receive visions of an object's past.

SHEPHERD One type of Consultant. The Shepherds are observers, thieves, and saboteurs that specialize in infiltrating a location and leaving unnoticed.

SOULBOUND A human who can channel the power of an Elder or a Kameira. These powers are contained in a Vessel, which is *bound* to a person during the Awakening process. Soulbound are rare and powerful because they combine the focus of human Intent with the miraculous power of inhuman beings.

Bliss, the Guild Head of the Blackwatch, is a Soulbound with the Spear of Tharlos as her Vessel. Therefore, she can borrow the reality-warping powers of the Great Elder known as Tharlos, the Formless Legion.

A person becomes a Soulbound by having a personally significant object Awakened. If the object has a strong connection to an Elder or Kameira, and if it is significant *enough*, then it can become a Soulbound Vessel.

See also: Vessel.

VESSEL An Awakened object that becomes the source of a Soulbound's power. Not all Awakened items become Soulbound Vessels, but all Vessels are Awakened.

In order to become a person's Vessel, an item must fulfill two criteria: it must be *personally linked* to the individual, and it must be invested with the power of a Kameira or an Elder.

1.) Personal link: A ring that you bought at a pawnshop three weeks ago could not become your Soulbound Vessel. It has not absorbed enough of your Intent, it is not significant to you, and it is not *bound* to you in any way. A wedding ring that you've worn for fifteen years and is significant to you for some reason—perhaps you pried it off your spouse's bloody corpse—could indeed become your Vessel, assuming it fulfills the second criteria as well.

2.) Power: A spear made of an Elder's bone could allow one to use that Elder's power of illusion and madness. If you bonded with a necklace of Deep-strider scales, you might be able to sense and control the ocean's currents as that Kameira does.

See also: Soulbound.

WATCHMAN A member of the Blackwatch Guild.

For more, see the Guild Guide.

THE GUILD GUIDE

A brief guide to the Ten Imperial Guilds of the Aurelian Empire, written by a licensed Witness for your edification and betterment!

THE AM'HARANAI

Also known as Consultants, the members of this mysterious brotherhood work behind the scenes for the good of the Empire...or for anyone with enough gold to pay them. Consultants are more than willing to provide strategic advice, tactical support, and information to the Empire's rich and elite, so long as it doesn't destabilize the government they've worked so hard to build.

Believe it or not, the Am'haranai were the first Imperial Guild, having existed in one form or another since long before the birth of the Empire. The next time you walk by the local chapter house of the Consultants, know that you're in the presence of true Imperial History.

The Consultants' local Guild Representative would not give us a definitive response to the less savory rumors surrounding this particular Guild. Juicy speculation suggests that—for the right price—the Consultants will provide a number of darker services, including espionage, sabotage, and even assassination. We can neither confirm nor refute such rumors at this time.

Consultants in the field are known to refer to each other by code names, to conceal their true identities.

Shepherds are their expert scouts, trained to watch, remember, and report.

Architects are the leaders of the Am'haranai, and typically do not leave their island fortress. They're the strategists, alchemists, tacticians, and Readers that make the work of the Consultants possible.

Masons are a truly terrifying order, though once again the Guild Representative put off most of my questions. They go undercover as everyday folk like you or me, living ordinary lives for months or years, and then providing information to their Architect leaders. Your best friend, your neighbor, that street alchemist across from your house...any of them could be a Mason secretly watching you!

Other, less credible reports suggest the existence of a fourth brand of Consultant: the **Gardeners.** The job of a Gardener is to "remove weeds." They are the black operatives, the pure assassins, the knives in the dark.

The Guild Representative had this to say on the matter: "There is not now, and never has been, an order of the Am'haranai known as the Gardeners. That's simple speculation based on our Guild crest, which is actually derived from our origin as humble farmers. Having said that, if you do have someone interfering with your business, it is possible that we could help you bring the situation to a satisfactory conclusion…for an appropriate level of compensation, of course."

Since the Emperor's death (may his soul fly free), I have no doubt that business has been very good indeed for this particular Guild.

Guild Head: **The Council of Architects.** No one knows much about the leadership of the Consultants, but it seems that the Architects collectively vote on Guild policy, coming to decisions through careful deliberation and long experience.

Crest: Gardening Shears

THE BLACKWATCH

Thanks to generations of legends and misinformation perpetuated by the Luminians, many of you have certain preconceived notions about the Blackwatch. They're hated by many, feared by all, and I urge you not to heed the rumors. Every Watchman I've ever met has been professional, focused, and inquisitive--very few of them actually worship the Elders.

Let me put a few of your unfounded fears to rest: no, they do not eat human flesh for power. No, they do not conduct dark rituals involving blood sacrifice. No, they do not kidnap babies from their cradles.

Yes, they do use certain powers and techniques of the Elders. That's no reason to treat them like cultists.

The Blackwatch was originally founded by the Emperor for two purposes: watching over the graves of the Great Elders, and studying the Elder Races to twist their great powers for the good of the Empire. It is thanks to the Blackwatch that Urg'Naut or the Dead Mother have not risen and devoured our living world.

Members of this Guild are known as **Watchmen.** They respond to calls for help and reports of Elder activity. Each Watchman carries seven long, black nails invested with the power to bind Lesser Elders for vivisection and study.

The goals of the Blackwatch often bring them into conflict with Knights and Pilgrims of the Luminian Order, who hunt down Lesser Elders with the goal of destroying them completely.

If the two would only work together, it's possible that Aurelian lands would never be troubled by Elder attacks again.

Guild Head: The current head of the Blackwatch is a young-seeming woman known only as **Bliss.** Her origins are shrouded in mystery, though tenuous evidence suggests that she was born in a Kanatalia research facility.

Like every Blackwatch Head before her, she carries the **Spear of Tharlos,** a weapon supposedly carved from the bone of a Great Elder. I have never interviewed anyone who witnessed the Spear in battle and survived with their sanity intact.

Crest: the Elder's Eyes (six eyes on a mass of tentacles)

THE CHAMPIONS

I doubt there is a single child in any corner of the Aurelian Empire who does not know some story of the Champion's Guild, but I will still labor to separate fact from romantic fiction.

The Champions as we know them today rose out of an old Izyrian tradition. In ancient days, before the Empire, the continent of Izyria was divided into a thousand clans. When two clans had a dispute, instead of going to war, they would send two representatives into a formal duel. The winner's clan, of course, won the dispute. These clan champions were often Soulbound, strengthened by some secret alchemical technique, and highly skilled fighters.

When the Emperor (may his soul fly free) originally crossed the Aion Sea with the aim of enfolding Izyria into his fledgling Empire, he created his own collection of duelists to defeat the natives at their own cultural game.

Thus, the Champions were born.

Champions became, as we have all seen, the best fighters in the Empire. They singlehandedly quell rebellions, reinforce Imperial troops in the field, and put down dangerous Kameira. And sometimes, when the Empire still needed to fight its own duels, the existence of this Guild ensured that the Emperor never lost.

Since the death of the Emperor, this Guild has become—dare I say it—a dangerous liability. Each Champion has largely gone his or her own way. The Guild still trains initiates according to the old traditions, but it doesn't have the organizational stability or control it once did.

Guild Head: **Baldezar Kern,** an undefeated duelist and the man who singlehandedly pacified the South Sea Revolutionary Army. Though he is known as a gentle man with an easy sense of humor, when he straps on his trademark horned helmet, he becomes a force of carnage on the battlefield like none I have ever seen. I had the opportunity to witness Kern on the warpath almost fifteen years ago, and the sight of this man in battle will haunt me until the day of my death.

Crest: the Golden Crown

THE GREENWARDENS

While the Greenwardens do protect us from wild Kameira and keep the Imperial Parks that we all know and enjoy, you may not be aware that they were originally intended to save the world.

The Guild of Greenwardens was founded at a time in our history when alchemy was first coming into its own, and we were afraid that a combination of alchemy, then-modern weaponry such as the cannon, and unregulated human Intent would tear the world apart.

Greenwardens were created to preserve Kameira, preventing us from driving them extinct, and to monitor and repair the effects of alchemical and gunpowder weapons on the environment. They each carry an Awakened talisman, which for some has become their Soulbound Vessel: a shining green jewel that they use to heal wounds and promote the growth of plants.

Guild Head: **Tomas Stillwell** is a practicing physician and a fully inducted Magister of the Vey Illai as well as the Guild Head of the Greenwardens, proving that no physical infirmity can prevent you from contributing to your Empire. Though he lost his legs in a childhood encounter with a wild Kameira, he never let that experience make him bitter. Instead, it drove him to study Kameira, their habits, and how they function. He is now one of the most famous natural scientists in the Empire, and he has done much to prevent the extinction of species such as the stormwing and the shadowrider.

Crest: the Emerald

THE IMPERIAL GUARD

I trust that all of you understand the purpose of the Imperial Guard: to protect the Emperor's person, and to shield him from attack and unwanted attention. Some suggest that they failed, that the death of the Emperor proves that the Guard were unequal to their task.

I can assure you that this is not the case.

Through a secret alchemical process known only to the Guild of Alchemists, the Imperial Guard replaces some of their original body parts with those of Kameira. Some Guardsmen have patches of armored Nightwyrm hide grafted onto their skin, or their eyes substituted with those of a Cloud Eagle. The process is said to be long and unbearably painful, and it results in guardians with the appearance of monsters.

However, in the twelve hundred years that the Emperor reigned, not a single assassination attempt reached his person. We owe that fact solely to the power and extraordinary sensitivity of the Imperial Guard.

I know that many outside the Capital are wondering what the Guard are up to, now that they have no Emperor to guard. Well, in the words of their Guild Head, "We may no longer have an Emperor, but we have an Empire. That, we will preserve until the sun rises in the west."

The resolve of a true patriot, gentle readers.

Guild Head: **Jarelys Teach,** a General in the Emperor's military and Head of his Imperial Guard, does not at first strike you as an imposing woman. I have met her on many occasions, and found her to be singularly devoted to her job. Popular legend says that she swallowed the blood of a Nightwraith, thereby absorbing its powers, but that's little more than speculation. It's a matter of Imperial record that she carries Tyrfang, the Awakened blade used to execute the Emperor's rivals over a thousand years ago.

Crest: the Aurelian Shield (a shield bearing the sun-and-moon symbol of the Aurelian Empire)

KANATALIA, THE GUILD OF ALCHEMISTS

As I write this guide, I sip a glass of enhanced wine that slowly shifts flavor from cherry to apple to lemon. A cart rumbles by my house, with a hawker loudly announcing his remedies for sale. A quicklamp provides my light, glowing a steady blue, never smoking or flickering like a candle.

Truly, one cannot escape the advances of alchemy in our modern society.

Though alchemists have existed since long before the Empire, Kanatalia is one of the more recent additions to the Ten Guilds. It was the first organization to unify the previously contentious brotherhood of alchemists, allowing them to collectively achieve what they never could separately.

Matches, quicklamps, potions, invested alloys, healing salves, enhanced soldiers, vaccines…practically every scientific advance in the past century, including the advance of science itself, can be traced back to Kanatalia's door.

Just don't ask too many questions. A true Kanatalian alchemist can be very protective of his secrets, and you might find yourself a drooling vegetable if you get on the wrong side of an experienced potion-maker.

Guild Head: **Nathanael Bareius** did not become one of the richest men in the Empire by relaxing on his inheritance. After receiving a substantial fortune from his late father, Lord Bareius went on to receive a full education at the Aurelian National Academy. He graduated as a licensed Imperial alchemist and a member of Kanatalia. At that point, he wagered all of his capital on a single risky investment: alchemy. He opened his vaults, spending every bit he had to make sure that every corner and crevice of the Empire had a licensed Kanatalian alchemist there to provide illumination, potions, medical care, and Guild-approved recreational substances.

Lord Bareius has personally earned back triple his initial investment over the past ten years, and is now poised as the most prominent leader in the

Capital. Even more significantly, he seems to have won the battle of public opinion—I haven't seen a street in the Capital unlit by alchemical lanterns, and no one has died of dysentery or plague since before the Emperor's death. No matter what you think of his politics, Nathanael Bareius has made great strides in moving our Empire forward into this new century.

Crest: the Bottled Flame

THE LUMINIAN ORDER

Ah, the Luminians. A more versatile Guild you won't find anywhere: they're responsible for building cathedrals, policing Imperial roads, hunting down Elders, and generally acting heroic.

Luminian Knights, the martial arm of the Order, march around in their powerfully invested steel armor, fighting deadly monsters chest-to-chest. Their swords are bound with light so that they reflect the sun even in the dead of night, burning through creatures of darkness.

The trademark representatives of the Luminian Order are **Pilgrims,** humble wanderers in simple robes. They are each Readers—some of them Soulbound—charged to remove harmful Intent and the maddening influence of the Elders.

The Luminian Order and the Blackwatch have each held a knife to the other's back for hundreds of years, arguing over the best way to protect the populace, to prevent the rise of the Great Elders, and to keep the Empire whole. Perhaps if one of them would learn to compromise, we would all feel safer after midnight.

Guild Head: **Father Jameson Allbright** is an old man, but his vigilance has never dimmed in the fight against darkness. He is one of the oldest Soulbound on record, wielding his shining Vessel to bring the purifying light to Elder worshipers and malicious Readers alike.

Crest: the White Sun (usually on a red banner)

THE MAGISTERS

Magisters are the most accomplished and educated Readers in the world. You probably grew up with a local Reader, who invested your knives and cleansed your graveyard of harmful Intent. Most small-town Readers are powerful and possibly even quite skilled.

But they aren't Magisters.

A Magister is a Reader who has received an extensive education inside the Vey Illai, an extensive forest in the Aurelian heartland, inside what was once the original Imperial Academy. They can use their Intent with a degree of focus, subtlety, and precision that an ordinary Reader could barely comprehend.

Magisters are in charge of regulating Readers and the use of human Intent, in much the same way that a father is in charge of preventing his children from misbehaving.

It's impossible for all Readers to study at the Vey Illai and become Magisters, because there are simply too many people with a talent for Reading. And of course everyone invests their Intent into objects, to one degree or another.

But the best and most powerful are called Magisters.

Guild Head: **Professor Mekendi Maxeus,** one of the most distinguished researchers at the Aurelian National Academy, retired from his lecture tour to the "relaxing" position as head of one of the largest Imperial Guilds. He isn't seen outside much these days, having received several disfiguring facial scars in the Inheritance Conflict five years ago, but he still lends his overwhelming power of Intent to the construction of new public monuments in the Capital. He carries a black staff, and I have personally witnessed him use it to blast a collapsed building off a pair of trapped children. I have met few heroes in my career, but this man is among them.

Crest: the Open Book

The Navigators

When I call the Navigators a Guild, I use the term loosely.

Navigators are the only sailors who can cross the deadly, shifting ocean at the heart of our Empire: the Aion Sea. We therefore rely on them for communication, trade, exploration, and transport between the eastern continent of Aurelia and the western continent, Izyria.

It's too bad that they're the most shifty and unreliable collection of pirates, confidence artists, mercenaries, and outright criminals the Empire has ever seen.

No one knows how they cross the Aion, with its hundreds of deadly Kameira, its disappearing islands, its unpredictable weather, and its host of lurking Elders, but anyone else who sails far enough out into the ocean either vanishes or returns insane.

The best way to recognize a real Navigator from a faker is to ask to see their Guild license, which is unmistakable and cannot be reproduced. Unfortunately, that only tells you which sailor is truly able to cross the Aion: not whether he can be trusted.

Guild Head: **Captain Cheska Bennett** is one of the few reliable Navigators left in this world. She owns *The Eternal,* a most striking ship with billowing red sails and a wake that trails flame. She commands truly shocking prices for her services, but if you hire her, you can be certain that every splinter of your cargo will remain secure between one continent and the other.

Crest: the Navigator's Wheel (a ship's wheel with a single eye at the center)

The Witnesses

I am proud to count myself among the honorable Guild of Witnesses, the final entry on this written tour of Imperial history. Witnesses are the official record-keepers of the Empire, having chronicled the entirety of the Empire's history since our inception. We also observe momentous events, record battles, produce educational reading materials for the general public, and notarize official documents.

As Sadesthenes once said, *"The Witnesses are the grease that allow the wheels of Empire to turn."*

Generally speaking, Witnesses travel in pairs:

As a **Chronicler,** I am a Reader with the ability to store my memories inside a special alchemically created candle. I burn the candle while I write, and as the memories flow out, I can record my thoughts without any margin of error even years after the events I have witnessed.

Always, I am accompanied by my **Silent One,** a trained warrior and my bodyguard. Silent Ones bind their mouths to symbolize their inability to betray secret or sensitive events, but contrary to popular belief, we do *not* remove their tongues. We're not barbarians. They are capable of speech, they are simply discouraged from doing so in the presence of outsiders.

Guild Head: The Heads of my own Guild are the twin sisters **Azea and Calazan Farstrider,** natives of exotic Izyria. Though they are young, having risen to prominence after the Emperor's untimely demise, I have never met anyone so dedicated to accuracy and neutrality. Azea works as a Chronicler, and Calazan as her attendant Silent One, though I can personally confirm that either sister can perform either role. Azea is a remarkable fighter in her own right, and Calazan a skilled Reader and clerk.

Crest: the Quill and Candle

WILL WIGHT lives in Florida, among the citrus fruits and slithering sea creatures. He graduated from the University of Central Florida in 2013, earning a Master's of Fine Arts in Creative Writing and a flute of dragon's bone.

Whosoever visits his website, *www.WillWight.com*, shall possess the power of Thor.

If you'd like to contact him, say his name three times into a candle-lit mirror at midnight. Or you could just send him an email at *will@willwight.com*.

(This paperback is made from 100% recycled troll-hide, for a sturdier finish.)